AMAGANSETT

MARK MILLS

G. P. PUTNAM'S SONS

NEW YORK

This is a work of fiction. Names, characters, places, and incidents either are
the product of the author's imagination or are used fictitiously,
and any resemblance to actual persons, living or dead,
businesses, companies, events, or locales
is entirely coincidental.

G. P. Putnam's Sons
Publishers Since 1838
a member of
Penguin Group (USA) Inc.
375 Hudson Street
New York, NY 10014

Copyright © 2004 by Mark Mills
All rights reserved. No part of this book may
be reproduced, scanned, or distributed in any
printed or electronic form without permission.
Please do not participate in or encourage piracy of copyrighted materials
in violation of the author's rights. Purchase only authorized editions.
Published simultaneously in Canada

Library of Congress Cataloging-in-Publication Data

Mills, Mark, date.
Amagansett / Mark Mills.
p.   cm.
ISBN 0-399-15184-2
1. Amagansett (N.Y.)—Fiction.   2. Social classes—Fiction.
3. Fishers—Fiction.   I. Title.
PS3613.I569A83   2004   2004044394
813'.6—dc22

Printed in the United States of America
3   5   7   9   10   8   6   4

This book is printed on acid-free paper. ∞

Book design by Stephanie Huntwork

For Caroline, Gus, and Rosie
And to the memory of John N. Cole (1923–2003)

I stand as on some mighty eagle's beak,
Eastward the sea absorbing, viewing, (nothing but sea and sky,)
The tossing waves, the foam, the ships in the distance,
The wild unrest, the snowy, curling caps—that inbound urge and urge of waves,
Seeking the shores forever.

WALT WHITMAN,
"From Montauk Point"

JULY 1947

Conrad knew it was a body the moment he started hauling on the net. The weight was there, rising and falling in the swell between the beach and the outer bar, but where was the familiar twitch of the line in his hands, the urgent pulse of fish thumping against the mesh? He said nothing to Rollo, but a stolen glance confirmed that his friend had sensed it too.

Some forty yards down the beach, Rollo's gaze was fixed on the bobbing cork line that arced through the ocean between the two men. He was searching the crescent of enclosed water for signs that he was mistaken— fleeting shadows in a cresting wave, the silver flicker of a surface break.

Conrad dug the heels of his waders deep into the sand and hauled hand over hand in unison with Rollo. He felt the chill wind of fatalism blow through him, calming. Further speculation was useless. In a few minutes the net and its cargo would be drawn into the pounding surf, raised high on a breaker—a momentary offering—then unceremoniously dumped on the beach.

1

"CONRAD. CONRAD . . ."

The first light of dawn was creeping over the horizon when Conrad was roused from his slumber by Rollo's hollering. Conrad only ever slumbered, he never slept, not the sleep of a child, dead to the world, its oversized surroundings. One small part of his brain kept constant vigil, snatching at the slightest noise or shift in smell. It no longer bothered him. He accepted it for what it was: a part of him now, like the scar in his side and the remorseless throb of his damaged knee.

The boards groaned under his feet as he shuffled from his shack onto the narrow deck that ringed it. The sharp salt air stabbed his lungs, raw from too many cigarettes the previous evening. As if in reprimand, an overflowing ashtray still sat on the arm of the slatted wooden chair out front. A book lay facedown on an upturned fish crate beside the molten remains of a candle and an all-but-empty bottle of cheap Imperial whiskey.

He had read deep into the night, the bugs dancing dangerously close to the candle flame until it had finally sputtered and died. The waxing moon, so high and prominent at dusk, had long departed, having run her early course; and for a further hour he had sat in the deep darkness, breathing in time to the beat of the waves beyond the high beach-bank, sleep rising up around him like the unseen tide, his mind numbed by the liquor, his body by the blanket of night dew settling over him.

Conrad stared at the chair, unable to recall the short stroll he must surely have made from the abandoned perch to his bed.

"Conrad. Conrad . . ."

The cries were closer now, carried on the breeze, but Rollo was nowhere to be seen among the tumbling dunes. Conrad guessed that when he finally appeared he'd be flailing his arms like a windmill. He always did, when he was excited or running. Right now, it sounded like he was doing both.

A few moments later Rollo hove in sight. Sure enough, his arms were slicing the air. He bounded down the face of the dune, hurdling a large clump of beach grass, stumbling momentarily but recovering his footing. He was panting, sucking in air, when he finally drew to a halt by the shack. Conrad waited for him to catch his breath.

Rollo's lank dark hair was streaked by the sun and the salt air as it always was at this time of year. When he finally looked up and smiled, his teeth stood out like bleached bone against the deep amber of his skin.

"You're not wearin' no clothes."

"Well, what do you know?" Conrad allowed a note of mild irritation to creep into his voice.

"Go get togged up."

"This better be good."

"Oh, it's good, it's good."

THEY PAUSED as they reached the top of the high dune that separated Conrad's isolated home from the ocean. Overhead, a handful of stars winked their final farewells in the brightening sky. Beneath them, the broad beach stretched off to the western horizon, one hundred miles of almost unbroken sand, straight as a yardarm, reaching into the heart of New York City.

A few miles to the east, beyond the sandy lowlands of Napeague where they now stood, rose the high ground of Montauk, a noble upthrust of ridged and pitted glacial moraine at the very tip of the South Fork—Long Island's last defiant cry before it tumbled into the oblivion of the Atlantic. Beyond lay nothing but water . . . and the lost dreams of the Old World.

The ocean was suspiciously calm and limpid, the towering breakers the only indication of the powerful forces that lurked beneath its pewter skin. Even from here, Conrad could see that the longshore set was still running west to east—a sporadic event that occurred when a tendril of warm water broke free of the Gulf Stream, snaking northwards, assisted on its lazy passage by a sustained southwesterly blow.

The marked rise in sea temperature was welcomed by the ever-increasing number of "city people" who populated the ocean beach from Memorial Day to Labor Day. It lured them beyond the relative safety of the crashing surf into the deeper water with its counterintuitive jostle of currents. Fortunately, the warmer waters were awash with bait, and with the bait came the predators, bluefish and striped bass, which in turn attracted an even larger predator—man.

Many owed their lives to the happy conjunction of treacherous swimming conditions and increased fishing activity off the ocean beach. Many were those who'd been plucked limp and spluttering from the water into one of the cumbersome little dories used by the local surfmen. Once deposited safely on the beach, embarrassment—more often than not—would get the better of gratitude, and they'd hurry off, eager to banish the memory, casting a few mumbled words of thanks over their shoulders as they went. This wasn't always the case.

Everyone knew the story of Gus Bowyer, how he had returned to his shingled home on Atlantic Avenue one afternoon to find a gleaming new motorcar standing beside the old barn out back. The handwritten note attached to the windshield meant little to Gus, who was unable to read or write, and he'd been obliged to wait two puzzling hours for his wife's return from Montauk, where she worked as a dispatch clerk for the Long Island Rail Road. Within a few minutes of crossing the threshold, Edna Bowyer informed her husband that they were now the proud owners of a Dodge Special Type-B Sedan—a gift from a gangling New York architect whom Gus had saved from near-certain drowning off the ocean beach the previous month.

News of the couple's windfall soon spread, and for the remainder of the summer, bathers who were even so much as tumbled by a wave would find themselves descended upon by a pack of alert and overly obliging local fishermen. Edna, a pillar of Puritan common sense, had urged Gus to return the overstated vehicle to the Halsey Auto Company in East Hampton and recoup the purchase price in cash. God knows, they needed the money. Twenty-two years on, they still needed the money, and Gus was still driving the hulking Dodge around the back roads of Amagansett.

"SHE'S ON THE TURN," said Rollo, meaning the set, not the tide. The wind had come around overnight. By noon the vast body of water in motion would grind to a halt, then slowly turn back on itself. The natural order would prevail once more with the current scouring the coast from east to west. Interesting, but hardly worthy of a predawn rousing.

"Remind me to be angry with you when I wake," muttered Conrad, turning to leave.

"Whale off!"

Everyone knew the call to arms, though it was no longer heard on the South Fork of Long Island, the days of shore whaling some forty years past. Conrad turned back slowly.

"Bound east'rd inside the bar."

"You sure?"

" 'Less you saw a fifty-foot bass before," grinned Rollo, pleased with his riposte.

They scanned the ocean in silence, with just the hoarse cries of a few black-backed gulls wheeling overhead on dawn patrol. Suddenly, Rollo's arm shot out. A patch of whorls and eddies ruffled the still surface of the ocean a hundred yards directly offshore. A few moments later, the whale broke water and blew—two distinct jets, fanned by the wind, caught in the sun's earliest rays.

"Right whale," observed Rollo, identifying the species from its forked spout. But Conrad was already gone, padding down the side of the dune onto the beach. The whale blew four more times before sounding.

For over an hour they tracked the leviathan on its journey eastwards, their faces warmed by the rising sun. They walked in silence, not needing to share their thoughts.

Right whales hadn't been sighted off Amagansett for decades. Hunted to near extinction, they had once been a cornerstone of life on the South Fork. Three hundred years previously, when a straggle of English families first appeared in the woods a few miles to the west, they found the local Montaukett Indians already preying on the migrating schools that roamed the ocean beach, going off through the treacherous winter surf in their dugout canoes. With the crude geometry of a child, those first white settlers pegged out a community around a slender marsh, fashioning cellar-shelters from the trees they had felled, naming their new home Maidstone, after the English town in the county of Kent where most had sprung from.

Fourteen years later, when the hamlet rechristened itself East Hampton, the dwellings had crept above ground, the early "soddies" replaced by New England saltbox houses clad in cypress shingles and insulated against the sharp winters with seaweed and corncobs; the marsh had been excavated to create the town pond; and the townsmen were in effective control of a small, burgeoning, and highly profitable shore-whaling industry.

"Away with you. Hoooo. Woooo."

Conrad was dimly aware that they'd passed the Napeague Coast Guard station. Now Rollo was striding towards the water's edge, waving his arms in front of him. The whale had altered its course and was heading inshore at an angle to the beach. With a lazy flick of its giant flukes, it sounded.

"She's goin' to beach," cried Rollo. He started running, set on heading the whale off.

When Conrad caught up with him, he was standing in the wash, oblivious to the waves breaking around him, scouring the ocean. Without warning, the whale surfaced beyond the white water to their left. At this short distance, the sheer bulk of the creature was overwhelming. It filled their field of vision, deadening all other senses.

"Hooo. Woooo. Yaaaaa. YAAAA—"

A rogue wave caught Rollo broadside, slapping the wind from his lungs, sending him sprawling. Conrad hauled him to his feet, dragging him up the beach, but Rollo pulled free, stumbling back into the wash. The waves became clouded with rile, churned sand where the whale had grounded.

Conrad was struck by the bitter irony of the sight—Rollo Kemp, grandson of the legendary whaleman Cap'n Josh Kemp, the last man to take a whale off the ocean beach; Rollo Kemp pathetically hurling handfuls of wet sand in a vain bid to save a creature his grandfather had devoted a lifetime to slaughtering. Laughter filled his head. It was a few moments before he realized the sound was coming from behind him.

Gabe Cowan, chief boatswain's mate of the Napeague Coast Guard station, stood chortling uncontrollably, his creased face like weathered oilskin. A good-natured man, and a first-rate fiddler till arthritis turned his hands to gnarled claws, Conrad's reproachful look seemed only to amuse him further.

"It's them krill," said Gabe.

"What?"

"Come up on the Gulf Stream then pushed inshore. She's feedin', off of the krill." He laughed some more.

Beyond the prancing figure of Rollo, the whale had turned parallel to the beach, sieving its breakfast from the ocean.

Conrad hurried over to Rollo. "Rollo, she's feeding . . ."

Deaf to his words, Rollo's face was wet with spray and tears. Conrad seized him, binding his arms to his sides, holding him tight.

"It's okay, she's just feeding on krill," he said gently. Rollo's struggles subsided, his eyes searching Conrad's face.

"Never seen it before," muttered Gabe, appearing beside them. "Sight to behold, boys, sight to behold."

Conrad only released Rollo when he started to laugh. "Go get 'em," he yelled. "Go get 'em krill!"

Maybe his cries startled the whale; more than likely she had had her fill; but with some difficulty she swung herself around and headed offshore, presenting first her small end and then the giant fan of her tail as she kicked below the surface. They waited, watching. She showed briefly just beyond the outer bar, blowing only once before disappearing for good.

A summer flounder flapped weakly at the edge of the wash, stunned by its encounter with the whale.

"Well, what do you know . . ." said Gabe, taking two nimble strides and stamping down with the heel of his boot. "Lunch."

THEY ACCOMPANIED GABE back to the Coast Guard station, reflecting on what they had just witnessed. As far as any of them knew, the coastal wanderings of right whales had always been confined to the colder months, June at the very latest. What was it doing here at this time of year? Had it been alone? Where was it headed? Conrad contributed his share of idle banter, but his thoughts were elsewhere. The episode was somehow emblematic of the times. It was as though the turbulence of the past years had infected the ocean as well, disturbing the natural rhythms, disorienting its occupants.

"You boys figure on haulin' down?" asked Gabe.

Rollo looked to Conrad to reply. They had planned to take the morning off, treat themselves to a well-earned rest, maybe set a gill net off Shagwong later in the day.

"Seeing as we're up," said Conrad, and Rollo beamed.

"Set's on the turn. Be one hell of a chop out there come noon."

"How else we going to make you earn that wage?"

"That ain't no wage, it's a goddamn insult."

"Man your age, scavenging for his lunch?" said Conrad. "The shame of it."

Gabe glanced at the dead flounder and laughed. "That's the truth."

Everyone knew that Gabe had squirreled away a small fortune over the years, largely thanks to a case of temporary blindness contracted during Prohibition.

"Wouldn't bank on much of a haul," said Gabe. "When the wind's from the east, the fish is least."

He wandered up the beach to the Coast Guard station, a grandiose weatherboard affair perched high on the frontal dune.

Conrad turned to Rollo. "Thanks," he said.

"Huh?"

"For waking me."

Rollo smiled. "Told you it was good."

THEY ATE a full breakfast on the front deck of Conrad's house as they did every morning, weather permitting. The menu never changed— pork belly and eggs fried side by side in a skillet, sourdough bread smeared with butter, and strong coffee, black as caulking tar, thick enough to float a nail. Afterwards, over a smoke, they would discuss the fishing prospects for the day ahead, trading the little hearsays that were the lifeblood of the fishing community. "Old Emmett took a full charge of cow bass on the Two Mile Hollow set, none of them under thirty pound," Rollo would say, or "Lindy says the bluefish is running off of Cedar Point."

To Conrad, there was something deeply pleasing about the mundanity of his morning routine with Rollo, its repetitive, unchanging nature. He would have been disappointed if, having hauled on his stiff black waders, Rollo hadn't promptly struggled out of them again, announcing that he needed to relieve himself—the click of the chest straps acting as some kind of Pavlovian trigger that also spared him the chore of loading the gear.

The equipment was stored in a barn behind the house. Windblown sand had banked up against its sides, giving the impression it had risen up out of the ground, pushing its way through the soft mantel. The barn's clean hard lines belied the muddle inside. Sails hung from its rafters like giant bats. Gill nets, drift nets, and haul-seines were bundled up all around. There were cod lines, drag lines, Greenport sloop dredges for scallops, basket rakes and bull rakes for clamming, oyster tongs, lobster traps and eel traps; as well as all manner of other paraphernalia for ensuring the smooth operation of the above—tubs of cork floats and lead weights, clusters of small anchors and marker buoys, spools of twine and coils of rope, buckets of nails, tins of grease, and barrels of tar.

Stacked in one corner of the barn was a jumble of obsolete whaling gear—lances, double-fluke and toggle harpoons, long-handled blades for cutting into blubber, block and tackle for prising the blankets free from the carcass, more blades for mincing the blubber, two cast-iron cauldrons for trying-out the whale oil, and large sieves for skimming off the bones and skin.

This clutter had come with the old whaleboat house—Rollo's

contribution to their enterprise—that now stood beside the barn. A twenty-six-foot whaleboat had also formed part of the package. They had hoisted the craft up into the barn's rafters where the beauty of its slender lines was revealed to maximum effect. It was the first thing Conrad's gaze would settle on each time he heaved open the double doors. This morning was different in that he found himself smiling as he stared up at the craft.

He singled out a short haul-seine, grappled it outside, and shouldered it into the dory. He was hitching the boat's trailer to the back of his battered old Model A Ford when Rollo appeared from the outhouse.

"Let's go get us a bunch," said Rollo, predictably, in words that never changed.

THE STRETCH OF OCEAN BEACH they planned to fish was no more than a few hundred yards from where they stood, but there was no breach in the tall dune that fronted the sea, no passage for a vehicle, and they were obliged to take the long route around—up the rutted sand track that connected Conrad's secluded world to Montauk Highway, a mile westwards into Amagansett, then down Atlantic Avenue to the beach landing and back along the shore.

At any other time, they would have been met at the landing by Sam and Ned Raven, the foul-mouthed sons of the equally foul-mouthed Joe Raven. A family of scallopers from Accabonac Creek, the quiet tidal backwater a few miles northeast of Amagansett, the Ravens were true "Bonackers," and proud of it. They did little to hide their resentment at having to sell their services to other fishermen from the wind-scoured days of March, when the adult scallops began to die, to the limpid days of late summer, when they could take to their sloop again in pursuit of the inshore pectens.

The boys had grunted halfhearted interest when Conrad offered to take them on for the short haul-seine season. "I don't know, a quarter share for haulin' another cunt's nets?" was how Ned had phrased his hesitancy.

Conrad figured they'd come around to the idea. The eelgrass was still dying back and the scallops had been down that winter. Most baymen had struggled to hit their daily limit of five bushels, and money was tight for the Ravens and their kind.

After a couple of weeks in Sam and Ned's company, Conrad had begun to wish the brothers had rejected his offer. The flood of blue speech that tumbled from their lips displayed an impressive and, at times, amusing grasp of the English language; but it unsettled Rollo, a devout Presbyterian and churchgoer.

Fortunately, the reduction gear on the Briggs & Stratton winch bolted to the bed of the Model A had given out a few days back, and Conrad had taken the opportunity to lay the boys off until it was repaired, buying a respite from the obscenities. This meant that he and Rollo were hauling by hand right now using a shortened eighty-fathom net, about a third the length of their usual seine. A two-man crew also demanded that they go off through the surf with only one oarsman, difficult and dangerous at the best of times.

The semi-inflated tires carved blunt furrows in the soft sand as the Model A slowly ranged the beach, Conrad teasing the stiff clutch to keep apace of Rollo who wandered the water's edge, scanning the ocean. He was looking for signs of fish: driven bait stippling the surface, like handfuls of sand cast upon the water, or a feeding slick that marked the spot where the larger fish were wreaking their havoc beneath the waves. Gulls and terns, ever-alert scavengers, would sometimes help guide the eye. If you were lucky. Most sets were made blind, based on some inexplicable feeling that the fish were there. Some called it smell, and Rollo came from a distinguished line of "long-nosed" Kemps. In the brief time they'd been in business together, Conrad had come to respect his uncanny instincts.

Rollo drew to a halt, squinting out to sea. Conrad eased the gear stick into neutral, letting the motor idle. He knew better than to say anything, and had time to roll a smoke before Rollo finally turned.

"I don't know," he said. "I don't know." He appeared puzzled that his sixth sense had deserted him. "Good a place as any, I reckon."

Conrad backed the trailer down to the water and they dragged the dory into the wash. As surfboats went, she was a little shorter than most—fourteen feet along the bottom—but in all other respects she was typical, her high, flaring sides climbing to sharp ends, fore and aft, that sliced through the surf when going off and parted the following sea around her stern on the equally perilous run to shore. Along with her oars and two nets, she was the only piece of his father's gear that Conrad still owned.

Hitching the inshore end of the net to the back of the Model A, Conrad pulled the vehicle up the beach until the line ran taut. He hurried back to join Rollo and they wrestled the dory through the thumping chaos of white water, fighting to keep its bow headed into the seas.

Conrad scrambled aboard. Moving fast, he slipped the oars into their locks and began to row gently, still standing, setting his stroke. His eyes were fixed on Rollo, chest-high in the water, doing his best to steady the dory. There was no need for Conrad to glance over his shoulder at the rearing seas. Everything could be read in Rollo's face as he waited for a slatch between two series of waves.

The next few seconds were critical. Rollo's judgment would determine whether they went off cleanly, or whether they filled up, broached to, or—God forbid—pitchpoled.

"Pull!" yelled Rollo, pushing off and struggling aboard in one graceless movement.

Conrad arched his back into the stroke. The dory slid up the face of the first capping sea. It broke over the bow, dowsing them, but Conrad was already well into his second stroke, shifting his weight, the oars biting deep, driving them down into the trough. His third stroke, long and measured, propelled them up and over the face of the next wave before it broke. They knew they were safe now unless Conrad popped an oar or the gods tossed a rogue wave their way. But the gods were in a good mood, and Conrad hadn't popped an oar in almost a decade.

Clear of the surf, Rollo could now concentrate on paying out the net, pitching the coils of lead line over the gunwale, the cork line dragged right along with it. Conrad settled down onto the thwart and eased into his long, distinctive stroke. Carrying so little twine, he soon began to turn the dory in a short, clean arc. The thicker mesh of the bunt began passing through Rollo's hands. This reinforced middle section housed the bag at the very center of the net, marked by a cork flag buoy. As soon as the bag was set, Conrad swung the dory parallel to the beach.

Rollo paid out the rest of the net until the offshore wing narrowed to a manila line coiled at his feet. This was Conrad's signal to turn again and begin their run to shore.

Speed and timing were everything when approaching the surf line. If Conrad lost momentum, the dory would slip back into the trough, floundering at the mercy of the chasing waves. If he came in too fast, the dory would hurtle down the face of a breaking sea, plant her bow in the sand and pitchpole forward, jackknifing over in one brief, heart-stopping moment, crushing her occupants.

Rollo was aft, his face a mask of concentration, applying just enough resistance to the net line whipping through his hands to keep the dory's stern headed seaward. If Conrad misjudged, coming in too fast, Rollo could yank on the line, stalling the boat's headway, buying them another shot at a clean approach. The line would skin his palms in an instant, but it was a small price to pay to avoid pitchpoling.

As it was, Conrad committed them to the surf on the back of large, lazy sea that lowered them kindly into the maelstrom of white water.

He boated the oars and seized the thwart to brace himself. As soon as he felt the jolt of the dory stranding, he was over the port side, Rollo over the starboard. They seized the gunwales and hauled the boat up the beach, assisted by the next breaking wave.

Exhausted, clinging to the dory for support, they laughed. It always felt good when they judged the seas correctly, going off and coming back without mishap.

They left the net to fish for a while, buying themselves time to recover from their exertions and share a smoke. Conrad had relished the last couple of days, the timeless, almost biblical, simplicity of the fishing—two friends, the beat of the sea, a net cast from a boat then hauled up onto the sand—no machinery, nothing to fall back on besides their experience and brute physicality.

After ten minutes or so they drew the offshore wing up onto the beach, closing the net. The semicircle of cork floats danced merrily on the building chop, the flag buoy at the apex not even a hundred feet beyond the breakers. They had yet to see any signs of fish. In all likelihood, the building heat combined with the shift in the longshore set had driven them into the deeper water beyond the bar.

"You okay?" asked Conrad.

Out of superstition, they never spoke when they sensed they were about to make a dry haul. But there was something else in Rollo's silence, the manner in which he mistrustfully regarded the ocean. He made to speak. It wasn't that he checked himself so much as gave up, unable to find the words.

"Meet you halfway," said Conrad. He headed off down the beach to the Model A and unlashed the onshore line from the back of the truck. They started to haul on their respective ends of the net, hand over hand, in unison.

Conrad felt the weight almost immediately, a particular kind of weight—deadweight—not the twitching load of fish breaking for deep water and coming up against the twine. A dead porpoise, perhaps. Another thought flashed through his mind. He shut it out, cursing himself for even considering it, for lending it any kind of credence or life.

He glanced along the beach and knew immediately that Rollo had also sensed something amiss. His rhythm had slowed and he was staring intently at the shrinking half-circle of water, their small bite of ocean enclosed by the net. Still no visible signs of fish. Just the inert load being drawn towards the crashing surf. Short of abandoning the haul, there was nothing either of them could do to alter the outcome.

They had been drawing ever closer together, measured steps to keep the bag centered, coils of sodden net snaking behind them on the sand. Only ten or so yards of beach divided them when a big sea caught hold of the bag, raising it from the bed. They hauled speedily, taking up the slack.

Conrad glimpsed a streak of white—the belly of a large fish?—buried behind the glassy face of the capping wave. It was lost to view as the wave broke, collapsing in a thunderous tumble of water.

The wash receded to reveal a body snarled in the bag—a woman, long blond hair braided with seaweed, sand crabs scurrying, sea robins flapping, drowning in air. Then she was engulfed by the next breaking wave. Instinctively, Conrad and Rollo used the momentum to drag the bag up the beach, beyond the wash.

Conrad stared, deaf to Rollo's religious mutterings and the crash of the surf.

The woman was lithe and long-limbed, wearing a navy blue swimsuit. She was lying facedown, her right foot cocked behind her left ankle, her right arm tight against her body, the left extended above her head, the fingers of her hand slightly splayed as if reaching for something.

She moved. Conrad hurried forward. She was definitely moving. Seizing her cold, pale shoulder, he turned her over. An enormous monkfish bucked and flailed beneath her. The bloated lips of its grotesquely broad mouth seemed to be reaching for the woman's, lunging for an embrace. As for the woman, her lips were blue, starved of oxygen, of life.

Conrad delved into the bag, seized the mollykite by the tail, and in one violent movement swung the creature high out over the breakers. He remained staring out to sea.

"Conrad," said Rollo helplessly, looking for guidance.

Conrad finally turned. "Help me take her out."

They peeled the net off the woman as best they could, swept the sand crabs from her face and body, and drew her out by the feet. She was completely rigid, unbending, as if frozen or hewn from a block of white marble.

Her hair snagged in the mesh. Rollo proffered his jackknife, but Conrad ignored him, finally freeing the woman from the clutches of the seine.

Rollo seemed reluctant to touch the woman again, so Conrad took her in his arms and carried her up the beach.

2

Tom Hollis lit another cigarette and turned to the sports pages. The Amagansett Bonackers had defeated the Hampton Bays by a score of 9–7 in Sunday's game. Some fellow called Lambert had gone four for five, knocking in two runs, and his batting was described as "spectacular."

"About what?" asked a gruff voice.

Hollis looked up to see the considerable bulk of Chief Milligan filling the door of his office.

"About what?" said Milligan, repeating himself.

Hollis frowned, still unsure.

"You said 'Who gives a damn?'" explained Milligan.

"I did?"

Christ, not only was he talking to himself now, he didn't even know it.

"Oh, you know, the baseball." He flapped the *East Hampton Star* vaguely in Milligan's direction.

"My boy made the winning run in the twelfth."

He should have remembered. He *did* remember. Young Tim played for the Bonackers. South paw. Swing like a caveman killing his lunch. It was coming back now. All too late.

"Think you could give a damn about this?" said Milligan, advancing. He slid a sheet of paper across the desk. Hollis scanned it.

His first thought was "There goes my lunch."

HOLLIS TURNED LEFT onto Newtown Lane from the East Hampton Town Police Department. From the junction with Main Street it was pretty much a straight run east of two miles into Amagansett, but as he cleared the town limits he swung the patrol car south onto Skimhampton Road, opting for the back roads.

He reached for the bottle of Gordon's in the glove compartment, steering with his knees while he unscrewed the cap. A bracing shot, he persuaded himself, because of what lay ahead. He didn't allow himself to recall the numerous other corpses he had confronted in his career without the aid of liquor.

The beach landing at the end of Atlantic Avenue was deserted except for a black sedan with New York City plates. Hollis pulled on his cap, squinting against the sun and the dust whipped up by the dry, stiff breeze. Even the beach appeared empty. Strolling down onto the sand he saw a gathering of vehicles and men about half a mile to the east through the thin haze of mist thrown up by the breakers. Half a mile. He'd only walked thirty yards and already his shirt was clinging to his chest. He removed his jacket and set off along the shore.

The body lay beneath a faded green canvas tarpaulin in the shade of a large truck, some kind of military transport converted for beach use. A dozen or so fishermen stood about in huddles talking. A few curious vacationers hovered on the fringes, morbid onlookers.

"Deputy Chief Hollis," he announced, approaching the group of fishermen nearest the body. Amagansett fell within the jurisdiction of East Hampton town, but he rarely ventured over here and didn't recognize any of the characters gathered around, regarding him coldly. He didn't blame them. He couldn't abide small-town cops himself.

He removed his cap and wiped his brow with the back of his sleeve. "Who found her?"

One of the men nodded over his shoulder. Thirty yards down the beach, a fisherman, tall and big-boned, was loading a net into a surf-boat hitched to the back of an old Model A flatbed. Another fellow—slighter, wirier, with lank, bleached hair—was helping him.

Hollis glanced back at the tarpaulin. "Don't worry," said one of the younger men, thin lips buried in a scraggy beard worn to conceal a weak chin. "She's fresh. A day, not even."

His reluctance to take a look was that transparent? Crouching, Hollis folded back the tarp.

Death had not completely obscured her beauty. Blond tresses matted with weed framed an oval face that descended to the delicate point of her chin. Her lips, though blue, were arched and full. Faint smile lines flanked her mouth. Her nose was sharp, her eyes wide-set and closed.

He resisted the temptation to force open the lids. Green, he guessed. He'd find out soon enough. There was a small scar etched into her left eyebrow, and pierce-marks in her ears. A beautiful young woman, her life cut short after no more than, what, twenty-five years? Thirty, maximum.

He examined both sides of her neck, instinctively, a vestige of his time in homicide. There was no bruising, but he did find something else, in the sand beside her head.

"Anyone recognize her?"

The fishermen shrugged, not bothering to reply. Hollis folded back the tarp and got to his feet. "Who took her earrings?"

They stared at him, their faces set in stone. He held up the gold back-stud he had found in the sand.

"I said, who took her earrings?"

He intended his words to have an edge of easy menace, but he knew they sounded petulant.

"What do you take us for?" From the one with the beard again.

Hollis let it go.

The two men who had netted the body exchanged a few words as he approached them. "Deputy Chief Hollis," he announced. The tall fisherman nodded an acknowledgment. His dark hair was cropped short, his mouth was wide, intelligent. Steel-gray eyes looked down on Hollis from beneath a broad, heavy brow.

"You were the ones found her?"

"Uh-huh."

There was something unnerving about the steady, unyielding gaze. The stillness of the fellow was in stark contrast to his companion, who shuffled his feet nervously as he glanced around him.

Hollis removed a small memo pad from the breast pocket of his jacket. "Your name?" he asked the taller one.

"Conrad Labarde."

Hollis looked up. "What is that, French?"

"Basque."

Basque. It rang a bell, some distant memory of a geography lesson.

"And you?" asked Hollis. The nervous fellow froze, then looked to his tall friend as if for assistance.

"Rollo Kemp," replied the Basque. Even Hollis had heard of the Kemps, an old dynasty of farmer-fishermen, one of those families that went back all the way.

"Cat got his tongue?"

"You make him a little jumpy is all."

There was no hint of aggression in his tone, no allocation of blame despite the phrasing. Hollis looked the Kemp boy over—something not quite right about him, he could see it now. Not "overburdened," as his mother would have said. The product of inbreeding, perhaps.

"You want to tell me what happened?"

Hollis took notes while the Basque, in an even monotone, described the events leading up to the discovery of the body. When he was finished, Hollis closed the pad and placed it in his hip pocket.

"Any idea who she is?"

"No."

"And what did you do with her earrings?" It was an old cop trick— a question charged with assumptions, asked ever so casually.

The Basque held Hollis's gaze, no trace of a flicker. Hollis showed him the earring back-stud.

"Wait here," said the Basque, making for the group of fishermen. Hollis followed, damned if he was going to be ordered around. The Basque stopped and turned.

"It's best," he said.

HOLLIS WAS TOO FAR AWAY to hear the specifics of the exchange. At a certain moment, the Basque must have mentioned Hollis, because everyone glanced over at him. Not long after, the young fisherman with the beard became agitated, raising his voice. With a dismissive sweep of his arm, he turned on his heel.

He had taken all of two steps when the Basque placed a restraining hand on his shoulder. The younger man spun back, swinging a roundhouse as he did so. More shocking, though, was the speed of the big man's reaction. He stepped inside the arc of the punch so that it fell harmlessly against his shoulder and in the same movement he pushed his assailant in the face with the open palm of his hand, so that he fell back onto the sand.

The Basque clamped a foot on the other's chest and held out a hand. The younger man rummaged in his pocket and handed something over. Only then did the Basque remove his foot and step away.

He wandered back over and placed a pair of pearl stud earrings in Hollis's hand. "What happens now?" he asked.

"The medical examiner's on his way from Hauppauge. They'll take her away."

"They'll bog down on the beach. We should move her to the landing."

Hollis nodded.

AN HOUR LATER, the Suffolk County chief medical examiner and his two assistants arrived at the beach landing in an unmarked van. Dr. Cornelius Hobbs was a stout, brisk man with gold-rimmed spectacles and a hairpiece that made little attempt to disguise itself as such. Jet-black, its curling fringes flapped wildly in the breeze like a young bird struggling to take wing.

"Deputy Hollis?" he asked, not waiting for a reply. "Let's see what we've got, shall we?"

His voice was pinched, nasal. Sinuses, thought Hollis, a welcome affliction for someone in his line of work.

The woman's body had been placed on the bed of the Basque's Model A. Without any consideration for the handful of onlookers, Hobbs seized the end of the tarpaulin and yanked it off.

"Mmmmmmm," he mused, lowering his voice as he turned to Hollis. "A fine figure of a woman. I believe a little mouth-to-mouth is called for. You never know, Hollis, you just never know." Like many of the medical examiners Hollis had known in the past, Dr. Cornelius Hobbs clearly enjoyed proclaiming his own ease when confronted with a corpse. He was still chuckling to himself as he used the trailer hitch to clamber up onto the back of the truck.

The Basque appeared at the side of the truck. "A little more respect, I think."

There was nothing censorious in his tone. Had there been, maybe Hobbs would have reacted differently; as it was, he simply frowned. "Don't I know you?"

"Not sure I've ever had the pleasure."

The reply brought a thin smile to Hollis's lips.

THE WOMAN'S BODY WAS LOADED into the van on a gurney by the two assistants. Hobbs closed the doors and turned to Hollis.

"They never learn."

"What's that?" asked Hollis.

"The sea's no friend of ours. Third drowning this week."

Here we go, thought Hollis.

"Had a lad down Mecox way, city people, father a banker. The boy gets accepted by West Point, has his friends up for the weekend to celebrate, big party on the beach. Swam for his college. Wasn't drunk, his blood tested clean. Sharks had themselves a nibble before he washed up." He nodded towards the van. "No, don't get much cleaner than that."

"How long do you reckon?"

"From the rigor . . . less than twenty-four hours. You'll have the autopsy report tomorrow, afternoon at the latest."

"I need a photo. For identification."

"Of course you do."

"Today would be good."

"Today, today, all I ever hear." Nevertheless, he clicked his fingers at one of his assistants. "Snap her."

CLUTCHING TWO FOUR-BY-FIVE FILM HOLDERS, Hollis watched as the van pulled away. Almost immediately the spectators started to dissipate. The Basque was rolling a cigarette by the Model A; the Kemp boy appeared to have left already. Hollis strolled over.

"Thanks," he said. "For the earrings."

"I figured it was important."

"Yeah?"

"How many women you know go swimming in their jewelry?"

Damn right, thought Hollis.

"What do you mean?" he said.

The Basque eyed him flatly, then slipped the rolled cigarette between his lips and lit it with a steel Zippo.

"Army issue?" asked Hollis, nodding at the lighter.

"See you around, Deputy."

The Basque climbed behind the wheel of the Model A, fired the engine, and pulled away. Hollis stood watching the vehicle, the trailer dancing over the ruts, until it turned east onto Bluff Road and was lost to view.

3

UNABLE TO JUSTIFY A FULL-TIME PHOTOGRAPHER, THE EAST HAMPTON Town Police Department subcontracted the work to a local man, Abel Cole. The sign in the window of his narrow shop next to Edwards Theater on Main Street read: *Portraits, Christenings, Weddings. "And Bar-Mitzvahs"* had been added beneath in a different shade of ink.

Many wealthy Jews from New York had built houses in the more exclusive beachside areas of town in the years preceding the war. They experienced little or no prejudice from the local people, who looked on all "people from away" as aliens, but if they expected their peers to leave their bigotry behind them in the city they were sorely mistaken.

The Maidstone Club, the sine qua non of social acceptability for the wealthy summer colonists, showed no signs of removing its ban on Jewish members. As a Jew, you could own a lavish mansion overlooking the manicured fairways of the Maidstone's links course, but if you wished to actually play golf you had to travel west to Wainscott.

Hollis had witnessed anti-Jewish sentiments at first hand, or at any rate their aftermath—a Star of David daubed in white paint on the front door of a Colonial-style residence belonging to a family called the Rosens.

It had been a sorry introduction to East Hampton for Hollis, occurring just two weeks after he'd taken up his position as deputy chief. A stark and malicious act, it was also quite unnecessary, since a large brass Star of David was already attached to the lintel above the door, nailed there by the Rosens when they had moved into their new home.

A search of the front garden had uncovered a size-10 patent-leather dress shoe speckled with white paint in a clump of hydrangeas—a discovery that Hollis had kept to himself, along with the name of the shoe's owner, clearly embossed on the inside.

The gentleman was a member of the Maidstone Club, the son of the club treasurer, no less. Hollis didn't need to summon the full force of his detective's training to piece together the events of the evening in question: a drunken dinner following the Maidstone's annual tennis tournament; the member's dress shoe; further sets of footprints in the flower beds; a property defaced with white paint that washed off easily—as easily, in fact, as the thin whitewash used to mark the lines on a lawn-tennis court. Hardly the stuff of departmental legend.

Hollis had stalked the shoe's owner for a few days until the opportunity presented itself for a word in private. When confronted with the evidence, the culprit pleaded high jinks. When Hollis informed him that a court of law would only accept a plea of "guilty" or "not guilty," he broke down in tears, right there in the changing rooms of a gentlemen's outfitters on Newtown Lane.

Two hours later, Jacob Rosen answered his door to a blond, red-eyed young man in a brand-new blazer, who handed him an envelope. Inside was a banker's draft to the order of five hundred dollars made payable to the Temple Adas Israel in Sag Harbor. The young man then asked for, and received, Jacob Rosen's forgiveness. He politely declined the invitation to take tea and cake with the family.

To Hollis's mind, the debt was only part-paid. Almost a year on, he still kept the shoe in a box beneath his bed along with a photo of the incriminating article, taken in situ by Abel Cole in his official capacity as the police department's photographer.

It was the first time the two men had met, but the signs of a fast friendship were there from the start. Hollis's plan for an unofficial settlement of the matter had required Abel's discretion and collusion. Indeed, it was Abel who suggested the outrageous sum of five hundred dollars by way of a penalty. He knew the family by reputation, knew the boy was good for the money but that it would pinch him hard enough to hurt. That very same week Abel Cole had added "And Bar-Mitzvahs" to the sign in his window.

Hollis entered the shop to find Abel photographing a stern-faced, middle-aged woman seated in a chair set against a mottled backdrop. A Persian cat lay curled on her lap, looking quite as unhappy and mistrustful as its owner. As ever, the sickly smell of darkroom chemicals hung heavy in the air.

Abel was stooped behind a tripod, peering through the viewfinder of his camera—a Graflex Speed Graphic. Hollis had seen hundreds, if not thousands, of the machines over the years—in front of precincts and courthouses, at crime scenes, bulbs popping on their side-mounted flashing units—but Abel's was different, trimmed in olive drab, witness to his time as a wartime photographer in Europe.

"She's got beautiful eyes," said Abel.

There was no reaction from the woman.

"And a fine, pert little nose."

"Yes, she has, hasn't she?" conceded the woman matter-of-factly.

Abel looked up. "I was talking to the cat."

Despite herself, the woman broke into a smile. Abel tripped the front shutter.

"Gotcha," he said.

"Edith Harper," explained Abel as soon as the door had swung shut behind the woman. "Lost her only boy in the Pacific, but she was a sour-faced old trout long before."

He took a pack of cigarettes from beneath the counter and offered one to Hollis. Six months back, Hollis would have glanced outside through the window to check no one was watching before accepting. He was way beyond that now.

Abel lit the cigarettes and pushed his long bangs out of his eyes. "Any luck?" he asked.

"No." After dropping off the film holders with Abel for developing, Hollis had returned to police headquarters to run a missing persons check through the neighboring force at Southampton, but had turned up nothing. "I was hoping you might know her."

"Seen her around," said Abel, reaching for a buff envelope on the counter. "Who could forget, face like that? But I don't know her name. City girl. Drives a swanky roadster. Ten bucks says someone'll know over at the coven."

"The coven?"

"You know . . . the Ladies' Vaginal Insertion Society."

The Ladies' Village Improvement Society was an organization of local women devoted to preserving and beautifying "the village," as they insisted on calling it. They had first come together to campaign and raise funds for the regular watering down of Main Street when it was little more than a dusty track at the mercy of the brisk summer winds. But they soon expanded their activities to include a program for the sweeping of the sidewalks and crosswalks, the installation of oil lamps, and the pruning of the huge elms that flanked the thoroughfare.

And so it had continued, their self-proclaimed remit extending beyond the main artery of the town like a river bursting its banks, swamping all in its path. Fifty years on, there was almost no aspect of life within East Hampton that lay beyond the scrutiny of the LVIS.

Abel was right, it was as good a place as any to start. Their numbers swelled in the summer months with the influx of wealthy New York worthies. More than likely, one of them would recognize the dead girl.

"Crying shame," said Abel, handing over the envelope. "Face like a Botticelli angel."

"Yeah," said Hollis, unsure what his friend was talking about.

HE DECIDED TO LEAVE THE PATROL CAR and walk down Main Street. Up ahead, two young girls pattered along behind a squat woman, their hair done in tight, stiff braids, faces scrubbed clean enough to shine.

Hollis wondered why he hadn't shared the news of the girl's earrings with Abel. It wasn't professional discretion on his part; there was little the two men kept from each other. Maybe he was getting ahead of himself, maybe she had simply forgotten to remove the items before going swimming. He had done a similar thing himself a month back, ruining a perfectly good wristwatch in the process, a gift from his wife.

Yes, that was why he had hesitated, for fear of looking foolish when it proved to be a blind alley. And yet the tightening in his stomach told him otherwise.

THE LADIES' VILLAGE IMPROVEMENT SOCIETY was based in the old Clinton Academy, beside the library on the north side of Main Street. The former school was now home to the East Hampton Historical Society, which, for a nominal sum, subleased the annex to the women.

Hollis paused before entering the old brick-and-wood building. From the apex of its gambrel roof rose a tall, pointed cupola, the bell it once housed for summoning the students long gone. The odor from an unruly clump of honeysuckle was almost unbearably sweet in the searing afternoon heat. Hollis wiped his brow before stepping into the shaded sanctuary of the covered porch.

The LVIS occupied two small, low offices at the rear of the building. They were a hive of activity, with women hurrying to and fro as if being blown by the black electric fans which adorned almost all the desks.

Hollis felt like a student entering the teachers' common room, summoned there for some misdemeanor then deliberately ignored to stew in his guilt and the anticipation of his punishment. Maybe it was the early history of the building somehow exerting its presence; whatever, no one paid him a blind bit of notice.

"Excuse me," he said to a woman in a floral cotton dress as she hurried by purposefully, a stack of papers under her arm. Without breaking her stride, she nodded towards a desk in the corner of the room.

So that was it, a strict pecking order, everything had to pass through Mary Calder, president of the LVIS. She was leaning forward in her chair, one elbow on the desk, the fingers of her right hand tugging at her sandy locks. In her other hand she held a phone receiver pressed to her ear.

"Yes, yes, I understand," she said irritably. "But the fair is only three weeks away and you still haven't *committed*."

The LVIS annual summer fair, hence all the activity, thought Hollis, relieved that they didn't always function at such a shaming pace.

Mary glanced up at him (reading his thoughts? he wouldn't put it past her). Her pale blue eyes registered his presence and she smiled. This threw Hollis. She had never smiled at him. In fact, she had only ever scowled at him in the past, usually when she was berating him for the mortal danger posed to village residents by speeding motorists, as if somehow he were personally to blame.

In fairness to Mary, accidents were an increasingly common occurrence, and it was little more than a year since one young resident had indeed lost her life, her coltish body shattered by a motor car, the impact so strong that she'd been thrown twenty feet through the air into the hedge beyond the shoulder.

The incident had occurred a few weeks before his arrival in East

Hampton, but he could still see the photo in the file—Lizzie Jencks hanging there in the hawthorn like some grisly scarecrow. The driver had stopped, scarring the surface of the dirt grade road, only to drive on, his identity destined to remain a mystery, as would the reason a fifteen-year-old girl was out walking a country road in the dead of night.

Mary rounded off the telephone conversation, the tone of her voice making it patently clear to the person on the other end of the line that their life wouldn't be worth living should they let her down. She hung up and made her way across the room towards Hollis.

He knew her to be in her mid-thirties, almost five years older than he, but she displayed fewer visible signs of encroaching middle age. She was tall, slender, healthy-looking to a fault, her tanned and freck-led face, devoid of makeup, witness to an active life spent outdoors. He had often seen her striding out along the wooded lanes north of town, sinewy calves protruding from clumpy hiking boots, a small can-vas knapsack on her back.

"You must think me a dreadful harpy."

"Excuse me?"

"Always complaining, always after something. You only ever see me at my worst."

"I'll take your word for it," he said with a wry smile.

Christ, thought Hollis, I'm flirting with her, stop flirting with her.

Mary cocked her head slightly, eyes narrowing, taking his measure. Hollis squirmed under her gaze; he had been way too familiar.

"Oh, you don't need to do that," she said. "Ask around, you'll see I'm not such a terrible old hag." Hollis's brain was racing too fast to fathom the implications of the last comment, so he searched for a way to move the conversation on.

"Can I have a word alone?"

"Yes, you may," replied Mary, stressing the "may" to correct his grammar. She paused before continuing. "Damn," she said, "you'll never believe me now."

———

HOLLIS WATCHED HER CLOSELY as she flipped through the photographs of the dead girl and knew immediately that he had just gotten a positive identification. They were standing in the shaded garden at the back of the building. A small fountain played nearby, humidifying the air around them. A climbing rose, loosely wired to a trellis, strained under the weight of its flowers. Birds chirped merrily and the wind lapped at the leaves of a tall birch tree. It was a tranquil spot, quite at odds with the expression on Mary's face.

Hollis was intrigued. From her very first glance she had clearly recognized the girl, but she insisted on viewing all four photographs, taking her time as she did so. When she was finished, she handed them back.

"Lillian Wallace. Her family has a house on Further Lane." Only now did she look Hollis in the eye.

"Thank you," he said.

Mary accompanied him around the side of the building to the street. She folded her arms across her midriff as if chilled by the eighty-five-degree heat. "She loved the ocean. I sometimes saw her there down at the beach, in the evening, when I walked the dog. She liked to swim there."

Strange, somehow she didn't seem like a woman who owned a dog. What would it be? Something devoted and fiercely loyal—a retriever, maybe, or a labrador.

"She was a good swimmer?" he asked.

"Not good enough, it seems."

"I appreciate it," he said, holding up the envelope. Mary watched him leave.

"I was sorry to hear about your wife," she called after him. Turning back, he groped for something to say. In the end he simply nodded then carried on his way.

Returning to the patrol car, he found a note from Abel on the driver's seat: *Dinner tonight. 7:30. Don't worry—I'm cooking!*

Hollis smiled, fired the engine and pulled away.

THE LENGTH OF THE YEW HEDGE that flanked the entrance gates of the Wallace property on Further Lane gave some indication of the scale of the plot, close on a hundred yards wide, while the height of the hedge concealed all else from prying eyes. The white wooden gates, discreet but imposing, were open, and Hollis guided the patrol car through them, slowing only to read the name painted in neat black capitals on a board—OCEANVIEW—proof that wealth and imagination didn't always make for natural bedfellows. All the properties on Further Lane gave directly onto the ocean at the rear.

He always found it strange when he entered the colony, this narrow belt of oceanfront the wealthy had claimed as their own. A mile to the south of Main Street, it was in East Hampton, but not of it. There were no stores, no filling-stations, no bars or boardinghouses. In fact, there was almost no trade whatsoever, nothing that might remind the residents of how they had amassed their fortunes. There were simply stretches of half-glimpsed residential grandeur, hedged and fenced, pegged out and parceled off.

Hollis had heard that some purchasers would happily pay too much for a house, inflating the value of surrounding real estate, thereby ensuring that the diminishing number of vacant plots would only ever be occupied by those of their kind. Maybe it was just rumor, but he somehow doubted it. There was a chilling simplicity to both the logic and the formula.

All you needed was the money, and for those with less than others there were alternatives—the roads once, twice, three times removed from the waterfront avenues that fronted the ocean and skirted the shores of Georgica Pond.

On the map, Georgica Pond always reminded him of a startled marsupial settled on its haunches, its upturned snout, pointed ears, forelegs, and tail formed by the larger creeks and coves which ran into the main body of water. At over a mile and a half in length from top to toe, pond was something of a misnomer. It extended from the highway to the ocean, effectively demarcating East Hampton from Wainscott and the other communities farther west.

Once open to the sea, a vicious hurricane had ripped through the area in 1938, and in a few brief hours scooped up thousands of tons of sand from the ocean bed, plugging the broad tidal gut as nonchalantly as a man might stop a bottle with a cork.

The summer colony had borne the full brunt of that freakish storm, exposed as the houses were on the high dunes and sandy bluffs that fronted the ocean. Nowhere suffered more than the Maidstone Club. Dozens of its colorful beachside cabanas were reduced to matchwood within minutes and littered across the slope leading up to the clubhouse. Paradoxically, the devastating force of the hurricane ensured the colony's survival. After all, was this not the very reason the wealthy had come here, to stare Nature in the face, to stand mute with wonder before Her? Besides, many of them had wisely overinsured their properties and duly snatched a tidy profit from the jaws of misfortune. The pioneering spirit rekindled and reinforced, an alarming number of industrialists, financiers, publishers, actors, and artists had blown in on the back of that hurricane, despite the advent of war.

Maybe the tide would turn again, as it had during the Depression. It was unlikely. Even in these uncertain times, Hollis had counted no fewer than four houses under construction on Pondview Lane while driving to the Wallace residence, the bearer of bad news.

Assuming the medical examiner's initial prognosis was correct, Lillian Wallace had drowned the previous day, and as he guided the patrol car down the serpentine driveway Hollis wondered why no one had reported her missing. He hated this moment, the nervous shuffle of his feet on a foreign doorstep, the downturned gaze, the mumbled words of comfort for a total stranger—"I'm sorry"—the unavoidable postscript, hopelessly inadequate.

He pulled to a halt a respectable distance from the main entrance, instinctively, as if the area immediately in front of the door were somehow reserved for the exclusive use of the family and their own motor cars. What had Abel said? Lillian Wallace at the wheel of a swanky roadster. There was certainly no sign of the vehicle out front.

Even with his untrained eye, Hollis could tell that the house, however imposing, was an ugly affair, uncertain of its identity, overblown, with all the discreet grandeur of a rooster puffing out its chest. It was as if the architect had thrown everything in his repertoire at the building in the hope that something pleasing to his client would stick. Over one hundred feet long, the walls were stuccoed in the English style and swathed in Virginia creeper. The vine-covered pergolas suggested an Italo-American villa, but the hipped and shingled roof was too steeply pitched for the effect to be convincing. The roof was interrupted at the sides by eyelid dormers from another stylistic epoch, and in the middle by twin gables that descended to a wide porticoed entrance. This central section looked as if it had been bolted on later, almost as an afterthought. Apart from its near symmetry, about the only thing the hybrid building had going for it were the exquisite formal gardens that rolled off in all directions.

As Hollis tugged on the bellpull, he spotted an elderly gardener observing him from beside a rose arbor, squinting beneath the brim of his straw hat, water arcing from the hose in his hand. There must be someone at home or he would have approached by now. Sure enough, there was the clatter of shoes on a wooden floor from inside the house, and the front door swung open to reveal a small, trim woman dressed in a maid's uniform. Her long, dark hair, laced with strands of gray, was pulled back tightly off her face. When she spoke, her voice betrayed a faint accent.

"Good afternoon." Almost immediately, her hand went to her mouth. "O Dio, no . . ." She had read it in his eyes.

"Is there . . . I mean, are the Wallaces at home?"

"Lillian. Where is she? Is she all right?" Her eyes pleaded with him.

Procedure dictated that he speak to the family first, if they were present. "Are they here, the Wallaces?"

"No," she choked.

It was Thursday. Still in the city, probably. Wouldn't be up till the weekend.

"What's your name?"

"Rosa."

"May I come in, Rosa?"

4

For the third time that day Manfred Wallace inhaled the heady scent of victory. He leaned forward over the backgammon board and stared at the dice. Six and five. The gamble had paid off.

"Goddamnit, Manfred."

"Language, Peter, I believe the chairman's within earshot."

Peter Carlson arched his long neck. Sure enough, Wheaton Blake, chairman of the club's Card and Backgammon Committee, was seated near the bar, observing them from behind a glass of chilled white port. Peter gave a coy smile and received a guarded nod of the head in return from the chairman: Apology accepted. This time.

"You lucky bastard," muttered Peter under his breath.

Manfred didn't believe in luck, or if he did, that it was the just reward of the skillful. Behind in the race almost from the first, he had played a faultless bar point holding game, gradually eroding White's advantage. Still ahead, Peter had been obliged to break his midpoint first, exposing himself to a double hit.

This was the one moment Manfred's bold stratagem had been geared towards—a pyrrhic victory or certain defeat to be determined by one roll of the dice. Ideally, he required six and five. He not only required them, he deserved them, he had earned them, they were his by right. The dice, it seemed, had agreed with him. Coming off the bar, Peter had tried valiantly to bring his two rear men home; but the game had slipped away from him along with the five hundred dollars riding on it.

"Whiskey?" asked Manfred.

"Why not?"

Manfred caught the eye of a waiter polishing glasses behind the bar, and the young man hurried over.

"Two whiskeys and soda please, George."

"Just a needle for me," said Peter.

"Of whiskey, sir?"

Peter shot him a look—soda, fool.

"Ignore him, George, he's sulking," said Manfred.

"Ignore me, George, I'm sulking."

George shed a helpless look and shuffled off. Peter pulled a checkbook from his pocket and began to write.

Manfred understood. It wasn't the money, it was the losing. Not once, but twice, first at squash racquets, now at backgammon. The squash had also been a close-run thing. Evenly matched ever since their days on the varsity team at Yale, Peter's fitness had dipped a little of late and Manfred had duly developed a hateful little dropshot. Their Thursday game was a regular fixture, and had been since the end of the war. Sometimes they played at the Yale Club down on Vanderbilt Avenue. More often than not the New York Racquet and Tennis Club was the chosen venue, as it was today. Built on a prime patch of Park Avenue, the vast building resembled a Florentine Renaissance palazzo, with rusticated arches and stone walls as thick as a prison, a prison designed to keep unsavory types out rather than in. The interiors were grand yet austere, the physical embodiment of the ideals of the gentleman sportsman, and members still stepped onto its hallowed courts clad in Brooks Brothers flannels, Oxford-cloth shirts, and Indian cotton jumpers.

Peter handed over the check. "You're going to have to make it up to me," he said.

Manfred smiled, reaching for one of Peter's cigarettes and lighting it. "Jarvis Steel Company."

"Never heard of them."

"They're based in Union, New Jersey. They make a range of tool steels, nickel-bearing alloys, that kind of thing. They've paid dividends every year since 1903. Very sound."

"Very boring."

"A little. Till now."

Peter leaned forward, intrigued.

"Their metallurgical laboratory in Reading has just patented a corrosion-resistant alloy," Manfred went on. "They're calling it Jarvis No. 10. I won't bother you with the technical details. Let's just say the results of the tests are, well, very impressive, according to my man."

"You and your men," smiled Peter. "Where on earth do you find them?"

Manfred shrugged.

"How much should I put in?" asked Peter.

At that moment, George returned with the drinks. Manfred waited for him to leave before replying.

"Forty thousand."

"It's a lot."

"Not as much as the hundred you'll make in a year, maybe two, not including dividends." Peter looked suitably impressed; one hundred thousand dollars was a lot of money even by his standards. It didn't come close to the sum that Manfred's family brokerage house had made that very morning.

It was Manfred, fresh from Yale, who had convinced the partners of Wallace, Greenwood and Company that they move into sugar when war ripped through Europe in 1939. Sugar was then selling at a paltry penny a pound. Prices had gone through the roof in the First

War and there was every reason to suppose the same would happen again.

In all, Manfred and his father had spent a month in Cuba before settling on a producer just emerging from bankruptcy and controlled by the Federal National City Bank of New York. It was another six weeks before the firm formally took control of the operation. They spent heavily on processing and refining equipment, an investment which had more than paid its way by the time America entered the war in 1941. Sugar prices continued to rise, the business prospered, buoyed up by wartime demand for ethyl alcohol, readily produced from sugarcane molasses.

The foresight, the risk, the hard work had all been theirs. Eight years on, it was time to reap the rewards, a staggering seventy-six-fold return on their investment. The deal had been finalized that very morning—Manfred's first victory of the day, indeed, his greatest to date. A few months shy of his thirtieth birthday, he was wealthier than he could ever have imagined. More important, though, for the grand design of his life, he had also made a lot of very influential people rich, and this was something they would never forget.

"Excuse me, Mr. Wallace." It was George again. "There's a phone call for you."

Manfred and Peter exchanged a look. No one ever phoned them at the club. It was a matter of principle.

"It's your father."

"My father?"

"He says it's important, sir."

Manfred tamped out his cigarette and followed George to the bar. He paused for a moment before raising the phone receiver to his ear. Something had gone wrong with the deal. No. Impossible. It was signed and sealed, he'd witnessed it with his own eyes just hours before.

"Father?"

His father's voice, when it came, was not its usual stentorian self, no bark, no bite. "Manfred, I'm afraid I have some terrible news."

Peter Carlson drained the last of his whiskey and turned in time to see Manfred replace the receiver on its cradle, groping for the surface of the counter to steady himself. His face was ashen, even the high color of his recent exertions on the squash court drained from it.

Peter hurried over. Manfred's blank eyes seemed focused on some distant, imaginary horizon. "Manfred, are you all right?" he asked. Only when he rested a hand on his friend's arm did Manfred appear to register his presence.

"My sister . . . she's dead."

"What? How? I saw her at El Morocco's only last night."

"Not Gayle. Lilly."

"Lilly?"

"She drowned."

Peter remained silent, not because he couldn't think of anything to say, but because in the twenty-two years he had known Manfred Wallace he had never once seen him cry.

5

As Hollis turned off Woods Lane, a dog darted into the road. He braked suddenly, stalling the car, and the small basket of chocolates spilled off the passenger seat onto the floor. He let them lie where they fell—already softened by the heat, the dirt clinging to them—then he restarted the engine and carried on along Highway Behind the Lots.

Abel lived in a modest cottage near the junction with Wireless Road. It was the house he had grown up in, the only house he had ever known. His father, an engineer with a New York firm, had moved with his wife and newborn son to East Hampton soon after the Great War to oversee the construction of a wireless telegraphy station on a plot just south of Cove Hollow Road.

By 1921, Henry Cole's work was done, but East Hampton had weaved its spell on him. A keen amateur photographer, he secured a loan for a down payment on a narrow store on Main Street, and for the remainder of his life devoted himself to photographic portraiture. Abel was nineteen years old at the time of his father's death, and it was natural that he take over the business. However, with money tight, he was in no position to move out of the family home, and he had to content himself with entertaining a string of local girls on the plum-velvet Victorian couch in the shop, the one reserved for family portraits. With his dark, broken looks, his languid manner and quick wit, there was never any shortage of young women willing to test the springs with him.

His mother died quite unexpectedly of a stroke the day after the German army entered Paris. The two events were not necessarily unconnected. Sylvie Cole had spent the first eighteen years of her life in a small apartment off the Square des Batignolles in the 17th arrondissement of that city, before boarding a ship in Le Havre bound for New York.

The only son of an only son, destined never to meet his mother's family, from whom she was estranged, Abel found himself alone in the world at the age of twenty-three with an ailing business and a small shingled cottage on Highway Behind the Lots.

Set some distance back from the road, the front lawn of the house was an untended meadow of tall grasses and wildflowers, Queen Anne's lace and black-eyed Susans. A narrow swath of clipped lawn provided the only access to the house, obliging visitors to run a gauntlet of butterflies and bees in order to reach the front porch, which was fringed with self-seeded hollyhocks, well over six feet tall at this time of year.

If Hollis knew the names of the flowers it was only because Abel's girlfriend, Lucy, had talked him through them on many occasions. Although they didn't live together, Lucy had staked her claim to the front and back gardens—wild, unruly kingdoms which belied the thought, expertise, and hard work behind them.

Lucy made a comfortable living maintaining the gardens of city people. Out of season she pruned their shrubs, cut back their perennials, planting bulbs and annuals so that their borders, pots, and window boxes were ablaze with color come the summer when they took up residence once more. The summer months were her quietest time of the year. She had a team of local boys, headed by her feckless nephew, to weed and water, and mow the lawns.

Lucy must have seen Hollis pull up because she appeared on the porch as he made his way towards the house. Slight, slender, and effortlessly beautiful, her long dark hair tied back with a ribbon, she was wearing an apron and clutching a wooden spoon. Hollis kissed her on the cheek.

"You look very . . ." He searched for the word.

"Yes?"

"Norman friggin' Rockwell!" shouted Abel from inside the house.

Hollis laughed. It was true, she was the very picture of benign domesticity, the smiling wife in the gingham apron, pure *Saturday Evening Post* front cover.

Abel appeared from the house and Lucy struck him with the wooden spoon, a playful but firm blow on the arm.

"Jesus, Lucy!"

"Any more of that and you won't be eating tonight."

"Chance would be a fine thing," mumbled Abel, wisely backing out of range. Lucy headed inside.

"I'm sorry," said Abel. "She insisted." He was referring to the fact that Lucy was wearing an apron. She was a woman of many talents; sadly, cooking wasn't one of them. It was an inescapable truth that Lucy sought unsuccessfully to refute with recipes of ever-increasing ambition and complexity.

In her defense, the dish she prepared for them that evening was far better than it sounded. Tomato aspic with cloves and beef tongue was certainly a first for Hollis, and it wasn't half bad, though there was no question it would have been far more appetizing had Lucy chosen to slice the tongue first. As it was, the pale, muscular appendage, spiked with cloves, lay suspended in its bed of rosy gelatin like some scientific curiosity preserved for posterity.

Abel was uncharacteristically restrained in his comments, even when Lucy cleared the plates and entered the house. They were eating at the table on the back terrace, the garden awash with warm evening light. Abel filled Hollis's glass with wine.

"You make any headway on the dead girl?" he asked.

"Name's Lillian Wallace." From Abel's expression, it rang no bells with him. "Her father's some Wall Street whiz. I spoke to him earlier, broke the news. The family's driving up tonight. There's a formal identification of the body set for noon tomorrow."

He didn't tell Abel that he planned to be at the morgue a good hour earlier to scrutinize the results of Dr. Hobbs's autopsy before the body was released to the custody of the family.

"Speaking of corpses," said Abel, reaching for his pack of cigarettes. "Any news from Lydia?"

"She called a couple of nights back."

"Collect?"

Abel had never liked Hollis's wife, a fact he had halfheartedly attempted to disguise while she'd been around. Now that she was gone, he felt no such compunction.

"Still with that stoop-shouldered fucker, is she?"

"Seems so."

"What did she want?"

"A divorce."

Abel looked at Hollis long and hard, weighing the news. "What did you say?"

"What *could* I say?"

"Knowing you, 'Come back, dear, all is forgiven.'"

"I said yes."

"You didn't?"

Hollis nodded.

"I'm trying not to smile."

"I can see that."

"Good on you, Tom," beamed Abel, raising his glass in a salute.

"To the stoop-shouldered fucker. May he soon come to know that your loss is not his gain."

The gentleman in question was a New Jersey artist of Scottish extraction, a competent watercolorist who had summered in East Hampton the previous year at a boardinghouse on Accabonac Road. Hollis had no idea how Lydia had come to meet Joe McBride. He didn't wish to know. It pained him to think of the numerous liaisons the pair had doubtless contrived behind his back; and it still puzzled him that he hadn't read the signs, the clues, he of all people. Hindsight offered no illumination. Even casting his mind back to that time he could recall nothing out of the ordinary. Had she taken special care over her appearance? Had she been more remote or bad-tempered with him than usual? Had she shown any undue aversion to sex? Probably, but nothing he could remember. It had simply happened, without his awareness, almost in his very presence.

This was the saddest indictment of their relationship, the unspoken pact of mutual indifference they had allowed themselves to sign up to. He had been immune to her, even as her heart soared. Could he really blame her for leaving?

One small part of himself clung to the notion that ultimate responsibility lay with Lydia, that things would have been different if she had only supported him in his hour of need, rather than chiding him for destroying his career, and their lives with it, on a matter of principle.

In his heart, however, he knew it was he who had betrayed their childhood dream, hatched in the gloomy passageways of the four-flight walk-up tenement where their families lived, vowing to each other that life would be better for them—no bedbugs, no roaches, no shared hall toilet stinking of C.N. disinfectant, no El trains hammering past outside, drowning out their whispers, the flat, dead eyes of the passengers staring in on their wretched lives. And so it had proved, their first halting steps on the ladder of self-betterment against the downdraft of the Depression years, ever upwards, until he had lost his footing, dragging her with him into the void.

At the age of twenty-nine, way before his time, Hollis had already faced the grinning demon all men must confront in their lives, the one who mocks you with the certain knowledge that you've climbed as high as you're ever going to, that you've scaled the peak, that from here the only way is down.

They were doomed even before they moved out to Long Island, he knew that now. Life in East Hampton—the village, its people, the cloying parochialism—became just another rod to beat him with. Lydia waxed sentimental about the city they had been forced to leave behind them, the same city she had spent the past twenty years of her life lambasting. She dreamed of Manhattan stores she had never shown any inclination to visit when they lived there: Macy's, Saks Fifth Avenue, Bonwit Teller. She subscribed to the Sunday *New York Times,* scouring its innumerable sections. Plaintively, she read aloud the reviews of Broadway plays as if theater were her greatest passion, and yet she showed no desire to attend the capable productions of the local Guild Hall Players.

Hollis had always tried to keep a wall between his work and his home life, to spare Lydia the daily round of depravity he witnessed as a detective. Since moving to East Hampton, he had maintained this wall, though for different reasons—to shield her from the banality of his work, to deny her the tools of further castigation.

As for himself, he had simply become inured to the desperate drudgery. He no longer bothered to return the smiles and waves while out on patrol. When called on to deal with some minor misdemeanor— the theft of a few hay bales or a family feud come to blows—he struggled to muster any concern, professional or otherwise, for the victims. The daily crowings and criticisms from Chief Milligan washed over him when once they had made his blood boil with impotent anger. He became an observer of a world he no longer inhabited although he moved through it: a muted world, clouded, like squinting at a painting.

That had all changed as of today when he saw the earring back-stud lying in the sand beside the head of Lillian Wallace. A moment of clarity, a detail, the world unexpectedly thrown into sharp relief. The Devil Is in the Details—the note pinned to the wall above his desk in the detective division task room.

"Have you heard of a fellow called Labarde?" he asked. "Conrad Labarde. He's a fisherman, in Amagansett."

"Why do you ask?"

"He was the one pulled the girl from the sea."

"Sure, I know him, to nod at. We crossed in high school. He got yanked out like most of the fishing kids. We didn't mix much, the East Hampton boys and the 'Gansetters, you know—a rivalry thing. I remember him, though."

"Carries a limp."

"A limp?"

"Left leg."

Abel shrugged. "Not back then. Hell of a ball player if I remember right. Could be he picked it up in the war."

"He's a veteran?"

"Not all of us managed to dodge the draft," said Abel with a wry smile. He knew this was unfair, that Hollis's job as a detective had excluded him from military call-up.

"We all passed through Camp Upton about the same time. I don't know where he ended up. Come to think of it, maybe he never saw action. He didn't show at the Memorial Day parade, this year or last." Abel stubbed out his cigarette. "Why all the questions?"

"No reason," said Hollis.

In truth, the tall Basque with the unsettling gaze had been preying on his mind all day. In the first place, he had also picked up on the woman's earrings—that was impressive—and then, when Hollis feigned uncertainty of their significance, he had simply smiled enigmatically, seeing through the front.

How had the fellow got his measure so quickly? And his parting words, the studied weight of the delivery—"See you around, Deputy." They had never met before, why should they ever see each other again? If it was a message, it was one that Hollis had yet to fathom.

"When you're ready," said Abel.

"What's that?"

"Come on, Tom, something's up. I can see you thinking—shit, I can almost hear it."

Hollis didn't reply.

"All I'm saying is . . . in your own time, if you want to talk about it."

At that moment Lucy appeared from the house, hurrying towards the table, the oven gloves barely a match for the heat from the glass dish she was carrying. Dropping the dish on the table, she shook out her scalded fingers.

Hollis and Abel stared: patches of ochre-brown paste showing through a husk of dirty white, like snow on a muddy paddock during the spring thaw.

"Lou, what in God's name . . . ?" muttered Abel.

"Sweet potato and marshmallow surprise," she replied proudly.

6

CONRAD FOUND HIMSELF COUNTING HIS STEPS AS HE WALKED—TEN PACES to every breaking wave, the spume washing around his bare feet. He resisted the urge to hurry ahead, the darkness not descended yet, measured strides over the tide-packed sand at the water's edge. One-to-ten, one-to-ten. The mental metronome of a route march, memories of the ragged hills east of Cassino invading his thoughts, the sound of the collapsing waves not unlike the hollow report of distant artillery fire, unseen shells reshaping the Italian landscape.

Looking up, he saw a couple coming towards him, arms linked, bodies pressed close, stepping out at twilight. He thought of turning away, veering off towards the dunes to allow them a clear passage along the shore, not wanting to intrude on their moment. But they had seen him now, and a sense of propriety drove them apart.

They approached through the blue-black light, eyes downcast, like guilty children.

"Good evening," said the man stiffly as they passed.

A thought occurred to Conrad, and he stopped in his tracks. "Excuse me."

The couple hesitated, turning.

"Do you walk here every evening?" asked Conrad.

"I'm sorry?"

"I was just wondering if you walked here most evenings."

"Why?" said the man.

"We're from Albany," said the woman. She uttered the words as if they were some kind of protective incantation.

Conrad took a couple of steps towards them. "Last night, were you here around this time?"

"Look," said the man, "we're very late."

"It's important," said Conrad.

"We weren't even here last night, okay? We got here today. And now we have to go." They turned and left, stepping briskly away.

Puzzled by their reaction, Conrad glanced down, taking in his appearance, aware for the first time that he was still in his fishing gear—the shabby twill trousers, patched and stitched and crusted with fish scales, plaid shirt protruding from the tattered hem of his jersey, once white, now stained with fish blood and streaked with tar. No wonder they'd been so anxious, confronted by a ragged, barefoot scrap of humanity.

He tugged the jersey up over his head and set off along the shore. After a few hundred yards, he cut inland, up the steep frontal dune. Beyond lay a tumble of sandhills, a tangled maze of crests and troughs, like an angry cross-sea. Narrowing to a point a few hundred yards beyond the Maidstone Club, this mysterious tract of vacant land extended four miles eastwards into Amagansett, widening considerably as it went, demarcated to the north by the steep inland bluff on which the wealthy had built their summer homes.

It was a world Conrad was well acquainted with, one that hadn't changed in all the years he'd known it. As kids, this had been their preserve, a private nether world where innumerable battles were fought, where Custer died a thousand deaths, yet, strangely, Jim Bowie and Davy Crockett always seemed to survive the storming of the Alamo.

Back then the old-timers still referred to the place as "The Glades," dim memories handed down of the time when the pockets of fresh-water marsh, fringed with phragmites, were deep enough for skiffs, and cranberry bogs abounded. The cranberries were still there, a wel-come source of pocket money for Conrad and his friends when they were growing up, though Arthur Bowles, the manager of Roulston's Store, always screwed them down hard on the price, his plastered smile masking a ruthless business head.

It was "down the Glades" that Conrad first met Rollo, wheeling around, lunging wildly, delightedly groping the air—a game of blind-man's buff—surrounded by a pack of shrieking kids, too young to know they were laughing at his expense, no sense yet that others saw him as different. That came later. Long summers spent roaming the sandhills in packs, squelching knee-high through the swales, forming tribes, alliances sealed in blood but soon reneged on, building camps thatched with dried reeds and cattails, whittling spears with gutting knives filched from unsuspecting fathers.

Sometimes they ventured beyond the southern frontier onto the beach; little Edmund Tyler—always Edmund, with his cherub face and see-no-evil eyes—coyly approaching a group of bathers, "Watch out for the sand snakes, it's their feeding hour," the others flat on their bellies in the beach grass at the top of the dune, howling with laugh-ter as the city people snatched up their belongings and scampered to safety.

One time, venturing farther still, into the west, to the Maidstone Club—the playground of the rich—the club itself too closely pa-trolled to risk an incursion despite the imagined lure of naked female flesh around the swimming pool, striking out across the golf course instead, sticking to cover, the eighth hole—par three, partially blind approach—Conrad racing from the scrub, staying low, scooping up a ball from the edge of the green and dropping it in the hole, not stay-ing to witness the celebration of the hole-in-one, knowing their laughter would give them away and ruin the prank, the unwitting victim still dining out on that magnificent drive from the tee, no doubt.

Conrad smiled, remembering. Then it occurred to him that four of the six boys present that day were now dead.

He banished the memories, pinched the burning end from his cigarette, and drove the stub into the sand with his finger.

It was night now, time to go.

Only fifty yards or so separated the wind-trimmed holly tree where he'd been sitting from the sandy bluff, and he could see the lights of the houses glinting through the oaks standing sentinel along the crest.

The moon lit his path as he picked his way across the sandhills and up the slope. He slipped the latch of the gate in the iron fence and stepped into the garden.

The air was cool and moist, rich with earthy scents where the borders had been watered. Somewhere out there in the night a dog barked and another returned its call. A low hum emanated from the small hut that housed the swimming pool's filtration system.

There were patches of water on the pool's flagstone surround, and a part-smoked cigarette in an ashtray beside a lounge chair. The cushions bore the moist impression of a person not so long gone.

He was right to have waited awhile.

He strayed as close to the house as he dared, positioning himself beneath the boughs of a tree at the edge of the lawn. From here he waited and watched, the figures moving behind the windows like marionettes on a nursery stage, until the lights were extinguished. A lone bedroom light was still burning bright behind the curtains when Conrad finally slipped away through the shadows.

He stopped as he passed by the swimming pool.

Crouching down, he dipped his fingers into the water and raised them to his lips.

7

"YOU'RE EARLY," SAID DR. HOBBS, DROPPING THE LIVER ONTO THE TRAY OF the hanging scales with a loud slap.

"I just wanted to make sure the paperwork's in order before the family get here," lied Hollis.

"Five pounds, four ounces," said Hobbs, reading off the weight of the organ to his assistant who was taking notes at a table. A sign on the wall read: *This Is the Place Where Death Rejoices to Teach Those Who Live.* The maxim was accompanied by an image of the Grim Reaper standing beside a blackboard, scythe in one hand, stick of chalk in the other.

The cadaver on the autopsy table was that of an elderly woman. Her large breasts, laced with veins, were splayed across her torso, hanging down over her arms so that they gathered on the enameled surface like wax at the base of a candle. There was a gaping Y-shaped hole in her abdomen where Dr. Hobbs had been at work.

Hollis's natural curiosity drove him towards the body, Dr. Hobbs evidently intrigued by his lack of squeamishness. "Want to hazard a guess at the cause of death?" he asked.

Hollis glanced at the weighing scales. "The shape of the liver, its color, weight . . ."

"Its weight?"

"Almost twice as heavy as it should be."

Dr. Hobbs raised an eyebrow.

"I don't know," continued Hollis. "Liver failure brought on by chronic alcoholism? The contusions on her knees and forehead suggest she collapsed forward onto the ground, the lividity in her face and neck that she lay there for some time."

Hollis regretted the words as soon as they left his mouth. As a rule, he played his cards close to his chest, finding it far more advantageous to be underestimated by his colleagues and associates. It was a sign of how low he'd sunk that he felt the need to impress the likes of Dr. Cornelius Hobbs.

"Local woman, Anne Hamel, notorious lush," confirmed Hobbs, "bottle and a half of gin a day. Neighbor found her on the bathroom floor." He removed the liver from the scales. "I can see you're something of a dark horse, Hollis, I'm going to have to keep my eye on you."

Yes, he should have kept his mouth shut.

"As for the paperwork on your girl," continued Hobbs, "I can't complete the death certificate or body release form before identification by next of kin. But then I figure you already know that, so you must be here to cast an eye over the autopsy report."

Hollis shrugged. "Just out of curiosity."

"Go ahead, it's on my desk, last office on the right down the hall." Hobbs couldn't resist a parting-shot as Hollis left through the swing doors. "You'll let me know if I missed anything."

THE OFFICE WAS SMALL, immaculately tidy, with windows onto the parking lot at the side of the building. There were graduation photos of two youngsters on the desk—gowns and caps, black tassels dangling— instantly recognizable as Hobbs's son and daughter, something that must have been a source of considerable consternation to the girl.

The autopsy report sat beside the phone, a sheet of ruled paper pinned to the front on which someone, Hobbs presumably, had writ-

ten in a neat, cursive hand: "Lillian Wallace (to be confirmed). Death
by Misadventure: death from drowning."

Hollis settled into the chair at the desk and picked up the report.
He paused a moment before starting to read. What was he looking
for? He wasn't sure. Maybe he was still grasping at straws. He admon-
ished himself for thinking that way, cleared his head, and started again.
Discrepancies. Yes, discrepancies between the report and what little he
knew of Lillian Wallace and the last hours of her life.

The few scraps he had to work with had been provided by the
maid, Rosa, the previous day. After breaking the news, Hollis had sat
with her for ten minutes while she tried to choke back the shock and
grief, tears pouring down her face.

When her sobbing had subsided, he gently prised his hand free of
hers and went and made a cup of tea for her. She joined him in the
kitchen, a room larger than the footprint of his whole house, with a
cathedral-cold stone floor. They sat at a table and she answered his
questions while he took notes in his memo pad.

Lillian Wallace had been twenty-six years old, the youngest child of
George and Martha Wallace, sister to Gayle and Manfred. Her mother
had died four years previously from cancer of the throat. Her father
had not remarried. Ordinarily, Lillian lived at her apartment in New
York, but she had been staying at the house in East Hampton since
January, following a separation from her fiancé, the engagement broken off.

When asked if Lillian was depressed, Rosa replied that she'd been
very low at first, but within a month or so she was her old self again—
spirited, full of life and humor. She said this in such a way as to warn
him off the notion that Lillian might have taken her own life.

For much of the time Lillian had been alone in the house. Rosa
lived with her husband and three children on the other side of town
and only stayed in the house on Friday and Saturday nights during the
season, when the whole family came out for the weekend. Since Lil-

lian had taken up residence, though, Rosa would come in for a few hours every morning to air the rooms, clean a little, make Lillian's bed, and prepare an evening meal for her.

Lillian kept pretty much to herself during the week, although Rosa said she played tennis with friends at the Maidstone Club every now and then. She read a lot, walked a lot, and swam whenever she could, in the swimming pool out back and in the sea.

Her evening dip in the ocean had been an established ritual. Even weekends, when her family was around, while the others indulged in preprandial cocktails on the terrace, Lillian would head off to the beach, out of the back gate in the garden and across the dunes. Rosa's eyes misted over again as she described this daily pilgrimage, the one that Lillian had never returned from.

Hollis had asked if he could take a look at Lillian's bedroom, and Rosa accompanied him upstairs. He would have preferred to inspect the room on his own, taking his time, but Rosa loitered protectively at the door.

There was nothing overtly feminine about the room, very little besides the clothes in the closet to suggest the gender of its occupant. The walls were painted cream and were hung with prints and etchings— a cart passing down a country lane, Montauk lighthouse, an abstract female nude by some well-known European artist whose name Hollis couldn't recall.

On the wall beside the bed was a framed photo showing a group of young women gathered on a stage. The caption on the mat read: "The Experimental Theatre, Vassar College 1942." Lillian Wallace stood out like a beacon, her beauty and the breadth of her smile animating the photo, lending life to those around her. The image was in stark contrast to Hollis's first sight of her, face frozen with rigor mortis, pinkish foam oozing from her blue lips.

He was left in little doubt as to what she had studied at Vassar. The shelves of a mahogany bookcase bowed under the weight of volumes of English and French literature, and there were more books stacked on the desk in front of the window. Hollis's eyes grazed over the clutter on the desk, looking for a suicide note. Despite Rosa's assertions, he didn't dismiss the possibility that Lillian Wallace had taken her own life.

There was no note, not on the desk, not on the nightstand, not in any of the drawers in the room. This didn't rule out suicide. Relatives or friends sometimes destroyed the suicide note of their loved ones. Sometimes this was done for simple, if misguided, reasons of decency. On other occasions it was no doubt done to protect themselves.

There was no denying the genuineness of Rosa's grief, but it didn't preclude her discovery of a note that morning when she had come to work. And as Hollis picked his way around the room, he was able to construct an alternative sequence of events—Rosa's horror on finding the note, the anxious hours spent waiting, praying that Lillian wouldn't see it through, that she would turn up, then the dashed hopes when he had appeared on the doorstep, the subsequent surge of emotion in Rosa indistinguishable from genuine surprise, and no less authentic.

This could also explain what Rosa was doing at the house at three o'clock in the afternoon, when, by her own account, she only ever came in for a few hours in the morning.

"Have you touched anything in here?" he asked.

"No."

"So the bed was already made?"

"Yes."

"Did that strike you as strange?"

"Strange?"

"You say you make her bed every morning. You come in one day and it's already made. Has it ever happened before?"

Rosa hesitated before replying. "No."

"So you must have been a little . . . surprised."

"Yes," she said, regarding him mistrustfully. Her mind was working hard, too hard.

There was a door in the corner of the room. Behind it lay a bathroom, painted pale blue. There were some cosmetics on the glass shelf above the basin, nothing elaborate. Across the room, a linen skirt and a white blouse lay neatly folded on a wicker chair, a pair of leather sandals on the floor nearby.

Sensing Rosa behind him in the doorway, he spoke without turning.

"This is where she would have changed?"

"Yes."

"Are these the clothes she was wearing yesterday?"

"Yes."

Hollis lifted the lid of a laundry hamper. It was empty. "Did she wear a brassiere?" Rosa, understandably, was a little put out by the question. "I'm just wondering where her undergarments are. They're not on the chair, not in the linen basket."

"They were in the hamper. I emptied it this morning."

Hollis ran the scene in his head. It's early evening, Lillian comes into the bathroom, she removes her clothes—first her blouse, then her skirt—folding them before placing them on the chair. She then takes off her brassiere and panties and puts them in the laundry hamper. Now she pulls on her dark blue swimsuit.

"The times you saw her leaving for her swim, what was she wearing?"

"A bathrobe."

"Shoes?"

Rosa thought before replying. "No."

"Did she take a towel?"

"I think so. Yes."

"And jewelry?"

"Jewelry?"

"Earrings, for example, did she keep them in or take them out?"

"Why are you asking me all these questions?" Her eyes were filling with tears again.

"I'm sorry, it's routine procedure."

"She didn't wear jewelry."

"Never?"

"Special occasions."

Well, death was certainly a special occasion.

"One more question, Rosa. What are you doing here mid-afternoon? You said before you only come in for a few hours in the morning." He felt bad springing this on her, given her state, but he had to know the answer.

"I wasn't worried at first," she said defensively. "I thought . . . I thought maybe she went out last night."

"And didn't come back? Stayed out? With someone?"

"You know how the young people are these days."

It bugged him that she chose to include him with her in the ranks of the elderly.

"I went home," she continued. "I made lunch for my family. Then I couldn't stop thinking . . ." She broke off, gathering herself. "Maybe she never came back from her swim."

"So you headed back here."

"She always leaves her swimsuit there, with the bathrobe." She pointed to a hook on the back of the bathroom door. "I should have looked earlier, I wasn't thinking, I should have looked . . ." She started to cry again.

"It wouldn't have made any difference," said Hollis gently. He made to rest a hand on her shoulder, but she hurried away, across the bedroom and out of the door, deep sobs resounding in the corridor. He didn't blame her for evading his touch; he had brought her to tears again with his persistent questioning, the mildly accusatory tone designed to unsettle, to dislodge the truth.

Well, at least he was able to throw out the theory of a missing suicide note. The deep affection Rosa clearly felt for her young mistress wouldn't have allowed her to return home to make lunch for her family if she'd discovered such a note that morning. He couldn't see it, it just didn't fit.

He turned back and surveyed the bathroom. Everything in order, as it should be, nothing that might lend weight to his gut feeling that Lillian Wallace's death wasn't an accident.

Feeling foolish, his heart already going out of the matter, he crossed to the sink, filled his cupped hands with cold water from the faucet and drank, splashing his face as he did so. He caught sight of himself in the mirror, and disliked what he saw staring back at him— a nondescript man, brown hair, brown eyes, average height—no distinguishing features besides a strong inclination to see the very worst in situations and in people. To question what most were happy to take in good faith. To doubt where others trusted.

And to what end? Not in the name of justice; that was a lofty notion he had abandoned within a year of leaving the academy. He knew that the true injustices in life lay far beyond the scope and remit of the police. They were merely flies buzzing around the dung heap, giving some semblance of order and activity.

No, he was as he was because he was good at it, because that's what he did best. And for the first time in his career he'd seen with blinding clarity that it was no longer enough of a reason to carry on doing it.

Casting his mind back to Lillian Wallace's bathroom, it occurred to Hollis that he wouldn't even be there, seated at Hobbs's desk in the morgue, if he hadn't wet his face with water at her sink. It was in the nature of destiny that you could trace your own back to the very smallest events.

Searching for a towel, he had spotted one hanging from a rail in the recess that housed the bath. Wandering over, he saw that there was also a toilet in the recess.

Only after he had dried his face and replaced the towel did it leap out at him: the wooden seat of the toilet was raised, suggesting that the last person to use it had been a man.

HOLLIS FINALLY OPENED the autopsy report and started to read. He made notes; to ask for a copy would only alert others to his interest in the affair.

The first section dealt with the external examination. In describing the general appearance of the corpse, Hobbs began by stating that rigor mortis was well established, suggesting a time of death somewhere between six and twenty-four hours previously. Starting at the head and working his way down the body, he noted small conjunctival hemorrhages in the eyes (green, as Hollis had guessed). These were evidence of asphyxiation, though not necessarily by water. The pinkish foam exuding from the mouth and nostrils, however, was strongly indicative of drowning and led Hobbs to opine that the victim had been alive at the time of submersion.

The report then turned to the abrasions over the prominent parts of the face and the anterior trunk. Apparently this was concomitant with drownings off the ocean beach. Hollis read on, intrigued. He knew that when a person drowned they soon sank to the bottom, where they remained until putrefaction filled their belly with gases that refloated them. He wasn't aware that the submerged corpse always lay suspended in the same position—facedown, with the head lower than the rest of the body. The abrasions were the result of Lillian Wallace's face and upper torso scraping along the sandy seabed as the currents carried her to and fro. The downward angle of the body also accounted for the faint and blotchy lividity in the head, neck, and anterior trunk.

The hands were next. The skin of the fingerpads and palms was blanched and wrinkled, what Hobbs called "washerwoman hands," a

direct consequence of prolonged immersion. The fact that this macera-
tion had not progressed to the backs of the fingers and the backs of the
hands led him to narrow his estimate of time of death to between
twelve and seventeen hours prior to the body's recovery from the ocean.

The passage of the report that dealt with the internal examination was far more technical, and Hollis was obliged to read it several
times over.

Core body temperature lent weight to Hobbs's revised time-of-
death estimate. The blue-purple discoloration of the bone of the
mastoid air cells was typical of drowning, though not proof of it.
However, a close examination of the stomach and the lungs placed the
matter beyond question. There was seawater in the stomach, with as-
sociated blanching of the gastric mucosa. The lungs were described as
bulky and ballooned, and as having a marbled appearance to the pleu-
ral surface, with blue-gray areas interspersed with pink-and-yellowish
zones of more aerated tissue—typical of emphysema aquosum. When
sectioned, seawater flowed from the lungs.

These appearances pointed to active inspiration of air and water
and could not be produced by the passive flooding of the lungs post-
mortem. This was further confirmed by the existence of hemorrhagic
subpleural bullae, resulting from tears in the alveolar walls, which also
accounted for the blood-tinging of the foam in the airways, nose, and
mouth.

There were further tests on the blood, bile, and vitreous humor.
These revealed low levels of alcohol, certainly not enough to have
played a contributory part in her death.

In conclusion, wrote Hobbs, the pathological evidence established
beyond any doubt that the decedent was alive when she entered the
sea, and that she drowned in it some time between 5 p.m. and 10 p.m.
the day before her body was found.

Hollis laid the document on the desk. He had misjudged Hobbs.
The report was as impressive as any he had read—authoritative and

thorough, circumspect in its judgments until the forensic evidence proved indisputable. What had he expected, some slapdash affair by a second-rate provincial medical examiner? Dr. Hobbs's jurisdiction covered miles of coastline noted for its treacherous waters. Drownings were commonplace, and he surely had more experience of them than the vast majority of pathologists. A little dejected, Hollis abandoned the idea of running the information by Paul Kenilworth, a former colleague back in New York.

A movement outside caught Hollis's eye. A brougham was pulling into the parking lot. Not seen as often since the war, it was the sort of vehicle that made a discreet yet unequivocal statement about the owner's wealth and standing. The uniformed chauffeur in the open driver's compartment guided the car to a halt. Getting out, he opened the rear door, offering his hand as he did so.

For a brief instant, it occurred to Hollis that the whole thing had been a terrible mistake, that Lillian Wallace hadn't drowned off the ocean beach. For there she stood, tall and slender, squinting against the sunlight.

It was a few moments before Hollis realized he was looking at Lillian's older sister, Gayle. Physically, there was little to distinguish between the two women. Gayle's hair was maybe a little longer and neatly coiffed so that it curled like two breaking waves around her neck and beneath the ears; but the oval face, the wide-set eyes, and the mouth were the same. What differences there were lay not so much in the physiognomy as the presentation—in particular the clothes.

Hollis had seen nothing in Lillian's wardrobe that came close to the elegance of the outfit Gayle was wearing. Her skirt was cut long and full in the new French style, her blouse was fashionably free of padded shoulders and tailored to accentuate her narrow waist.

A gentleman who could only have been George Wallace was next out of the car. Of medium build, he was dressed in a dark gray summer suit, white shirt, and blue necktie. For a man who must have been into his sixties, he was remarkably well preserved, displaying very little extra weight around the midriff, and a full head of silver hair, parted at the side. He stood tall and straight, exuding the easy patrician air of a long-standing member of the privileged class.

The same could not be said of his son, who was the last to exit the vehicle. The poor fellow was clearly upset and doing his best to conceal the fact, but the set of his brow and the stoop of his shoulders betrayed him. What was his name again? Hollis turned to his memo pad. Manfred.

Looking back through the window, he saw George Wallace direct a few words to his son, who then visibly pulled himself together, smoothing his sandy hair. Manfred smiled weakly at something his sister said, then she took his arm and they started making their way towards the building.

HOLLIS ARRIVED IN THE LOBBY as they were entering through the main door. "Mr. Wallace? Deputy Chief Hollis. We spoke on the phone yesterday."

George Wallace accepted the hand with a cold, firm grip. "My daughter, Gayle. My son, Manfred." There was something soothing about the depth and resonance of his voice.

"I'm sorry we had to meet under these circumstances," said Hollis. He felt insincere uttering the line he had used on many such occasions in the past. "The medical examiner will be with us shortly. Please, take a seat."

They glanced disapprovingly at the diminutive waiting area, where a lean, shabby young man was sucking dejectedly on a cigarette. It struck Hollis that this must be one of the few instances in their lives where they had little choice but to do as others did, sit where others sat. Ordinarily, they lived sheltered from the world, moving between their houses, clubs, and offices, cocooned in chauffeured limousines, supported wherever they went by a loyal staff who shopped, cooked, cleaned, laundered, and generally shielded them from the less appealing realities that most accepted as an elemental part of life. Maybe he was doing them a disservice, but somehow he couldn't see any of them waiting in line at a grocery store for a pack of cigarettes or haggling with a taxi driver over the fare.

Here at the county morgue, however, there were no private boxes, no members-only enclosures, no first-class Pullman compartments. It was a low, ugly, antiseptic building where all and sundry were obliged to mingle. Death, the Great Leveler.

Gayle picked nervously at the out-of-date magazines on the low table. Manfred removed a pack of cigarettes from his pocket, offering one to his sister, who declined. Unexpectedly, he then held the pack towards the young man who had just put out his own cigarette.

"Don't mind if I do," said the man. From his eyes it was clear he had been crying. Manfred lit the fellow's cigarette, and then his own, with a gold lighter.

"Who d'you lose?" asked the young man.

"My sister."

"Mother," said the young man. And that was the end of the conversation, to the evident relief of George Wallace, who observed with a cool, dispassionate eye. Hollis looked at the young man, considering the likelihood that the woman with the swollen liver had been his mother.

"How does this . . . work?" asked Manfred.

Hollis turned. "One of you will need to identify her."

"We would all like to see her," said George Wallace, though Gayle's expression suggested otherwise.

"You'll then need to sign the body release form, and that's it."

"That's it?" Manfred said.

"The funeral directors can then take her away. I imagine they'll be coming up from the city."

"She wanted to be buried here," said Gayle.

"We don't know that," interjected George Wallace.

"Father, we've already had this conversation."

"She loved East Hampton." Manfred's words were directed at Hollis but intended for his father's ears. George Wallace had evidently conceded defeat on the matter, but had wished to flag his disapproval one final time.

"Can you recommend a local funeral home?" Wallace elder asked.

"I'm afraid I'm not allowed to do that. There are several in town."

"Livingstone's is best," interrupted the young man. "Buried my nan, grandpa, and my old man, good and deep, no frills, don't need 'em, not where they gone."

"Thank you," said Manfred.

"Ain't no skin off my nose."

Hollis suspected that, thanks to the young man, Livingstone and Sons now stood little chance of attracting George Wallace's custom.

At that moment, the receptionist manning the front desk approached. "Mr. Hamel, like I said, it's going to be several hours before we're ready for you. There's really no point in you waiting around." The young man looked at her long and hard. If he suspected he was being moved on for the benefit of the others, he gave no indication of the fact.

"So long," he said, getting to his feet and leaving. The receptionist waited for the door to swing closed behind him.

"I'm sorry about that," she said. "Can I get you something to drink?"

Hollis had been wrong. Even here in the morgue, the Wallaces and their kind received preferential treatment.

"No thank you," said George Wallace.

"A glass of water, please," said Manfred.

"Yes, water, thank you," said Gayle quietly.

The receptionist left without even glancing at Hollis.

He placed a brown-paper parcel on the table. "These are Lillian's, her bathrobe and towel, from the beach. I went down there when I was at the house yesterday."

Following in her final footsteps, he had wandered past the swimming pool, out the back gate in the garden, down the bluff, and across the sandhills. He hadn't expected to find anything, but a short search revealed the bathrobe and towel folded beside a clump of beach grass on the frontal dune. They were clearly visible from the beach, and it was evidence of the class of bather frequenting that stretch of shoreline that in almost twenty-four hours no one had taken them.

He had approached the spot carefully, but the soft, windblown sand had absorbed any tracks there might have been. Back at headquarters, a closer examination of the articles had revealed nothing out of the ordinary, just a hair band and a brush in the pocket of the terry-cloth bathrobe.

Hollis removed two documents from his pocket and laid them in front of George Wallace. "A personal effects form, to say you've received them." George Wallace took the pen offered him and signed both copies. Hollis replaced one in his pocket.

"There'll be another form to sign for the effects found with her." He threw in a brief pause. "Her swimsuit . . . and her earrings." Mention of the earrings triggered no reaction.

"Do you know what happened exactly?" asked Manfred.

"It's hard to say. There were no witnesses that we know of. I'm sure you're aware, the currents can be pretty dangerous. The autopsy confirms that she drowned."

Manfred straightened in his seat. "The autopsy?"

"Yes."

"You mean you cut her up?!"

Hollis took a moment to formulate his response. "An internal examination was conducted by the medical examiner. The law calls for it in all cases of unattended deaths."

"Unattended deaths"—what was he thinking, reducing the tragic loss of their loved one to a piece of police-manual jargon?

"Jesus Christ," said Manfred, "they cut her up!"

"Manfred . . ."

"Don't you at least have to ask for our consent or something?!"

"Manfred." This time, George Wallace raised his voice.

"They should have asked for our consent."

"It's not required," said Hollis.

George Wallace turned to him. "All the same, it would have been good to know."

Hollis had to concede the point. It was an oversight on his part, and one he wouldn't have committed if he hadn't been so caught up in his own private speculations. "You're right," he said, "I apologize."

"What exactly did you do to her?" Manfred's tone remained accusatory.

"Manfred, the gentleman has apologized," said George Wallace firmly. "He has explained the situation and he has apologized."

Thankfully, at that moment the receptionist reappeared with the glasses of water. "The medical examiner will see you now, if you'd like to come with me."

Manfred stared forlornly at the glass in front of him. Without touching it, he got to his feet and followed his father.

Gayle lingered a moment longer, sipping from her glass. "I'm sorry," she said. "They were very close."

As she left, Hollis called after her. "Miss Wallace." She turned back. "Try Yardley's Funeral Home. They're on Newtown Lane."

"Yardley's. Thank you."

And she was gone.

8

Oyster shells crunched beneath the tires as Conrad turned into the parking lot. The lone headlight swept over the other vehicles already gathered there, before settling on a space in the shadows, beyond the pool of light thrown by the lamp above the door of the ramshackle oyster house.

Conrad stepped from the vehicle. It was a still, warm evening, humid and close, the breeze too light to cool the skin. He could hear the hum of raised voices from inside the hall, then a barked reprimand calling everyone to order.

He shouldn't have come, but what else was he going to do, sit at home with his swirling thoughts? He needed distraction and this was as good as anything on offer. He pulled the tobacco pouch from his pocket, laid it on the hood of the Model A, and started to roll a cigarette.

The moon cast an inviting trail across the grand sweep of Gardiner's Bay, connecting the steep bluffs south of Accabonac Creek to Promised Land, where Conrad now stood. This was the northern limit of Napeague, the narrow thread of land that connected the high ground of Amagansett to that of Montauk.

Not even half a mile to the south lay Conrad's house and the battered Atlantic coast. Here on the lee shore it was an altogether different world, a place of calm and shelter where the southwesterly winds came in fits and starts, broken up by their passage across the upland, and the waters lapped lazily at the arcing sand beach.

The fishermen weren't fooled by this. They knew from hard experience that the bayside sea could still turn on you in the beat of a heart. One winter just before the war Conrad had been helping Milt Collard run building stock out to Gardiner's Island when the wind suddenly backed around to the northeast. With a crew of twelve workmen and a belly full of bricks, Milt's old cut-down schooner, the *Osprey,* was already slung low in the water when they set off from Three Mile Harbor, the big 671 diesel straining under the load.

Ten minutes out, the wind turned suddenly and breezed up. An angry chop soon gave way to battle lines of whitecaps, four feet high, which advanced on the *Osprey,* slapping into her with remorseless regularity. In no time at all these had grown to six feet. Ice cakes left over from the big freeze began surfing down the face of the waves and shattering against the schooner's bow.

By now they were pumping and bailing by hand, a bucket brigade of men fighting to keep the vessel afloat. Milt stood in the small pilot house in the stern, fighting the wheel, water flooding knee-high around him each time the *Osprey* slumped into a trough.

"Ditch the cargo!" he screamed. "Goddamnit, ditch the goddamn cargo!"

You never saw a bunch of men move so fast. Instead of water, they now started heaving bricks over the side, no formal chain this time, half of the crew scrabbling in the hold, the others ducking the hail of bricks; the blind panic of men looking death squarely in the eye. There were no life jackets on board, not that they'd have done you any good in water that cold. No, if the *Osprey* went down, you'd have been better off grabbing an anchor and getting it over with.

It was a close call, but they had made the shelter of Gardiner's Island, riding out the vicious squall. The wind dropped abruptly, and Milt swung the *Osprey* around, heading back to Three Mile Harbor.

Not one word had been shared by the ashen-faced crew since Milt first barked his order at them.

"You lazy sonsabitches," he now said. "Two hours to load, two minutes to offload. Now I *know* you been leadin' me a dance."

A handful of men, Conrad among them, erupted in fear-tinged laughter. They quickly figured from the look in the eyes of those who knew Milt a whole lot better that any humor in the remark was entirely of their own imagining.

Milt later admitted that he'd never seen anything quite like it out on Gardiner's Bay, and this from a man who'd skippered bunker boats out of Promised Land for more than twenty years. Fair weather or foul, the long steamers would put out from the dock in search of the spiny little menhaden fish—bunkers, as they were known locally—that clogged the waters off the South Fork during the warmer months. The Smith Meal Company had a dock and a clutter of hangars where endless tons of the fish were processed. Hauled from the depths in giant purse-seine nets, they were boiled to extract their oil, the remaining pulp scooped from the vats, dried and ground down into fish meal. It was a gut-wrenchingly malodorous process, one that had given Promised Land its name, for the place stank to high heaven—a smell so pungent it tarnished the silver coins in the pockets of the workers.

When the plant was in production, the tall smokestacks belching clouds of fetid steam, the residents of Amagansett lived in dread of an easterly breeze. The stench would descend on the village like a curse, clawing at your nose and throat, clogging your pores. Even during the winter months, when the vats lay cold and still, there was no escaping the smell out at Promised Land. Over the years it had permeated the wooden cladding of the factory buildings and the shanties thrown up for the hordes of itinerant laborers, it had seeped into the pale sand, and it seemed to drip from the branches of the pitch pines.

The fish meal plant sprawled on the edge of Gardiner's Bay like a rancid dishrag beside a sink, and yet its presence there had safeguarded the area. For who in their right mind would want to build in the shadow of such a foul-smelling beast? The low dunes behind the curving beach were unencumbered by houses. More important, the fragile hinterland of Napeague had been spared the usual depredations of development. Its deerfeed flats, pine copses, and dune hills were still laced with freshwater bogs that rang with the sound of peeper frogs in early summer. Cranberry, blueberry, and sundews were in abundance, along with curly-grass ferns, staghorn lichens, Hudsonia, tiny orchids, and strange, edible fungi highly prized by those of Italian and French descent, who'd been known to come to blows during the short picking season.

Napeague meant "Water Land" in the language of the Montauketts, and the area was a living testament to the happy coexistence of both elements. The relationship, tentatively forged over the centuries, recalled an era when Napeague had been open water separating the hills of Montauk from the main body of Long Island.

Some disputed this notion, but Conrad was convinced of it. How else to account for the skeletal remains of the whale he had discovered while out roaming one spring morning? The bleached vertebrae, each as big as a water pail, lay part-buried beneath a tangle of bearberry bushes a quarter of a mile inland at a spot where Napeague was half a mile wide. The only explanation was that the creature had been cast up on a shallow bar linking the two landmasses, and that over the many years this slender umbilicus had grown inexorably through a process of accretion, sand layered upon sand, scoured from the ocean bluffs of Montauk and deposited by the ocean.

Conrad was an eleven-year-old boy when he first stumbled across the bones, and to his wildly imaginative mind the find was proof that the great Flood as described in the Book of Genesis had indeed occurred. The whale must surely have found itself stranded high and dry when the waters that God sent to punish the wicked finally receded. As far as Conrad was concerned, discovering those bones was the next best thing to finding the ark itself atop Mount Ararat.

The possessiveness of the young led him to guard his secret closely. He persuaded himself there was no need to share the discovery, not even with his closest friend—Billy Ockham—who would have been with him that day had he not been forced to trim hickory spiles for his father's pound traps. Instead, Conrad carefully covered the exposed bones with sand, returning home with just the one vertebra, informing his father and stepmother that he'd found it on the ocean beach.

He had rejected the idea of hiding the precious object, partly because he needed his father's expert confirmation that it had indeed come from a whale, but mainly because his older brother, Antton, would most likely have discovered the bone, then destroyed it— ceremoniously, before his tear-filled eyes—for no other reason than that concealment was proof of Conrad's affection for it.

For years the vertebra lay casually discarded in a corner of the attic bedroom the brothers shared, Conrad feigning indifference to it. However, when he was alone he'd pick it up, turning it in his hands, tracing its soft, porous contours with his fingertips.

Even when his faith abandoned him some years later, the bone lost none of its iconic power. Twenty years on, he still kept it in his bedroom. It was the last thing he registered before fitful sleep descended upon him, and the first thing his eyes searched out when he woke each morning. It had become the touchstone by which he tested his life. Somehow, it seemed to enshrine everything that had happened to him since he first pried it from the packed sand.

When he looked at it he saw himself romping with Billy on Napeague, grubbing for cherrystone clams that they cooked up on a steel plate over a fire-pit on the beach, digging holes and hauling up fresh water in a nail keg to see themselves through the long hot days of summer, or sneaking out at night to watch the Coast Guard cutters chasing the rum runners all over Gardiner's Bay, tracer bullets and the muzzle flashes from the big three-inch guns lighting up the night sky, better than the Fourth of July. Other times, he saw Billy torn apart by machine-gun fire, clods of flesh flying, on some nameless rock in the Pacific, thousands of miles from home, fighting for a people who had sought, with considerable success, to annihilate him and his kind.

Good times and bad times, the lump of whalebone had absorbed them all like a thirsty sponge. Given the events of recent years, he now wondered if the bone hadn't begun to favor the bad over the good, somehow attracting ill luck to itself, and he questioned whether he was to blame for this. Maybe it was a cursed object, blighted from the moment he first removed it from its natural resting place.

He didn't dismiss such ideas. Like most fishermen he was given to superstitions—no talk of pigs or knives around the boat, no women or preachers aboard, no whistling in a breeze. He even knew a Swedish lobsterman in Sag Harbor who refused to put to sea in the company of a Finn, but that had as much to do with ancient rivalries between the two nations as it did arcane beliefs. Men for whom death was a daily and very real possibility were inclined to respect the precautionary wisdoms, however curious, of those who'd gone before them. It was the reason Conrad still cherished the cawl that had masked his blunt, newborn face.

The patch of diaphanous skin, moist and clear when he was first dragged into the world, now lay dry and crinkled like a piece of old parchment in the shallow wooden pine box made specially by his father to house it. Prized as a potent charm against drowning, deep-sea whalemen used to pay big money for a baby's cawl to carry with them on their perilous voyages, though most found themselves rounding the Horn with little more than a scrap of cow's afterbirth in their pockets, sold to them by some unscrupulous type wise to the lucrative trade.

That Conrad should have been born with a cawl was as good a portent as any fisherman could wish for his son. It meant that the child was somehow touched, that the gods looked favorably upon him, that this was one boy who would never get to share the company of Davy Jones. Whether there was any truth in this, who could say? All Conrad knew was that he was still alive while others had been taken by the sea.

A sharp pain in his hand brought Conrad to his senses. He flicked the cigarette butt away and turned towards the oyster house, aware again of the noisy debate taking place inside.

IT WAS SOME YEARS since the beds off the north shore had yielded oysters of sufficient number or size worthy of the New York market, and little remained in the cavernous hall to indicate the building's original function. The long benches for cleaning and packing the oysters had been stripped out—bought by old Mabbett for a song when he had expanded his fish-packing business—and the community of Amagansett men who followed the sea now referred to the rickety building as Oyster Hall. It was where they collected to while away the slow, fragmented winter months in idle chat. When the weather was too severe for even the most reckless among them to put to sea, the place would be packed with bodies. Right now there were fifty or so men gathered inside, but not one of them turned as Conrad entered.

Some were on their feet, gesticulating wildly, disturbing the pall of pipe and cigarette smoke hanging below the rafters. Others hurled insults at each other. The meeting had degenerated into a free-for-all.

"Shut it off!" bellowed Rollo's father, Ned Kemp. He was seated behind a table on the far side of the hall, flanked by Jake Van Duyn and Frank Paine. Beside them, on a worn square of zinc nailed to the floor, stood the big airtight stove, its long and rickety pipe snaking above their heads, suspended by wires from the ceiling. Grabbing a poker, Ned beat on the pipe.

"Shut it off, goddamnit!" The deafening sound restored some kind of order to the assembly.

Ned advanced through the rows of men ranged on chairs before him, brandishing the poker. "You, Osborne, bring your ass to anchor." Art Osborne duly did as he was told.

"God in heaven," snapped Ned. "What do you think the sports'd say if they saw us now. I tell you what they'd say, they'd say they got the battle won, and they'd be right, you sorry sonsabitches."

Conrad caught sight of Rollo standing with his brothers against the wall in the corner, looking completely puzzled. His father wasn't naturally given to profanities.

"We got to get us organized," Ned went on. "Else we don't stand a snowball's chance in hell of beating the bill, that's sure enough."

The bill in question was a proposed amendment to the state fisheries law sponsored by the growing lobby of sportsfishermen. Like the bill narrowly defeated before the war, it called for a total ban on all fishing by means of nets, traps, and trawl lines within the tidal waters of New York State, ascribing natural fluctuations in all fish populations to wholesale pillaging by the commercial fishermen. When it came to it, though, everyone knew the real reason the rod-and-line men were calling for action. They wanted to board the train at Penn Station in New York at 3 a.m. on a Saturday morning in the knowledge that no one else had tampered with their precious waters off Montauk since the previous weekend.

Conrad had witnessed the "Fisherman's Special" pull into Montauk station only once, but it wasn't a sight you were ever likely to forget—hundreds of grown men, many of whom had been on their feet for the past four hours, grappling with their gear and with each other to get off that train, leaping from the carriages, scrabbling through windows, anything to beat their friends-turned-rivals to the favored spots on the boats lined up along the Union News Dock on Fort Pond Bay, a short but sapping sprint away.

To THE FISHERMEN OF THE SOUTH FORK, the building crusade against them was an affront of such profound impertinence it made the blood

beat in their ears. These were men whose families had fished the waters off the East End for as long as anyone could remember, for twelve
generations in the case of the older Amagansett clans. They were
the representatives of a tradition reaching back hundreds of years, and
many still spoke with the same Kentish and west country inflections of
their seventeenth-century English ancestors who had first settled the
village.

Ned Kemp understood that these romantic notions counted for
nothing in Albany. The sportsfishermen were wealthy, they could afford the best lawyers, and they were accustomed to getting their own
way. It was the reason Ned had called the meeting at Oyster Hall, to
urge the fishermen to meet like with like, to act with level-headed
pragmatism. But the discussion had clearly become mired in a collective venting of the spleen.

"I know I ain't a tub of wisdom," said Noah Poole, too old now to
do anything but grub for piss clams in summer. "The way I sees it
though, God Almighty put the fish in the water and the birds and animals in the woods for the people, and when you make any fool laws
that stops the people from using 'em, then God Almighty makes 'em
scarce."

"You're right . . ." said Jack Holden. Noah accepted the compli-
ment by smoothing the few lonely wisps of hair on his head. ". . . You
ain't no tub of wisdom," continued Jack.

This triggered a chorus of sniggers from the other young men he
was seated with.

"You boys got nothin' better to contribute," said Ned, "you might
as well clear off."

"What's to say? This crap them sports is trying to put over on us, it
burns me up," said Jack. "Sometimes the fish don't run so good. There's
good and bad seasons for fish just like crops to a farm."

"Yeah."

"The bass and blues is down right now, come next year they'll be running like a damn army, that's just the way things is."

"Always has been."

Ned looked down at the younger men, deep furrows in his lean, dark face, his white hair clipped so short it sat like a dusting of frost on his square skull. "We know that," he said. "Now we got to show it. Prove it."

"How'n the hell we gonna do that?" came a voice from across the hall.

"First off, I say we cooperate with that young fellow who's around right now."

"You mean that screwball who keeps wanting to scrape scales off of my fish?"

There was a smattering of laughter from around the hall. The source of their amusement was a young fisheries biologist with the New York State Conservation Department. Sheepish, bespectacled, and with a nose like a cobbler's awl, the poor fellow had become something of a whipping boy for the local fishermen who openly referred to his biological survey as the "diabolical survey" whenever he dared show his face.

"I been talking to him," said Ned. "He's a log of stuff to learn about fishing, but what he don't know about bass ain't worth knowing." He ignored the incredulous puffs from his audience. "It's all in the spawning, he says, the Hudson and Chesapeake. The conditions ain't right for the cows in the estuaries, ain't no point in us and the sports even arguing, not one of us is going to see a fish off the East End."

"Fact is the sports is takin' more bass than us anyhows."

"Goddamn pinhookers."

"Yeah, what we take don't amount to nothin'."

"He knows that, he's with us on it. Like I say, the problem don't lie here, it's in the estuaries, the pollution from the factories."

"Factories owned by them politicians and their friends."

"Yeah, what good's a sorry scamp like that going to do against them lot?"

"If anything can drive you crazy or into evil it's politics."

"That's the truth."

"I say him being here don't spell nothin' good."

"No, not by a damned sight."

And so the discussion continued, despite Ned's best efforts, whirling, reeling, spinning in circles, until Conrad's head was swimming with words he no longer heard. The hall suddenly felt very small and congested, the atmosphere heavy and stifling. He steadied himself against the rear wall with a hand. He needed air.

THE DOOR SWUNG SHUT behind him as he stepped outside into the night. A cloud of bugs buzzed around the tin lamp above the door, and for a moment it seemed to Conrad that they too were embroiled in some feverish, futile debate.

He drew a few long, deep breaths, but they did nothing to clear his head. He picked his way cautiously down the steps and towards the truck, each stride an act of concentration. Halfway across the lot he heard the door of the hall swing open then bang shut again. He didn't turn till he heard the footsteps crunching behind him on the carpet of crushed shells, a pace and purpose to the tread.

Three men were advancing towards him, shoulder to shoulder, back-lit by the lamp above the door. The jug-eared silhouette of the fellow on the right marked him out as Ellis Hulse. As they drew closer, he recognized the other two as Charlie Walsh and his squat, none-too-intelligent brother-in-law, Dan Geary. And he knew then what was coming.

If there was any doubt, Ellis and Dan moved away from Charlie, drifting lazily off to the sides. Charlie drew to a halt, scraping at the shells underfoot with the toe of his boot. "So what do you think?" he asked, nodding over his shoulder. "You think we'll beat the bill?"

Conrad could feel the lightness shifting from his head to his stomach. "Go home, Charlie."

Charlie looked at him as if seriously weighing the suggestion. "Shit on that," he said.

Dan Geary grunted with amusement, moving, still moving, around to the left. Ellis was circling to the right, obliging Conrad to retreat a little to keep them both in view.

Charlie advanced a few paces. "Just wanted to say I'm sorry, for before." His mouth was twisted between self-pity and bitter contempt. Conrad toyed with the idea of further conciliation but rejected it, not because he doubted it would work—that much was certain—but because he no longer wanted it to.

"So you should be," he said, "stealing off the dead."

"A pair of damn earrings. What the hell does she care?"

"What if it was your sister?" fired back Conrad.

It took a moment for Dan Geary to register that Charlie's sister also happened to be his own wife, but once the thought had lodged itself in his brain it appeared to bother him. He looked at his brother-in-law uncertainly.

"What?" snapped Charlie.

"Nothing, Charlie."

"Good, 'cos it's time we taught this foreigner some goddamn manners."

Charlie Walsh wasn't flame-headed like his father, but he still had the fire in him. Conrad could see it sparking in his eyes as he turned back, balling his fists. Conrad could remember his father telling him once, in his labored English: "You just got to get an Irish down 'n' beat shit out of him, then he's the best friend you got."

Even if they ganged him, as they clearly planned on doing, Conrad stood a fair chance of putting Charlie Walsh down, but he seriously doubted they'd ever become friends because of it. No, he set more store by the other piece of advice his father had offered up at the same time, much to the consternation of his stepmother. If you're ever outnumbered in a fight, he had said, keep your eyes on one man, but be sure to land your first punch on another.

And this is what Conrad did.

His eyes never left Charlie's, but the punch, when it came, was a scything right across the body that caught Dan Geary square in the face, crumpling his nose and stopping him dead in his tracks. Conrad didn't wait to see him hit the ground, he was already spinning back, shifting the weight to his left foot, swinging his right arm as he did so.

Caught off-guard, Charlie wasn't set when the forearm struck him in the head, knocking him sideways. He probably would have kept his footing if Conrad hadn't pile-driven a knee into his hip a split second later. Charlie snatched at Conrad as he fell, seizing hold of his shirt. Conrad pulled free, but he was off balance, his back now turned to Ellis. In two strides, Ellis was in range.

The boot caught Conrad in the side of the chest just below the rib cage and he heard something crack. He raised his arms protectively in front of his face as he doubled up, and the second kick glanced off his elbow. He tried to back away, but Charlie was hauling at his trouser legs now, doing his best to bring him down. From here, things quickly degenerated into a close-quarters dogfight—fists flailing, fingers clawing at faces and snatching at hair. There were a few small satisfactions—at one moment his elbow met Charlie's mouth, splitting the lip clean open and dislodging some teeth—but Conrad started to wilt under the hail of blows. A few moments later, he found himself brought to the ground, the side of his face impacting with the crushed oyster shells.

Charlie took a step back, setting himself for a swing of his boot. It was clearly intended for Conrad's head and there was nothing he could do to avoid it; Ellis was all over him, pinning his arms. He closed his eyes in anticipation of the searing white pain and the black void of unconsciousness.

But they never came.

He heard a sound like a sack of grain being dropped from a trailer, and opened his eyes in time to see Charlie collide with a truck, another man wrapped around him.

It was Rollo. Conrad had never seen him so mad. In fact, he'd never once seen Rollo mad. Mute with frustration on a couple of occasions, maybe, but never like this, possessed by rage. He was screaming, pummeling Charlie with his fists.

If it had been a less shocking sight, Conrad might have been the first to react. As it was, Ellis had the edge. Conrad lunged at his leg but missed, looking on helplessly as Ellis snatched a length of two-by-four from the back of a truck.

"Rollo!" cried Conrad.

Rollo turned, saw the piece of lumber raised high above Ellis's shoulder, and he froze.

"No!" It was Charlie Walsh who screamed, blood spraying from his mangled mouth. "Don't!" He extended his arm to ward off the blow, and Ellis truncated his swing at the last moment. Despite the heat of the fight, Charlie knew better than to strike a Kemp, especially Rollo. There would be the devil to pay.

Conrad was on his feet now, moving to be with Rollo. Charlie and Ellis backed off warily, helping Dan to his feet as they left. For the duration of the scuffle he'd been sitting on his ass, staring perplexedly at the blood sluicing from his nose into his open hands.

Charlie Walsh gunned the engine of his truck, the tires spitting shards of shell before biting on the packed sand beneath. He didn't even glance over as he roared out of the lot.

Rollo watched the taillights disappear into the night. "He's a hard-shell sinner, that one."

Conrad laughed, then winced from the pain.

Despite Rollo's protestations, Conrad insisted on returning home. He knew he had fractured a rib, possibly two, but it wasn't as if it was the first time. Doc Meadows—in his inimitable, cranky way—would only strap him up, tell him to take it easy, and maybe give him some aspirin to dull the pain. The first of these Conrad was quite capable of doing himself, the second was out of the question, the third he had no desire for.

He wanted to feel the stab of pain in his side, he wanted it to endure, to aggravate him as he went about his day, to wake him at night each time he rolled over in bed. It would act both as a nagging reminder of what had occurred and as a call to arms.

Already he could feel a clarity of thought descending on him, a determination as clean and hard as the steel of a new blade.

Leaving the parking lot, he found himself swinging the wheel of the truck to the left, heading east on Cranberry Hole Road. Home was to the west.

The handful of rundown shanties clustered on the western shore of Napeague Harbor where it opened to the bay was dubbed Lazy Point by the locals. There was indeed an air of langor about the residents, who scratched a living from the surrounding beaches, bars, and flats. But when they sold their services to others—shucking scallops, skinning eels, or baiting cod trawls with skimmer clams in winter for the ocean crews—they worked with impressive speed and dexterity.

When it came to it, Lazy Point was so called because of its appearance. Aside from a few straggly hedgerow weeds there was hardly a flower to be seen in the place. Instead, the front gardens of the houses were cluttered with fishing paraphernalia, most of it well beyond use, or even repair. Ancient lobster pots lay abandoned in heaps, woven through with tall grasses. Small rowboats were propped up on logs, their rotten timbers destined never to be replaced. Out front of one house there was even a rusting horse-drawn hay rake, a relic from the last century when the nearby salt meadows were cropped for winter grazing.

As for the buildings themselves, not one was painted the white or cream of their counterparts in Amagansett. At best, they received an annual baptism of bunker oil to protect their rough, salt-bleached cladding. They were low, ramshackle structures, some cobbled together from the old sugar boxes once used for shipping fish. Come a hard winter blow, large sections would detach themselves and take wing, only to be located the next day and bolted right back on again. Like an old garment fondly preserved with patches, these humble dwellings were unsightly to all but their owners.

In amongst the dilapidation, one home stood out like a pink ribbon on a sow's ear—a neat little weatherboard shack with a shingled roof, set back from the road down a rutted track. And it was in front of this building that Conrad pulled the truck to a halt.

He hesitated, allowing the engine to idle, suddenly doubting his decision to have come here. He would have pulled away again if Sam Ockham hadn't opened the front door of his home, raising one hand to shield his eyes from the glare of the truck's headlight. His other hand was clamped around the collar of his dog, restraining it.

Conrad killed the engine. "It's me, Conrad," he called, stepping down from the truck.

"Bed," snapped Sam, and his dog scuttled back inside. "You near scared hell outta me."

"I thought you didn't believe in hell."

"Are you crazy? I live it most days."

Conrad smiled, stepping into the swathe of light thrown by the kerosene lamps inside.

Sam squinted at him. "You been brawlin'?"

"I guess."

"Get yourself in here. I'll fix you something to stop that eye closing up."

"Forget it, it's okay."

"Easy for you to say, you don't got to look at you."

Half an hour later Conrad was sitting in a chair, a compress
strapped to his eye, the pad smeared with some pulpy substance concocted by Sam from the strange herbs and weeds he always had to
hand.

Conrad glanced around the single-room shack while Sam clattered
away in the corner, clearing up the residue of his preparations, always
clearing up. Little had changed in all the years Conrad had known the
place. The old double-barreled ten-gauge with the rabbit-ear ham-
mers still hung above the mantel on pegs, loaded, ready for action.
The surface of the pine table was, as ever, scrubbed white with wood
ash lye, clean enough for a surgical operation, the chairs neatly tucked
in around it. A curtain embroidered by Sam's wife just before her
death shielded the sleeping area with its iron bed from the main body
of the room.

The only notable additions in the past two decades were a good-
quality battery radio set and a framed photo of Billy in military uniform, both on the side table next to the old captain's chair where Sam
spent a good deal of his time. Taken by some backstreet photographer
in Manila, the grainy image had been posted home by Billy, along
with a letter. They had arrived at Lazy Point, the letter partially cen-
sored, two weeks after the Western Union telegram announcing Billy's
death in combat.

Sam shuffled over with two glasses of clear liquid and thrust one
into Conrad's hand. "Potato grog. One of my best yet."

It burned a streak down Conrad's gullet. Sam lowered himself into
his chair and set about packing his pipe.

"How's the hip?" asked Conrad.

"Better this time of year, I can stir around more, do a little net fishing. Sand dabs is running strong right now." Sam looked up. "If you knows where to look," he added mischievously.

Conrad stared at his old friend and felt an overwhelming sense of sadness: alone in the world, his wife and son gone, his body failing him, clinging to what little dignity his circumstances allowed him. He knew Sam was having difficulty making the payments on his lease to the town trustees, that there was talk of moving him out of the house.

As he lit the pipe, Sam glanced up, his drawn eyes reading Conrad's look. "It ain't so bad," he said.

"I can help."

"I don't want no charity from any man."

"I'm not just any man."

Sam hesitated. "No."

"I'll see you good with the trustees till spring."

"Can't do it."

Conrad's lone eye flicked over to the photo of Billy on the side table, drawing Sam's gaze with it. "That last summer he fished on shares with my father," said Conrad. "You remember? Couldn't put an oar in the water without striking a bluefish."

Sam smiled. "Yeah, Billy done real good that year."

"Should have done a whole lot better."

Sam looked at him long and hard, drawing on his pipe. He exhaled slowly. "It's a fool bends a dead man's name to his own ends, good or bad—a tenfold fool if that man's his father."

"Name me one cap who didn't split a catch his own way given half a chance, not when there's more than enough to go 'round." Conrad paused briefly. "I fought him on it, would've done the right thing by Billy at the time if I could have."

"Would've if you could've," said Sam for no apparent reason.

"Now I can."

Sam didn't say anything for a few moments. "Spring it is . . . when the swamp maples flower."

Conrad nodded.

"Now why don't you tell me why you really come here."

He should have known Sam would see it in him, the man missed nothing. He sneaked another sip of the home brew, stalling for time.

"You're hurtin', that much is sure, and I don't mean them bruises."

Conrad knew that once he'd spoken there'd be no turning back, his course would be set.

"They killed a friend of mine," he said.

Sam removed the pipe from between his teeth. "Who?"

"I don't know who."

"I mean the friend."

Conrad hesitated. "A girl. A woman."

"Do I know her?"

"No."

"What kind of friend?"

"A good friend." He felt the pain welling in his gut, and he fought to keep it there. "They say she drowned swimming in the ocean, but she didn't."

"I hear the currents is awful tricky right now."

"She knew that."

Conrad drew a long breath to steady himself. Then he told Sam how he'd explained the dangers of the shift in the longshore set to Lillian Wallace just a few hours before she supposedly went for that final swim.

He didn't say that she had been lying in his arms at the time, in his bed, his house, or that she had laughed then kissed him, touched by his concern, when he made her swear by all she held dear that she wouldn't swim off the ocean beach again until he told her it was safe to do so.

9

THE TURNING AREA WAS JAMMED WITH CARS, AND HOLLIS WAS OBLIGED TO park up along the driveway, the offside wheels on the verge. Among the vehicles jostling for space in front of the house was a florist's van with green-and-gold livery that discreetly proclaimed a Park Avenue address. The rear doors were open, revealing an assortment of wreaths and other floral displays on wooden racks.

As he approached the entrance porch, the front door swung open, and an elaborate arrangement of pink, yellow, and white roses stepped from the house. A casket spray, thought Hollis, moving aside to allow the young man a clear passage through to the van. Hundreds of dollars worth of fresh-cut flowers shipped up from the city so the Wallaces could make their selection on site—a small fortune destined to go to waste, the funeral still five days off.

Hollis glanced at the bellpull, but decided against it, crossing the threshold unannounced, making straight for the kitchen in the east wing.

She was busying herself at the counter, topping and tailing green beans, and didn't see him enter.

"Hello, Rosa."

She turned suddenly, startled.

"The door was open. Are the Wallaces in?"

Rosa laid the knife aside and began to untie her apron strings.

"It's okay, I'll find my own way."

He headed for the door on the far side of the room, pausing as he passed the oven. "Lamb?"

"Beef."

"Never had much of a nose."

He made to leave, hesitated, as if stopped in his tracks by an afterthought. "Oh, the gardener. What's his name?"

"Derek."

"Derek . . . ?"

"Watson."

"Is he in today?"

"Yes."

"Every day?"

"Not weekends."

"What time does he work till?"

"Five o'clock."

Hollis nodded, then left the kitchen.

Guided by the sound of voices, he found himself in the drawing room. He had passed through it on his last visit, but had failed to appreciate the enormity of the space, his mind on other matters then. Some forty feet in length, a run of French windows gave onto the back terrace, which was shaded by a vine-woven pergola, bunches of grapes dangling above a long table draped in a white tablecloth and set for lunch.

The room was effectively divided into three by a central seating area—an overstuffed sofa and armchairs, all upholstered in matching blue damask, which fronted the marble fireplace. To his left, a woman was seated at a writing desk, speaking on the phone in thoughtful, grave tones. There were more ticks than crosses beside the names and accompanying telephone numbers on the list lying before her.

"I'm afraid he's not available right now," she said. "Yes, of course I shall. Yes. Until then. Good-bye, Mrs. Elridge." Another tick. Her finger tapped the phone cradle, and she asked the operator to put her through to a number in Boston.

The far side of the room had been given over to a library, the walls lined with tall bookshelves. George and Manfred Wallace were in discussion with a woman around a table laden with yet more flower arrangements, the florist taking notes in a file.

"Richard," called George Wallace. "How many windows in the church?"

"Ten," came a disembodied voice from the terrace. "Eleven including the apse."

"Ten or eleven?" George Wallace turned irritably, catching sight of Hollis as he did so.

"I tried to call," said Hollis. "The telephone was engaged." He moved deeper into the room. "I thought we should talk about the traffic. I imagine there'll be a fair number of cars."

Chief Milligan had assigned Hollis to the problem of congestion that would inevitably arise at a society funeral, issuing the order with relish, keen to point out that Hollis had done "such a damn good job on the Memorial Day parade." To the chief's evident disappointment, Hollis hadn't fought him on it. He welcomed anything that brought him into contact with the Wallaces right now.

"Richard."

A middle-aged man materialized from the terrace as if from the wings of a stage. There was a polish and grace about him that hovered on the edge of effeteness. Trim and slight, his dark hair was receding neatly at the temples. His features were clean and even. Keen dark eyes peered out on the world from behind gold-rimmed spectacles that lent him a scholarly air, and a cigarette smoldered between his slender fingers. Hollis remarked that, despite the heat, his shirt remained buttoned, the knot of his necktie unloosened.

"This is . . ."

Hollis took his cue from George Wallace, who had clearly forgotten his name. "Deputy Chief Hollis."

"He wants to talk about numbers at the funeral."

The man approached, offering a hand. "Richard Wakeley."

His grip was surprisingly firm. The smile appeared to be genuine.

"Richard's a friend of the family," said George Wallace. "He'll fill you in."

A courteous dismissal, if ever there was one.

"Shall we?" said Wakeley, steering Hollis towards the terrace.

"Deputy Hollis." He turned to Manfred Wallace. "I'm sorry for the other day . . . at the morgue, I mean. I wasn't myself."

"Forget it," said Hollis, aware that Manfred could well have said nothing and spared himself the look of mild astonishment from his father.

THEY STROLLED THROUGH THE GARDEN, sticking to the shade, Wakeley sipping homemade lemonade, Hollis regretting that he'd declined the offer of a glass.

The service was set to take place at the First Presbyterian Church on Main Street, the burial to follow immediately after at the Cedar Lawns Cemetery on Cooper Lane. This would mean traversing the railway tracks at the top end of Newtown Lane, and Hollis made a mental note to contact the stationmaster about train schedules. It wasn't a grade-crossing—no danger of the Cannon Ball broadsiding a carload of mourners—but it still wouldn't look good if the barriers came down, sundering the long, creeping cortege as it wormed its way northwards.

Wakeley anticipated about two hundred people attending. Hollis pledged the full cooperation of both the East Hampton town and village police forces. Main Street, Cooper Lane, and Further Lane would all have to be kept clear of cars so that the armada of vehicles could park. Moreover, every junction on the route would have to be manned by an officer holding up other traffic.

Wakeley appreciated the scale of the operation, graciously thanking Hollis for the inconvenience to which the force would be put. There was something reassuring, calming even, about the man—the mellifluous tones of his voice, the way in which he handled himself, deferring to Hollis's expertise. He was a consummate manager of men, and certainly more than just a friend of the family, that much was clear. The silk necktie, the monogrammed shirt, the black leather oxfords, all suggested a person on equal standing with the Wallaces; and yet the highhanded manner in which George Wallace had addressed him earlier spoke of a different relationship. What was he exactly? Something less than a friend and peer; more than mere employee.

Hollis's musings were interrupted by a piercing female scream. It was followed closely by a loud splash. They had strayed to the end of the garden, where the swimming pool was located. More playful shrieks now emanated from behind the yew hedge that screened the pool on three sides. Hollis moved to take a better look.

"Shall we head back?" said Wakeley.

Hollis permitted himself two further steps, but they were enough.

Gayle Wallace was reclining on a lounge chair beside the pool, wearing a dark swimsuit, straw hat, and sunglasses. She was smiling wistfully at the antics of an attractive young couple frolicking in the water. Another couple was seated on rattan chairs in the shade of an umbrella, sipping drinks.

"Shall we?" said Wakeley, more firmly. Hollis briefly locked eyes with Gayle as he turned and followed.

They were halfway back to the house when Gayle came hurrying up behind them.

"Deputy Hollis." She had pulled on a light chiffon robe that barely concealed what lay beneath, not that it had ever been designed to do so. Even without shoes she was a shade taller than Hollis.

"I just wanted to thank you for the recommendation—the funeral home, I mean."

"Funeral home?"

She frowned momentarily, then remembered and smiled. "Oh yes, I'd forgotten." She turned her gaze on Wakeley. "Deputy Hollis isn't supposed to make recommendations about such things, but you won't tell anyone will you, Wakeley?"

"Of course not."

Wakeley, thought Hollis—definitely more employee than friend.

"Have they finished inside?" asked Gayle.

There was nothing in the question that demanded a response. It was a thinly disguised order, and Wakeley read it as such.

"I'll see you before you go," he said to Hollis.

Gayle waited until he was out of earshot. "You needn't worry, discretion's his middle name."

"Oh, I don't really care."

"No? Can't they demote you or something?"

"I suppose." He realized his honesty was starting to sound like swagger, or worse: self-pity. "Anyway, I'm glad I could help," he said.

"There's something I wanted to ask you."

Of course there was. Why else had she dismissed Wakeley?

"The fishermen who found my sister . . . found Lilly, I'd like to meet them, to thank them."

"The one to talk to is Conrad Labarde." He couldn't see her getting much out of the Kemp boy. "He lives just back from the beach off Montauk Highway, beyond Napeague Lane. No address, but I don't think there's much else down there, just dunes."

"Do you mind writing it down for me?" Hollis scribbled down the details, tore the sheet from the memo pad and handed it over.

"You're left-handed. Lilly was left-handed."

He searched for something to say, but there was no need.

"Thank you," she said.

"I can take you over there if you like."

"Excuse me?"

"To see the fisherman." It would be a good excuse to meet the big Basque again, survey his world, get more of a sense of the man.

"It's okay, I'm sure I can find my own way."

She left, stepping lightly across the lawn, her long, narrow feet leaving impressions in the spongy grass.

Hollis returned to the house to find the florist and her assistant gone. George and Manfred Wallace were seated with Wakeley at the table on the terrace. All three nursed glasses of chilled white wine while Rosa moved around them, arranging cutlery.

"I don't suppose you're allowed to," said Manfred, meaning the wine.

"Maybe a glass of water."

Rosa poured him a glass from a jug. No one spoke while he downed it, the silence oppressive, each gulp resounding in his ears.

"One more thing," he said. "The press."

George Wallace frowned. "What about them?"

"We'll do our best to keep them at bay, but with limited re-sources . . ."

"It's a good point. Richard?"

"I'll get on to it," said Wakeley.

Hollis drained the rest of the water and placed the empty glass on the table. "I'll be in touch in a few days once everything's arranged." He turned to Rosa. "Thanks for the water."

She met his look with something approaching defiance, enjoying the protection of her employer. This only confirmed his suspicions. She feared him, not in the way that many feared a police officer— irrationally, believing that the uniform somehow conferred on him the power to see into the dark caverns of their conscience. No, he had rumbled her in the kitchen, creeping up on her like that, surprising her. The momentary flash of apprehension in her eyes had betrayed her. She definitely knew more than she was letting on.

As he strolled around the side of the house, his mind was racing, filtering impressions. He could dismiss the gardener for now. Rosa had displayed no telling signs of unease when he'd sprung the subject of the old man on her. Whatever her secret, it was unlikely she shared it with—what was his name?—Derek, yes, Derek Watson.

He climbed into the patrol car, lit a cigarette, and added the name to his memo pad along with that of Richard Wakeley. It was an old habit. Names on a page obliged you to consider connections your mind might normally pass over, like deciphering a crossword anagram by writing the letters in a circle.

Watson and Wakeley side by side. It was an unlikely association, but you never knew, not till the affair had played itself out.

Hollis slowed as he passed the Clinton Academy, but his courage failed him at the last and he drove on down Main Street. Fifty yards along he was given the opportunity to reconsider.

Mary Calder was walking towards the center of town, stepping through the dappled shade cast by the tall elms. He drove past her, then swung the wheel, carving a long turn and pulling up at the curb.

"Maybe I'm mistaken," said Mary, "but wasn't that an illegal maneuver?"

"Was it?"

"Bylaw eighteen, I think you'll find."

Shit, maybe he'd misjudged their last exchange; there was still no trace of a smile.

"I'm on official police business," he said.

"Oh?"

"In pursuit of a suspect."

She held up her hands in mock surrender. "I demand to see my lawyer." And there it was—the smile—clutching at his breast.

"Where are you going?"

"Home," she said. "For lunch."

"You want a ride?"

She glanced around her. "Whatever will people say?"

"You're right. It's more than your reputation's worth."

She laughed.

"What?"

"Well, you obviously know nothing about my reputation."

True. He didn't.

"All right," she said suddenly, as if surprised by her decision. She crossed to the other side of the car and climbed into the passenger seat.

"Where do you live?"

"Three Mile Harbor Road."

"It'll mean making another illegal maneuver."

"Not if you head up Dayton Lane there."

This time she wasn't joking.

THE HOUSE WAS SET SOME DISTANCE back from the road down a cinder track. It was a large, squat, two-story farmhouse with a shed-roof extension on the side and two end-wall chimneys jutting from the shingled roof. Behind it stood a barn, dwarfed by an enormous tree with a dark crown. Beyond lay a paddock—a neat square of pasture hacked out of the dense oak woods and enclosed by a white post-and-rail fence.

"A farm," said Hollis, pulling the patrol car to a halt.

"That's very observant of you."

"So where are all the animals?"

"Well, there's a truculent old goose called Eugene, but he takes a nap about now—lucky for you. He doesn't like strangers."

"And your dog?"

She hesitated before replying. "She's with my son. He's staying with his father."

Ah, thought Hollis, that is news; two big pieces of news, in fact.

"Now I'm offended," said Mary.

"How's that?"

"You really haven't checked up on me, have you?"

He had done a bad job of concealing his surprise, and an awkward silence settled around them.

"Thanks for the ride," said Mary, getting out of the car.

Hollis felt bad. He wanted to make amends for his reaction, to tell her that he didn't care, but he couldn't find the words.

"Do you always drive so slow?" she asked.

It was a fair question. He had meandered through the maze of roads north of Main Street, crawling along, the needle barely nudging fifteen miles an hour. He had asked her about the LVIS summer fair, less than three weeks off now, and she had pattered away indulgently.

"I was enjoying myself." No lie there, he hadn't wanted it to end, the low hum of the engine, her voice washing around him.

"Well if you're lucky, next time we meet I'll fill you in on the rummage drive we've got planned for September."

He laughed, relieved that he'd been able to turn the situation around.

She was halfway to the side door when he called after her.

"Mary."

She turned back.

"The times you saw Lillian Wallace down at the beach, was she ever with anyone?"

She weighed the question for a moment. "Once. About a month ago. There was a man, a young man, tall, rangy. Why?"

"Blond?"

"No. Auburn hair."

Well, that excluded the brother, Manfred, but it hardly narrowed the field of lanky young men who moved in the elevated circles of the

Maidstone Club. Only an hour before he had seen two such speci-
mens at the Wallace's house, friends of Gayle.

"Why do you ask?"

"It's nothing," he shrugged. "Are you going to the funeral?"

"I think so."

"I'll see you there. Chief Milligan's got me on traffic duty."

Her eyes held his for a moment. "Don't let him get you down," she
said, "he's just a big old blowhard."

Hollis laughed.

"What?"

"I don't know. Yes, I suppose he is, isn't he?"

Driving away, his thoughts returned to the scene he'd glimpsed at
the Wallace's swimming pool—the young couple romping in the water, the other couple observing from the shade, Gayle stretched out in
the sun, all limbs, her face shaded by the brim of her straw hat.

People dealt with grief in different ways, but somehow he couldn't
see himself lounging by a swimming pool just four days after his dead
sister had been plucked from the ocean in a fisherman's net.

10

CONRAD UNCOILED. THE CANE ROD BOWED UNDER THE STRAIN THEN whipped through the air, the reel singing as the lead weight arced high up over the surf into the flat water beyond.

Not as far as the last cast, but far enough if they were out there.

He started to reel in—inexpertly. When it came to rod-and-line fishing, there was a certain truth to the phrase "beginner's luck." The jerky, unskilled actions of a child were, if anything, more likely to attract a fish to the bait.

It was a lesson first learned on the stubby harbor breakwater at Guéthary, back in the old country. His first fish, caught under the watchful eye of his father—a three-pound sea bream—enough to feed the family that evening. Conrad on his father's lap at the table in the kitchen, swollen with pride, his father's meaty paw wrapped around his little hand, steering the gutting knife. His mother slashing the sides of the fish then grilling it over coals, serving it with a garlic sauce, the cloves browned in a pan then crushed in the stone mortar. Everyone agreeing that it was the finest sea bream they had ever tasted, though the same couldn't be said of the local txakoli, the sharp, dry white wine made by their grandfather, and which both boys were permitted to taste for the first time. The wine driving them to early slumber, curled at their mother's feet while she read to them, the logs in the hearth crumbling to embers.

Was that really how it had been? Or had sentiment got the better of him over the years? He no longer knew, or cared. He was entitled to the memory, for it was the last pleasing one he had of his mother before she was taken from them.

The menace, when it came, was from a completely unexpected quarter. The war rumbling away in a distant corner of France had barely touched their village, their lives. It was spoken of, but not feared. One boy, the mayor's son, had headed north, carried on a tide of patriotism, only to lose a leg on a muddy hillside near Amiens. Remarkably, he survived and was shipped back to Guéthary.

In view of what followed, it would have been far better for all if that German artillery shell had caught Tomas Errekart squarely between the eyes, for when he returned home he carried Death with him.

In Guéthary, it became known as "Spanish flu." A few miles to the south, across the frontier in Spain, it was referred to as "French flu." The disease itself respected no boundaries, spreading like wildfire, laying waste to whole communities in a matter of days. To the puzzlement of all, "La Grippe" appeared drawn to those in the prime of their lives, passing over the young, the elderly, and the infirm; and the end came fast to those touched by its hand. A burning fever rapidly gave way to a crippling pneumonia that flooded the lungs.

Conrad's father was the first in the family to be struck down. By then the whole village was firmly in the grip of the disease, and Doctor Barron was able to do little more than pay a cursory visit and wish their mother well in the trial ahead.

Terexa Labarde nursed her ailing husband for two days and nights, the boys ferrying buckets of icy water from the well in the yard. On the morning of the third day, she was too weak to wring out the rags with which she cooled his body. Breathing hard, her own clothes sodden with perspiration, she pleaded exhaustion and asked the boys to take over, instructing them from a chair across the room.

Just before noon, she slid silently to the floor.

She didn't die immediately, but lay there on her back, the shallow rise and fall of her chest almost imperceptible, a reddish foam oozing from the corners of her mouth, the veins in her slender neck standing out like cords of rope. Antton insisted that he go for help, but she wouldn't release his hand, a feat of superhuman strength given her condition. She wanted to die with her boys at her side. And that she did, just a few minutes later. Mikel Labarde, lost in delirium, did not witness his wife's passing.

Antton displayed great presence of mind for a seven-year-old, turning his attention once more to their father, placing Conrad on bucket duty. Just before dusk he went for help, only to return an hour later in tears. The mayor, the doctor, even the priest, they were all dead. Guéthary was like a rudderless ship, with everyone looking to their own affairs, their own survival. Antton had been driven off, at gunpoint in one case, by people he'd known all his life.

The boys hacked ham from the bone in the pantry and settled in for another long night.

Mikel Labarde's fever broke at dawn the next morning. He woke to find his naked body covered in damp rags, his two sons intertwined on the bed beside him, fast asleep, and his wife dead on the floor in the corner of the room. He was too weak to do anything but cry; and Conrad and Antton were woken by his sobs.

Life never returned to normal, not for their father. He became sullen and withdrawn. In spring of the following year, when a second, more deadly wave of the disease swept the country, Guéthary was spared. But while others gave thanks for this, their father remained plagued by thoughts of those who had spurned his son that day.

It was something for which he could never forgive them, especially the *lehen auzo,* the "first neighbor." Basque custom dictated that the occupants of the nearest house be treated as kin, and in return behave as such when the situation called for it. The *lehen auzo* had thought only of himself and his family when he turned Antton away; he had reneged on the relationship, causing mortal offense.

In a clear and vindictive break with tradition, it was their father, not the *lehen auzo,* who carried the cross the day of their mother's burial. Still weak from the flu, his black mourning cloak billowing in the stiff November breeze, he stumbled and fell twice at the head of the procession as it threaded its way from their house to the church.

In August, he abruptly announced to the boys that they were moving away—to America. This news wasn't as startling as one might have imagined, even to their young ears. Basques had been crossing the ocean since the Middle Ages, voyaging to the rich cod fisheries of the Grand Banks and pursuing whales into the treacherous subarctic waters off Greenland. Indeed, John Cabot's celebrated discovery of Newfoundland in 1497 was greeted by the Basques with something approaching wry bemusement, for it was hardly a new-found-land, two of their own captains having dropped their anchors off the very same coast over one hundred years before. The Basques felt no need to justify this claim, nor did they doubt for a moment that the Vikings had been there well before themselves. *Amerika* had made rich men of many Basques over the centuries; and the belief that it still could was firmly embedded in their culture.

The boat and the gear sold promptly and well to a fellow tuna fisherman. The house would have gone for more had the highest bidder not happened to be the same individual who'd leveled his rifle at Antton less than a year before.

They sailed from Bordeaux on a converted whaling ship mobbed with American servicemen returning from the war, still drunk on victory. The crossing was rough, enough to blunt the merrymaking and fill the narrow steerage compartments with the rank odor of seasickness. Sixteen days after she put to sea, and following a brief stopover in Havana, the *Chicago* crept past the Statue of Liberty and sank her anchor into the deep Hudson River mud.

On disembarking, they were immediately ferried from the quay side over to Ellis Island. Conrad could only recall brief moments of the lengthy processing. He remembered being tagged, doctors prodding and poking, sticks of blue chalk raised menacingly, those marked with a cross screaming in protest as they were led away. And he could remember thinking, his heart drumming a terrified tattoo in his breast: What if they mark me and not Antton or Papa? They'll take me away, I'll never see them again, and then there'll be nobody, not till I die and we all meet again in heaven. And the prospect of seeing his mother again washed through him, and suddenly things didn't seem quite so bad.

Then there was the vastness of the registry room with its seething mass of outlandish humanity—men in dresses, others with whiskers that reached to their waists, women with their faces shrouded in veils, children with pointed shoes that curled at the end—the deafening clamor of their unintelligible voices rising to the rafters as they slowly shuffled forwards. A man behind a tall desk fired questions at their father, and then they were out, down the stairs, into the rain.

They were greeted warmly in their own tongue by a man with a kindly face. He ruffled the boys' hair and thrust candy into their hands, helped them recover their baggage then led them over to the Manhattan ferry. Valentin Aguirre was something of an institution for Basque immigrants, many of whom passed through his New York boardinghouse, Eusko-Etxea, on their journeys westwards to Nevada and Idaho. Most of the guests were single young men looking to make their fortunes in the New World. Others were married, with wives and children back home, who would be joining them once the cost of their passage had been earned out West. A widower with two young sons was a novelty, drawing bucketloads of sympathy from the serving girl in the dining room, who kept seizing Conrad and Antton to her ample bosom, until one joker proclaimed, to everyone's amusement, that his mother was also dead.

Guests tended to stay no more than a few days, time enough to recover from the crossing while Valentin arranged their railroad tickets for the onward journey. And it would have been no different for them if their father hadn't struck up conversation in the barroom with a fellow by the name of Eusebio Landaluce. He was tall, with a stooping gait and a feral expression that belied his good nature. He laughed heartily at the slightest inducement and he was immensely proud of his black Borsalino hat, which, he swore blind, was made from the hairs of wild Argentinian rabbits. He plucked coins from behind the boys' ears, stuffed his silk kerchief into his fist only for it to vanish before their disbelieving eyes. He made his ears dance, his nose wiggle, and he could break wind on command.

After they had been dispatched upstairs to bed, Eusebio regaled their father with tales of woe out West. He told of Basques reduced to little more than slavery by the owners of the big sheep companies, pitchforking hay and mucking out lambing sheds from dawn till dusk. The winter camps of the sheepherders were a sight to behold, he said. He had seen families dumped in the mountains with no more than a patched tent, some bedrolls, a potbellied stove, and a 30/30 rifle for fending off the bears, wolves, coyotes, and cougars. And when you weren't defending yourself or the flock against wild animals, there were the cowboys to contend with. Fierce feuds raged between the ranchers and the sheepherders over the best pastureland. Then there were the kids in the street, the ones who'd spit on you and call you "black bascos" or "dirty Catholic." And so he went on, misery heaped upon hardship and suffering, a grim catalog of wretchedness.

When their father woke them the next morning and announced that they would be staying in New York, that Eusebio was going to find a place for them to live, they greeted the news with enthusiasm.

Of course they did. They hadn't laughed so much in over a year, not since their mother died. Even when they set eyes on the pitiful little apartment that was to be their home, their opinion of Eusebio never faltered. It later emerged that he had vacated the place that very morning, that the sums he took off their father by way of rent were excessive, to say the least, and no doubt more than covered the cost of the improved accommodation to which he'd decamped. All this they forgave him, and more besides, for he was true to his word.

He found a woman, Irena, to care for the boys during the day, to cook for them and teach them English. She was a spry little Lithuanian with a fierce temper and a questionable grasp of the language, but she quickly grew fond of them and let them know it. Obsessed with personal hygiene, she was always dragging them off to the public showerbath on Eleventh Street between Avenues A and B. It was Irena who introduced them to the neighborhood, pointing out the whores and the hustlers, the crazies and the pickpockets as she scuttled along, her bag clutched tightly to her breast.

On her days off, the boys would roam farther afield, heading for South Street, the East River waterfront, with its forest of masts, the windjammers and clippers gathered cheek by jowl, their bowsprits sticking out over the street, sailors and longshoremen scuttling to and fro, offloading cargo or filling their bellies with chowder at the small eating places across from the pier houses. They didn't know what drew them here, not at the time. Only later did they realize that the sea was already in them.

Irena's presence lent a much-needed order to their lives, as well as freeing their father to pursue his "business" with Eusebio. It was an improbable partnership, almost comical—their father grave and thoughtful, Eusebio a babbling bundle of nerves—and for several months there was little to show for it. Then, suddenly, the apartment started to fill with furniture, and meat appeared on the table with increasing regularity.

The source of their newfound wealth was one of the many harebrained schemes Eusebio was always hatching. Most of them foundered, the triumph of wild optimism over common sense. This one was no different, except that it worked. They bought show programs from theater doormen, selling them on at a profit to errant husbands or wives in need of an alibi for their whereabouts that evening, something to drop in front of their unsuspecting spouses. As the business grew, they extended the service to include used ticket stubs from senior ushers. Clients were sourced through a spreading network of saloon barmen, and runners were employed to handle the distribution.

Reduced, as they became, to the position of overseers, Eusebio and their father spent more time around the apartment. Dinner was always a riotous affair—laughter in the home was more precious than gold plate, Eusebio used to say—and it was generally followed by several hands of *mus*. Conrad was always paired with Eusebio against his father and brother, which stung a little but invariably resulted in victory, *mus* being a game of bluff and deception, Eusebio being a master of both.

The business continued to prosper, the money kept rolling in, and before long they moved to a much larger, three-room apartment on the second floor. This was a matter of grave concern for Irena, who believed that to relocate downwards in the same building brought bad luck.

She was wrong.

At midnight on January 16, 1920, the Eighteenth Amendment to the Constitution came into effect.

PROHIBITION, THOUGHT CONRAD, without Prohibition I wouldn't be standing here on the ocean beach, casting into the surf. Not with much success, as it happened. The prospect of landing a fish for his supper was fading fast.

He reeled in, cut a fresh length of squid and fastened it to the hook. Five more casts, he told himself, then he'd throw in the towel.

On the fourth cast he felt a bite and struck. The line thumped taut; the rod craned its slender neck. Big enough for supper, and then some. But what was it? Was he right? Could they be here already, so early in the season?

"Damn. Hell. Damn. Damn . . ."

He glanced left. Twenty yards down the beach, a woman was hopping around at the water's edge, straining to examine the sole of her bare foot. She lost her balance and tumbled backwards onto the sand. She looked over at him helplessly, and as she did so, the tension went out of the rod.

The fish was making a play for freedom, running at the shore. It hadn't slipped the hook, there was still life in the line, he could feel the tremor in it. He reeled in as fast as he could, just fast enough as the fish broke to the westward. Any more slack and the ploy would have worked. But he had her now, she was tiring, resigned to the inevitable. No. She broke again, running eastwards this time, stripping twenty yards of line from the reel. A fighter. Experienced.

"Excuse me."

Not the first time she's felt the sharp taste of steel in her mouth. He felt bad that it wasn't going to work this time, that her bag of tricks wouldn't save her.

"Excuse me."

Did the fish have as strong a sense of who he was, connected as they were by the line?

"Excuse me." The indignation of the delivery struck home this time. He couldn't afford to turn away, but answered nevertheless.

"Yes?"

"I've cut myself. I'm bleeding."

He was drawing the fish into the surf now. It leapt briefly and he smiled. "Ha!"

"Is that all you can say? Ha!?"

"Give me a minute."

"A minute?"

"Less."

He hauled the fish up onto the sand beyond the wash, pinned it there, then struck it behind the head with the handle of his knife. Hard. Only then did he turn.

"Let's take a look," he said.

Beneath the blood he could see that the cut was long but not deep, running from the ball to the heel of her foot. It would mend itself without assistance, no need for stitches.

The offending spear of metal was poking from the packed sand just nearby.

"Flotsam," said Conrad.

"Oh really? Not jetsam?"

"Wreckage from a boat, probably a merchant ship. We still get a lot of stuff cast up. From the war, you know, the U-boats."

"That's very interesting. And what about my foot?"

Conrad pried the object from the sand. It was a small lump of wood pierced by a jagged shard of metal—shrapnel embedded there by some mighty explosion, a fossilized moment of devastation.

"You'll live," he said.

She used him as support until they reached the steepest part of the frontal dune, where she grew too weak to hop farther. Conrad abandoned the rod by a clump of beach grass and took her up in his arms.

She carried the fish.

"You live here?"

"Yes."

"By yourself?"

"Uh-huh."

"Don't you get lonely?"

"No."

She looked around the room. "I didn't know there was a place here."

"Not many people do. You can't see it from the beach."

"Are those your books?"

"No."

"You stole them?"

"They're my stepmother's. She was a teacher."

"Was? She's dead?"

"Moved away. California."

Her eyes scanned the shelves. "Have you read them?"

"No." He opened a tin and removed a bottle of iodine. "This is going to sting."

He was right. It did. He held her ankle tightly as he dabbed at the wound, carefully removing the sand, dropping the bloodied swabs into a bowl.

"You have long toes."

"Excuse me?"

"But then you're tall."

"Do you mind not talking about my feet? I don't think I've ever discussed my feet with anyone, and I can't see that I should start now."

"Not another word."

He placed a sterile pad over the cut and began binding it in place with gauze.

"I hate them," she said.

"Huh?"

"My feet. They're too big."

"You think?"

"How many women you know take a size nine?"

"Not a whole load."

"Exactly."

"They don't look big, maybe because they're narrow. Any wider and they could look big."

"You're doing it again."

"I'm sorry."

He secured the gauze with a safety pin.

"Where are your shoes?"

"At home."

"Where's home?"

"East Hampton."

"I'll run you back."

"Could I possibly have a drink of water? You do have water, don't you?"

"Sure."

He poured a glass from the pitcher on the table and handed it to her.

"You seemed very intent on catching that fish."

The fish lay on the table, slick and metallic, its armored rainbow sides speckled with black dots, its fins and tail yellow, almost as if they belonged to another species altogether.

"It's a special fish—a weakfish."

"Really? It looked like it was putting up quite a fight."

He smiled politely at her joke.

"What makes it so special?" she asked.

"It shouldn't be here yet, not till May. But then everything's early this year, the shad bushes, dogwoods, birchwood violets, even the oaks. Now the fish."

For the past few days he had seen gannets circling off the ocean beach, gulls doing the same in the bay: unseasonable indicators that the fish had already started their annual run up the coast and would soon be hitting the beach.

"What will you do with it?"

"Fry it in beer batter."

"Is it good?"

"You've never had weakfish?"

"Not to my knowledge."

"You should try it sometime."

"I'll be sure to," she said a little curtly.

He took a filleting knife from the drawer in the table and began sharpening the blade on a stone. "You can share it with me if you like."

"I wouldn't want to put you to any more trouble."

There was a hint of annoyance in her voice that the offer hadn't been immediately forthcoming.

"As you like," he said, enjoying the game. "I have to do this now or the flesh will spoil."

He sliced open the fish's belly and pulled out the guts. He cut down to the backbone just behind the head, turned the blade and worked it towards the tail. The first fillet came free. Flipping the fish over, he repeated the process, aware that she was watching him with a look that hovered somewhere between intrigue and revulsion.

"Beer batter, you say?"

"Deep-fried cubes. We call them frigates."

"And they're good?"

"The best."

"That's quite a claim."

"I tell you what," he said, turning to look her in the eye, "if you don't agree, you're allowed to say so."

"Deal."

He sliced the skin from the fillets.

"If I'm going to stay for supper, shouldn't I know your name?"

"Conrad."

"Lillian," she said. "Lillian Wallace."

11

THE MODEL A BUMPED ALONG THE ROAD TO THE BEACH LANDING, ITS chassis groaning, the beam from the headlight dancing up ahead.

Conrad pulled the vehicle to a halt. He knew what to expect as he rounded the bend: the sandy lot, fringed with trees and bushes, rising up to the shallow breach in the dune, the ocean out of sight beyond. But he needed to try and see it with fresh eyes. The eyes of a man looking to dispose of a body.

She hadn't been put in the ocean in front of the Wallaces' house, of that he was certain. The strength of the longshore set at the time she was supposed to have drowned would have carried her farther eastwards overnight, beyond the spot where they'd pulled her from the water the next morning. He knew from experience that the ocean could do strange things with a drowned body, taking it on an improbable journey that seemed to defy all natural laws. But that was rare.

It was some distance from the house to the beach, down the bluff and across the dunes, an exposed walk, moonlit on the night in question. Too far to carry a dead weight, and too risky. That was probably the reasoning. Maybe there had been kids on the beach. It was a popular stretch for clambakes at this time of year, the deep sand at the base of the frontal dune pockmarked with the blackened remnants of the nocturnal feasts.

Whatever, he was fairly sure she had been taken elsewhere in a car and then dumped in the ocean. Fortunately, there were a limited number of spots nearby where this might have happened.

Two Mile Hollow landing seemed unlikely. Although closest to the Wallaces' house, it became a rendezvous for lovers once night fell, a place of furtive exchanges and steamed-up car windows. Likewise, he had dismissed Egypt landing. Right next to the Maidstone Club, there would have been too many other cars coming and going, and there was the added risk that club members often strolled down onto the beach at night.

The small landing at Wiborg's Beach, on the other hand, a little farther along, would have been ideal—remote, squeezed in beside the wasteland of the club's west course. The village tryworks for rendering whale oil had once stood there, and since much of the big house just back from the dunes had been torn down, local people had started using the track again to gain access to the beach.

Conrad wrenched the Model A into gear and pulled away. He knew that what he was doing served no concrete purpose, nothing could possibly come of anything he found, it was simply that he needed to know: for himself, and for Lillian.

Rounding the bend, the small landing opened up in front of him. He found himself drawn to the gloom beneath the boughs of an oak, the natural spot to park up if you had something to hide. He turned the engine off, reached for the flashlight on the seat beside him and got out.

What would he have done next? Strolled up onto the beach, probably, to check the coast was clear. Returning to the car, he would then have shouldered the body and hurried as best he could towards the breach in the dune. No. This would leave him vulnerable for—what?—thirty or forty seconds, prey to the headlights of an approaching vehicle. Far better to cut through the undergrowth on the right. It offered perfect cover. If he happened to be surprised, he could easily drop out of sight and hide there, undetected, until the danger had passed.

Conrad pushed his way through the hawthorn and dogwood, the thin, poor soil underfoot giving way to sand as he neared the back of the dune. He swept the rise with the beam of the flashlight, but the dense carpet of beach grass concealed any tracks there might have been leading up the incline.

The crest of the dune, however, was bald of any vegetation, and he found what he was looking for almost immediately; so quickly, in fact, that at first he doubted what he was seeing.

There was a shallow but distinct patch of flattened sand where the killer had laid her on the ground after the climb—carefully, no doubt, so as not to mark the body. Indistinct footprints disturbed the area around.

If this had been the movies, he would have discovered a cigarette butt nearby—some rare Turkish brand that would identify the culprit. But all Conrad could see were two tracks in the crusty, wind-packed sand leading down the face of the dune onto the beach.

The scene presented itself to him: the killer hooking his arms beneath hers and hauling her backwards down the dune, her heels furrowing the sand in neat, straight lines.

The tracks led out across the beach a short distance before dissolving in the swathe of disturbed sand where others had strolled in the intervening days.

He carried on past to the water's edge.

The waves were breaking low and clean to the east, their curling crests catching the light of the moon—strips of silver traveling gently along the shore.

So this was it, the place. He must have drenched himself in the process, dragging her out there beyond the break.

He had thought in terms of just one killer up until now, finding it easier to focus his confusion, his hatred, on an individual rather than a cast of conspirators. It was now clear he'd been right to do so. The lone set of footprints flanking the furrows confirmed it.

He wandered back to the dune, settled himself down, and rolled a cigarette. His Zippo wouldn't light, out of gas, and he slipped the smoke into his shirt pocket.

He laid his hand on the sand, feeling the contours of the indentations left by her heels.

It caught him like a rogue wave, a big sea surging up from the depths, unexpected, overwhelming. He choked, trying to keep it down, but it swept him before it, engulfing him, deep sobs racking his body, tears coursing down his cheeks.

12

"ABEL, FOR CHRISSAKES."

Hollis moved to block his friend's path. Abel shimmied left, right, left again, brandishing his camera.

"No photos."

"Tell that to my editor." Moonlighting for the *East Hampton Star* was another string to Abel's bow.

"I meant to," said Hollis. "I forgot."

"I can't be held responsible for your failings as a police officer."

"Is there a problem?" They both turned at the voice.

A squat, bullnecked man approached, his dark suit straining at the seams.

"No problem, thanks," said Abel chirpily.

The man drew on his cigarette and exhaled, his porcine eyes shrinking to pinpricks as they fixed themselves on Abel.

"It's okay," said Hollis.

The man turned away grudgingly and sauntered back to the huddle of chauffeurs smoking near the curb. Beyond them, the run of parked cars stretched off into the distance down Main Street.

"Who's the gorilla?"

"The guy who's been hired to break the back of anyone taking photos in front of the church."

"Nice work if you can get it."

Abel glanced over at the church, then up at the sun, judging the exposure. "Must be almost done in there."

"For me, Abel, as a friend."

"Oh come on, Tom, don't pull that one. You don't call, you don't write . . ."

"I've been busy."

"So I hear." The knowing look was accompanied by a faint smile. "You and Mary Calder, eh?"

He shouldn't have been surprised—it was a small town, tongues wagged freely and readily, he knew that.

"All I did was give her a ride."

"There's a joke there, but I won't demean your love for her."

"Christ, you can be infuriating."

At that moment, the organ inside the church piped up and the mourners broke into song: "Dear Lord and Father of mankind, forgive our foolish ways . . ."

"Breathe through the hearts of our desire," said Abel distractedly.

"What?"

"It's 'breathe through the *heats* of our desire,' but people always sing 'hearts.' Have you noticed that?"

"No."

"What about the cemetery?"

"Out of the question. Anywhere else is okay."

Abel looked over at the chauffeurs. "No photos in front of the church, eh?"

He was gone as the words left his mouth. Hollis could only watch helplessly as Abel approached the group and addressed himself to the Wallaces' muscle. The man squared off at first, then the tension went out of his bulky frame and he nodded, acquiescing. The group returned to their discussion, albeit a little self-consciously, while Abel circled around them, snapping with the Graflex, issuing instructions to his models.

Hollis turned back to the church. The two towers flanking the facade were so disproportionate to each other—one low and delicate, the other wide, clumsy, monumentally tall—that he found himself wondering what had driven the builders to shun symmetry in favor of such glaring discord.

The unseen congregation launched into another verse of the hymn.

"Breathe through the hearts of our desire," they sang, "thy coolness and thy balm."

ABEL BEHAVED. He was gone by the time the doors opened and the pallbearers shuffled from the church with the coffin. Manfred Wallace was paired at the front, his moist eyes glistening in the sunlight.

His sister, Gayle, head bowed and face veiled, walked behind the coffin, her arm hooked through her father's. George Wallace stood tall and upright, his features devoid of any expression.

Hollis scanned the faces of the mourners as they trailed down the steps of the church.

Where was Mary?

He had arrived as the service was beginning, so he didn't even know if she was inside.

He cursed himself. He'd been too quick to assume she'd turn up. Foolish, when so much was riding on her attendance. Now he was facing the prospect of losing a possible lead.

He didn't recognize her at first, and it took him a moment to figure out why that was. She was wearing makeup, not much, but enough to distort her features, somehow enlarge her already full lips and overwhelm her pale eyes. It didn't suit her, he thought, a little guiltily.

A crowd gathered hesitantly near the hearse, as if unsure whether they should be observing this particular stage of the operation. Undertakers swooped to assist as the pallbearers maneuvered the coffin from their shoulders and slid it into the vehicle.

"Hello."

Mary turned. She was standing on the fringes near the back.

"Hello."

So what if her face didn't light up? It was a sombre occasion.

"You look great."

"Thanks," she said flatly. She seemed almost annoyed with him.

"Quite a turnout."

"Yes."

People were dispersing now. He had to be quick or the moment would be lost.

"She had a lot of friends."

Not good, but it was the best lead-in he could think of.

Mary looked him clean in the eye.

"You could just ask me straight, you know, it's less insulting."

"What?"

"You want me to point him out—the one I saw her down at the beach with. It's why you're here."

All Hollis could manage was a feeble look.

She nodded towards a group of young people. "The tall one over there on the right."

He was talking to a girl, a diminutive creature a good foot shorter than him—an almost comical pairing, not unlike the towers of the church facade. He was handsome in an unremarkable way, his features refined by generations of selective breeding to the point of blandness. If it hadn't been for his height, Hollis might not have recognized him.

It was the same young man he had seen slouched in a rattan chair beside the Wallaces' pool earlier in the week.

"Happy now?" asked Mary, not waiting for a reply.

"I'm sorry."

Mary turned back. Nothing in her expression suggested she wanted him to expand on the apology; in fact, she looked utterly unconvinced by it. He was a little surprised, therefore, when she asked, "What are you doing next Friday evening?"

"Nothing."

He was working the night shift, but he could always get someone else to cover—young Stringer, maybe, always so eager to please.

"I'm having some friends over for a drink. From seven o'clock."

"Sounds good," said Hollis. "Maybe I'll get to meet Eugene this time."

"Pray you don't."

He smiled, but his mind was already elsewhere, figuring both where and how to make his approach.

BOB HARTWELL WAS STANDING near his patrol car opposite the cemetery entrance on Cooper Lane, turning his cap in his hands. Hollis pulled in beside him.

"It's going to be tight, Bob. Best get the first cars to park up right down the end there."

"Sure."

"I'll wave them through to you."

Hartwell wandered off. Hollis knew he had planned to spend the afternoon on the water, sailing with his kids in Three Mile Harbor, and yet he hadn't so much as flinched when Hollis announced that he'd be directing traffic instead. He was a good man, smart, unflappable. Even when Chief Milligan chose him as the target for one of his sudden and quite unexplained broadsides, the abuse seemed to wash right over him. Afterwards, he might say something like "Guess who didn't get any last night?" or "The market must be down," but that was the extent of his ill feeling. He was the closest thing Hollis had to a friend on the town force, albeit a friend with whom he had never broken bread or even shared a beer.

The hearse crept around the corner into Cooper Lane, trailing cars. It turned into the cemetery, followed by the next four vehicles—Richard Wakeley had been very specific—and Hollis directed the others on down towards Hartwell at the end of the road.

He noted that the tall young man whom Mary had pointed out was traveling in a chauffeured limousine. That was good.

THERE WAS NO DISGUISING THE FACT that the plot where Lillian Wallace's bones were to rest for eternity had been hastily put together. The low privet hedge that ringed it was set in freshly turned earth. Within this perimeter, the lines were still visible in the green and sappy turf.

It was a large plot, a family plot, wide enough to take at least three abreast, though it was doubtful that the soil on either side of her grave would ever be disturbed. She had expressed a wish to be buried in East Hampton, Hollis knew that, but somehow he couldn't see another Wallace choosing to keep her company.

No, George Wallace had done the very best by his daughter—as in life, so in death—and he wanted people to know it. For her there would be no slender patch of ground off one of the avenues that sliced the cemetery north to south, squeezed into the seried ranks of humble little granite headstones pushing up through the overgrown grass. She would lie in this pleasing little copse, this shady reserve of the wealthy, with its yew trees and cypress trees and ornamental hedges and its names carved into the finest white Italian marble.

Hollis had attended many burials over the years—family, friends, fellow police officers, even a hobo on one occasion—but somehow the experience never lost any of its impact. Weddings, those you became inured to with the passage of experience: the same hymns, the same vows destined to be overlooked or broken. But there was something about the physical act of lowering a body in a box into a hole in the ground that always struck home. There was no other sound quite like that of a handful of earth hitting the lid of a coffin. It reached to the core of your being and shook you.

As he glanced around at the faces of those gathered near the grave, it struck Hollis that he was not alone in feeling as he did. It also occurred to him that the person responsible for Lillian Wallace's murder was, quite possibly, among those mourning her passing at the graveside—right here, right now—not even twenty yards from where he was standing.

How could he be so sure she'd been murdered? He deflected the question. At this stage of an investigation, the material facts were often stacked deep and high against you—an autopsy that revealed no evidence of foul play, for example. All you had to go on were your instincts, the little whispers at the back of your mind.

This was not one of those murders committed rashly, in the heat of the moment, then hastily covered up. The planning and execution were to be respected, if not admired. Mistakes had been made—they always were—and it was in the nature of an intelligent crime such as this, carefully conceived, that the lapses, however small, were all the more glaring for it. Like a lone dent in the faultless bodywork of a new car, they drew the eye.

Hollis felt a chill of excitement run through him, for it was becoming clear that this was exactly the kind of investigation at which he had once excelled, on which he had built his name.

One case had set him on that path, bestowing upon him a mantle of notoriety that would never be shrugged off. He could recall every detail of it, his first hesitant steps over the threshold, the two technicians from the Broome Street crime lab on their hands and knees in the living room, the ashen-faced patrolman accepting a cigarette from a colleague in the kitchen. And he could still taste the rust in his mouth, the metallic vapors of the blood that speckled almost every surface in the apartment.

The woman lay on her back beside the sofa, her throat opened to the bone. The man was in the bedroom, slumped in a corner, a bewildered expression on his face, as if still coming to terms with the fact that he was dead. There were several stab wounds in his chest, along with a deep gash in his shoulder. A picture of what had occurred was already emerging, for another man, the gentleman of the house, had survived. Horrifically wounded, Gerald Chadwick had been rushed to the hospital, giving officers a sketchy account of the carnage before being sedated for surgery. By noon of the following day his story had been confirmed by a thorough examination of the crime scene. Door-to-door questioning of the other residents of the smart block only lent further weight to it.

The dead man in the bedroom was a neighbor of the Chadwicks', Samuel Kuhn, a wealthy widower, withdrawn and private, but prone to raging outbursts against the other occupants of the building. A feud had sprung up recently over the issue of the Chadwicks' cat, which Kuhn claimed was fouling the common parts. When the poor animal was found hanging from the Chadwicks' door handle, the police were called. It was clear from the patrolman's report that he sided with the Chadwicks—a respectable insurance man and his petite, attractive wife—but he was bound to let the matter drop through lack of evidence. This incident had occurred some two weeks prior to the killings, and in the intervening period Samuel Kuhn had, by all accounts, grown more cantankerous and vocal than ever, accusing anyone unfortunate enough to cross him in the hallway of conspiring against him.

Then one evening he cracked. Taking up a long paring knife from the drawer in his kitchen, he wandered upstairs and vented his spleen on the Chadwicks. He gained access to their apartment on the pretext that he wished to apologize to them, but on entering the drawing room he went berserk, slitting Julia Chadwick's throat before turning his attention on her husband. Badly wounded, Gerald Chadwick fled down the corridor to the bedroom, where he managed to wrest the knife from Kuhn's grasp, turning it on him and stabbing him several times in the chest, killing him. Bleeding profusely, Chadwick then called the police from the bedside phone.

It was an entirely plausible account of the horror that had unfolded in the apartment. Analysis of fingerprints, blood distribution, and blood types all supported it. The multiple lacerations to Gerald Chadwick's palms, forearms, and face were concomitant with defense wounds sustained in a knife attack, and would lead to unsightly, lifelong scarring. Moreover, the knife was undeniably Samuel Kuhn's, one of a matching set discovered in his kitchen.

The Homicide Bureau was satisfied. And this was their case. Had Hollis not been responding to a break-in at a pawnbroker's when the call came in, he might have got there ahead of them and been able to stake a claim—his precinct, his watch. Unlikely, though. The bureau detectives would never have allowed a high-profile, open-and-shut case like this one to slip through their fingers without a fight. No, they would have muscled him out, a precinct detective, and a third-grade one at that. Either way, his was always going to be a lone voice of dissent struggling to make itself heard, if only because he couldn't put his finger on exactly what it was that was troubling him.

All he knew was that he had a sense of unease about the case—an itch, a niggle—something he had seen, heard, imagined? He couldn't rightly say. His persistence drew hoots of derision from Lieutenant Gaskell, who refused to share Hollis's misgivings with the Homicide Bureau. Gaskell was an incompetent, a man who had made lieutenant before they required you to sit an exam, but he was no fool. He had his record to think of.

The night before the crime scene was due to be cleaned up, Hollis gained access to the apartment, spinning some yarn to the uniform on duty at the door. He wandered the rooms and corridors deep into the night, working every angle he could think of. No idea was too preposterous; and not one of them bore fruit. He was smoking his last cigarette, pacing through the events of that evening one final time, when it hit him. It was almost as if it had teased him enough and out of pity had decided to reveal itself to him. One moment it wasn't there, and then it was, as it had always been, since that first day. He dropped to his hands and knees in the corridor, peering at the wooden floor.

Gerald Chadwick maintained that he had fled down the corridor in fear of his life, hotly pursued by a knife-wielding maniac. The spots of blood on the floor were indeed Chadwick's—that much had been established—but if he'd been traveling at anything more than a walking pace, the impact pattern of the drops would have betrayed this fact, with jagged, toothlike projections extending forwards.

The uniform, almost perfectly circular shape of the drops in the corridor suggested that Gerald Chadwick had in fact been strolling towards the bedroom.

In one blow, it was now possible to construct an altogether different scenario for the evening in question: Gerald Chadwick somehow luring Kuhn to the apartment, Gerald Chadwick slitting his wife's throat in the drawing room, Gerald Chadwick slashing himself with the knife then calmly trailing his terrified guest down the corridor to the bedroom.

Why? It didn't matter. That would follow. Gerald Chadwick had lied, and to Hollis's mind that suggested Gerald Chadwick was guilty of murder.

Two hours after his arrival at the Homicide Bureau headquarters on Centre Street, and following further examination of the bloodstains, Harry Beloc, the chief of detectives, announced that Hollis might be on to something. By now, word had filtered through to Lieutenant Gaskell, who showed up in Beloc's office, backing his boy, and keen to point out that he'd done so from the very first. He changed his tune when Hollis suggested they go straight for a confession.

"Gaskell, shut the hell up," Beloc had snapped. "This could be your meal ticket. Might even get your name in the *Daily News.*" Beloc had made up his mind by the time the laughter subsided. He handled the matter himself, paying Chadwick a visit in his recovery room at Bellevue Hospital. Chadwick crumbled under questioning. Too weak to be moved, he spent that night in the hospital, but two floors down—in the Department of Correction's prison ward.

The story made the front pages, and Lieutenant Gaskell did indeed get his mention in the *Daily News.* Hollis didn't. That was okay, though; it was the way things worked. Besides, those who mattered knew that the breakthrough clue and the subsequent strategy had been his. Three months later, he was promoted to detective second-grade, which meant an extra two hundred dollars a year. Lydia celebrated by promptly spending a sizable portion of this sum on clothes. They dined out on Broadway, the Great White Way unnaturally dim and moody because of the wartime blackout restrictions, and they toasted their future with an overpriced bottle of French champagne.

There was cause for real cheer; Hollis had turned a corner in his career. Gaskell had already pulled him off the petty larcenies—the sneak thieves, pennyweighters, and pickpockets—and if he continued to make the lieutenant look good on the bigger cases he might even get a call from the Homicide Bureau in a year or two. He hadn't seen or heard from the chief of detectives since that day in his office, but he knew Beloc had registered his existence.

But if Hollis felt good, it wasn't so much for his growing status— Lydia was covering that base—as the fact that he was beginning to believe he might actually have a gift for detective work, a nose.

So young, so earnest, so thoroughly self-absorbed that he hadn't even noticed his enemies already ranging themselves against him in the shadows of his victory, his vainglory.

———

HOLLIS WAITED UNTIL THE MOURNERS DISSIPATED, heading for their cars, before making his move.

"Mr. Penrose?" he said, approaching from the rear.

Getting the name had been easy, requiring no more than a casual exchange with the chauffeur; figuring where he'd heard it before had taken a little longer. He'd found it eventually, scrawled in the memo pad among the notes taken at his first meeting with the maid, Rosa: *Lillian W. moves to East Hampton in January following split from fiancé (Penrose).*

"Yes?"

"Justin Penrose?"

"That's right."

"It's about Lillian Wallace. I have a few questions."

"Questions?" frowned Penrose.

"You knew Miss Wallace well." It was a statement, not a question.

"We were together for a time if that's what you mean. Why?"

"I believe you were engaged, no?"

"Yes."

"When was the last time you saw her?"

"I don't know, a month or two ago."

"Up here?"

"Look, what's this all about?"

"In East Hampton?"

"Yes, in East Hampton."

"This was the time you went swimming with her off the ocean beach."

Penrose visibly stiffened. "You know," he said firmly, "I really don't think I have time for this right now."

"Of course. We can do it later if you want."

Penrose glanced around him. Cars were beginning to pull away from the curb, making for the reception at the Wallaces' house. He turned back to Hollis, resigned to having the conversation.

"How did she appear to you?"

"Well, a lot better than just now." Embarrassed by his flippancy, Penrose added solemnly, "Look, she seemed well. Very well indeed."

"Were you worried about her, I mean, her leaving the city, coming up here over the winter?"

"Yes, I was worried about her. We all were. But as I say she seemed very well, much better."

"Do you mind me asking why you broke off your engagement?"

Penrose weighed the question. "As a matter of fact, I do. I don't see that it's any of your business. In fact," he added, "what *is* your business?"

"I'm just trying to get a picture of her state of mind. It's routine in cases of unattended deaths."

That phrase again.

"What are you saying?" asked Penrose. "That you think she took her own life?"

"Oh no, Mr. Penrose, I know she didn't."

This was the moment he had been heading for. A guilty man would recognize it for what it was: Hollis laying down his hand. Penrose's expression was impossible to read. A poker player, no doubt about it. And a good one.

"Then why are we having this talk?" said Penrose.

"Like I say, it's just routine. Thank you for your time."

Hollis stood his ground, waiting to see if Penrose glanced back at him before climbing into the limousine.

He didn't.

But Hollis did see Bob Hartwell observing him from down the far end of Cooper Lane. He turned away when Hollis caught his eye.

13

CONRAD GLANCED AT HIS WATCH. UNLESS THEY WERE RUNNING LATE, THEY'D be putting her in the ground about now. He had no difficulty picturing the scene, because he'd passed by the cemetery the previous day.

It was a large plot, shaded, pleasingly so, the earth heaped up beside the fresh hole. She would have approved of the headstone, nothing too ostentatious, no ornamental frills, just her name, date of birth, and date of death carved into some kind of pale stone, softer than marble. He had frowned as he did the calculation. Twenty-six years old. She had lied to him about her age, adding two years. Why?

He had struggled with the question then, and he did so again now as he lay curled on his bed, fully clothed.

With time, no doubt, she would have offered up an explanation.

With time.

Did he really think their relationship would have continued on its course indefinitely? Had he ever allowed himself to believe that it could? It would have been easier to lie to himself and say no; but there had been signs from the beginning, almost from their very first exchange. They had discussed it later, or rather she had discussed it, pushing him to admit that he had sensed it too. And he had flatly denied any such immediate feelings.

That was their game. Their dance. On other occasions, he took the lead and she did her best to step on his toes. The truth was, they'd both known they would see each other again after that first chance encounter. And they had, a little less than a week later.

It was dusk, and Conrad was by the barn, tarring a fyke net in the old cauldron once used for trying-out whale oil, racing to beat the creeping darkness.

She materialized ghostlike from the gloom, clutching a bottle of whiskey.

"Hi."

"Hi."

"How's the foot?"

"Better. Not true. It keeps opening up."

"I told you not to walk on it."

"I'm not good at taking orders." She glanced at the cauldron. "What's cooking?"

"Tar."

"This is for you."

The whiskey was his brand—Imperial—noted and logged on her last visit.

"It's by way of thank-you for coming to my aid . . . albeit a little slowly at first."

"You want some?" he asked.

"Is it any good?"

"No."

"I didn't think so. It was the cheapest one in the liquor store."

She tried it nonetheless, mixed with Coke. As soon as he had cleaned up and changed his clothes, he joined her on the deck and poured himself a glass.

"It's my birthday," she said.

"Happy birthday."

"Thank you."

"Shouldn't you be out celebrating?"

"That's exactly what my father said when I spoke to him earlier."

"Sounds like a wise man."

Lillian smiled.

"I'll do something over the weekend," she said. "My brother and sister are coming up. They're throwing a surprise party for me."

"Some surprise."

"My cousin let it slip. Poor Alice, she was never the brightest flame."

They sat in silence, staring at the stars.

"I don't have a present," said Conrad, "but I can offer you supper."

"Well, that depends what's on the menu."

"Lobster and caviar?"

"You're joking."

"Where'd you think they came from?"

"I don't know. Lobsters, I suppose, but caviar . . ."

"It's been a good year for sturgeon."

"You catch them here?"

He pointed at the ocean, adjusting a little to the southwest. "About there. Got six hundred fathoms of net fishing just off the bar. We'll haul the gear tomorrow, set it again, keep it up till the spring runs drops off at the end of May."

"I had no idea."

"Come with me."

He fired up the generator and led her over to the old whaleboat house beside the barn. It was here that they prepared the sturgeon roe. He talked her through the operation, demonstrating how they separated then salted the eggs. When she asked if they did good business, he shrugged. He didn't tell her that they'd made enough in the last month alone to see them good till the end of the year. Before leaving, he took a couple of tins of their own caviar off the shelf, gifts from a grateful buyer at the Fulton Fish Market eager to do more business with them. Then he plucked two lobsters from a wooden tub and asked her to choose between them.

"I reckon we're good for both," she said. "Don't you?"

She set the table while he cooked. She remarked on the beauty of the sideboard, and he told her that it was made from the wood of one of the tall elms on Amagansett's Main Street felled by the '38 hurricane. He explained that the house too was a victim of that apocalyptic storm. It had started life in East Hampton, on the western shore of Georgica Pond, put up as a summer home by a New York publisher at the turn of the century. Shattered by the high winds, it had lain derelict throughout the war before Conrad bought it, transporting it along the beach on skids to the plot of land he'd just purchased on Napeague. A section of the roof, the back bedroom, and one corner of the main room were all missing, and all were replaced with timber and shingles recovered from the old Amagansett Gun Club, sold off by the members when they decided to upgrade their bunking quarters out on Montauk.

The barn had arrived a few months later, dismantled in Amagansett then reerected, piecemeal, beside the house. After more than two hundred and fifty years of service, the Van Duyns no longer had need of it. Ten generations of the family had stored their hay in the barn, and many more generations of cows had brushed against its sturdy uprights, rounding them off, buffing them smooth as glass.

As for the whaleboat house, the third side of the open yard formed by the buildings, that had been Rollo's contribution to their joint enterprise. For as long as anyone could remember it had stood, sleek and low, just back from the beach at the end of Atlantic Avenue. If Conrad had offered to take Rollo on simply as a member of his crew, it would still be standing there. But he hadn't; he had proposed that they go into business together—a true partnership, equal shares, riding out the highs and the lows together, the good years and the bad.

After Ned Kemp had overcome his initial reservations and con-
sented to the venture, he insisted that Rollo bring something to the
table. Conrad was, after all, providing the dory, the catboat, and a
whole bunch of other gear. Rollo had never wanted for anything, but
nor had he ever received payment for his labors, either. He was
housed, clothed, fed, and cared for, and in return he did what was
asked of him—working the farm, crewing on the *Ariadne* during the
bunker season, dragging for yellowtail flounder in fall, codfishing off
the ocean beach in winter. There was no injustice in this, it made
sense to everyone, not least of all Rollo, and it worked. Or, rather, it
had up until then.

When Conrad refused to accept a cash payment from Captain Ned,
Rollo chipped in his only asset, his inheritance, gifted him ahead of
time by his father. It was never in doubt that Rollo, of all the brothers, would be the one to inherit the whaleboat house. Since childhood
he had been drawn to the building and its mysterious contents, dusty
and disused, his fascination fueled by the thrilling tales of derring-do
learned at the knee of his grandfather, Cap'n Josh.

By the age of ten, Rollo had become the official repository of all
matters relating to the Kemps' long association with inshore whaling
off the East End. He was a storehouse of anecdotes, too young to detect the whiff of embellishment clinging to them. Had a right whale,
a notoriously sluggish creature, really dragged six men in a twenty-
eight-foot boat two miles out beyond the bar in as many minutes?

Rollo knew of every rally made by the Kemps off the ocean beach.
He knew who had first sighted the whale, who had raised the weft
above their house on Bluff Road, and who had crewed for them. He
could tell you the sea and weather conditions at the time, as well as the
exact course taken by each whale after it was fastened on to. And he
could describe in detail the nature of each kill, clean or messy, depending on the accuracy of the man administering the coup de grâce
with the lance, and the ferocity of the exhausted animal's death flurry.

His accounts only became sketchy when it came to the contribution made by the other crews who had participated in the rallies. Inshore whaling was, necessarily, a collective affair. How else to tow sixty tons of dead whale ten miles back to shore in a heaving sea? Rollo wasn't to blame for the omissions in the stories he told. He was only repeating his grandfather's words, and Cap'n Josh had never been renowned for the high regard in which he held rival whalemen. At best he had a grudging respect for the Van Duyns who worked the other end of the village. This diminished by degrees the farther west one headed. The East Hampton crews were barely worthy of consideration or comment, and as for the "Wainscott dumplings," as he called them, well, they were fit only for ridicule, putting to sea in those clumsy, oversized dories of theirs.

It was all bluster, of course. Any man who has thrust iron into a creature a thousand times his own size is inextricably bound to others who have done the same.

Conrad and Billy were eleven years old when Rollo first shared with them the secrets of the whaleboat house. It was a Friday, after school, a sunny, windblown afternoon, with choppy waves thumping against a stunt beach, and they'd had to clear the sand banked up against the doors before they could enter.

The whaleboat held center stage, like a dusty sarcophagus in some ancient tomb. Around it lay an armory of weapons to ensnare a boy's imagination—harpoons, lances, axes, grapnels, and blades of every description for cutting into blubber. But Rollo directed their attention to the boat itself. He made them trace the sheer lines of its white pine hull with their fingertips. He pointed out the sharp stern end, explaining that the ability to retreat rapidly without turning was vital during the whale's flurry, when a crashing blow from the vast flukes could tear the boat and its occupants apart. He showed them the wooden tholepins trimmed with leather to deaden the sound of the oars, of approaching doom; and he demonstrated how, in time-honored tradition, the boat-steerer switched places with the boat-header in order to deliver the death stroke.

Most impressive, though, was the change in Rollo. What had happened to the nervous, downturned gaze, the halting speech, the struggle to put names to all but the most commonplace objects? He spoke with a confidence he had never once displayed in the classroom, plucking technical terms from the air at will.

Conrad and Billy must have passed the test, for they were invited to return time and time again. Together they reenacted the stories handed down by Cap'n Josh to his grandson, Rollo standing tall and proud in the stern, barking orders to his depleted crew of two—"Slack back!" . . . "Hold water!" . . . "Spring ahead!" . . . "Stern all!"—before hurling the harpoon into a big burlap sack of hay conscripted to play the whale. With time, willing crew members were found to man the other oars. Then numbers climbed beyond the capacity of the boat, and tales of inshore rallies made way for grander, more epic yarns of deep-sea, round-the-horn whaling that could accommodate a larger cast of characters.

There was never any shortage of adventures to be played out. As a young man, Cap'n Josh had sailed from Sag Harbor on the oceangoing whaleships, the last of three generations of Kemps to do so. He had made three trips in all, visiting both frosty ends of the globe, rising through the ranks from pimpled greenhorn to chief harpooner. When gas lighting finally put paid to the demand for whale blubber, he returned to the wife and young family he hardly knew, a respected man, and a rich one.

Like others in Amagansett and East Hampton fortunate enough to have survived their time aboard the whaleships, he'd had to content himself with sporadic rallies off the ocean beach in late winter. After the speedy finbacks and hostile sperm whales of the southern oceans, the local right whales—long on blubber and bone, short on speed—made for easy quarry. Then, suddenly, some years before the Great

War, the whales disappeared. Inshore whalemen up and down the coast hung up their harpoons. All the gear was stowed away, forgotten.

The Kemps' boat hadn't seen the light of day for almost twenty years when Rollo, Conrad, Billy, and the pack of other local kids first heaved it out of the whaleboat house under the approving gaze of Cap'n Josh. The building itself was to double as a whaleship, its boxy construction not unlike the square-sterned, blunt-bowed vessels that used to clog the quayside in Sag Harbor—"Built by the mile and cut off in lengths as you want 'em," Cap'n Josh had said, before dispatching two men into the mastheads to keep watch for whales.

"Ah blow-O!" they hollered from the roof.

"Where away?"

"Sperm whale, two points off the weather bow, sir, four miles away."

"Stand by to lower."

And so it continued, Cap'n Josh marshaling his troupe of young actors, feeding them their lines, directing the chase of a particularly feisty sperm whale encountered in the South Pacific, which, once ironed, had proceeded to strip all three hundred fathoms of manila line out of the boat before dragging it on a heart-stopping Nantucket sleigh ride (Cap'n Josh rocking the boat fiercely to mimic the effect of it crashing over the waves). The whale had fought till the last, capsizing the boat on two occasions before finally expiring.

That wasn't the end of it, though. They had lost sight of the whaleship on the long pull back. Then the wind breezed up from the sou'west. They were six men in a cockleshell boat tossed on an angry sea, many hundreds of miles from land, rowing blind in a fading light, dragging a dead whale. When the last vestiges of day dipped below the western horizon, hope went with them. Some among them began to pray, not for succor, but final prayers, beseeching forgiveness for sins committed.

And then they saw it, a beacon in the night—the distant fires of the tryworks burning on the deck of their mother ship—and the strength returned to their backs and arms. Safe alongside at last, one of the oarsmen, a Scotsman, cursed then kicked the whale that had almost cost them their lives. Too exhausted for further labor, others were assigned to undertake the cutting-in while they recovered on the deck, smoking their pipes. When the first blanket piece was hoisted aboard from the carcass, the block made fast to the main masthead came free, and two tons of suspended blubber felt the fierce grip of gravity.

The scene was enacted in somber silence, the whaleboat's lugsail doubling as the blanket piece, Billy playing the unfortunate Scotsman on whom it landed. The message was clear, though Cap'n Josh spelled it out for the younger ears. Even in death the whale had sought satisfaction for the disrespect shown it by one of its hunters. It was a lesson they would all be wise to remember.

These expeditions to far-flung corners of the globe were played out almost every weekend for a year. Then Cap'n Josh suffered a seizure, and after a brief, humiliating struggle turned up his toes. That he died well after his time was poor consolation to Rollo, who withdrew into himself. The whaleboat house fell dormant once more, until given new life on Napeague almost twenty years later, taking its place between Conrad's house and the barn. It was pleasing to Conrad that all three buildings had experienced previous lives. It somehow made them one with the landscape, the ever-changing sands on which they were perched.

None of this he had any intention of revealing to Lillian, but she drew it from him in the way that only a stranger can, fueling him with questions. At a certain point, though, she grew silent, pensive.

"What?" he asked.

"The stories."

"What about them?"

"I don't have any to tell. Nothing that comes close, at least."

"I doubt that's true."

"It is. But it doesn't matter."

"They're just stories," he shrugged. "Maybe I made them up."

"Now you're just trying to make me feel better."

"If I am, it's not working."

His words brought a smile to her lips. She lit a cigarette and looked at him intently.

"What are you doing here, Conrad?"

"What?"

"Why not over there with everyone else? Why out here on your own?"

"It's my home."

"You made it your home."

He felt himself coming to, like waking from a dream, the cold wash of reality bringing him to his senses, suddenly aware of the shattered lobsters on their plates.

"It's late," he said. "I should drive you back."

She asked if she could borrow a book and he told her to take her pick.

"Is this any good?" she asked, plucking one off the shelf.

"Not bad."

She turned to him. "I thought you hadn't read them."

"That one I've read."

"I hear it's tough going, but worth it."

He didn't take the bait, but he did reach for a pen and write in the flyleaf: *To Lillian, on her . . .*

"How old are you?"

"Never ask a lady her age," she said, but told him anyway.

. . . 28th birthday, he wrote.

"Aren't you going to say who it's from?"

"You'll know," said Conrad.

They barely spoke on the drive back.

"Thanks for the book," she said as they pulled up in front of her house.

She reached for the handle, but hesitated. Turning back, she leaned over and kissed him on the cheek.

"That's the best birthday I've had in years."

And the last she would ever have.

SUNDAY WAS A BETTER DAY.

He rose early, venturing outdoors for the first time in two days. There was an ominous groundswell running, with waves breaking over the bar and banking up in their eagerness to strike the shore, the outer ripples of some distant Caribbean storm.

He stripped off and fought his way through the break, struggling against the pain in his ribs. It had diminished little in the past week, though the bruising had lost some of its lividity, dulling to a grayish purple tinged with yellow. He still welcomed the injury inflicted by Ellis Hulse's boot. It had offered him the perfect excuse to lay off the fishing for a while, to be alone, no need to keep up appearances of normality.

That changed a few hours later, when Rollo showed up fresh from church in his ill-fitting suit and clutching a Bible. He had brought some aspirins with him to speed along Conrad's recovery.

Rollo had spent the past week crewing for his father on the *Ariadne,* a 110-foot subchaser from the Great War, the fastest rig in the Smith Meal bunker fleet. The fishing had been good—Conrad had seen pods of menhaden darkening the waters off the back side all week—but Rollo seemed unwilling to talk about it. This meant only one thing: a spell on the ocean in the company of his father and brothers had undermined his confidence.

No doubt they'd had him working the winch, or below decks in the engine room manning the old Fairbanks-Morse, awaiting instructions from the pilot house. Nothing too challenging. Never anything too challenging.

Conrad announced that he'd be ready for action by Wednesday, and Rollo visibly came to life, rolling a smoke and demanding a coffee.

"We'll be into them Wednesday, get us a bunch, you'll see," he said when he finally left, taking off towards the beach.

Conrad watched him all the way.

Rollo turned as he crested the frontal dune, jerking his thumb over his shoulder. "Looks fishy to me!" he yelled.

Conrad waved, and he was gone.

Wednesday was pushing it, but it would force him to dig himself out of the irremediable gloom into which he had sunk. Something needed to change, and fast. He'd taken to muttering to himself as he shuffled around the house like a soul in limbo.

Maybe things would be different once he'd visited her. He felt ready to. That in itself was something. He checked his watch. Still too early. The cemetery would be milling with people paying tribute to their dead.

By midday they should all be gone, driven indoors by the building heat.

HE PARKED ON THREE MILE HARBOR ROAD and walked the last couple of hundred yards. He was wearing fawn twill pants and the white shirt reserved for special occasions. He had even dug out some lace-up shoes.

He felt foolish in the clothes, and no doubt he looked it, too. He knew Lillian would have laughed at him, but somehow he didn't care. In fact it brought a smile to his lips, picturing the glint of playful mockery in her eyes.

The cemetery was deserted except for a scrappy-looking dog loping about, forlornly nosing the ground, as if aware that all those bones were down there but far beyond its reach. Bouquets of fresh flowers laid that morning studded the ground like colorful pins in a green felt board. The sun was high, intense, and it cast his shadow black on the ground at his feet.

Her grave was buried beneath a deep blanket of wreaths and other flowers, and it struck him that even now they were shielded from each other. He clamped his eyes shut in the hope of blotting out the scene. But dim shapes took form in the darkness, coalescing to produce her features, set in repose, a low, gloomy light cutting across them. Her wide-spaced eyes doomed to collapse in on themselves, her lips to draw back into a hideous rictus grin, her tongue to protrude, the flesh of her barely freckled cheeks predestined to blacken, blister then liquefy, consumed from within by the very organisms that had struggled so hard to ensure the body's survival.

He knew what happened to the body after death, he knew that decay was, in fact, life for a multitude of other creatures. He knew that the deeper you buried a corpse, the slower the process of decomposition. He knew that in the heat of summer it raced ahead, and in the bitter chill of a mountain winter it ground almost to a halt. He knew all this because he had gone out at night to recover the bodies of his fallen comrades.

They were rarely whole. Often days would have passed before any attempt at recovery could be made, time enough for the scavengers that inhabited the dense Italian *macchia* to feast away at leisure, to drag off the limbs, or bits of limbs, cleaved away by a mortar blast or a burst of fire from a German 88.

Had his unit not been operating behind enemy lines for so much of the time, there would have been others to perform the grisly task. But the boys from the Grave Registration Service were deemed lacking in the necessary skills to move around undetected in enemy territory, and only one of their number had been assigned to Conrad's company. He was a young corporal from southern Illinois by the name of Harold Bunt, although everyone called him the Professor, because he'd broken off his studies to go to war.

The Professor's orders were to coordinate the retrieval and dispatch of the dead from the safety of their own lines, assembling the bodies as best he could, then shipping the canvas-wrapped packages back down the mountain on mules. He soon ignored his orders, though, extending his remit to assist in the recovery of the dead. He did this selflessly, aware of the terrible toll it was taking on the soldiers.

To the Professor, those weren't his buddies out there, they were just KIAs, brave men killed in action, who'd earned the right to a decent burial and a small white cross with their name on it. Circumstances permitting, he extended the same respect to the enemy, burying their dead in shallow graves where they'd fallen, to be recovered at some future date by either side, depending on which way the territorial pendulum swung. This courtesy was the cause of some surprise to the fighting men, boiling over into anger on a couple of occasions. But the Professor assured them it was customary practice for the men of the Grave Registration Service and he saw no reason to abandon it now.

He kept to himself, eating alone, wary of forming friendships, conscious that his role made him a figure of some suspicion. As a scout, Conrad came to know him better than most, guiding him over the hostile terrain on nocturnal forays whenever there was a lull in the fighting. Nothing pleased the Professor more than sneaking past an enemy foxhole—hearing the voices, smelling the cigarette smoke—in order to bring a KIA home. It amused him to imagine the look on the Germans' faces the next morning when they discovered the body was gone.

For Conrad these missions were a welcome change from the normal demands of a night patrol. It was a relief to just slip by in the darkness, no obligation to draw his knife, drop into the hole, and silence the enemy's murmurings.

They started spending more time together, playing chess with a set the Professor had recovered from the rubble of a bombed-out farmhouse. Each time the regiment advanced, they split the chess pieces between them so that only half the set would have to be replaced should either man step on a mine or take a direct hit from a mortar or a shell.

For the first few weeks, their games were conducted in near silence, each man alone with his thoughts, his strategy. But with time, their friendship found a precarious footing, the only kind possible under the circumstances. Experience dictated that to know a man too well was only to store up unnecessary grief for the future.

As the fighting increased in ferocity, Conrad came to appreciate the true value of their chess games. They permitted him to keep functioning at a certain level of aggression, the right combative pitch. He feared what might happen if he ever allowed himself to come down in between the firefights, to think about what he was doing, what he had done. Chess, it seemed, was his way of dealing with things, of keeping going. Others had theirs.

Some talked big and brave and carved notches into their rifle butts. Others retreated into themselves, drawing on resources they never knew they had. Others sought refuge in humor, black as the night at a new moon. You did what you did to get through, that was all. The Professor was no different, turning to science for his crutch, laying his theory on Conrad late one night while they sheltered in a church.

Men died, said the Professor, and when they died, the microscopic creatures that inhabited their bodies suddenly turned on them and consumed them. Everyone knew that they came first—the microorganisms, the protozoa, the bacteria. That's what all life had once been about. But maybe it still was, maybe the evolution of life was a load of bunk. Life, the life that mattered, was the same as it had always been: microscopic. Only its external appearance had changed, the husk it had molded around itself, the tendrils it had sent out—legs to carry it to better feeding grounds or away from danger, hands to kill on its behalf and nourish it. We were like servants, he went on, laboring under illusions of self-importance, convinced that they're the true masters of the house. In truth, we nourish the bugs, and then we die, and then they devour us, their vehicle, before moving on.

Conrad could remember thinking at the time that what the poor fellow needed was a spell of leave, a few days furlough in Naples—take in a show or two, flirt with some Red Cross girls. But now he found himself reaching for what the Professor had said that night, trying to see sense in it, draw some kind of solace for what had happened to Lillian, for what was happening to her in that coffin.

It didn't work.

And he knew then that he would break the pledge he had made to himself, the vow muttered through clenched teeth in the garden of the English hospital, beneath the dying heat of a September sun, the long grass in the orchard littered with fallen fruit.

In that moment, he saw with absolute certainty that he would take another human life.

"Hello."

Conrad spun around, startled. An elderly woman was standing behind him, frail and stooped, her thinning silver hair as light as goose down.

"Did you know her?" she asked.

"No."

He saw his lie reflected back at him in her rheumy eyes. How long had he been standing at the grave, adrift on his thoughts? Five minutes? Twenty? More? Hardly the actions of someone with no association.

"She drowned," he said. "I found her."

"Oh, you're the fisherman."

"One of them. I just came by to pay my respects."

She seemed satisfied with his response, and turned towards the grave. "A tragedy. She was a right beauty."

The *East Hampton Star* had run a small piece, along with a picture of Lillian taken at some charity event at the Guild Hall, smiling as always.

"Kind with it. Always found time to speak to an old lady."

Conrad cast an eye over the washed-out colors of her dress, the cheap handbag, the swollen feet squeezed into scuffed shoes, and he tried to imagine her moving in Lillian's circle.

As if reading his thoughts, the old lady turned to him. "I used to see her here."

"Here?"

"I come every day, sometimes twice. Hubert likes me to come, you see, even if it's for a few minutes, just to say hello. Oh, I know it sounds silly, and maybe it is, but I live close, on Osborne Lane, just along from the crossing, so it's no great hardship, though sometimes my joints protest when the wind's off the ocean."

Out of politeness, Conrad allowed her to finish.

"She used to come here?" he asked. "To the cemetery?"

"Who?"

He nodded towards the grave. "Lillian Wallace."

"Oh yes, almost every week. To visit someone over there."

She pointed towards the northeast corner of the cemetery.

"Almost every week," she repeated. "Always with flowers."

"What kind of flowers?"

"Just . . . flowers. I don't know."

The directness of the question had unsettled her. Why should he care what variety of flowers Lillian Wallace had brought with her?

"I best be going." She shuffled off, casting a suspicious glance over her shoulder as she went. Conrad waited till she was lost to sight on Cooper Lane before making for the northeast corner of the cemetery.

Apart from the names, there was little to distinguish the headstones from one another—a scattering of rough-hewn granite blocks with polished faces. The resting place of the poor. Poor but not forgotten. Flowers adorned many of the graves.

Which one had drawn her here? And why? Who among this silent gathering of the dead had she known or cared about enough to warrant her making regular visits?

It didn't make sense, not unless it was something to do with a member of the household staff. The maid, Rosa, perhaps. They were close, very close, he knew that. Could Rosa have lost a son, a daughter? No, Lillian would have said something to him. He would have known.

He silently hoped that he didn't stumble upon an innocent explanation. He wanted the reason for her visits to have a bearing on her death. More than that, he needed it.

He had dredged the memories of their times together for clues, but had turned up nothing. The father she feared, the ambitious brother, the sister who had always belittled her, the fiancé who had left her for another woman. Hardly a happy life, but commonplace stories nonetheless, unremarkable. All he had to go on was a faint impression of disquiet in her last weeks, a remoteness that would settle on her face like a veil when she was off her guard. If she hadn't been more eager than ever to spend time with him, he might have assumed she was having misgivings about their relationship. He certainly now wished that he'd pushed her a lot harder on the matter.

He glanced around, reading off names at random—familiar names, names still carried by the living—but the answer didn't present itself. There were just too many to choose from.

He fought the frustration building inside him and cleared his head. Think. If she'd left flowers around the time of her death, they would have to be over a week old, well past their prime, dead even. That excluded most of the graves. In fact, it left only a handful of candidates.

He moved slowly between them, dismissing them in turn: a woman some twenty years dead, Agnes White's stillborn daughter, Orville Hatch, who had lost both legs to poor circulation before the end. No obvious connection there.

The name on the next headstone stopped him dead in his tracks.

Being a long-lived flower, the lilies had stood up pretty well, though a scattering of petals lay around the rusted metal vase. He approached slowly, crouching down.

One lily for every year of the short life memorialized in the cold granite. Lilies, a symbol of purity and innocence. He knew that from the somber print that used to hang on the landing of their house, the one his stepmother had brought with her when she moved in with them, the one entitled "The Annunciation"—the Virgin Mary on her knees before the angel, clutching a single lily.

He could sense Lillian's mind at work, her hand at play. More than that, though, he had a dim recollection of a conversation, an idle question, or so it had seemed at the time: Lillian asking him if he had known Lizzie Jencks.

Yes, had been his reply, but not well. His father had fished with her father once, setting gill nets off the ocean beach.

Young Lizzie, hair the color of copper wire, always so ready to spring a smile on you, her cheery disposition snuffed out late one night on a lonely lane, victim of a hit-and-run driver.

14

HOLLIS HAD NEVER HAD CAUSE TO VISIT THE MAIDSTONE CLUB BEFORE, AND the appearance of a police officer was clearly something of a novelty for the members as well. Four of them gathered on the green abutting the parking lot broke off from their golf game and stared as he pulled the patrol car to a halt. Words were exchanged, and a ripple of laughter passed between the men.

The interior of the clubhouse was cool, dark, and strangely dank, the moist air heavy with the odor of wood polish. The desk clerk peered over the top of his spectacles as Hollis approached. "Good afternoon," he said coolly.

"I'm looking for Anthony Cordwell."

"I wouldn't know if he was here. Members aren't required to sign in."

"And I suppose you can't leave the front desk to check."

"I'm afraid not," came the reply, heavy with false regret.

"Then I guess I'll just have to take a look around myself."

He was a few steps shy of the doors leading to the back terrace when his path was blocked by the desk clerk.

"I'll see what I can do. If you'd be so good as to wait over there." He indicated some club chairs before disappearing.

Hollis lingered at the doors, curious to get a glimpse of the wealthy at play. From its vantage point at the top of the steep grassy slope, the clubhouse offered a wide vista over the swimming pool complex with its sandy sunning areas, restaurant, bar, and dining patio. Beyond, two long runs of cabanas arced through the broken dunes towards the beach like arms reaching out to embrace the ocean. All around, people were gathered beneath striped umbrellas, finishing lunch or sleeping it off. Only a handful of youngsters were braving the sun, frolicking in the pool, diving for hoops.

Hollis felt a little cheated; the Sunday afternoon scene before him was hardly different from those being enacted all over the country, though the setting was surely grander than most.

"May I help you?"

The gentleman from the front desk had reappeared. He was accompanied by a colleague, a younger man with a thin, reedy voice.

"I don't know, can you?"

"You want to see Anthony Cordwell."

"I think we've already established that."

"Is there a problem?"

"Not unless you don't go get him for me."

ANTHONY CORDWELL HAD BEEN PLAYING TENNIS, and, judging from his complexion, he was being given a run for his money.

"Oh, it's you," he said warily.

"I won't take up much of your time," said Hollis. "Though it looks like you could do with the break."

Hollis was led through to the bar, which to Cordwell's evident relief was deserted. Cordwell wiped his face with a towel.

"Couldn't this have waited?" he asked

"You're a bright boy. You'll think of something to tell them."

Hollis handed him a buff envelope. Of the two photos inside, the first was a close-up of a dress shoe, Cordwell's name clearly embossed inside. The second showed the shoe beside a hydrangea bush, the

Rosen's defaced front door visible behind, the crude, dripping white Star of David clearly in focus.

"What is this? Blackmail?"

"Think of it as a gift."

Cordwell eyed him suspiciously. "And in return . . . ?"

"I have a few questions, then I'm gone. Those stay."

"And the negatives?"

Hollis patted the breast pocket of his uniform. "When we're done talking."

Cordwell nodded, as if accepting a deal from the Devil himself.

"Justin Penrose, you know him?"

"Yes."

"Well?"

"As well as anybody, I suppose."

"Meaning?"

"He's what you might call private. Why?"

"How long was he with Lillian Wallace?"

"A year, two years."

"Try and be more specific."

Cordwell thought on it. "Just under two years."

"Why did they break off their engagement?"

"Differences. I don't know. She ended it."

"You must have heard something."

"You know," said Cordwell, casting his mind back, or at least appearing to, "it really wasn't discussed." He paused. "It was never going to be easy, what with Gayle."

"Gayle Wallace? What about her?"

"They were an item once, Justin and Gayle."

"What are you saying, he switched horses in midstream?"

"It was over with Gayle by then, but she still wasn't happy when she heard about Lillian."

I bet she wasn't, thought Hollis.

"What does Penrose do?"

Cordwell snorted, amused by the notion. "He doesn't have to *do* anything. His family has a bank."

"And what do *you* do, Mr. Cordwell?"

"Me?"

"Aside from persecuting Jews?"

Cordwell was too angry to manufacture any kind of response at first. "Are we finished here?" he asked sharply.

"No, we're not. Penrose came to see Lillian about a month ago."

"Did he now?" sighed Cordwell.

"Why would he do that?"

"What do you mean?"

"I mean did he still carry a torch for Lillian?"

Cordwell hesitated before replying. "It's possible. He was pretty upset when it ended."

It was a hard image to conjure up, Justin Penrose upset by anything.

"What's this all about?" asked Cordwell.

"I'd appreciate it if you didn't mention this conversation to anyone."

"And I'd appreciate it if you gave me those negatives now."

Hollis handed them over.

If Cordwell had bothered to examine the negatives before slipping them into the envelope he would have noted that they didn't match the incriminating photos. Rejects from the batch of shots taken by Abel, one was of the Rosens' daughter, a raven-haired beauty with whom Abel, in characteristic fashion, had been mightily and momentarily taken; the other showed Hollis on his hands and knees in a flower border, the crack of his ass just showing above the waistband of his pants.

A print of this last shot now hung on the wall of Hollis's kitchen. Framed up and presented to him at the time by Abel, the handwritten title on the mount proclaimed: "The Thin Blue Line."

15

As he mounted the steps to the library, Conrad's knee buckled under him. He swore, then gathered up the books that had spilled from beneath his arm.

"Good morning, Mrs. Emerson," he said, approaching the front desk.

She looked up from the typewriter, peering at him over the top of her spectacles. "Mr. Labarde. Returning, are we?"

"Yes."

"Overdue, are they?"

"How did you guess?"

She pulled the sheet of paper from the typewriter and handed it to him. He scanned it.

"I was going for a note of mild outrage," she said.

"Mild, huh?"

She smiled.

"I've a confession to make," said Conrad.

"Unless you want the whole town to know, I'm probably not the person to share it with."

Conrad handed her one of the books. "I think I just broke the spine."

"No," she said, examining it. "You *definitely* broke the spine."

"I'll replace it, of course."

"What, and deny Mrs. Cartwright the challenge? She's a whiz with the glue, you know."

Conrad settled the fine, then asked where the back copies of the *East Hampton Star* were stored. Because the dates he was after were more than six months old, he was sent through to the reading room, Mrs. Emerson appearing a few minutes later with two bound volumes on a trolley.

Conrad hefted them onto the table. He could see her itching to ask what he wanted them for, and he'd prepared an answer for her, but it wasn't required. She fought her curiosity, returning to the front desk.

Conrad took a seat and stared at the spines: April–June 1946, July–September 1946. He found the initial newspaper report without any difficulty. News of Lizzie Jencks's tragic death had, of course, made the front page of the *Star*. Two issues later, the story still warranted the front page, though it had been relegated to the bottom right-hand corner, rolling over into a handful of column inches on page three.

By now, Chief Milligan of the town police department was reluctantly conceding that the investigation had produced no concrete leads in the past couple of weeks, and possibly never would. The incident had occurred on a Saturday night, when the roads of the South Fork were notoriously infested with drivers who had flooded in for the weekend from up-island or New York City. Questions remained, however. The medical examiner had placed the time of death at somewhere between midnight and two o'clock in the morning, and no one seemed to know what a young girl was doing walking a country road at that hour of the night.

Come August, coverage of the story had all but petered out. The last mention Conrad could find of it was in an editorial that leveled its sights at the "people from away" crowding this quiet corner of Suffolk County. The piece had the hollow report of a blind, scatter-gun blast into the night, the intruder long gone.

Conrad worked his way back through the newspapers, sifting for signs. The first issue with news of the incident had come out on the Thursday, young Lizzie already five days dead. In the same edition, there was a brief report of a wedding that had taken place in Sag Harbor on the Saturday in question. The festivities, complete with impressive fireworks display, had rolled on into the early hours of Sunday morning. The names of the happy couple, not known to Conrad, suggested summer people, the kind of society event Lillian might have attended.

The geography was wrong, though. There was no way you could end up on Town Lane when driving from Sag Harbor to East Hampton, not unless you had completely lost your way. Still, it was the best he could come up with, and certainly better than nothing.

He almost left it at that. Thankfully, he cast a quick eye over the Thursday issue from the week predating the accident. Buried on page seven was a small announcement, no more than a few lines, announcing the first dinner-dance of the season at the Devon Yacht Club on Gardiner's Bay, set to take place that Saturday night.

The Devon Yacht Club, one of Lillian's favored haunts.

He experienced no surge of relief, no sense of elation. Rather, he felt a chill descend upon him, the stillness and clarity a hunter experiences when first sighting his quarry, his world narrowing to a point, the periphery blurring, all else forgotten.

He stared at the page for a good while, not focusing on the print, but deep in thought, weighing his various options. They shared one piece of common ground: whichever way he chose to proceed, it was time to start drawing Deputy Hollis into the hunt.

16

HOLLIS HAD SEEN CHIEF MILLIGAN ANGRY BEFORE, BUT NEVER LIKE THIS—
puce with rage, spittle flying.

He's just a big old blowhard, he said to himself. Mary Calder's description of Milligan had proved a source of comfort in recent days, somehow consigning the chief to the ranks of the ridiculous, emasculating him. Confronted with the volcanic presence before him, however, her words had lost their sting.

"Well?!" bellowed Milligan.

Hollis groped his way back to reality. An official complaint from the Maidstone Club. Unseemly conduct. Hollis throwing his weight around.

It wasn't looking good. Just one thread of hope. There was a chance the complaint hadn't come from Anthony Cordwell. No. Odds were the complaint had come from the club itself, probably without Cordwell's knowledge.

"Well?! What in the hell do you have to say for yourself?"

"It's a bit embarrassing, sir," he said, buying himself time to think.

"Embarrassing? Is that what you call it? I've got the president of the club on the phone accusing you of goddamn intimidation."

"I was acting in the club's best interests, sir."

He had it now, a story that should just about hold up.

"Stop mincing your words, man."

"It's like this, sir. The night of Lillian Wallace's funeral I was on duty here in town. There was an incident on Main Street involving two young ladies. One of them had her dress torn."

"What?"

"She was pretty upset."

"Just tell me what in the hell happened."

"I didn't witness it, but it seems they were approached by a group of young men who'd been at the Wallaces' place, you know, the funeral reception. They were a little . . . upset."

"You mean tight."

"As drums. Anyway, they invited the girls to a bar, and when they refused there was some kind of scuffle. That's when the dress got torn and the men ran off."

Milligan was going off the boil now. It was time to start boring him into submission with details.

"I went looking for them, saw four men in a car fitting the description, and tailed them. They ended up at the Maidstone Club. Maybe I should have, but I didn't do anything at the time. I talked the girls into not pressing charges if the dress was paid for. That's why I went back to the club the next day, looking for this Anthony Cordwell."

"Cordwell, huh?" Milligan clearly knew the name. "Still, it didn't give you the right to storm right on in there."

"Cordwell had been dodging me all morning. If I hadn't leaned on him he'd be up on a charge of assault right now, along with his friends. This way everyone's happy. Everyone except the Maidstone Club, it seems."

"You didn't tell them what you were after Cordwell for?"

"It didn't seem right, fair. Sure, they were drunk, they messed up, but they'd just seen their friend put in the ground."

It was good, good enough, especially the last bit—the note of sympathy for a bunch of grief-stricken drunks tearing at a girl's dress. That was the sort of thing Milligan could relate to.

"Why didn't you come to me with this?"

"It was Sunday, I didn't want to bother you."

He was safe now, but it wasn't over yet. Milligan would have the last word. He always did. Hollis could see him working up to it as he rounded his desk and settled into his chair.

"I don't like you, Hollis. Can't say I ever have. And it's not 'cos you're a weasely know-it-all little prick." He paused for effect. "It's 'cos I know what you are."

Hollis felt the blood drain from his cheeks.

Milligan smiled. "That's right. You think I'd have them dump you on me and not check you out? I know people, don't think I don't." He began playing with a letter opener, twisting the point into the palm of his hand. "Hell of a cover story you New York boys came up with," he said, laying the sarcasm on thick. "Damn near fell for it, I did."

Hollis was helpless. Anything he said would be shot down in flames. Milligan mistook his silence for fear.

"Don't worry, it stays in this room. Last thing I need is the good people of East Hampton knowing there's a crooked cop on the force."

"Yeah, one's enough for any town."

Thankfully, the words died before they reached Hollis's lips. It would have meant the end. He didn't care about the job, but he was damned if he was going to jeopardize the investigation, even if it did mean taking abuse from a hypocrite. It was well known that the fortunes of the Milligan household had experienced a marked upturn during Prohibition.

"Go on," said Milligan, "clear out."

Hollis stopped at the door and turned. "It's not true. What you heard about me."

"Now how did I know you were going to say that?" smirked Milligan.

As Hollis crossed the squad room, Bob Hartwell shot him a sheepish glance.

Hollis entered his office and pushed the door shut behind him. He shed his jacket, reached for the mug of cold tea on his desk, but thought better of it. He didn't want to sit, he didn't want to stand; he didn't know what he wanted to do.

The breeze through the open window rattled the blind against the frame. He wandered over, peering down through the slats at the street below. A few people came and went, entering and leaving the post office, which occupied the ground floor of the building. Across the way, a dog cocked its leg against the wheel of a parked car.

Cursed.

It would pursue him for the rest of his life.

The crooked cop.

It had tracked him down, sniffed him out, even out here. Why should it ever let up?

It was so ridiculous. If people only knew the truth.

But that wasn't the way things worked. Once tarred with the brush of scandal, there was little to be done to allay their suspicions—not even a full exoneration could do that—some small splinter of doubt always remained lodged in their brains. His parents had been no different, not that he blamed them; he had rubber-stamped his own guilt when he'd signed up to the lie: a detective second-grade looking for a quieter life on a country force.

Milligan was right. As a cover story, it stank. With the passage of time that much had become evident, like so many other things. It was clear to him now that he should have stood and fought, gone down fighting.

As the memories crowded in on him, he smiled at the absurdity of it all. Making a stand on the hoary issue of police corruption was one thing, but he could at least have chosen one of its grander battlefields on which to lay down his career. For Christ's sake, there were any number to choose from. But no, he in his wisdom had chosen to impale himself on the blunt dagger of black-market gas-ration stamps. It hadn't been easy, but he'd still managed it.

The scam was well established and widespread. Ration stamps filched wholesale from local price administration offices were sold on to garages and gas stations for a few paltry cents apiece. The profits were enormous, though, because of the huge scale of the operation. People were involved at all levels, Hollis knew that. Yet he'd still been shocked when a snitch dropped him the name of a precinct detective from the Seventeenth.

The snitch, a pickpocket who worked the Sunday museum crowds, was looking for a break. Well, he got one—a snapped neck in an alleyway at the edge of the Gashouse District.

When Hollis visited the dead man's girlfriend, she went at him with a knife, accusing him of murder. It was a while before he figured she was right. In mentioning the pickpocket's name to the captain back at the precinct he had effectively signed the man's death warrant.

He went to Gaskell with his suspicions, ignoring the lieutenant's advice to let the matter drop. A few days later, a batch of stolen ration stamps showed up in Hollis's locker. When word came through of a couple of lowlifes ready to testify to his involvement in the scam, Hollis knew he was lost.

Whether Gaskell was in on it from the start, he never found out. One thing was clear, though, the lieutenant had never forgiven him for going straight to Beloc at the Homicide Bureau with his theory on the Chadwick case. He wasn't a team player, said Gaskell, never had been, never would be. The offer of a role on a provincial force— ostensibly to avoid an unseemly scandal—was their way of shutting him up and clearing him out. Turning it down hadn't even been an option at the time.

Hollis forced his thoughts back to the Wallace investigation, but even that denied him any consolation. Wherever he turned he was confronted with his own eagerness to believe in some sinister plot. What did he really have to go on? The earrings, the raised toilet seat, the nervousness of the maid, the visit paid to Lillian Wallace by her ex-fiancé a month before her death—each and every one of which he had chosen to interpret in its darkest possible light.

He was driven into the chair behind the desk by the weight of the realization: any investigation that existed was entirely of his own invention. He had brought it into the world, breathed life into it through an act of sheer will. He had wanted it to exist, and it had duly obliged.

There was a light knock at the door.

"Yes."

It was Hartwell. "I swear to God," he said, "one day . . ."

He was angry, uncharacteristically so. Hollis stared at him, unable to match the outrage Hartwell felt on his behalf.

"This is for you. She called while you were with him."

Hollis took the piece of paper. Verity Brandon. The name meant nothing to him.

"She said she's with the medical examiner's office."

He remembered now—the nameplate on the front desk at the county morgue, her failure to offer him a glass of water. What did she want?

"Tom," said Hartwell, "is something up?"

"Up?"

"I don't know . . ."

"Nothing's up, Bob."

"Okay," he said, then left the room.

Hollis felt a little bad. It was probably nothing to worry about, but he could still recall Hartwell watching him from afar the day of the funeral, just after his conversation with Penrose.

He reached for the phone and asked the operator to put him through to the morgue in Hauppauge. She answered on the second ring.

"Suffolk County Medical Examiner's Office."

"Mrs. Brandon?"

"Miss."

"It's Deputy Chief Hollis, from East Hampton."

"Ah, yes. Wait a minute, please." He could hear her searching through some papers. "I have it here somewhere . . . a strange request . . . I mean, we get them sometimes, but they're rare. I just thought you should know."

"What kind of request?"

"Dash it," she said.

"Miss Brandon . . ."

"Someone has asked to see the autopsy report on that poor girl who drowned. A member of the public. It's their right, you know, we can't stop them."

"Yes, I know."

"I told him he has to wait a month."

"Who?"

"I have his name here somewhere."

"Conrad Labarde," said Hollis quietly.

"Excuse me?"

"Conrad Labarde."

There was a silence on the other end of the phone. "Well, yes," she said, "I think that *was* his name."

"Best to be sure though."

"Of course. Like I say, I have it here somewhere."

17

GAYLE WALLACE HAD SWUM IN THE POOL, TAKEN A BATH, WASHED AND DRIED her hair, and all but finished her breakfast when Manfred stepped gingerly from the house onto the terrace.

"Christ it's bright."

"You look dreadful," said Gayle.

"Thanks."

"Worse than I've seen you in quite a while."

Manfred picked up her discarded sunglasses and put them on. "Better?" he asked.

"Much."

Manfred dropped into a chair and poured himself a cup of coffee from the jug.

"It's cold," said Gayle.

"It's coffee." He took a gulp, grimaced. "Justin stayed late."

"I know."

"We didn't keep you awake, did we?"

"I don't mind. You play well when you're drunk . . . even if it is Dinah Shore."

"There's nothing wrong with 'Shoofly Pie and Apple Pan Dowdy.'"

"Not if you have your head buried under a pillow."

Rosa appeared with some fresh toast and some hot coffee.

"Thanks, Rosa," said Manfred, "you're a lifesaver."

Rosa smiled, then left.

"So what did you end up deciding?" asked Gayle.

"What do you think?"

"It's going ahead."

"Father grew pretty adamant after you went to bed."

"I'm not against it, Manfred. It's just that it seems a little . . ." She couldn't find the right word.

"I know."

"I understand how important it is to you. I do."

"It's hardly going to be a riotous affair. It never was. Far from it."

Over dinner the previous evening, the conversation had turned to a sensitive subject, one they'd all been dodging for the past couple of weeks: that of the house party arranged months before and set to take place the following weekend.

It had never been in question that Manfred would one day make a move into politics—that decision was taken on his behalf while he was still wet from the womb—but no one had anticipated the ease with which he would navigate the course charted for him from birth. At prep school he had excelled himself, surpassing even their father's expectations. He was captain of the varsity soccer and baseball squads, secretary of the student council, chairman of the student deacons and editor of the school newspaper, the *Phillipian*. These accomplishments heaped up with little or no apparent effort on Manfred's part, and their father used to say that in this lay Manfred's greatest achievement. For people mistrusted overt ambition, it threatened them, obliged them to take a stand for or against you.

There was only one thing more important than winning, and that was appearing not to care about winning. It was a credo that had been instilled in them from an early age, an article of faith vigorously contested by Lillian, silently accepted by Gayle, but dutifully observed by Manfred. And it had served him well, both at Andover and Yale.

It wasn't until he went to university that Gayle actually witnessed Manfred in action. She was present in the mahogany-paneled hall when he got to his feet as captain of the Yale debate team to deliver his summation speech in defense of the resolution: An oppressive government is more desirable than no government.

He opened by stating that he was a little mystified by his rival speaker's arguments in favor of no government, as he had it on good authority that the fellow was actively seeking a position in government on his graduation. Delivered with a sly smile, his tone devoid of any malice, this won him a large laugh and proved to be the final nail in the other man's coffin. Manfred had already argued a difficult position with a compelling mix of conviction and crowd-pleasing humor.

When he finally stepped away from the lectern, it was Lillian, chauffeured in from Vassar for the night, who was first to her feet, applauding loudly. Shrugging off their mother's efforts to silence her, she triggered a standing ovation. The motion was duly carried by a large majority.

In the heady aftermath of his victory, it became clear that Manfred had delivered no more or less than had been expected of him. Yes, his peers mobbed him and showered him with compliments, but only as teammates might congratulate a star batter who can always be relied upon to pull a winning homerun out of the bag. There was no mistaking the fact that he was already a figure of some considerable standing among his Conservative Party cronies, admired and respected by the sons of some of the country's most influential men, a few of whom also happened to be present that evening.

Gayle could still recall her father's largesse with the Champagne in the bar of the Taft Hotel afterwards, the expression on his face as he surveyed the proceedings. It was a look not so much of paternal pride as of deep satisfaction. He had invested everything in Manfred, and Manfred had more than repaid the confidence placed in him.

Bathed in his reflected glory, Gayle and Lillian had found themselves surrounded by a pack of attentive young men, until ushered to the relative safety of a corner booth by Justin Penrose, Manfred's closest friend. At midnight, when their parents finally pried them away from the rowdy gathering, Gayle was left in little doubt that Justin wished to see her again. And her father let it be known that he thoroughly approved.

America's entry into the war two years later, though a little inconvenient, was barely a setback to their father's plans. It also meant that Manfred could enter the political arena with the added kudos of a sound military record.

The scene was now set. Gayle wasn't sure of the exact details, though she knew there was talk of skipping over the State Assembly and making a play straight for membership of the New York State Senate. With elections coming up, it was time for some serious decisions to be made. Hence the weekend house party—an opportunity for some of those backing Manfred's political career to put their heads together and determine the exact course of his candidature.

In truth, Gayle had known for several days now that the gathering would go ahead regardless of Lillian's death. It would have been postponed well before if it was ever going to be. No, the discussion over dinner the previous evening had been a mere formality, the decision a foregone conclusion.

The most gratifying aspect of the evening had been Justin's attitude towards her. Had she imagined the flutter of his fingertips against her waist as he stooped to kiss her cheek on his arrival? Had the kiss itself been less perfunctory than usual? Possibly. In the privacy of her bedroom, she had dismissed any lingering doubts. She knew the signals; she had, after all, been on the receiving end of them before. This was the reason she had been unable to sleep, the events of the evening tugging at her thoughts, even before Manfred and Justin started banging out numbers on the piano.

"Father thinks we should take Senator Dale fishing," said Manfred.

"Fishing?"

"Game fishing, for tuna. Next weekend. You know, charter a boat in Montauk, make a day of it."

"Business and pleasure," said Gayle indifferently.

"You think it's a bad idea?"

"I really wouldn't know."

"Anyway, Richard's going to look into it." He heaped some strawberry jam onto a slice of toast. "Where's Father?"

"Playing golf."

"Who with?"

"Don't worry, I don't think you're missing out on anything." The words came out wrong, the tone more aggressive than she had intended, but Manfred didn't appear to notice. "He said he'd meet you at the club for lunch," she added.

"You're not coming?"

"I'm going to see the fishermen, the ones who found Lilly."

"That's right, I'd forgotten. Do you want me to go with you?"

"It's okay." She paused. "I want to take them something, but I can't think what."

"Champagne. Raid the cellar."

"Champagne seems a little . . . celebratory."

"We served it after the funeral."

"That's true."

They sat in silence for a moment, then Manfred reached out, took her hand and squeezed it.

"Gayle, you haven't really talked about what happened. About Lilly." Gayle didn't reply. "Maybe it's not my place to say, but you might feel better if you did."

"You're right," she said, removing her hand from his. "It's not your place to say."

SHE SPOTTED THE TURNING ON HER THIRD PASS, just as she was about to give up and go home. A sandy track, barely wide enough for a vehicle, snaked off through the pines on the south side of Montauk Highway.

There was no sign on the shoulder, nothing to indicate that some-one lived at the end of the narrow trail. She was beginning to doubt that they did when, after a hundred yards or so, the trees petered out, giving way to an expansive view, the top of a barn showing in the dis-tance above the crests of the rolling dunes.

She teased the car forward, steering to avoid the ruts. This proved to be her undoing. The front wheels of the roadster sank into the soft sand beside the track, losing all purchase. The more she gunned the engine, the faster the wheels span and the deeper the car settled.

"Damn."

She grabbed her handbag and the two bottles of Champagne, and set off on foot. Almost immediately she kicked off her shoes and tucked them under her arm.

She was sweating now, irritable, and it occurred to her that she must look like some slattern searching for a party.

THE FISHERMAN DIDN'T SEE or hear her approach. He was bent over the front of a battered truck, head in the engine, revving the motor loudly. He was wearing only a pair of tatty cotton trousers, and she could see the muscles in his shoulders bunching beneath the skin as he worked.

She didn't call out; her shadow alerted him to her presence, star-tling him.

"I'm sorry, I didn't mean to surprise you. I'm looking for Conrad Labarde."

He reached into the engine and killed the idling motor.

"You just found him."

"I'm Lillian Wallace's sister."

"Yes . . ."

He must have spotted the resemblance. There was oil on his hands, and what she first took to be oil smeared around his right eye and along the side of his chest. She quickly realized that what she was staring at was bruising.

"Some gear fell on me," he said, reading her look.

"These are for you, you and your friend, by way of thank you."

He took the bottles of Champagne from her.

"You look hot," he said. "Are you thirsty?"

"A little."

"Come with me." He wandered off, leaving her little choice but to follow.

The house wasn't at all what she'd been expecting. What *had* she been expecting? There were pictures and books and fine old pieces of furniture, albeit of a rustic nature. He obviously felt no inclination to make idle chat, and she browsed around while he washed his hands at the sink.

"Here," he said, handing her a glass of water.

She had every intention of leaving as soon as she'd quenched her thirst, but when he indicated a chair at the end of the table she found herself sitting. He took a seat near her.

"I'm sorry about your sister."

"It could have been worse."

"Worse than death?"

"If you hadn't caught her in your net she might never have been found." She paused. "Does that sound silly?"

"No. We all look for small consolations at times like this."

We. He was sending her a message that he, too, knew about loss, that he knew what she was going through. But he didn't. Even if he thought he did, he didn't. And she resented the complicity he was forcing upon her.

As if sensing this, he changed the subject. He asked about Lillian, remarking that since she had been buried in East Hampton she must have loved the place. Gayle found herself warming to the conversation, eager to talk. There was nothing pushy about his questions; he drew responses from her effortlessly. At a certain moment it occurred to her that she was satisfying a need in him, that his desire to understand the person he had only ever known as a corpse was a necessary part of putting the experience behind him. Against his wishes he had been written into the last chapter of Lillian's life, and he had a desire to know the details of the story preceding his involvement.

There was something calming about his presence. He was considered in his comments, articulate when he made them, and his attentive gray eyes never left hers, not even for a moment.

She felt a momentary twinge of disappointment when he suggested that she must have things to do. He got to his feet.

"I'll get a tow rope," he said.

"How did you know?"

He smiled. "Happens all the time."

As she followed him from the house, he turned to her. "I want to show you something first."

He struck out across the dunes towards the ocean. She followed, intrigued, the hot sand scorching the soles of her feet, obliging her to tread lightly and quickly behind him.

Along the beach a scattering of people were huddled beneath their sun shades, sheltered from the midday sun. A dog scampered to and fro at the water's edge, barking at the gulls.

Gayle hurried to the wash and cooled her feet in the spent waves.

"That's where we found her," he said, pointing down the beach. "About a hundred yards along."

Gayle stared at the spot, aware that he was watching her intently.

"I'm not sure I wanted to know that," she said.

"Why not?"

"I don't know."

"Did you see her?" he asked. "At the morgue?"

His tone had changed. In fact, his whole appearance had changed. He suddenly seemed very big. And very threatening.

"I wanted to, but when it came to it, I couldn't."

He glanced back down the beach. "Maybe with time you'll be glad you knew," he said, more gently.

She doubted it, but said nothing.

THE ROPE WAS IN THE BARN, coiled and hanging from a wooden peg.

"You use all this . . . stuff?" she asked, awed by the amount of equipment on display.

"Pretty much."

"What's this for?"

"It's a scallop dredge."

"And that?"

"Eel trap."

As he led her to the truck, he asked, "You eat fish?"

"Yes."

"If you want, I'll drop some by. Maybe a bluefish or two."

"That's very kind, but you really don't have to."

"I'd like to."

He hauled open the passenger door, removed a sleeping cat from the seat, and helped her climb up.

HE ONLY UNTIED THE TOW ROPE once he'd seen her safely back to Montauk Highway.

"Thanks for the Champagne," he said, then added with a smile, "I'll try to remember Rollo gets his bottle."

She found herself not wanting to leave, and watched as he swung the truck around on the highway, negotiating his way past her and back down the track.

A thought suddenly occurred to her and she punched the horn several times. He pulled to a halt, leaning out of the window.

"How much do you know about game fishing?" she called.

"Game fishing?"

"For tuna."

18

"You're kidding me," said Abel.

"No."

"Mary Calder's invited you to a party?!"

"Don't sound so surprised," said Lucy, coming to Hollis's defense.

"Yeah," said Hollis.

"Come on, Tom, you've got looks, brains, a sense of humor, but not a whole lot of any of them."

"Abel Cole!" snapped Lucy, kicking him under the table.

"Jesus, Lou."

"He's just jealous," said Lucy, turning to Hollis. "She's one of the few women in town who never succumbed to his dubious charms. And, believe me, he tried."

"Is that what she told you?"

"I *remember* you trying."

"I meant the bit about not succumbing."

Hollis laughed. Abel was indomitable in these situations.

"Don't," said Lucy, "you'll only encourage him."

At that moment the waiter appeared at their table with the bottle of wine. He cast a surly eye over their unopened menus and left.

"It's okay, we'll pour," said Abel, just loud enough for the departing youth to hear.

Hollis filled their glasses and insisted that they order whatever they wanted from the menu—it was his treat. There was nothing magnanimous in this gesture. He was painfully aware that he'd been living off their hospitality since Lydia had left him. A meal out was the least he could offer them.

His stated intention of getting them around to his house had somehow amounted to nothing, maybe because he had lost the desire to prove to himself that life went on. It didn't. He knew that now. It stalled, shuddering towards inertia.

He was shocked by the speed with which the house had descended into a state of dereliction. Dust heaped up in corners he could swear he'd just swept. Clutter multiplied, begetting yet more clutter with no apparent involvement on his part. Without Lydia to spur him into action, hinges creaked, windowsills leaked, taps dripped, and bulbs went unchanged.

At first Hollis had battled bravely against this creeping decay, but at a certain point he had conceded defeat, contenting himself with an uneasy coexistence, singling out a room and concentrating all his efforts there, allowing the dust and detritus free run of the other areas of the house. The kitchen had been his first place of refuge, then the living room, but he'd recently retreated to the bedroom. He had plans to break out soon and reclaim the kitchen. But right now, Number 4 Indian Hill Road was not a fit place to entertain one's friends—in fact, it was hardly a fit place for anything—hence the dinner at the 1770 House.

Hollis and Abel opted for the steak; Lucy ordered the bluefish before announcing that she was going to "powder her nose." Abel suggested she take a leak while she was at it.

"You want to tell me what's up?" asked Hollis as soon as she had left.

Abel lit another cigarette and eyed him suspiciously, almost aggressively. "Who said anything was up?"

"You seem a little edgy is all."

"Yeah?"

Hollis didn't mind being shut out. He knew Abel well enough to accept that he'd tell him in his own time. This turned out to be about twenty seconds (and three large gulps of red wine) later.

"She mentioned the M-word."

"Ah," said Hollis.

"A couple of nights back. Just dropped it in there. Caught me on the hop. Guess I'm still hopping."

"Marriage, huh?"

Abel winced at the word. "Don't do that."

"You brought it up."

"*She* brought it up. I'm just . . . relaying it to you. Forget I ever mentioned it, okay?"

"Okay," said Hollis. He waited, relishing his friend's discomfort, trying not to smile. Abel snuck a look at the rest room door.

"So what do you think?" he mumbled.

"About what?" asked Hollis innocently.

"You know . . . the M-thing?"

"What do I think? I think she's crazy."

"Come on, Tom, seriously."

"Abel," he said despairingly. "She's smart, talented, funny, and very, very beautiful."

"I know, I know."

"She's too good to be true. And she's chosen you."

"That's the point."

"What?"

"Don't you see?"

"No."

"I wanted . . ." He hesitated. "I don't know . . . to amount to something first. Then think about it. Maybe. Or not. I don't know."

"Abel, you're a great photographer."

"Bullshit. And I'm not fishing for compliments."

"Let me lay some on you anyway."

Abel wagged a hand, cutting him dead. Hollis didn't persist. It wasn't as if they hadn't had the conversation before. Abel judged himself far too harshly. How many other photographers would have been mortified at getting their work on the front cover of *Life* magazine? How many would actually have given thanks for the fact that the photo wasn't credited directly to them but to the U.S. Army Signal Corps? Most would have had that front cover framed and hanging on the wall of their shop for all to see, not moldering among a pile of other magazines on a shelf back at their house.

It was Lucy who first drew Hollis's attention to the magazine cover. Lydia was also present at the time. Abel wasn't. He was in the kitchen, preparing dinner—their first dinner together, two couples tentatively getting to know each other. Taken in a small town in Germany, the photo showed a GI leaning against a half-track, muffled up against the cold, and smiling. Abel's reaction when he wandered through and found the three of them bent over the copy of *Life* almost soured the evening. He dismissed their compliments, cutting Lydia quite dead, something for which she never really forgave him.

Abel explained that the officer in the photo had bugged him to fire off a couple of shots, and he'd only done so to shut the guy up. The reel of film was then tossed into the photographic pool, and that was the last he expected to hear of it. Next thing he knew, there was the smiling GI on the front of *Life,* some idiot at the War Department having decided that his grin struck just the right note of cheeky triumphalism for the folks back home. Abel rated the photo as one of the blandest he had taken during the long push eastwards from the beaches of Normandy—devoid of any technical or artistic merit—but what annoyed him most was its dishonesty.

The man whom he'd immortalized for the homefront readership had played no part in the fighting they'd just come through, the hell that was the Battle of Hürtgen Forest. He was from a relief unit sent in at the end, 33,000 men having already died or been incapacitated in a few brief months, swallowed up in five hundred acres of densely wooded real estate of little or no tactical value.

Some weeks after that first dinner, Abel dug out and showed Hollis a folder of shots he had taken in Hürtgen Forest—photos he'd held back for himself rather than consign them to the near-certain oblivion of the photographic pool.

The forest itself was the stuff of fairy tales, those of the more nightmarish kind—a dark, dense underworld, the dwelling place of witches and wolves. Towering pine trees, tight-packed so that their branches interlaced, formed a gloomy canopy through which stray shafts of sunlight barely penetrated to the forest floor. What the photos didn't show were the German antipersonnel mines lurking beneath the spongy carpet of pine needles, or the trip wires rigged to the assault course of fallen wood that anyone passing through the forest was obliged to negotiate. The greatest danger, Abel explained, came from above, from the deadly hail of wood unleashed by artillery tree-bursts. In one of the shots a soldier was literally hugging a tree, while all around him death whirled like a blizzard. It was an image that brought to mind a terrified child clutching at his mother's thigh.

Most of the photos, though, were of GIs at rest, stuffed into slit trenches and foxholes, tending to their feet or their weapons, seeking comfort in the little routines of life. One GI was even plucking at his nose hairs, using the inside of a tobacco tin as a mirror.

By the time Hollis had worked his way through to the end of the batch, the forest was all but gone, the noble pines reduced to matchwood, their shattered trunks poking through the surrounding debris. Light flooded the photos, the roll of the land was revealed. The final shot was of three tall pines outlined on a bald crest, beheaded and stripped of all but their lower branches. There was no mistaking the parallel with the three crosses of Calvary.

Abel had been right. The photo selected for the front cover of *Life* magazine was inert and empty when set alongside those other images. But he was wrong if he thought he had yet to prove himself as a photographer.

"It's a poor excuse," said Hollis.

"What's that?"

"Your work. For not getting married."

"Right now it's the best I can come up with."

"What if she leaves you?"

"That's her choice."

"I hope she does."

"You fancy a shot at her yourself?"

"Then you'll know what a damn fool you've been."

"You're not her type, Tom."

"Will you just listen to me for a moment."

Abel spread his hands: fire away.

"Too late," said Hollis. "She's coming."

Abel stubbed out his cigarette.

"Thank Christ for that," he said.

HOLLIS GROPED FOR THE ALARM and shut it off. Three aspirin and a cup of reheated coffee later, the little man jackhammering at the base of his skull downed tools.

Abel was to blame. If he hadn't taken Hollis to task over the amount he was drinking, then he wouldn't have got angry, and he wouldn't have reached for the bottle of brandy when he got home. He guessed there was a hollow logic to this thinking, so he tried not to dwell on it too much.

He tracked down the binoculars eventually, though how they'd found their way to the back of the airing cupboard he couldn't rightly say.

HE HAD BEEN UP at this hour many times before, the duty rota demanded it, but he'd never found himself down on the ocean beach just after sunup.

The fishermen, he knew, rose early. One time he had attended the scene of a bar brawl on Montauk. By the time the matter had been resolved, the participants in the fracas agreeing to split the costs of the damage, there were already dim little figures creeping from their shacks around Fort Pond Bay, rowing out to where their boats were moored, lanterns like fireflies in the fading night.

From the top of the frontal dune at the Atlantic Avenue beach landing, Hollis could make out two crews of fishermen working the shoreline to the east. The Basque's Model A was not among the vehicles gathered on the beach.

It lay to the west, a mile or so away.

Hollis lowered the binoculars. Better to drive around to Indian Wells landing and walk from there.

THEY WERE EMPTYING their net, dragging fish up the beach by the gills, big fish, their tails trailing in the sand. If the Basque was surprised to see him, he didn't show it.

"Morning," he said, tossing two fish into the back of the truck. Hollis waited and watched while they went about their business. When the net was empty, the Basque turned to the Kemp boy.

"Rollo, you want to go get that other seine from the barn?"

"Sure."

Hollis took this as a sign that the Basque wished to be alone with him, but as the truck pulled away along the beach he wandered down to the water's edge. Hollis followed. He hadn't noticed before, but there was a shark wrapped in the sodden net.

The Basque picked up a baseball bat lying nearby and rinsed the bloodied end in the wash. "Thresher," he said. "Chewed up the seine some bad. Mostly they go right through. This one got snagged."

"They come in so close?"

"How many people would go swimming if they knew, right?"

The Basque seized a hold of one end of the net.

"You mind?" he asked.

This was not how Hollis had imagined the encounter going: helping the Basque to drag a dead shark up the beach.

When they were done, the Basque set about rolling a cigarette.

"You asked to see the autopsy on Lillian Wallace."

The Basque didn't react, didn't even look at him.

"Why?" asked Hollis.

"Curiosity."

"Curiosity?"

"That's right."

"You're going to have to do better than that."

Now the Basque looked up. " 'Cos you're a cop?" For a brief instant Hollis was scared by what he saw behind the gray eyes, or rather the lack of it, of anything, the emptiness. "I don't owe you nothing," said the Basque. "It's best you understand that now."

"Now" was the word that leapt out. It suggested that this was the start of something. But what exactly?

"I've seen the autopsy report," said Hollis. "She died from drowning."

"I'm not saying she didn't."

"So what's your interest in it?"

"Could be they missed something."

"What if I told you they didn't?"

"I'd say, 'What are you doing here?'"

Hollis pulled his cigarettes from his pocket and lit one. The aspirins were wearing off; the little man was back at the rock face, hammering away.

"Follow me," said the Basque.

The boat sat at the water's edge a little way along the beach. The Basque seized the bow and swung it around in the sand.

"Best take those fine leather shoes off," he said.

"What?"

"And the jacket."

"I'm not going out there."

The Basque ignored him, tugging the boat into the wash.

"I can't swim," said Hollis.

"You'd be surprised how many fishermen can't."

"That's supposed to make me feel better?"

The Basque smiled. "Nothing's going to happen, not with the surf all flattened off."

It was true—the waves weren't at their most menacing—though "flattened off" was hardly the phrase Hollis would have used.

The Basque was waist-high in the water now, waiting.

Hollis heaved a sigh, shrugged off his jacket, kicked off his shoes and waded in.

"Hold the stern steady. When I give the word, shove off and climb in." The Basque clambered into the boat and began to row gently, glancing over his shoulder at the ocean.

A wall of white water slapped into Hollis, almost wrenching him free of the boat.

"Now," said the Basque, pulling hard on the oars.

Hollis pushed off, hooking both elbows over the side. And that's where he stayed. Each time he tried to swing his leg up over the side a wave would drive it back under. His strength fading, it was all he could do to hold on in the face of the relentless onslaught.

When they were clear of the breakers, he found he was too exhausted to haul himself aboard. The Basque abandoned the oars, seized the back of his pants and plucked him out of the water. He lay limp and drained in the bottom of the boat, his heart racing, as much from fear as exertion.

"Not bad," said the Basque. "For your first time."

"You mean my last time."

The Basque smiled, rowing them out to sea.

It was unexpectedly quiet, just the slap of the oars, the dull thump of the breaking waves receding with each stroke. It struck Hollis that he'd never seen the land from the ocean before. He'd taken a ferry once from Sag Harbor over to Shelter Island with Lydia—a Sunday jaunt when they were still poking at the carcass of their relationship—but that had been more familiar, more welcoming, with its bays and inlets and islands and little sailboats. Here on the ocean side you were left with an altogether different feeling. It was as if God in a fit of pique had used a ruler to divide two of His elements—a clean, stark battle line stretching from one horizon to the other, the conflict to roll on for all eternity. It wasn't something that could be fully appreciated when viewed from the land.

"First time off the back side?"

Hollis turned. "The back side?"

"That's what we call it out here," said the Basque, releasing the oars.

"What are we doing here?"

The Basque pulled a tin pail from beneath his feet and tied a length of rope to the handle.

"Fishing," he said.

He tossed the pail over the side. It slowly filled with water and sank from view. The Basque reeled it in and handed it to Hollis.

"What do you see?"

"Water?"

"Look again."

Hollis peered into the pail. "Sand," he said quietly. Sprinklings of silver in suspension.

He looked up at the Basque. "What are you saying?"

"You tell me. They won't release the autopsy yet."

DOCTOR CORNELIUS HOBBS WAS OUT on a call, and wasn't due back at the county morgue till two o'clock.

He appeared at one-thirty, which was why he found Hollis in his office, going over the autopsy report on Lillian Wallace.

"Well, well, well," he said, with as much indignation as he could summon up.

"Sit down," said Hollis.

"You're in my chair."

"Sit down," repeated Hollis firmly, indicating the seat across the desk from him. Hobbs hesitated, to press home his point, then did as he was told.

"There better be a damn good reason for this."

"Let's find out, shall we?" said Hollis. "Correct me if I'm wrong, but it's common in cases of drowning to find foreign material in the airways and lungs, material that's in the water."

He knew this to be the case. Before driving out to Hauppauge he had phoned Paul Kenilworth, an old friend from police pathology back in New York.

"That depends," said Hobbs guardedly. "What kind of material are you talking about?"

"Sand, for example. Sand thrown up by heavy surf."

Hobbs smiled, the smile of an adult indulging a child. "Oh dear,

Deputy Hollis, I can see where you're going with this." He leaned forward. "As it happens, I did find traces of sand in her airways. I might not have recorded them, though."

"I can tell you, you didn't."

"Believe me, they were there."

The news was a blow, and if Hollis hadn't discussed the matter at some length with Paul, it might well have ended right there, as Hobbs evidently thought it was about to, judging from his self-satisfied grin.

"Where exactly was this sand?"

"Her pharynx and trachea."

"The larger airways, then."

"Yes," said Hobbs, a distinct note of annoyance creeping into his voice.

"It's possible, isn't it, for debris to enter the larger airways after death has occurred, while the body's under water."

"It's possible."

"In fact, the sand you found in Lillian Wallace's airways proves nothing about the exact circumstances of her death, only that she was submerged in the ocean."

This was the moment Hobbs lost his temper. "Are you questioning my expertise? Read the report, man. She drowned. Everything points to it. Everything."

"I can see that."

"She drowned in the ocean."

"Now that we don't know for sure."

Hobbs grabbed the autopsy report, turned to a page near the back, and slapped it down in front of Hollis.

"The results of the salinity test on the water in her lungs."

"Yes, I know."

"So what more do you want?"

"Just one thing. Evidence of sand in the terminal bronchioles and alveoli. It would have been drawn deep into her lungs when she drowned."

It was pleasing to see Hobbs stopped in his tracks, silenced.

"You didn't check, did you?"

"The facts speak for themselves," stammered Hobbs, jabbing his finger at the report.

"Did you check? Yes or no?"

Hobbs couldn't bring himself to actually utter the word.

"It would have been there."

"Speculation."

"Deduction. Based on sound scientific evidence and twenty-two years of experience. There is no other explanation for her death."

"Try this on for size. She drowned in salt water and her body was placed in the ocean afterwards."

Hobbs weighed his words. "That's ridiculous."

"But it fits, right?"

"That's not the point. Where on earth is she going to drown in salt water, if not the ocean?"

From Hobbs's expression, it was clear that the answer occurred to him as soon as the words had left his lips.

BOTH CARS WERE GONE within a minute or so of Hollis's pulling up, his decision to turn on the flashing blue light no doubt precipitating their departure. He stepped from the patrol car as the taillights disappeared into the night. He could picture the occupants of the vehicles, panic giving way to relief, still adjusting their clothing.

He was alone in the silence, just the lazy pulse of the waves breaking against the shore. He glanced up at the night sky—an even dusting of cloud, enough to mute the glow of the moon; no need for a flashlight, though.

The most direct approach to the house from the beach landing was along the base of the bluff, but he opted for the long route around, down onto the beach, along the shore then back across the dunes. He needed time to marshal his thoughts.

As he walked, he tried to persuade himself that the investigation would remain intact even if this trail turned cold on him. But he knew he was only preparing himself for the worst. He soon found himself at the spot where he had discovered Lillian Wallace's bathrobe and towel neatly folded on the frontal dune some two weeks before. If she hadn't placed them there, then someone else had—someone with a detailed knowledge of her routines and habits, someone close to her, someone who wanted her dead.

He was getting ahead of himself now. Even if she had drowned in the family swimming pool, it wasn't necessarily evidence of foul play. This was the line he had fed Hobbs, anyway. In fact, he'd openly dismissed the idea of murder to Hobbs, suggesting that the body had been moved for more innocent reasons. There were, after all, no indications of physical violence on Lillian Wallace's corpse. Hobbs's silence had been bought with the inducement that if anything came of Hollis's investigation he would credit the medical examiner with first drawing his attention to the anomaly in the autopsy.

The tactic seemed to have worked. If Hobbs was going to spill the beans to Milligan, he would have done so by now.

He paused to catch his breath at the top of the bluff. The sound of a vehicle broke the silence. From his vantage point he could see headlights sweep the lot of the beach landing, passing over the patrol car, then accelerating away up Two Mile Hollow to Further Lane.

The sooner he was gone, the better.

Entering the garden through the gate in the rusted iron fence, he crept through the shadows and found himself poolside.

The pump suddenly kicked in, causing his own to skip a couple of beats. Dropping to one knee, he scooped up some water and raised the cupped hand to his mouth.

There was no mistaking the taste, the briny tang.

As he hurried away, there was no feeling of exhilaration, but a curious sense of inevitability. He hadn't landed here by chance. Like a blind man guided across a road, he had been led by the elbow.

19

THE BEACH NEAR FRESH POND WAS DESERTED. CONRAD HAULED THE sharpie to the water's edge and lashed the sail-bag to the foredeck. Drawing the stumpy little craft out into deeper water, he clambered awkwardly aboard and began to paddle.

The tide was on the ebb, the wind stiffening from the southwest as it always did at this time on summer afternoons, catspawing across Gardiner's Bay, its invisible hand slapping the surface at intervals.

Today it carried with it the playful shouts of children leaping from the end of the long jetty at the Devon Yacht Club, hurling themselves off the wooden rail, skinny brown limbs scything the air before impact. He could just make out the dim tock tock of a tennis ball being struck on an unseen court behind the low clubhouse.

The Junior Yacht Club was out on the water, a flotilla of boxy little Knockabouts running dead before the wind. A motor launch was in attendance, an instructor barking orders through a loud hailer. As the dinghies came about, Conrad ranged alongside the catboat.

The *Demeter* had been his first purchase on his return from Europe—a twenty-five-foot Gil Smith from the turn of the century, a masterpiece of design, and a dream come true. The elegance of its sheer lines aside, the shallow, wide hull, almost eleven feet in beam, provided the perfect working platform for a bayman. It was the first boat Conrad had ever crewed on, working the culling board with Antton, plucking out scallops from the eelgrass and the crabs and the culch dredged from the seabed. Conrad had never concealed his interest in the craft, and when old Josaiah Fullard died in 1943, the *Demeter* had languished at her moorings in Accabonac Creek, awaiting Conrad's return from Europe. Even when the news arrived that he'd been killed in action, Josaiah's sons had held out a little longer, just in case.

Now the *Demeter* was his, more beautiful than ever—new running rig, new sail, new yellow-pine hull. He always felt good when seated at the helm, teasing the great barn door rudder, beating before the wind, the canvas snapping like a rifle shot each time he tacked. Even now she seemed to understand him, responding with ease, compensating for his distraction.

With any luck, the last few pieces of the puzzle were waiting for him in Montauk, he'd have them by the end of the day.

Before he knew it, the buoy at the mouth of Napeague Harbor was bearing down on them. He thought about entering the channel and making for Lazy Point, but decided against it. He didn't want to see Sam right now. It would only mean turning down his offer of assistance for a second time. Once had been hard enough. He was already regretting having shared the truth with him. The last thing he wanted was for Sam to get caught up in an affair that could only end badly.

He leaned on the tiller and came about on the port tack. That's when he saw it, lying in the bilges—Lillian's jadeite hair clip, a gift from her brother. She had mentioned to him that she'd misplaced it, and they had searched his bedroom, and they had searched her bedroom, and then he had remembered that she'd been wearing it the last time they took the *Demeter* out, and they had laughed, remembering that night, then all the other nights they'd taken the *Demeter* out, right back to that very first night.

She had phoned as he was halfway to the truck, and although they hadn't seen each other for a week, not since the evening of her birth-day, he sensed it was her and he hurried back to the house.

"Hello."

"It's me," she said.

"Hi."

"Hi."

"How was your surprise party?"

"Oh, you know . . ." said Lillian. "What are you up to?"

"I was about to go firelighting for fluke."

"Firelighting for fluke?"

He explained.

"Sounds to me like you could do with some help," she said.

He picked her up at her house and they drove to Promised Land. It was a warm night, with the lightest of breezes, perfect for the task in hand. Safely aboard, the gear loaded, he edged the *Demeter* away from the dock and out into Gardiner's Bay, the five hundred square feet of canvas sucking up what little wind there was. Nearing Cartwright Shoals, he rigged the lantern from the stern of the boat and lit it.

"Wow," said Lillian, peering over the side.

Beneath the glassy surface, the seabed was laid bare.

"Those are wild oysters," said Conrad, pointing. "They're pretty much gone now."

"Why?"

"Who knows? That's a horseshoe crab."

"Where?"

"There. And that's a fluke, over there by the eelgrass, the flat fish."

"With the spots?"

"With the spots."

Taking up the spear, he slid the barbed head beneath the water and stuck the fluke. He tossed it to the far end of the cockpit, where it flapped wildly in the bilges.

"A third of that's yours," said Conrad.

"Only a third?"

"The boat gets a share."

"If I'd known, I wouldn't have come."

"Okay, I'll go fifty-fifty, but you'll have to earn it," he said, handing over the spear.

They talked while they fished, drifting across the shoals. Conrad explained that he'd learned the technique from Billy, who had learned it from Sam, who in turn had learned it from his father—a family tradition reaching back to well before the arrival of the first white faces on the South Fork.

"Billy's an Indian?"

"He's dead. But yes, a Montaukett."

"I didn't know . . . I mean . . ."

"There aren't many of them left," said Conrad.

He told her how, within living memory, the Montauketts had been lured off their tribal lands with promises of payments which had never materialized; how they had been chased away at gunpoint, shot at, killed in some cases, by the same men who had assured them they could return to fish and hunt on Montauk whenever they wished; and how the Suffolk County court had then dismissed their suit against these blatant injustices on the grounds that the tribe had ceased to exist, that it was now extinct.

He told her how Sam had been present in the courtroom when Judge Abel Blackmar handed down his ludicrous verdict, declaring that he saw "no Indians there," apparently blind to the fifty or so Montauketts cramming the public gallery that day, clad in full tribal regalia.

He described how he had stood with Sam and Billy on Signal Hill in Montauk one blustery summer's day in 1926. The community was in the firm grip of construction fever, with hundreds of workers bulldozing, blasting, and building away, racing to bring to life Carl Fisher's dream of turning Montauk into "the Miami Beach of the North." The centerpiece of his vision was Montauk Manor, an enormous mock-Tudor hotel perched high on the hill above Fort Pond. The location offered unrivaled views to the west, and it was no coincidence that the site was already occupied by an ancient Indian burial ground. The Montauketts always buried their dead on high ground, in a seated position, facing west—the direction of their journey into the afterlife.

Fisher had given his word that the burial ground wouldn't be disturbed by the construction work. But that brisk summer's day, with the clouds whipping by overhead and the rush of the wind drowning out the sound of the earthmovers, it became clear that Sam's advice, and that of the other Montauketts who knew the precise compass of the sacred site, had been ignored.

There were scraps of rough-woven cloth, dank and dirty, in the mounds of earth. And there were bones.

"That's terrible," said Lillian.

Conrad shrugged. "Maybe not." He explained how two months later, a hurricane had ripped through Miami Beach, devastating Carl Fisher's greatest creation; how later that year the headquarters of Fisher's Montauk Beach Development Company had burned to the ground, blueprints and all; and how the stock market crash in 1929 had then killed off Fisher's Montauk dream for good.

"He died poor and unhappy," said Conrad. "But Sam still said a prayer for his soul when he heard."

They were heading back to the dock now, the *Demeter* gliding across the surface.

"You think there's a connection?" asked Lillian.

"I don't know. I like to think so. If Fisher hadn't desecrated the ground, if he'd pulled it off, everything out here would have changed for the worse."

"Yes," said Lillian, smiling, "it's a pleasing irony."

Back at the dock, they unloaded the fluke into crates, then he ran her back to her house on Further Lane.

"When do I get my cut?" she asked as they pulled up.

"Couple of days, week at the most. I'll ship them down to Fulton tomorrow."

"You know," she said, "it'll be the first money I've ever earned." She glanced across at him. "I'm not proud of it."

"No, I can see."

"But I do think it calls for a celebration."

THEY TOOK THEIR DRINKS to the end of the garden and they sat on the bluff overlooking the ocean.

"This is my favorite spot in the world," she said.

They never finished the drinks.

A little while later, she placed her hand on his, the charge of her touch shorting out all other thoughts, smiling at him with a mixture of tenderness and certainty that left no room for doubt or maneuver. Not that he was considering either. He leaned across to meet her lips, and she drew him down onto the ground.

Later, when it was over and they were lying entwined in the grass, she pressed her face to his neck and inhaled.

"You have a very particular smell."

"It goes with the job."

"I like it," she said. "Eau de fish."

Conrad laughed.

Lillian's fingers sought out the long ridge of scar tissue in his side, tracing its smooth contours.

Maybe she felt him tense under her touch, or maybe she just knew him well enough already, but she didn't give voice to her curiosity.

THE MONTAUK FISHING FLEET was back in, and Fort Pond Bay was a
hive of activity. Sloops and draggers were making for the docks where
others were already packing out, unloading their catches, separating,
boxing and icing the fish, hammering the tags of their favored dealers
to the sides of the cedar crates.

Conrad ranged alongside Duryea's Dock and made fast. He
checked that the *Demeter* was good there till the morning, pushed his
way through the crowd, and set off along the great scythe of beach.

Waves lapped at the pebbly sand. Out on the water, two boys were
floundering away in a little craft cobbled together from fish boxes and
corrugated iron. The caulking at the seams had failed and they were
shipping water fast, bailing furiously with their hands. As the gunwales
dipped below the waves, they saluted, going down with their stricken
vessel. Their shrieks of laughter carried clear across the water as they
kicked for the shore.

Just back from the beach, some young kids were playing baseball on
the same sandy lot where Conrad had once swung a bat with their fathers. The crude baseball diamond hadn't changed, but Trail's End
restaurant and the post office, which had once sandwiched the lot,
were gone, moved away on skids at the outbreak of the war.

The navy had decided that the broad, clean sweep of Fort Pond
Bay offered the perfect location for a torpedo-testing range, and had
duly slapped a compulsory relocation order on every family in the
fishing village. Some had rolled their houses down to vacant lots on
Edgemere Road and Flamingo Avenue. Others had simply abandoned
them, taking the $300 compensation on offer and buying or building
anew.

The navy succeeded where the hurricane of '38 had failed, deliv-
ering a blow from which the fishing village looked unlikely ever to recover. What buildings remained trailed around the shore like a broken

line of walking wounded returning from battle, and only a handful of people had returned to the homes they'd been forced to leave.

Hendrik Morgan was one of them.

He was sitting out front of the two-room shack his father had first built, knitting a funnel for a lobster pot. More pots were stacked around him. Straggly shrubs demarcated the small patch of shingle that was the front garden, and a weather-beaten vine clung precariously to the side of the building. These few plaintive stabs at adornment were undermined by the rancid stench of bait fish setting in a barrel nearby.

"*Goddag.*"

Hendrik looked up and smiled. "*Hej.*"

"How's it going, Hendrik?"

"Good," he said, getting to his feet. "Good."

He took Conrad's hand warmly, clamping his other hand on top. He stood at least as tall, his lank blond hair flopping in front of his blue eyes.

"You got time for a cold one?" asked Hendrik.

"Sure."

Hendrik headed inside, returning a few moments later with another chair and a couple of bottles of beer. He popped the tops, and they settled down in the sunshine, looking out over the bay.

"How's the lobstering?" asked Conrad.

"Easier now I got me a new boat."

"Yeah?"

"The *Alice T,* a thirty-foot western rig out of Stonington. Got a fair few miles on her keel, and trims a little heavy by the stern when loaded, but she's a real beauty."

"How many pots you fishing?"

"Hundred and fifty, more on the way." He nodded at the oak laths and other lobster pot stock piled up nearby. "Two hundred and fifty should do it."

"And some."

"Yeah, first year back's been good to me."

"You deserve it."

Hendrik smiled. "Wish it worked like that, but we both know it don't."

Hendrik's family had been plagued by a run of mud-luck for well over a decade. The Depression had been tough on everyone, but it had coincided with a sharp drop-off in the lobsters, obliging Hendrik and his father to abandon their operation for other work, chopping wood for the WPA and filling ruts for the Highway Department—anything to scrape together a few precious dollars a day. This was how Conrad and Hendrik had first got to meet, odd-jobbing in East Hampton one winter, thrown together in the gardens of city people, spreading manure on the flower borders, the heat rising up through their boots. Left to their own devices, Hendrik would take every opportunity to snoop around the summer homes. He claimed he never touched anything, though how he came across the selection of riding crops tucked beneath the bed of a well-known movie actress remained to be answered; and there was always a faint but distinct whiff of mothballs about him whenever he returned from his prowls.

From shoveling shit in East Hampton they had moved to the woods north of Amagansett, where they felled oaks for a couple of months, reducing the trees to cords of wood. Then it was on to Promised Land, where they tarred the roof joins on the fish factory buildings at Smith Meal, daubing obscene doodles—only visible from the air, they calculated—to relieve the monotony. When the shimmering pods of menhaden reappeared in late spring, they descended from their lofty perch and lugged hundredweight sacks of fish meal, still blisteringly hot from the driers, out to the boxcars on the railway siding. The only white men in the human chain of seasonal southern workers, they soon picked up the songs and learned to take the ribbing in good humor.

They grew tight, sharing stories as they toiled. Hendrik's father was

a tough little Welshman who had ended up in Montauk by way of
Nova Scotia. It was here that he met his bride, Hulda, a towering
Swedish blonde who waitressed at Parson's Inn. It was a typical tale of
Montauk folk: two people from different corners of the world, thrown
together at this windblown outpost. There were Norwegians and
Finns, Spaniards, Danes, Dutch, and Portuguese. Many of the Italians
had worked on the Long Island Rail Road, laying the final miles of
track out to Montauk, only to marry and settle down. There were
workmen left over from Carl Fisher's doomed enterprise to develop
Montauk, and there were navy men left over from both wars. Then
there were the Irish, of course, not for any particular reason, just because they seemed to turn up pretty much everywhere.

Many in East Hampton and Amagansett looked down on the tatty
little community of transients, apparently forgetting that their own
villages had started life in exactly the same way. It was natural that
Conrad and his family take Montauk to their hearts. After all, their
story was no different—first-generation immigrants lured to the eastern end of Long Island by a twist of fate. In their case, they owed it all
to the intervention of a loose paving stone. If one of the men who
made the weekly booze run out to Montauk hadn't turned his ankle,
then Conrad's father wouldn't have had to stand in for him, and he
would never have set eyes on Amagansett.

Two years into Prohibition, his father and Eusebio had secured a
lucrative little slice of the trade in illegal liquor, running the stuff into
the city from the tip of Long Island, where the foreign schooners
moored just beyond the twelve-mile limit, the booze hustled ashore
by a fleet of local boats. On the night in question, Conrad's father had
found himself on the ocean beach at Amagansett, hefting cases of
Golden Wedding whiskey into the back of a truck.

The way he told it, he experienced an epiphany of near-religious
intensity. As he took in the unbroken strip of moonlit sand backed
by dunes, he found himself transported back to his Euzkadi, to the

beaches north of Biarritz, which he'd fished since childhood. The same ocean, the same waves breaking against an identical stretch of coastline. And he made a vow to himself: if he couldn't go back to the old country, he would at least return to the old ways. As soon as he had saved up enough money, he would move with his boys to Amagansett and take up fishing once more.

That moment arrived, quite unexpectedly, a few weeks later. While pushing their way along a crowded downtown sidewalk one night, Eusebio yelped then span around, searching the faces in the throng. He grabbed their father's arm and urged him to hurry along. Within a block, Eusebio was leaning on him for support, steering him into an alleyway. That's when their father saw the bib of blood soaking the back of Eusebio's pants.

It was a warning, a single thrust of a stiletto blade into the back of the thigh; but the assailant had messed up, striking an artery. Eusebio felt the life slowly draining out of him and he began to talk. He admitted that he hadn't been entirely honest in his dealings with their father, excluding him from certain profits, certain transactions, one of which had just backfired on him. He told their father to disappear, and quickly; it was just a matter of time before the people in question came knocking on his door. He barely managed to reveal the whereabouts of his ill-gotten gains before drifting into unconsciousness. Death followed moments later. Their father left Eusebio where he had fallen, curled on the cobbles. He would have taken his friend's black borsalino hat with him, but Eusebio had always joked that he never took it off for fear his Maker wouldn't recognize him when his time came.

Conrad had a dim recollection of being hauled from his bed in the dead of night, of their father thrusting a thick roll of notes into the hands of a tearful Irena, of being bundled into a car. They woke the next morning to find themselves in a field on the outskirts of Hempstead.

By late afternoon, they had moved into their rooms on the third floor of Sea View House, the only hotel in Amagansett at that time.

The money from Eusebio was enough to buy a house, a boat, and some gear; and their father's first act on taking possession of the two-story lean-to on Miankoma Lane was to carve his name into the lintel above the front door, according to the Basque tradition.

Their sudden appearance on the scene, to say nothing of their father's deep pockets, piqued the interest of the community. But suspicion soon gave way to wary acceptance, largely thanks to the intervention of Cap'n Josh. When word trickled through to the old man that the newcomer was a Basque, Conrad's father was summoned to the Kemps' large house on Bluff Road. Cap'n Josh's mother was still alive at the time, though you wouldn't have known it to look at her, and four generations of the family were living under one roof, the oldest and youngest both in diapers.

The two men retired to the study, where they traded stories for most of the evening over a bottle of King George rum. When they finally emerged, Cap'n Josh announced to his sons that the Labarde family was to be welcomed into the fold. He had worked alongside Basques on the whaleships and knew them to be one of the oldest seafaring peoples, God-fearing and hardworking, proud and reserved, their ancient homeland divided by a border not of their choosing.

All this was more than enough to recommend them to Cap'n Josh. However, he did suggest that their father spend that first winter cod-fishing with the Kemps. It would give him a chance to learn the ways of the local surfmen.

Antton and Conrad were placed under strict orders to tell no one about the source of their wealth, even when it became clear that many in Amagansett were lining their pockets with booze money. It was an oath Conrad had broken on only two occasions—once with Lillian, the other time with Hendrik.

"Was that the *Demeter* I saw out there?" asked Hendrik, nodding towards the bay.

"Yeah."

"You'll be wanting a bed for the night, then."

"The floor will do."

"I got a mess o' clams and a bluefish needs eating. I'd boil up a lobster, only I'm sick to the hind teeth of the damned things."

Hendrik cooked up the clam chowder on the kerosene stove, and they ate it off their knees, watching the sun slip behind the bluffs on the western shore of the bay.

"Heard you had a run-in with Charlie Walsh," said Hendrik.

"Yeah?"

"Don't want to talk about it?"

Conrad shrugged. "Just bad history going back a ways."

"That's good of you to say. But I heard what he done with them earrings off of that girl you found. He's rotten like a pumpkin hit by a frost then melted in a harvest sun."

Conrad smiled.

"I knew the girl, you know," continued Hendrik, reaching for his beer. "From the yacht club, when I was working bar last summer."

On returning from the war, Hendrik had taken a job at the Devon Yacht Club that first season to raise some cash to replace his neglected lobster pots. It was very likely he had met Lillian during his stint at Devon.

In fact, Conrad had been banking on it.

"Fine-looking and funny with it, always quipping," said Hendrik. "Had a smile could tear the insides out of a bear."

It was Conrad's cue, the reason he had come here, but he felt her hair clip in his pocket, pressing against his thigh, and he found he was unable to speak. He looked to change the subject, anything to regain his composure.

"Hendrik, I need a charter boat for this Saturday. There's a party wants to go tuna fishing."

"Tuna fishing, huh?"

"Best if it's someone who works out of Montauk Yacht Club."

"Rich folk, eh?"

"Money no object."

Hendrik thought about it for a moment, then came up with a name.

THEY TALKED ABOUT THE OLD TIMES until the moon was high overhead. They skirted around the subject of the war, dipping their toes in from time to time, but never taking the plunge. That was the way of it, though. Only the ones who hadn't been through the real meat-grinder liked to go over their adventures.

Moving inside, Hendrik insisted that Conrad take the cot while he bunked down on the floor. Lying there in the darkness on his back, Conrad toyed with how best to tackle the subject. There was only one way—front-on.

"There's something I got to talk to you about, Hendrik."

"I didn't want to ask."

"What's that?"

"I ain't seen you in months, and you don't need me to find you a charter boat."

"Last year," said Conrad, "at the Devon Yacht Club, were you working the night of the first dinner dance?"

"Sure I was. It was a big do, all hands on deck."

"Was Lillian Wallace there?"

It was a moment before Hendrik replied. "Yeah."

"You remember who she was with?"

This time, the silence lasted longer.

"There was a whole gang of them," said Hendrik.

"Her brother?"

"Sure. And her sister. They was always there together."

"What about her fiancé, Justin Penrose?"

Conrad heard a match strike. Light from the kerosene lamp flooded the shack. Hendrik was looking at him intently, his eyes demanding an explanation.

"I can't," said Conrad. "Not yet."

Hendrik nodded. "What do you want to know?"

"Who she left with. And when."

20

Hollis had never been assaulted by a goose before.

"Eugene!" snapped Mary, hurrying over from the house.

Either Eugene was deaf, or Mary estimated her authority over the big bird far too highly; possibly both. Hollis found himself backed up against his car, trying to parry the thrusting beak with his leg.

He thought about taking refuge inside the vehicle, but Mary's other guests gathered on the lawn were all staring now in rapt amusement, and the idea that they would witness his ignoble withdrawal was too humiliating to even consider.

"Eugene!" barked Hollis.

"Don't," said Mary, "you'll scare him."

"What?!"

He only took his eyes off the goose for a split second, but it was enough for Eugene to get a good one away—a sharp nip to the thigh.

"Christ!"

Mary placed herself between Hollis and Eugene.

"That's enough," she said firmly. "Barn." She pointed.

Hollis could have sworn Eugene shot him a look before skulking off, one that said "Saved by the bell, buddy."

"That's strange," said Mary.

"What?"

"I've never seen him so angry before." There was definitely something in the tone of her voice that suggested Hollis was to blame in some way.

"I didn't do a thing," he bleated.

"Maybe you didn't need to. You know what they say about geese."

"That they taste damn good with orange sauce?"

"That's not funny."

But she smiled.

HOLLIS WAS IMMEDIATELY COLLARED by a large woman in a noisy print dress who proudly announced in a gruff baritone that she was chairman of the Apron Booth at the upcoming LVIS summer fair. She also happened to be the secretary of the Roadside Committee, and proceeded to spend the next half hour singing the praises of Tufor weed killer in the society's ongoing drive against poison ivy, ragweed, and sumac. She wasn't as alarmed as some about the threat posed to the local verges by the recent surge in the dandelion population.

Hollis was finally rescued by her appetite, the smell of the lamb flame-grilling on the barbecue luring her away. It left him free to fill his glass at the drinks table and survey the gathering. It seemed to be divided into two clear and quite discordant camps—Mary's associates from the LVIS, and a younger crowd, dressed more casually. Strangely, they seemed to be mingling quite happily.

"I see you met Barbara."

Hollis turned.

"She doesn't like me," continued Mary, filling her glass. "She thinks I'm too young to be president."

"She didn't say anything."

"She's far too diplomatic, knows I'll demote her to the Candy and Cigarette Booth if I hear any rumblings."

For a moment Hollis thought she was being serious, but as she raised the wineglass to her mouth, her lips curled into the faintest of smiles.

"Why do you do it?" he asked.

"It's easy to laugh, I know, but I think it's important, where we live, how we live." She paused briefly. "And it keeps me out of mischief."

She took another sip of wine, then said, "I see from your look that you've finally done your research."

She was right—he had. Abel and Lucy had filled him in on the story, or rather the scandal. Mary's husband, an engineer, had been spared military service because of their son, but had volunteered to help retool the machines at the Grumman aircraft plant in Bethpage. During his lengthy absence, Mary had struck up an affair with an army liaison officer based out of Camp Hero at Montauk Point, where the big guns were. His job, it seemed, was to develop relations with the locals, a task he had clearly taken to heart.

Opinions were divided when it came to the allocation of blame. Mary's husband was a man known for his fierce temper and his wandering eye.

"Does it bother you?" Mary asked.

"Why should it bother me?"

"The fallen woman."

"Maybe I'm fallen too," said Hollis.

The moment was broken by the arrival of a man dressed in a navy blazer and gray flannels. There was a rakish elegance to his colorful bow tie and the matching kerchief gushing from his breast pocket. His silver mustache was flecked with pieces of potato chip.

"This is my cousin, Edgar," said Mary. "He's a keen sailor."

"Vice-commodore of the Three Mile Harbor Sailing Club," added Edgar, pumping Hollis's hand.

"Tom. Tom Hollis."

"Tom's with the town police."

"Ah yes," said Edgar knowingly. "Didn't recognize you in your civvies. You're the one whose wife slipped her moorings."

HE DIDN'T INTEND TO BE the last to leave, but when he found himself alone with Mary, the final set of taillights disappearing down the track, he was struck by a sense of inevitability, that somehow they were always going to find themselves in this situation.

Or not.

Maybe he was deceiving himself. It wasn't as if he had much experience of such matters. It was quite possible he'd imagined the unspoken complicity, the words behind her eyes.

"I should be going," he said.

"What, and leave me to tidy up on my own?"

They carried everything inside to the kitchen on trays. She washed up; he dried, putting crockery and glasses away in the cupboards according to her instructions. It was an ordered kitchen, spotlessly clean, and he vowed to himself that he'd make an assault on his own the very next day.

She suggested a nightcap, and they retired to the veranda with their glasses, where they sat on wicker chairs, their knees almost touching.

"Are you working tomorrow?" she asked.

"No."

"Sunday?"

"The night shift."

"Do you have any plans?"

He tried to think of something, anything.

"I thought I might take in a movie tomorrow night." He hesitated, mustering the courage. "Do you want to come?"

"I can't."

"Oh."

"I'm going walking."

"At night?"

She smiled. "Tomorrow, but I'll stay over in Springs. I sometimes do."

"Friends?"

"A friend."

"Oh." He swirled the wine around his glass, suddenly aware how
late it was, and wishing he was gone.

"Do you want to come?" she asked.

"Excuse me?"

"With me. Walking."

"Walking?"

"You'll pick it up quick, it's very easy."

He smiled. "Sure. Why not?"

"Tom."

"Yes."

"Do you want to kiss me?"

He hesitated. "Yes, I think so."

"You don't have to."

"No, I'd like to."

"Your glass."

"Oh. Yes."

He put it down beside the chair.

They both leaned forward and their lips met.

For a moment he felt ridiculous, detached, as if observing himself
from on high. He could see the small patch of thinning hair on the
crown of his head as he craned his neck, her hand sliding up his arm,
taking a hold and drawing him closer. Then her tongue forced its way
between his lips, and he dropped back into himself.

Only two tongues had breached the barrier of his lips before. One
had belonged to Lydia, the other to a downtown whore he'd arrested—
a pasty young Ukrainian who had lunged at him in a bid to secure her
release. That time, the kiss had lasted no more than a couple of seconds,

though he still wondered whether that wasn't just a little longer than had been absolutely necessary.

Unlike Lydia, who kissed like she was stoking a fire, Mary's tongue was soft, gentle, probing. And then gone.

"Mmmmmmmmm," she said, smiling, looking deep into his eyes.

"Yes."

They kissed some more. When they broke off again, she said, "I set off early."

"Huh?"

"To beat the heat."

"Oh."

"You can stay if you want."

"Isn't that a bad idea?"

She shrugged. "I'm all out of good ideas."

"I'm thinking of you."

"I know you are."

He sat back in his chair. "I don't know, Mary."

She took his hands in hers. "Let me put it another way," she said. "Edward—that's my son—comes home in just over a week. He's only seven, and I love him . . ." Her words tailed off.

"But . . . ?"

"But he's difficult. If this doesn't happen soon it's never going to."

"Difficult how?"

"Think Eugene then add a bit."

"Where's the bedroom?"

THEY UNDRESSED IN SILENCE in the near-darkness, Hollis perched on the edge of the bed, Mary standing near the window, silhouetted against the moonlight striking the blind.

He was the first to slip between the sheets. They were crisp and fresh, as new.

"That's my side," said Mary.

"Sorry."

"No, don't move."

She climbed in beside him, facing him. He ran his hand along her thigh, up over her hip, down into the dip of her waist. A different contour, a different landscape to Lydia's—more rugged, angular.

"He knew," said Mary.

"What's that?"

"Eugene. He knew. That's why he went for you."

"Be quiet."

"Okay."

They made love, slow and tender, taking their time.

When it was over, she said, "Well, that was quick."

"Was it?"

He was a little stung, but genuinely curious; he really had very little else to judge it by.

"I enjoyed it a lot," she said, stroking his face.

"Did you?"

"Couldn't you tell?"

She had certainly seemed to enjoy it, but in truth he'd been a little distracted, his mind straying to other matters, such as how firm she was, how taut, just how slack and baggy he felt beside her, on top of her.

She took his hand and placed it between her legs, the oily warmth, the matted hair. "You see. Feel how wet I am."

She didn't release his hand.

This time they took longer, though he couldn't say just how long. His desire—unchecked and unruly this time—pushed all other senses to the periphery of his world. She uttered words he'd never heard spoken by a woman, and her whispers sped him towards a conclusion she would then deny him.

The release, when it finally came, was somehow not his, or theirs for that matter. It belonged to the thing that had swallowed them whole.

He lay on his back, drifting in and out of sweet slumber, her arm draped across his midriff, her breath cooling the skin of his chest. He felt like a man who had unearthed a hidden mystery. He told himself it was only sex, but his heart rejected the words.

Had he really spent so many years of his life not knowing?

When he felt an involuntary twitch of sleep in her leg, he gently extricated himself, tugged on his pants, and headed downstairs.

He pulled the car behind the barn, where it couldn't be seen from the road.

As he slipped back into bed, she said, "That's very thoughtful."

"Go to sleep."

"I can't."

He fought the urge to ask how it had been for her.

"How was that for you?" he asked.

"Christ, Tom, look at me. I'm a wreck."

He looked at her, then kissed her, overcome with tenderness.

"Your ankles crack when you walk," she said.

They talked for quite some while. He wallowed in the intimacy of feeling her body while asking her about her life. She seemed to be related to pretty much everyone in the area, worryingly so, but that was the way with the older families, she assured him—they were all "cousins" of some sort or another. She had inherited the farm from her uncle, who had died childless, and she lived off the rent from the land. The eldest of three girls, her two sisters and her parents lived in East Hampton, all within a few miles radius. She said that since they now knew each other carnally, it was only right he should meet them all the next day. His face dropped, but she was only joking.

They discussed his work, and she told him several amusing anecdotes about Chief Milligan, which he hadn't heard before. Though he knew it wasn't the moment to ask, he couldn't help himself.

"Do you know Conrad Labarde?"

"The one who found Lillian Wallace?"

"Yes, the fisherman."

"I met his stepmother a few times. Maude. She used to be a teacher at the school in Amagansett, a good woman. My mother was on the same charity committee as her."

"Where's she now?"

"She moved away when her husband died. It was a couple of years ago, just before the war ended. She wasn't from here. There was a brother—Antton, I think—he died too."

"How?"

"Some kind of fishing accident before the war. He drowned off the beach. I know they all took it hard."

Hollis tried to picture it: the Basque returning from the war in Europe to find his father dead, his stepmother gone. He knew the Basque had served in Europe during the conflict, because he had paid a visit to the Veterans of Foreign Wars office in East Hampton. They didn't have the details of the outfit he'd ended up with—only a record of his enlistment and dispatch to Camp Upton along with all the other local men—but the post commander had heard that he'd seen action in Italy. Maybe the American Legion in Amagansett would know more. Hollis made a mental note to check with them.

"Tom."

"Yes."

"I don't want to know what this is about."

"It's nothing."

"Don't lie to me. First you ask me about Lillian Wallace, now it's the man who found her."

In the silence that followed, he tried to formulate a response, enough to satisfy her, nip her curiosity in the bud. It wasn't required.

"I mean it," said Mary. "I don't want to know. But there might come a time when I do. And then I'll expect you to be honest with me. Okay?"

"Okay."

"May I have my breast back now?"

He removed his hand and she rolled onto her side. He snuggled up behind her and kissed the nape of her neck, inhaling her scent.

"I'm sorry," he whispered.

"Just tell me one thing. Is it important?"

"Yes."

"Then you're forgiven."

21

THEY ARRIVED AT THE MONTAUK YACHT CLUB AT SEVEN O'CLOCK SHARP, TWO chauffeur-driven cars pulling up near the clubhouse and disgorging their occupants.

Conrad made his way along the dock to greet them.

He recognized her father, brother, and Justin Penrose from photos she'd once shown him at the house. Her sister, Gayle, was talking to a small woman with long dark hair tied back off her face. Her appearance fitted what Lillian had told him of the maid, Rosa. This was confirmed when Conrad drew closer to the group.

"Help Rosa unload the food, will you," said George Wallace to one of the drivers.

Gayle effected the introductions and Conrad shook hands with father and son. George Wallace thanked him for recovering Lillian's body from the ocean, and for arranging the charter boat. It didn't seem to occur to him that there was anything odd about juxtaposing the two events in the same sentence, but at least he got them in the right order of priority.

Conrad made a point of gripping Manfred Wallace's hand a little more firmly than was necessary, and of staring deep into his blue, almost aquamarine, eyes. He was rewarded with a satisfying flicker of unease.

Another man introduced himself as Richard Wakeley. They had spoken on the phone when Conrad first called Gayle to say he'd found a boat for them. Steering Conrad a little to one side, Wakeley peeled off the sum they'd agreed on from a wad of bills.

Conrad tucked the cash into his hip pocket. "Not coming with us?" he asked, taking in Wakeley's neatly pressed slacks and leather shoes.

"I can't stand the ocean."

"She's a cruel mistress, old Mother Atlantic. As Lillian learned to her cost."

The overfamiliar use of her Christian name was intentional.

"Indeed," said Wakeley.

IN ALL, THERE WERE SEVEN in the party—the Wallaces, Justin Penrose and his father, another man, and an attractive brunette a little younger than Gayle, with dark pools for eyes.

They all seemed pleased with the boat, the *Zephyr*—a low-sided, beamy forty-four-footer. There was plenty of room around the two fighting chairs bolted to the aft deck, as well as a shaded eating area in the large, open pilot house, which had been vacated by the skipper for the running bridge above.

Conrad knew that Captain Whitman B. Chase wouldn't disappoint, and he didn't. His grizzled face was shaded beneath the long bill of his swordfisherman's cap; and his gruff, almost dismissive greeting of his customers as they clambered aboard was no less than they'd expected, or hoped for.

"Stow your gear down below. There's ice in the fish hold," he growled. "And shake a leg, else we'll miss the ebb tide."

They exchanged amused glances, delighted at being taken in hand by this grumpy old sea dog.

As Conrad helped load the platters of food, the boxes of drink, crockery, and cutlery, he sensed an unease in Rosa. She seemed to be doing her very best to avoid his gaze.

Taking a large dish of deviled chicken from her, he said pointedly, "Thanks, Rosa."

There was no mistaking the alarm in her eyes.

She knew. Lillian had told her about them.

Turning away, he tried to assess the impact of this revelation, feeding the information into the equation. There was no way of knowing how it would affect his plan, if at all.

She certainly hadn't told her employers, that much was clear from the way they were treating him. And if she hadn't told them by now, then she was unlikely ever to do so. Lillian had probably sworn her to secrecy, and there was no reason for Rosa to break that trust, even now. Just to be sure, though, he kept a close watch on her until they were ready to leave.

Chase fired the engines, and a great cloud of fumes billowed out of the stern.

"Cast off," he called.

Rollo freed the lines, leaping aboard the *Zephyr* as she slid away from the dock and out into the basin of Montauk Lake.

"Good luck," shouted Wakeley, waving them off.

Rosa stood beside him. She wasn't waving.

THEY STEAMED OUT OF THE CHANNEL, then ran east. The sea was glassy calm with a gentle groundswell running, and they bowled along at a steady clip, driven by the throaty GM diesel.

Rollo worked his way to the end of the narrow swordfish pulpit that extended some twenty feet clear of the stem. He stood there, his hands on the rail, facing into the rising sun, the wind whipping his hair, and Conrad wished for a moment that he had a camera with him.

"Do you want some coffee?"

He turned to see that Gayle had joined him on the foredeck. She hadn't found her sea legs yet, and probably never would, certainly not in those heels.

"Thanks."

He glanced up at the flying bridge where Chase was rolling a plug of tobacco around his mouth.

"Hey Cap, coffee?"

"Makes me shit liquid."

"I think that's a no," said Conrad. He nodded at Rollo riding the wind beyond the bow wave. "He'll have some when he's finished."

"What is that thing?"

"A pulpit, for harpooning swordfish."

"Oh."

Gayle started making her way around the pilothouse.

"Best take those off." He nodded at her shoes. "One big swell and you'll be swimming."

She reached for him to steady herself as she slipped off the shoes, her fingers pale against his forearm. She was flirting with him, just as she had the other day when she showed up at his place. This time, though, he didn't resent her quite so much for it. From what Hendrik had told him, it seemed unlikely she was involved.

"Thanks," she said when she was done.

"No problem," he replied, tearing his eyes away from her feet.

They could just as well have been Lillian's.

THE ONLY EXPERIENCED FISHERMAN among the party was the gentleman who proved to be the father of the brunette. The older men called him Marshal; Manfred Wallace and Justin Penrose addressed him as senator; to his daughter he was just plain Pappy.

The senator had come armed with his own rod, its reel as big as a dinner plate, and he had every intention of telling the others how things were done. Depositing himself in one of the fighting chairs, his instructions were clearly secondary to the real purpose of the exercise: that of discussing his past exploits. For him, "the one that got away" was a six-hundred-pound bluefin he'd hooked off the Outer Banks of North Carolina, an excellent winter tuna fishery known to few, he claimed.

"I was in the chair for an hour before the first mate took over. When he folded, I put in another half hour. That monster never tired, not once, kept running back and forth beneath the boat. We could have been there till nightfall and still not brought it to gaff. Yes, she earned her freedom, that one," he conceded magnanimously, through gritted teeth.

As the stories ran on, the others hanging on his every word, it was becoming increasingly clear that the trip had been organized primarily for the senator's benefit.

And that, thought Conrad, presented an opportunity for a bit of sport.

THEY WERE FIVE MILES SOUTH OF BLOCK ISLAND when the order came down from the flying bridge to start trolling. Rollo took a couple of menhaden from the live well. They hooked the fish up to the lines and trailed them over the teakwood transom into the wake.

Chase slowed the *Zephyr* to six or seven knots. At this speed, the tuna would take the live baits for the real thing. Not that getting bluefin to strike was the problem. What you did with them once they had was the name of the game.

It had already been decided that Justin Penrose's father should take the first turn in the other chair beside the senator.

Conrad adjusted the drag on Penrose's reel.

"If you get a hit, don't do anything. The skipper will throttle up to set the hook. I'll talk you through it from there." He started strapping him into the harness.

"Is that necessary?" asked Penrose senior.

"Never know what's out there."

"You wouldn't be the first to go over the side, Everett," chuckled the senator.

"That's the truth," called Chase from the bridge. "Ask old Eric Doucette, he'll tell you. If you can find him. No one's seen him since."

Penrose shifted nervously in his chair. "What happened?"

"Worked a commercial boat out of Old Harbor on Block Island. Experienced bluefin man. Been fishing 'em since ever, them Nova Scotians. Hooked a large giant out there in the mud hole, just last year it was. Anyhow, he fights it to the boat and it's laying there in the water, dead as mutton, or so he thinks. He's wiring it up when that fish comes to life, takes off straight down. Only thing is, Doucette's got the wire looped 'round his arm. Gone in a flash. Straight over the side. Still down there probably, cruising around. Who knows, maybe it dropped him off back in Nova Scotia."

"That's terrible," said Gayle Wallace.

"That's bluefin for you, don't want to mess with 'em."

Chase was right. For sheer brutish power and endurance the bluefin had no equals among the big-game fish. For all their leaps and fancy acrobatics, marlin and sailfish tired quickly, and it was often said that once you'd hooked a giant bluefin nothing else would do.

Conrad rested a reassuring hand on Penrose's shoulder. "You'll be okay. Just keep the rod butt in the gimbal and your hands away from the reel."

He turned his attention to the senator, whose eyes were fixed on his bait some thirty yards astern of the boat.

"What line are you carrying?" asked Conrad.

"Hundred-pound."

"Won't be much fun if we hit some thirty-pound schoolies."

"A fish is a fish," said the senator.

Asshole, thought Conrad.

"What's the record this year in these waters?" asked the senator.

"Cap, what's the record this year?" called Conrad to the bridge.

"Seven hundred and thirty-six pounds," came back the reply.

"Sweet Jesus."

"Pappy!"

"A third of a ton," muttered the senator. More than enough to put the demon of that giant North Carolina bluefin to rest. He adjusted himself in his chair and waited.

And waited.

Half an hour later they were still trolling back and forth on the off-shore grounds, the only consolation being that none of the other boats they could see appeared to be hooked up.

The girls had lost interest by now and had retreated to the shade, where they were chatting and flipping through magazines. The men, all five of them, were smoking cigars and talking about Yale. Rollo had climbed to the masthead where he was perched on the old automobile seat that served as a lookout. He was scouring the ocean for telltale signs—a surface break, or a darkened patch, like the shadow of a cloud, indicating a school of baitfish.

"What do you say we anchor up and try chunking them?" called the senator to the bridge.

They'd come prepared with a tub of mashed menhaden chum, but Chase wasn't ready to start heaving it over the side.

"They're out there, I can smell 'em. And the troll bite's been holdin' up good all season."

"Did he say he can smell them?" asked Penrose senior.

Manfred Wallace blew out his cigar smoke. "He doesn't mean it literally."

"Don't be so sure," said Conrad.

Manfred Wallace didn't appreciate the comment, or the tone. It rankled him, though not enough to warrant a response.

"I don't know," called the senator to the bridge. "My guess is they're settled in."

Chase didn't reply. He didn't need to. The fish did the talking for him. The water just behind the senator's bait erupted in a blur of blue and bronze.

"Holy shit . . ."

The senator's reel came to life, whirring to a mist as the tuna made a blistering run to starboard. Chase eased the throttle forward to set the hook, then span the wheel hard and opened it up.

Conrad seized the back of the senator's chair, turning it to keep the fish lined up. The others gathered around, staring, mesmerized by the sheer speed of the fish—a hundred yards, two hundred . . .

"Look at it go," said Manfred.

"It's not going anywhere," said the senator.

The bluefin stripped two hundred and fifty yards off the reel before sounding.

"You get a look at it?" asked the senator. "All I saw was the hole it left."

"I don't know," said Conrad. "Not a giant. Maybe fifty pounds."

"Seventy," called Chase.

Either way, the senator was right—it wasn't going anywhere, not attached to hundred-pound test line. It was simply a matter of cranking it in, something the senator was clearly quite capable of doing. Twice Conrad spotted him back off the drag on his reel, allowing the fish to make another rush. This was done for the benefit of the spectators, to make him look good—man and fish locked in battle.

It was all over in ten minutes, the fish alongside the boat. Conrad gaffed it under the chin and Rollo secured a strap around its tail. Together they hauled it up over the gunwale. It flopped onto the deck, its flanks flashing iridescent blue in the sunlight, grading through bronze to the silver of its belly.

"Poor thing," said Gayle Wallace.

"It's your daddy I'm after," said the senator.

"Bait off the port bow," called Chase.

Conrad hurried aloft. In the distance, birds were flocking, with more arriving by the second.

"Big school of bait comin' up fast."

"What do you think's driving them?"

"Well it ain't lobsters," grinned Chase, edging the throttle forward.

As they drew closer, Conrad said, "Jesus."

"Even he couldn't walk on that lot," muttered Chase.

The surface of the ocean was churning with life. And death. Gannets and gulls swooped and slammed onto the water from above, snapping up sparkling baitfish, while hundreds of frenzied school tuna flashed to and fro, their distinctive sickle fins scything through the chop. Every now and then one would break clear of the water in its eagerness to kill, jaws snapping at the silver mist of baitfish leaping before it. There were other fish present too, striped bass and bluefish, both fearsome hunters, and also ready to take to the air for their prey, but no match for a speeding bluefin. A couple of sharks lazily patrolled the fringes of the melee, biding their time, allowing the tuna to tire themselves out.

It was as if two invisible hands had corralled all living creatures from the surrounding waters into five acres of ocean and ordered them to fight it out among themselves. Conrad had once seen a school of large stripers rip through a pod of menhaden—and a shocking spectacle it had been—but he had never witnessed anything on this scale, the whole savage cycle of life in the ocean laid bare for human eyes.

And in that moment, staring down from the flying bridge, Conrad saw himself reflected back: blind, raging, unmerciful. Inhuman, but not unfeeling. That was the worst of it, what marked men out, their curse—the clean, sweet taste of vengeance, the deaths of those you had known atoned for on the altar of the battlefield, their lives memorialized in the letting of yet more innocent blood.

"Well?" said Chase.

"Huh?"

"I said best go ready them rods." He spat a stream of tobacco onto the boards at his feet. "And the idiots what's holdin' 'em."

THE *ZEPHYR* EDGED INTO THE FRAY, and they took their place in the upper orders of the food chain. It was merely a matter of dropping a live bait over the side; the hit would happen within a matter of moments.

Chase nosed the boat back and forth through the seething waters, glancing over his shoulder every so often, swinging the wheel to keep the lines from tangling. By the time the other charter boats arrived on the scene, each member of the party had hooked and boated a tuna, including the girls.

It wasn't enough, though. They wanted more. And they got them. For almost an hour they got them. They were small fish, in the thirty- to fifty-pound range, but after hooking a half dozen of them, even the senator was ready to vacate his chair.

The bite dropped off when the sharks moved in, scattering the tuna. The chop gradually subsided. Apart from a few gulls swooping for scraps, there was little evidence of the carnage they'd witnessed, and shared in.

Conrad dropped the tuna into the hold, piling ice around them, while Rollo swabbed the deck, slick from the blood of the throats they'd cut.

The Wallaces and their guests celebrated with Champagne, faces flush from exertion and exhilaration, talking excitedly. Glasses were raised to the skipper and his crew, though not offered to them, and when the table was laid for lunch Conrad and Rollo withdrew to the flying bridge.

Rollo had come armed with sandwiches made for him by his mother, which he insisted on eating at the end of the swordfish pulpit, legs dangling either side of the narrow gangplank. He was more withdrawn than usual, and had been all day. Conrad observed him, concerned.

"He's a good boy," said Chase. "Not the sharpest chisel in the toolbox, but a good boy." He proceeded to give an account of his association with the Kemps over the years, and his rags-to-riches rise from Jersey plumber to Montauk charter boat captain.

Chase enjoyed the sound of his own voice, which was fine by Conrad; it allowed him to keep one ear on the conversation rising up from below. The talk shifted from the economic regeneration of Europe, to Communists, then to politics and presidents. Manfred Wallace said it was unfair to expect the nation to choose between an ex-haberdasher and a man who resembled one of those little grooms on top of a wedding cake. This was the cause of much amusement, with the senator laughing the loudest. The discussion then turned to Manfred, to upcoming elections, to his candidacy. There was talk of the State Senate and of District 26, of the New York City Tax Commissioner and of other favors that could be called in.

Conrad felt the bile rise in his gullet. Thinking that the heat was getting to him, Chase suggested that he put on his cap. The clatter of crockery gave way to the smell of coffee, and Conrad pictured the scene, pictured himself heading below, what he would do, how easy it would be.

"Conrad!" It was Rollo at the end of the pulpit, pointing towards the southeast.

"You see 'em? Swordfish!"

Chase was on his feet now, squinting. "Well, damned if they ain't," he said.

Some half a mile away two swordfish were finning, lazing on the surface.

"You want to break out the gear?" asked Conrad.

"You're kidding me."

"I crewed for Jake Minton back in 'thirty-nine."

"He still owe you money?"

"Uh-huh."

"Damn right he does. Tightest son of a bitch that ever lived. You know what he said once, to his own brother? Ed's broke, busted flat, needs to borrow a bit, but Jake says he can't help out, says he's got this deal with the bank, an agreement, says the bank won't go into fishing if he don't go into lending money! You believe that?!"

"What about it?" said Conrad.

It was the opportunity he'd been waiting for, the scene already playing itself out in his head.

"Swordfishin'," muttered Chase. "I don't think so."

"The boat gets to keep the fish and there's another fifty in it for you."

"Let's go swordfishin'."

HEADING BELOW, Conrad addressed himself directly to the senator so the outcome would be assured.

"Senator, you ever harpoon a swordfish?"

"No."

"Want to give it a shot?"

"Damn right I do."

What else could he say? He hadn't hooked the giant fish he was after, and he wasn't going to now, the tuna bite being pretty much played out by noon.

"There's a couple finning nearby."

"Show me," said the senator with swagger, laying aside his glass of Cognac.

As they all made their way to the foredeck, Conrad collared the Wallaces.

"The captain's asking for an extra hundred."

"A hundred dollars?!" said Manfred.

"Not a problem," said his father.

It was a twelve-foot harpoon, light and well balanced. Conrad demonstrated how to hold it. He showed them how the little bronze dart at the end came free at the moment of the strike, twisting as it did so, lodging itself in the flesh. The dart was attached to a wooden keg by several hundred feet of manila line, neatly coiled down in a tub. The keg was tossed over the side as the line ran out. After that, it was simply a question of tracking the keg, waiting for the fish to tire itself out or to die from the wound.

It was a perfect day for swordfishing—a dead calm sea and a searing, windless heat. They would find other fish, and Conrad could afford to take the first turn on the pulpit. He removed his overshirt before doing so, and regretted it almost immediately.

"Regimental tattoo?" asked the senator.

The red arrowhead was clearly visible just beneath the arm hem of his T-shirt.

"Yeah," replied Conrad, busying himself with the harpoon, clearing the line, hoping that was the end of it.

"Did you see action? My boy saw action—Guadalcanal. He didn't make it back."

"Sorry to hear that."

Conrad made his way to the end of the pulpit, terminating the conversation. They were bearing down on the swordfish now with the sun astern to keep the glare from blinding Conrad. It was a large fish that looked likely to tip the balance at around four hundred pounds.

"Keep her off half a point," called Conrad.

"You tellin' me my business?" growled Chase.

"Sorry, Cap."

Chase put him directly over the fish and Conrad threw his full weight behind the harpoon, thrusting down into the dark, lacquered body, ironing the creature in the thick muscle right behind the dorsal fin.

The ocean erupted, the swordfish making a scorching run to starboard, the line burning out of the tub, singing. Rollo hove the keg over the side. A second later, the line snapped taut and the keg tore across the slick surface. They set off in pursuit.

With the lily firmly set, the rest was a formality. They trailed the keg for half an hour until it finally bobbed to a halt, inert.

"Reckon he's about drowned out," said Chase.

They hooked the keg aboard and dragged the swordfish up from the depths. It had no fight left in it; in fact, no life at all. It had expired from the wound Conrad had inflicted. It was best to be sure though. Taking up the lance, he turned to the girls.

"You might want to turn away."

But they didn't, and he thrust the lance into the gills. They fastened a strap around the tail and hoisted the fish inboard using a block and fall, laying it on the deck.

Everyone stared in mute wonder at the beauty and the enormity of the creature.

The senator ran the toe of his shoe along the sword. "My God."

"Are you still game?" asked Conrad.

"Are you joking?"

Conrad turned to Manfred Wallace. "You want to tend the warp and keg for the senator?"

"Sure."

It was another ten minutes—time enough to cut out the lily and recoil the line—before Rollo hollered from the masthead, "Fish on the lee beam!"

There were two of them, finning close together this time. Keeping the sun at their backs meant coming at them head-on. Conrad accompanied the senator to the end of the pulpit and handed him the harpoon.

"They may flare off at the last second, but you'll still get a shot. Here . . ." He adjusted the senator's grip on the pole. "Remember, just behind the dorsal fin else you'll bone the dart. And don't look them in the eye."

"Why not?"

"They'll freeze you with their stare."

"Really?"

"Trust me."

The senator nodded gravely and Conrad made his way back to the stem of the boat where the others were gathered.

"Good luck, Pappy!" called the senator's daughter, all afluster.

Conrad wandered aft, picked up an axe, then returned to the foredeck. He let the axe hang inconspicuously against his thigh.

What the senator lacked in style he more than made up for in determination. He almost disappeared over the pulpit rail in his bid to stick the fish, but it was a clean hit.

"I got him!" he yelled in triumph, raising the harpoon high above his head.

The swordfish took off at a breathtaking clip, heading directly astern of the boat. Conrad couldn't have asked for more. Everyone turned instinctively to observe its passage, including Manfred Wallace, which meant he took his eyes off the tub.

Conrad glanced down at it, the manila line hissing out, the wooden rim starting to smoke.

"The keg!" he shouted, when he judged it was just too late.

To Manfred's credit, he didn't freeze. Spinning back, he lunged at the keg, only to see it snatched from his fingertips.

It flew across the foredeck, upending Penrose senior and scattering the others, before crashing into the starboard rail, ripping out one whole section as it continued its journey aft. Conrad leapt forward, swinging the axe, severing the line.

Chase hauled back on the throttle lever. "You stupid son of a bitch!" he yelled. "The one thing you had to do—toss the goddamn keg!"

"I—" stammered Manfred.

"No excuses," said Conrad. "You screwed up."

Manfred turned his gaze on him, and for the briefest of moments, deep in his crystalline eyes, Conrad caught a glimmer of what Manfred was capable of.

"Look at my goddamn boat!"

"We'll cover it," said George Wallace. "Whatever it costs."

"Damn right you will," said Chase, beginning to soften, the prospect of padding out the costs already dampening his anger.

Mr. Penrose was helped to his feet. He hopped around and rubbed his shin and declared himself to be okay. The senator looked far from okay.

"Did I stick her right?" he asked Conrad.

"You stuck her right."

"I'd have had her."

"Oh, you'd have had her."

Manfred Wallace felt the full force of the senator's glare. Assuming, as you certainly could, that the senator had grossly exaggerated the size of the North Carolina bluefin that got away, then he'd just lost the biggest fish of his life, and through no fault of his own.

Only when he caught Rollo looking at him did Conrad realize he was wearing an expression of deep satisfaction. He didn't care that Rollo had seen him laid bare. He didn't care that someone could have been far more seriously injured by the keg, or that somewhere out there a four-hundred-pound swordfish was being driven mad with the agony of a bronze dart buried in its back. He didn't care, because he knew this was as close as he was ever likely to come to witnessing the humiliation of Manfred Wallace.

It was a dismal end to a perfect day for the Wallaces and their guests. As the *Zephyr* pressed towards home, the conversation was muted, with Gayle doing her best to lighten the mood. Manfred was silent, suitably chastened, and by the time they reached the breakwaters at Montauk Harbor he'd been forgiven.

The senator mock-punched him on the jaw and laughed as he recalled the spectacle of Penrose senior going ass over elbow. The swordfish might have given him the slip, but he had a far more entertaining tale to tell because of it, and that realization was just beginning to dawn on him.

The late-afternoon buzz at the Montauk Yacht Club swept aside the last vestiges of the incident, the dockside thronging with people eager to view the catches of the returning boats. Their swordfish was hoisted onto the scales at the end of the dock. At four hundred and forty pounds it wasn't large enough to cause a real stir, but the number of tuna they'd hooked, stacked up on the dock like so much cordwood, was impressive by any standards. It made Chase look good, it made his party look good, and the moment was trapped for posterity by a photographer.

Conrad cleaned and dressed a couple of tuna and packed them in ice for the Wallaces. The rest were sold to the same buyer who took the swordfish off Chase's hands.

Manfred announced he was off to phone home, to let the drivers know they were back. Conrad slipped away, tailing him towards the clubhouse.

"There's the extra hundred for the swordfishing," he called.

Manfred stopped and turned. "I thought I'd just add it to the cost of the repairs."

"I'll take it now if that's okay with you."

It was twice as much as he'd promised Chase, but he doubted any tips would be forthcoming after what he was about to say. He didn't care for himself, but there was no reason Rollo should be denied his dues.

Manfred handed him the cash, and Conrad stuffed it into his hip pocket without looking at it.

"Whose idea was it?"

"Excuse me?" said Manfred.

"Going fishing, your sister still warm in her grave."

Manfred didn't respond immediately, unsure if he had heard correctly. "How dare you," he flared.

Conrad took a step towards him.

"I know about Lizzie Jencks."

Manfred recovered quickly, but not quickly enough. His eyes had betrayed him.

"Lizzie who?"

"And that's not all I know."

"I have absolutely no idea what you're talking about," said Manfred with way too much indignation.

Conrad smiled. "I'll be seeing you."

He stood his ground, obliging Manfred to walk away first. But he didn't.

"Who the hell do you think you are, hurling accusations around?"

"Accusations?" said Conrad. "I thought you'd never heard of Lizzie Jencks."

22

HOLLIS HAD BEEN TRYING HIS HARDEST TO APPEAR INTERESTED, SO HE WAS A little surprised when Mary said, "You don't seem very interested."

"Don't I? Maybe it's the blisters."

"The blisters?"

"I have a few."

It was an understatement; his heels and toes were rubbed raw. This was due in part to the old pair of walking boots she'd lent him, her ex-husband's feet being a good couple of sizes larger than his own. Mainly, though, it was because of the considerable distances they'd covered since their dawn departure. He had never walked so far in one day, not since a tramping trip in the Catskills with the Brooklyn Boy Scouts many years before. On that occasion the heat had been bearable, the terrain forgiving, and they'd had the roving hands of a buck-toothed scoutmaster to spur them onwards.

Mary, he'd soon discovered, was a keen believer in treading the thorny path. Without so much as a word of warning she would leave the trails that threaded the oak woods north of town, striking out through the brush and briars over uneven ground deliberately designed to turn an ankle. He'd had little choice but to follow. The treasures she sought were only to be found deep in the woods.

She showed him square indentations in the forest floor—the cellar holes of dwellings abandoned centuries before. She pointed out large, flat stones buried in the undergrowth, etched with initials, that had once served as boundary markers for these early homesteads. And as they weaved through the oak, hickory, maple, and birch, she drew his attention to clusters of pear and apple trees, gnarled and wretched— the vestiges of orchards considerably older than the trees that now towered around them.

She explained that at one time the early settlers had so denuded this rolling landscape that they'd been forced to drive their cattle and sheep into the kettle-holes whenever the English ships appeared off the coast looking to restock. The East End, she said, was pockmarked with these deep depressions, footprints of the vast blocks of ice left behind by the glacier when it retreated. She insisted on making a detour to show him one such hollow, its steep sides descending to a sun-dappled pool, the water clear yet somehow black as pitch. And he imagined the farmers cowering there with their beasts, safe from the hungry eyes of the enemy, their former countrymen.

She showed him the graves of those early herders, small family burial plots reclaimed by the forest, the bones of the dead woven through with the roots of the same trees that had dislodged and toppled the weathered headstones. The names, eroded by time, had been destined for obscurity until Mary came along and recorded them, clearing off the lichen, taking rubbings with wax crayons, pulling out onto rice paper names no longer discernible to the human eye.

Some were names that hadn't survived the years, the male lines cut short at some juncture, although some part of their blood still flowed in the veins of the living, trickling down through the generations via the womenfolk, mingling through intermarriage, surviving in every-thing but name.

Mary wasn't a Calder; her husband was a Calder—from Scotland via Madison, Wisconsin—and he was new to the East End of Long Island.

Or rather he had been until he left. Mary was a Northfleet, a family to be reckoned with in and around East Hampton ever since Samuel Norfleete first showed up on the scene from England. And just as Mary could trace her descent right back to the very earliest days of settlement, so they now retraced the footsteps first taken by her ancestor as he headed through the North Woods in search of an inlet or cove with a deep enough draft to accommodate the seagoing vessels that would transport his timber, cattle, and tanned hides to new and lucrative markets. He found the ideal spot at what was now called Northwest Landing, and he became wealthy on the back of the venture, though you wouldn't have known it to look at the place almost three centuries on. All that remained of the warehouse and the wharf he had built was a handful of blackened stumps poking through the mud of the silted-up little creek, barely visible through the murky water.

It was while he was peering at these few pathetic remnants of the wharf pilings that Mary said to him, "You don't seem very interested."

It wasn't the blisters, not if he was honest. And it wasn't that he was bored. He had enjoyed listening to her stories of days gone by, even if she did have a tendency to talk with earnest, almost irritating, enthusiasm at times. It wasn't even that her tales of hardy pioneers hacking out a life for themselves unsettled him—the noble clans of farmers and fishermen, with their ancient lineages and deep-rooted traditions, wedded to the land and the ocean. It didn't bother him that he knew almost nothing of his own heritage, except that he sprang from an undistinguished jumble of different races and religious creeds. There was a German great-something (or was it a great-great-something?) who had worked as a stonecutter in the granite quarries of Vermont, and a Danish wetnurse, then some whispers of Jewish blood on his mother's side, topped off with a large shot of Brooklyn Irish and a dash of Jesuit French.

No pure pedigree for him. He was a mongrel, genuine homegrown fare, and there seemed no reason to deny it or be embarrassed by it.

For all their lofty claims, people were people. Even here in East Hampton, with their time-honored bloodlines, they would still have their share of bastards and backroom abortions and cuckolded husbands blithely bouncing other men's children on their knees.

No, if Mary sensed a certain distraction in him it was because it was five o'clock on a Saturday—weekend cocktail hour—and by his calculation they had another hour and a half's walking ahead of them before they reached their destination.

HE WAS WRONG.

Some unseen clock was striking eight as they crossed the bridge spanning the creek in Springs. This was the heart of the little community, though you wouldn't have known it to look at the place. There was no Main Street as such, just a couple of road junctions, an open expanse of land bisected by a creek, and a few isolated buildings, randomly placed, as if someone had blindfolded a founding father and asked him to stick pins in a map. There was a church here, a schoolhouse over there, a barn, a hall, and a lone store on the south side of the bridge, in front of which a group of local men was now gathered, chewing the fat. Mary greeted a couple of them as they passed by.

Beyond the store, a blind lane led down to the edge of Accabonac Harbor and what appeared to be an abandoned boatyard. Closer inspection revealed a few desultory signs of activity—a small rowboat upturned on wooden stays and half painted, an outboard motor stripped down to its component parts, a torn fishing net in the process of being repaired.

Across the yard, on the shore of the creek, stood a small shack, the water lapping at the base of the veranda. An old man was seated in a spring-rocker examining a small round object between his thumb and forefinger.

"Joe."

He turned and his furrowed face cracked a smile. "Mary. And with a beau in tow."

"Just a friend," said Mary, stooping to kiss him on the cheek.

"If you say so." He eased himself to his feet, extending a crooked and calloused paw. "Joe Milne."

"Tom Hollis."

"What's that?" asked Mary.

Joe handed her the small ball. "You tell me."

She turned it in her fingers. "I don't know," she conceded, handing it on to Hollis. It was hard and textured.

"Flo Barratt back in the woods there, she's got her an army of cats, that old heifer, scores of the damn things runnin' all over, pissin' on the couch and all sorts. Some of 'em's gone missing of late. Now I know why." He paused. "It's a fur ball out of that great horned owl I keep for huntin' crows."

To have dropped it then and there would have been impolite. Thankfully, Joe took it off him.

"Must have developed hisself a taste for kitty meat. Best dispose of the evidence while I figures what to do." He lobbed the fur ball out into the creek.

Hollis noted that it floated.

Joe suddenly clamped a hand on his shoulder. "There's a clam pie needs eatin' and some cold beers to wash it down with."

Thank you, God, thought Hollis.

THEY WENT AND DUNKED THEMSELVES in the creek before dinner to wash away the sweat and the grime, stepping gingerly through the rushes, the mud oozing between their toes. Hollis was forced to confess to Mary that he couldn't really swim. He knew that at a push he could flail his way to the side of a swimming pool, because he'd been forced to do so once on a day trip to Coney Island, when his father had tossed him into the deep end of the marble pool in the Pavilion of Fun. But the atavistic impulse to survive which had driven him through the water that day had little in common with the pleasure others appeared to get from swimming.

He stood near the bank up to his chest in water while Mary stroked around leisurely in the dying rays of the sun, glancing over every so often to check that he hadn't lost his footing and slipped beneath the surface. He was warmed by her concern, and surprised by the force of the urge that welled up inside him when she stepped from the water.

She slapped his hand away and told him to behave.

They ate dinner inside by the light of a kerosene lamp hanging from a beam. The clam pie was hot and the beer, as promised, cold—manna and nectar after a day's hiking.

"So, bub, you get to see the sights?"

"I think we covered pretty much everything between East Hampton and here."

Joe laughed. "It's the one comfort now that my legs is goin'—Mary don't get to drag me around with her."

"He's lying," said Mary. "Everything I showed you Joe showed me first."

"Have you lived here all your life?" asked Hollis.

"Since the war, the one with the South. 1861. Born right over there in back of Hog Creek."

"Don't tell me," said Hollis, "she's related to you too."

"Goin' back some, but they don't like to talk of it, them Nor'fleets." Unseen to Mary, he winked at Hollis.

"That's not true," she said indignantly.

"We're Bonackers, you see, us Milnes—clam-diggers. We was poor as muck when we first come here to tend sheep for them Gardiners out on the island; three centuries on we still ain't got enough real estate to put in a flower pot. There's some things you can't change, I guess. What mule ever had another mule for a ma or a pa?"

"Excuse me?" said Hollis.

"You can't breed mules from mules," said Mary. "And you can stop bellyaching for one," she continued, turning back to Joe.

"Why not?" asked Hollis.

"What?" asked Mary irritably.

"Why can't you breed mules from mules? I mean, where do they come from?"

"They're horses crossed with donkeys. They're sterile."

"Oh."

"I'm proud of my Bonacker blood," said Mary to Joe, defensively.

"I know you is. And *you* know most in these parts ain't of your mind."

It was the low point of the evening, watching Mary brought to heel, Joe retouching the rose-colored picture she had painted for Hollis over the course of the day. But he loved her all the more for the speed with which she recovered, abandoning her pout for lively banter designed to draw him into the conversation.

He was being presented to Joe—that much was clear—for the old man's scrutiny, his seal of approval. Normally, he would have kicked against such a test, but he rose to the challenge without effort, assisted by the bottle of whiskey that landed on the table with a welcome thump once the plates were cleared. And when it came to explaining how he'd come to join the East Hampton Town Police Department, he almost believed his own lies.

It was Mary who brought the evening to a close, attending to the dishes at the sink, prompting Joe to insist that she let them alone. Armed with a couple of extra blankets, they were banished to a large hut out back. It was a shed used for shucking scallops in season, Mary explained, and the mountain of empty shells heaped up outside gleamed white in the moonlight.

They used the blankets to enlarge the bed Joe had made up for her, and they undressed by the glow of a paraffin lamp that cast their shadows around the timber walls.

"Lie back," said Mary reaching into her knapsack. She removed a pot of Pond's cream and scooped some onto her fingertips.

Hollis closed his eyes, anticipating some delicious prelude to a sexual romp. The cream was cool against his chest, his neck, his face, his arms. It was all becoming a little too matter-of-fact, her attentions drifting away from the center of his body towards the extremities.

He opened an eye.

"For the mosquitoes," said Mary. "They can be pretty fierce around here."

She wasn't joking.

23

"ARE YOU SURE YOU HEARD HIM RIGHT?"

"For God's sake, Richard, of course I'm sure."

"Tell me again exactly what he said."

Manfred drew hard on his cigarette and exhaled. "He said he knew about Lizzie Jencks. And he said it wasn't all he knew." His head snapped around towards Wakeley. "I'm not imagining it. He was at me all day, nothing obvious, small things, niggling. He knows. Believe me."

Wakeley considered his words for a moment. "It's not impossible."

Manfred laughed—a short, incredulous expulsion of air. "No, I'll say it isn't!"

"But how does he know? And what exactly? Was he there when it happened?"

Three unanswered questions strung together, and yet Manfred found them strangely reassuring. Richard was already displaying more clarity of thought than he had been able to muster all evening.

Dinner had been a living hell, spinning in the void of his own head while trying to do the right thing by their house guests. Richard had only returned from visiting friends as cocktails were being served, and there had been no opportunity to share the burden with him until now. But standing there on the bluff at the end of the garden, over-looking the ocean, the others safely in bed, he felt better already. Not exactly restored, but beginning to believe it might just be possible to shore up the crumbling edifice of his life.

Richard could have that effect on you. Even in the most adverse circumstances he remained reassuringly calm, utterly insightful. It was the reason he had been hired in the first place, the reason they still paid him so handsomely almost twenty years on. They had made him rich, rich enough not to be tempted by the rival offers of employ he must surely have received over the years. And he had earned every penny of his small fortune, isolating and ironing out problems on their behalf.

When the unions had threatened production at the Cuban sugar plantation, Richard had advised against the strong-arm tactics em-ployed by the other operators, opting to fly to Havana himself. He did nothing for the first week other than inform himself about the enemy—the personalities, the politics, and, most important, the rival-ries, both within and between the two labor organizations in question.

And then he had destroyed them from the inside. Not completely—that would have proved self-defeating in the long term—but just enough to undermine the workers' confidence in their representa-tives. He fueled tensions, ambitions, turning stewards against bosses, splitting committees, oiling the wheels of discord with cash "dona-tions," which he then ensured were brought to the attention of the workers.

Concessions were made; they had to be. Men were given two days paid holiday on the birth of a child. A nursery was provided free of charge, in the knowledge that few would expose their children to the coarse language of the cane-cutters' buses. A literacy program was in-troduced, not that anyone in their right mind would want to spend their precious lunch break in a classroom. The cost of these measures was carefully calculated to fall well short of the losses the company had been facing. Moreover, the initiatives created a false impression of

high-minded munificence: the caring face of capitalism. It had been a
Machiavellian masterstroke on Richard's part.

And when the girl had stepped in front of the car on that dark,
lonely lane, Richard was the person he had turned to—Richard, who
always knew what to do, who never disappointed.

Whatever his counsel had been that night, Manfred would have
followed it unswervingly. As it was, he found himself driving the
length of Long Island in the early hours of the morning, a traumatized
Lillian sitting beside him. Their destination was a run-down gas station
on the outskirts of Jamaica Bay. Two men were waiting for them near
the pumps. One wordlessly got behind the wheel of the damaged
Chrysler and disappeared into the night. The second drove them to a
taxi rank on Broadway. He was under instructions, he explained, not
to take them home. It was better that he knew nothing about them:
better for them, better for him.

The cover story was in its infancy, but already hatched and finding
its place in the world. It would undergo certain refinements once
Richard had thought it through from every possible angle, but the
skeleton was there from the first. The version of events he told them
to think about and add texture to was this: Manfred had gone to the
dinner dance at the Devon Yacht Club with Lillian and Gayle around
seven-thirty. At nine they were telephoned at the club by Justin, who
had only just arrived at his house, having been obliged to stay late in
the city. They told him the evening was proving to be something of a
dud, and it was decided that they leave and join him at his place. Gayle
stayed on at the club.

Up until this point in the story, the presence of witnesses demanded that truth and fiction run the same course. They now parted
company and Richard's imagination came into play.

If asked, Manfred and Lillian were to say that they'd been at Justin's
for no more than half an hour when an argument broke out between
the two men. Upset with her fiancé's behavior, Lillian left with Man-

fred when he stormed out. Manfred was still fuming when they arrived back at their house on Further Lane, where he announced he was returning to the city. Lillian offered to accompany him back. They packed their bags and left well before midnight, something Richard would attest to if called on to do so. A few hours later, as they were entering the outskirts of New York, Manfred's car broke down. Forced to abandon it, they thumbed a lift with a stranger to a taxi rank on Broadway and a cabbie drove them the final leg to Lillian's apartment.

It was a good story, which had stood the test of their remorseless scrutiny, a remarkable achievement by Richard given that he had fabricated it in a little under ten minutes. He was assisted by a few pieces of good fortune, the chief one being that Justin was the only member of his family staying at the house that weekend, so no one saw the three of them leave the place at one o'clock in the morning, drunk and in two cars.

They hadn't set out to race, but maybe it was inevitable. Justin had spent a good part of the evening making fun of Manfred's new Chrysler, a Town and Country Convertible. The mahogany doors and trunk lid, trimmed with white ash, made it look like a mobile sideboard, he said; and while he was sure it would draw admiring glances from every carpenter between Park Avenue and Montauk Point, it really wasn't a fit vehicle for a man of taste to be seen driving around in. He conceded that the car had its advantages. Should Manfred ever break down in the wilderness, he would always have a ready supply of kindling to hand for a warming campfire.

He kept returning to the subject, laughing more raucously each time he did so. Manfred took the joshing in good grace, although he didn't appreciate Lillian's disloyalty, chortling at his expense. It was maybe out of guilt that she chose to ride with him when they decided to head over to their house on Further Lane.

Justin led the way in his Packard, heading south down Old Stone Highway, the narrow road weaving its way through the oak woods. As they rounded a bend, a short straight presented itself to them. Lillian, with her uncanny sense for reading his mind, said, "Go on. If you must."

Manfred floored the throttle, and the Chrysler swept effortlessly past the Packard. Justin was better acquainted with the road, but Manfred knew it well enough to head him off each time he came back at them and tried to pass. The turning onto Albert's Landing Road whistled by on their left—a flicker in the headlights, a vertical break in the trees.

A little farther on, Manfred slowed for a sharp left-hand bend. The Packard closed, Justin anticipating the straight that lay beyond, but at the last second Manfred swung the wheel, turning into Town Lane. It was a hard right-hander that seemed to go on and on, the road almost doubling back on itself, the tires screeching in protest, Lillian doing a good job of mimicking them. Manfred couldn't afford to take his eyes off the road, but he didn't need to, he could see the headlights of the Packard sweeping over them, still in pursuit.

Justin had taken the bait. It was a mistake. If he'd kept on going he might well have beaten them back to Further Lane and justifiably claimed victory. As it was, they would pull away on the long straight that was Town Lane, ground that Justin would never be able to make up.

The Chrysler didn't disappoint. As soon as they were clear of the woods shrouding Quail Hill, the headlights revealed a road as straight as a city avenue, and the car came into its own, powering away from its pursuer through open countryside. Manfred permitted himself a satisfied chuckle.

"That was damn stupid!" snapped Lillian above the rush of wind.

"Don't worry, it's over now."

But his foot remained pressed to the floor. The needle nudged eighty miles per hour. He glanced over his shoulder to see the Packard falling behind, its headlights barely penetrating the clouds of dust thrown up in their wake.

"Manfred!"

The idea that time slowed down in such situations Manfred now knew to be a myth. It didn't. If anything, it speeded up, compressing moments into an instant: his head snapping back to the road, the ghostly figure frozen in the headlights and the sickening thud of the impact.

The body was hurled heavenwards, clipping the top corner of the windshield as it span off into the darkness at the side of the road. Manfred could remember turning instinctively and thinking that nothing could possibly spin so quickly in the air, certainly not a body, whirring like the blades of a fan.

He hit the brakes and the car slewed dangerously before coming to a halt. Justin overshot them by a good hundred yards.

"Oh my God," gasped Lillian.

"I didn't see him."

"It was a girl."

The figure had made no attempt to move, but had just stood there, facing the oncoming car.

"She stepped into the road," gasped Lillian, "just stepped into the road . . . Oh my God."

Manfred was aware of a sound filling his head, building in volume. It was the scream of the Packard's reverse gear. Justin drew alongside.

"Wait here," he said.

He swung the Packard around, the headlights cutting through the night, settling on something in the hedgerow, surprisingly close. Despite appearances, the impact had propelled the body some considerable distance back down the road.

"Don't look," said Manfred as Lillian made to turn.

Justin was out of the car now, approaching on foot. There was no need to get too close. The angle of the limbs placed the matter beyond any doubt.

Justin hurried over. "Manfred, look at me. I said look at me. You have to follow me. Can you do that?"

His hands were trembling, but he appeared to have control of them. "Yes," he said.

Lillian only spoke once on the seemingly endless drive through the back roads to their house on Further Lane.

"What are we going to do?" she asked.

"Richard will know."

Richard was asleep, flat on his back in his bed, arms by his side, like a body lying in state. Manfred was a little surprised to find him wearing a hairnet, but any embarrassment Richard might have felt was soon forgotten as Manfred described the events of the past fifteen minutes. When he was done, the questions began, rapid-fire: Did anyone at the yacht club know where you were going? Yes. Was there anyone else at Justin's house? No. Was the girl killed? Yes. Did you take her pulse? No. How's Lillian taking it? How do you think? Is Gayle back yet? No, I don't think so.

Richard thought for a moment then said, "Move the car into the garage then pour yourself a large whiskey. I need a little time to think."

A little time proved to be less than ten minutes, during which he made a call from his room, judging from the small ping given off by the phone in the drawing room. When he came downstairs, he had swapped his silk pajamas for slacks and an open-necked shirt, crisp and clean as always.

Justin was seated beside Lillian on the sofa, his arm around her, comforting her. Richard deposited himself in a chair and waited for her to compose herself.

"You said to Manfred that she stepped into the path of the car."

"Yes," said Lillian.

"Deliberately."

"I don't know. That's how it seemed."

Richard turned to Manfred. "You've been drinking, I assume."

"Yes."

"If you'd been sober, would it have made any difference?"

"I don't know. I don't think so."

"Lillian?"

"No. It all happened too quickly."

Manfred suddenly saw it, Richard's strategy. He was playing to Lillian, the weak link in the chain, steering responsibility away from them and onto the girl, planting the belief that their only error lay in being in the wrong place at the wrong time.

"This will destroy you, you know that, Manfred, don't you?"

The words were meant for Lillian's ears and Manfred dutifully took his cue from them.

"There was nothing I could do."

"That's clear."

"They were racing," said Lillian.

"And who was the one who told me to overtake in the first place?" retorted Manfred.

"I'm not sure you should be looking to blame each other," said Richard.

"If we're doing that," interjected Justin, "then I'm at fault, for making fun of your car in the first place."

"We're all to blame," said Lillian. "A girl is dead!"

"Maybe that's exactly what she intended," said Wakeley.

"We don't know that."

"Lillian, listen to me." Richard's tone was calm, measured. "You see a car hurtling towards you at night on a country lane, what do you do? You hug the hedgerow; you do not step out in front of it just when it draws level with you. Think about it. From where I'm sitting, I'd say you're lucky to be here at all. She might have killed you both."

It was clear from Lillian's expression that he'd convinced her, for now at least.

"Here's what's going to happen," said Richard. "And it's going to have to happen fast."

The mastery of the plan swiftly hatched in his bedroom only became clear at a later date; for now they just did as they were told. Justin was instructed to return home by a roundabout route. While Manfred and Lillian hurriedly packed their bags, Richard took himself off to the garage, where he examined the damage to the Chrysler and cleaned off the gore as best he could. Fortunately, the nearside headlight was intact, reducing the risk of being pulled over by the state troopers on the long drive back to the city.

The main danger now was that Gayle would return, catch them in the act, and have to be won over. Fortunately, as they later discovered, she had chosen to go home with the handsome but dull copyright lawyer who'd been making a play for her at the dinner dance.

As instructed, they kept to the back roads until clear of Southampton. Soon after, they telephoned Richard at the house. He gave them the address of the gas station in Jamaica Bay, where they were met by the two men.

Manfred waited a couple of days before informing the garage that housed and serviced the Chrysler that it had broken down on the outskirts of the city, by which time he had received details of where it could be found. The Chrysler was duly towed back into the city, its bodywork as new, but with a clogged carburetor.

As long as they all stuck to the story, there was no reason it shouldn't hold up. No one could attest to Manfred and Lillian's presence in East Hampton during the critical, incriminating early hours of Sunday morning; and the temporary absence of the Chrysler could now be convincingly accounted for.

That was pretty much the last they heard of the matter. A few weeks later, Justin was visited by a local cop following up on the case, working his way through the guest list for the Devon Yacht Club dinner dance. Justin confirmed that Manfred and Lillian had visited him a little after nine on the Saturday night in question, returning to their house on Further Lane less than an hour later—well before the time of the girl's death.

And that had been that; at least until Lillian had started behaving strangely. Now the ghost of Lizzie Jencks was back to haunt him in yet another guise—that of a local fisherman—only this time it just didn't make any goddamn sense.

"IT DOESN'T MAKE ANY GODDAMN SENSE," said Manfred, lighting another cigarette off the first, not wanting to mess around with matches in the stiff breeze coming off the ocean and rustling the leaves above their heads.

"It makes sense, we just can't see it yet." Richard paused, thoughtful. "How does he know? Either you told him, I told him, or Justin did." He paused. "Or he heard it from Lillian."

"What are you saying?"

"I'm saying he wasn't there when it happened; otherwise why wait till now to say something?"

Richard paced back and forth for a while, as he often did when working through problems.

"Yes. Why wait till now? That's the key. Because he's only just found out. But how?"

"All I'm hearing is more questions."

Richard ignored him, pacing, pacing, head bowed. He stopped abruptly and looked up.

"You know, I doubt he really knew for sure, just enough to bluff it out of you."

"I didn't admit to anything. I didn't *say* anything."

Not true. He had messed up with that line about hurling accusations around.

Richard must have read the lie in his eyes. "It doesn't matter," he said. "He would have known from your look when he sprang her name on you."

Manfred stared at the ocean. "Christ, what have we done, Richard?"

"No more than we had to. It'll be all right."

"I'll pay you whatever it takes."

A cloud of disappointment passed across Richard's face. "It's not about the money, Manfred. It never has been."

Richard looked away suddenly, as if embarrassed by his words.

"I need time to think this through," he said, "find out more about this Conrad Labarde."

"He's a veteran, I can tell you that."

"How do you know?"

"He's got a regimental tattoo on his arm, some kind of arrowhead, a red arrowhead."

"Are you sure? A red arrowhead?"

"Yes I'm sure. Why?"

"It's nothing," said Richard, not wholly convincingly.

24

Conrad knew something was wrong when Rollo failed to show for work first thing Monday morning. He was never late. If anything, he was early. Conrad would often wake to find him sitting on the deck, waiting patiently, whittling a piece of driftwood or just staring into the distance.

Maybe he was ill. Unlikely. Conrad couldn't remember the last time he'd been sick.

The answer arrived as he was finishing his breakfast. Two trucks pulled up beside the house. Four men got out. And Conrad knew immediately that he was in for a hard time.

He nodded at Rollo's father. "Ned."

"Conrad."

The other men cast their eyes around the buildings. None of them had visited before now; they'd never had reason to. Cap'n Jake Van Duyn showed particular interest in the barn, which was hardly surprising, seeing as his brother had sold it to Conrad a little over a year before.

"Looks okay," he said.

He was a kindly man, blunt-spoken and fiercely proud of his Dutch origins. When he was in liquor, he still railed against the politicians back home who had sold his ancestors down the Hudson River, trading New Amsterdam to the English for a handful of spice islands in the East Indies.

"You know Jacob, Francis, Edwin," said Ned.

"Sure." Though not well enough to call them by their Christian names. The familiarity of the introductions had an ominous ring to it.

"You want some coffee?"

"We'll not stay long," said Ned.

"Coffee would be good," said Cap'n Jake.

"Why not?"

"Sure."

Ned wasn't happy about being overruled, but he didn't protest.

CONRAD FELT CURIOUSLY DETACHED serving coffee to the headmen of the oldest Amagansett clans. The Kemps, Paines, Songhursts, and Van Duyns were known as the First Four. It was their forebears who had settled the village, dividing up the land among themselves, land that would prove to be the mainstay of their families' enduring wealth and influence.

If the Gardiners—with their island out in the bay, a manor held by royal grant since the earliest days of settlement—represented the aristocracy, then the men sitting around Conrad's table were the gentry of Amagansett. Other families had come and gone over the centuries, some even challenging their ascendancy, but they had ridden out the years ahead of the herd.

There was nothing overt about the hold they exercised over the village. Like the wind that turned the blades of the artesian wells and twisted the weathervanes, you couldn't actually see it, but you knew it was there. It percolated the village, touching councils, committees, the school board, even the Ladies' Society of Busy Workers.

And like the wind, if it turned on you, if it really turned on you, there was nowhere it couldn't reach.

"You have any idea why we're here?" asked Ned.

"Sure he does."

Conrad looked Frank Paine hard in the eye. He was known for chewing cloves to hide the smell of alcohol on his breath. He was doing it now.

"The girl who drowned," said Ned. "Rollo's got it stuck in his head it don't add up."

"Yeah?"

"That's what he says. Says she couldn't have drowned where they say she did and ended up off the beach here. Says the set was too strong, she'd have been carried a ways down."

"The ocean can do strange things," said Conrad. "Remember Elsie Bangs."

Elsie Bangs was a neighbor of Sam Ockham's down at Lazy Point who'd gone clamming at the mouth of Napeague Harbor one evening a few years before the war. Her family went hungry that night. It was assumed that she'd lost her footing near the edge of the deep channel and gone under. She certainly drowned. Two weeks later her badly decomposed body was washed ashore at Dead Man's Hole on the back side. She was identified by a stocking garter stitched for her in school by her daughter.

Once people had overcome their surprise at the idea of Elsie wearing stockings to go clamming, they began remarking on the extraordinary journey her body had taken. Against the prevailing currents, she had traveled east, past the Montauk fishing village at Fort Pond Bay, rounding Montauk Point and bearing west along the ocean shore, hugging the bluffs, before being cast up at Dead Man's Hole, a distance of some fifteen nautical miles from where she'd disappeared.

"It ain't often the ocean plays tricks like that," said Edwin Songhurst, old but not yet stooped, still husky and rawboned.

"Take your brother," added Ned. "He showed up right where we said he would."

Not exactly true. One small part of Antton—an arm, one shoulder, and his head, all still attached to each other, but barely—had been washed ashore a little to the east of the area they'd been searching in.

"Why'd you go at Charlie Walsh over them earrings off the girl?" asked Frank Paine.

Conrad turned to him. "What would you have done? Pocket them yourself?"

"Let's keep this civil," said Ned. "We know you knew her, Conrad. Rollo saw you two together."

Conrad tried to think straight, but failed, his thoughts collapsing in on themselves.

"When?" he asked.

"It don't matter when?"

"He's no cause to lie."

"And nor do you."

It can't have been rehearsed, but it worked—a gentle yet firm assault on all fronts, each chipping in their bit, having their say.

"Yeah, I knew her."

It explained a lot, Rollo knowing. It explained his reaction when they'd pulled Lillian from the ocean—silent, shrinking, living Conrad's horror. It explained his blind fury when he came to Conrad's aid in the parking lot at Oyster Hall, and his attentiveness in the following days. It explained a lot he should have picked up on before, but hadn't, and he wondered what else he'd missed.

The current, for one. If Conrad knew her body should have been carried farther eastward by the longshore drift, then Rollo certainly did. He could read the waters off the back side better than anyone.

"Where's Rollo?" he asked.

"He's okay," said Ned. "A little upset is all."

"How's that?"

"I had to work it out of him. He's been acting odd for a bit now; was worse than ever Saturday after you two went tuna fishing."

"Yeah?"

"He thinks you've got a problem with the girl's brother."

"Her name's Lillian."

"Do you?" demanded Cap'n Jake.

Conrad felt a sudden urge to unburden himself, but as he looked into their eyes he saw what he already knew: that they hadn't come here for him, they'd come here for themselves.

"Yes, I knew Lillian Wallace," he said. "As for the rest, I couldn't say, you'll have to take it up with Rollo."

"What passed between you and this . . . Lillian is your business," said Cap'n Jake. "Anything else is ours too."

Conrad got to his feet. "Are we done here?"

"Not if that's your attitude," said Frank Paine.

Conrad fastened his eyes on him. "You don't understand. I'm asking you to leave."

Glances were exchanged, but what could they do? A man was entitled to call the shots in his own home.

Conrad made a point of holding the door open for them. Ned lingered while the others headed to the trucks.

"I done some asking," he said. "They're rich folk them Wallaces, powerful folk, with pull. You think we don't already have us enough problems with that bill comin' up in Albany?"

"This isn't about fishing."

"You're a fisherman. You do anything rash, we all look bad. You know that."

In the last year there'd been a marked rise in hostilities between the local fishermen and the recreational anglers, who had taken to dumping scrap iron in the favored dragging spots so the nets got hung up and torn. Gear left on the beach overnight would be sabotaged. Any kind of retaliation had the sports racing for the State Assembly in Albany, like the school bully running to teacher with a bloody nose. Just the month before, Seth Tuttle had taken a knife to the tires of a surf-caster's sedan. The lawyers pushing for the bass bill were all over it still.

"They'll bend it any way they like if you give 'em the excuse," said Ned.

"They don't need an excuse. One thing I've learned: money takes what it wants then comes back for more."

"We'll beat them."

"This year, maybe. Next too. But they'll keep coming back, they'll win in the end, they always do."

Ned glanced over at the others waiting in the trucks.

"I'm sorry for the girl," he said, looking back. "I am. But if anything happens to Rollo, you'll have me to answer to." He paused. "You put a mark on my word, you hear me?"

Conrad nodded.

"He won't be pitchin' up for work no more. If he shows, you turn him away."

THE MOMENT THE TRUCKS LEFT, Conrad felt the strength drain out of him through his boots. He set about tidying away the cups, but found himself reaching for a chair and slumping into it.

Rollo was the closest thing he had to kin. He was alone—the way it had to be, he knew that—but he hadn't seen it hitting so hard. At least it had come from Ned, at least he'd been spared the task of driving Rollo off. His plan had been to lie, fall back on the ribs as an excuse, to suggest they take a break for a week or so while he fully recovered, by which time it should all be over.

He had played the scene with Rollo in his head, but he hadn't thought about how it might hit him. There was no solace in the seclusion, just one scrap of comfort: Rollo was safe now; he couldn't be damaged by the misfortune that seemed intent on dogging Conrad, circling him, sparing him while picking off those around him, almost in mockery.

He had never discussed it with anyone, fearing that his words would only breathe more life into the specter. It was the men of his company in Italy who had first forced the issue into the open.

He wasn't the only one to survive the grueling assault on Monte la Difensa—their first bitter taste of combat in Italy—but few who had been in the thick of the fight had emerged completely unscathed. Twice he'd been lifted clear off his feet by the vacuum of a shell from an enemy 88 snapping past his head. He had cowered like all the others as lead from the MG-42s tore into the icy rock around them, but not once had he been so much as nicked by one of the lethal shards of flying granite. He had seen the aluminum fin of an enemy shell embed itself in the forehead of a man crouching beside him in a German slit trench they'd only just occupied; and against all apparent logic he'd witnessed a good friend disappear in a plume of scarlet vapor when the fellow was standing farther from the mortar burst than himself.

At night, the time when they did most of their work, it was as if an invisible hand was swatting away the tracer bullets arcing through the darkness towards him, like shooting stars fallen to earth. One time, returning from a raid, he had been bounding over the rocks back to his lines when he collided with an enemy soldier coming in the opposite direction. Thrown to the ground, they both spilled their weapons in the darkness. The German was first to react, snatching up the nearest gun, which happened to be Conrad's M-1, beating him to the draw. The M-1 jammed. The German's Schmeisser didn't.

"You're one lucky son of a bitch," Dexter had remarked one night during a welcome lull between barrages. By now they had secured the summit, repelling numerous German counterattacks, and were preparing for an assault on the saddle below so the British could have a crack at the peak of Monte Camino. It was a cold night, with a light sleet falling, and they were hunched beneath their ponchos, spread out in foxholes along the first line of defense.

"I want her number, Labarde," called Crane.

"Who's that?"

"Your fairy godmother."

"Me, I got a lucky rabbit's foot," came another voice.

"Not so l-l-l-ucky for the goddamn r-r-r-abbit."

The laughter built quickly along the line until they were all creased up—young men; boys, most of them—finding a vent for their confusion and fear.

Maybe the German forward observers heard them, maybe not, but the mortars started landing again. They really worked them over this time. When it was done, the joker in the night—the stocky lumberjack from Wyoming, with the stammer—had bought it from a direct hit.

Dexter hurried over to his foxhole to check on him. "He's like God."

"You mean *with* God," said someone.

"I mean God is everywhere."

Not long after, with their combat casualty rate nudging sixty percent, they were pulled out of the mountains and assigned to the thirty-two-mile-long stalemate that was the Anzio beachhead. Caught unawares by the amphibious landing deep behind their lines, the German army had soon retrenched and began throwing everything they had at the Allied forces, intent on driving them back into the sea. Penned in like cattle in a narrow corral, they were strafed and bombed from the air. Long-range 88-mm and 170-mm artillery shells rained down on them day and night, as did the flak from their own anti-aircraft guns, almost as deadly.

That first month, shell fragments accounted for almost all of their casualties. When a lone shell burst killed the three Canadians with whom Conrad was playing a game of horseshoes one dismal gray afternoon, the other men in the outfit began avoiding him.

No one ever voiced it straight to his face. They didn't need to; it was clear what they were thinking. In its apparent eagerness to spare Conrad, Death seized those around him instead. Even the young, poorly trained replacements shipped in to bolster their dwindling ranks knew of his reputation and kept their distance.

Only the Professor sought out his company, and only then in order to play chess. Driven below ground into the warren of trenches and dugouts by the constant aerial assaults, they relieved the torpor of static warfare by rigging radio sets from razor blades, using pilfered tank headsets to tune into Axis Sally's broadcasts. They made light of her taunts, while being strangely drawn to the sultry lilt of her voice. They speculated about her looks, settling on a pleasing confection of Jeanne Crain and Lana Turner—part girl-next-door, part smoldering temptress—and they described in salacious detail exactly what they would do if given a few hours alone with her in the suite of a top ho-tel. Above all, though, they tuned in to her because of the music. You might be huddled in a damp hole on the edge of the Pontine marshes, but thanks to Sally you could still listen to the very latest songs from back home.

Their standing as a commando force to be reckoned with had been secured by their successful assault on Monte La Difensa, where the U.S. 3rd Infantry, the 36th, and the British 56th had all tried and failed before them. They now raised that reputation further on both sides of the front line with their deep-penetration night raids out over the Mussolini Canal, stepping gingerly through the minefields, employing a little psychological warfare of their own, leaving calling cards on the foreheads of their unsuspecting victims emblazoned with the message *Das dicke Ende kommt noch!*—The worst is yet to come.

They came and went like ghosts in the night, using their guns only as a last resort, their weapon of choice being the combat knife. A fear soon took a grip of the enemy troops ranged directly across from them on the eastern flank of the beachhead. They learned from German prisoners that they were known as the "Black Devils" or "the Devils in Baggy Pants," because of their loose, billowing mountain fatigues.

They didn't take as many prisoners as they might have, but then the nature of the lightning raids didn't allow for it. Likewise, any of their number captured while on patrol was more likely to end up on the Killed In Action roster than on a truck bound for a German stalag. The first infringement of the Geneva Convention that Conrad witnessed was committed by a man in his own unit—a part-Indian fur trapper from Vermont. It had proved impossible to sustain his levels of disgust, though, for within a week he too had joined the club. You told yourself that that was war, and maybe some even believed it. Others suspected and feared that the reasons lay closer to home, in some darkened corner of themselves.

It was a dirty conflict, a war of attrition, and by the time the order came through for the breakout from the beachhead, many of those whom Conrad had originally trained with in the mountains of Montana were dead, maimed, or otherwise unfit for line duty. Exhaustion and disease had claimed a fair number, mental imbalance more than you could ever have predicted.

One night, after a particularly severe pounding by the German 88s, Reg Horley had stripped off, hurled himself into the Mussolini Canal, and started swimming in circles, kicking beneath the surface every so often. When he was finally dragged from the water, he explained, between racking sobs, that he was looking for his father's wristwatch. It was a mildly amusing incident, but they knew they were in trouble when the medics started losing it.

The Professor was one of the few beacons of sanity in the madness unfolding around them. Some warned him about his association with Conrad, but the Professor seemed content with their games of chess and their nocturnal forays to recover the bodies of fallen GIs. They rarely touched on the subject of their other lives, placed on hold on the far side of the world. The one time they had done so, it hadn't gone well.

"What do you hunt?" the Professor had asked while they were setting up the board one night.

"What do you mean?"

"Last night when you picked off that Jerry trying to outflank us. Swing-lead-squeeze," he said, demonstrating. "One shot, no waste. I figure you hunt, you know, back home."

"Black duck, quail, coot, some deer," said Conrad. "You?"

"Canada geese. We get a lot in southern Illinois, though we near wiped them out twenty years back, squeezed the season down to a month."

Conrad told the Professor about Sam and Billy Ockham—their little hunting trio—tramping through the frosty underbrush on winter mornings, crouching in duck blinds, rowing their sharpies out to Cartwright Shoals for some open-water coot shooting, and poaching wild turkey in the primeval forests of Gardiner's Island during the Depression.

A little while later, the Professor looked up from the board. "It's the first time I've seen you kill a man," he said.

"I guess."

"How does it feel?"

Conrad could have shrugged the question off, played on in silence, but he stepped through the door the Professor had opened, regretting it later. "I can't remember," he said. "How it feels."

"I couldn't do it."

"You might have to."

"Some things you know."

"Don't be so sure."

"It's not a criticism. Don't take it as a criticism. It isn't."

"So what are you doing here?" asked Conrad.

"Helping."

"Clearing up our mess?"

"Someone's got to. I don't have a problem with death."

"That's right, I forgot, we're all just vehicles for bacteria."

"Don't be like that. I couldn't do what you do, that's all I'm saying."

"But you bought yourself a ringside seat. Why is that?"

"Conrad . . ." said the Professor gently.

"Who do you think you are, Florence fuckin' Nightingale?"

"Conrad . . ."

"No, screw you!" He swept the pieces off the board onto the earth-packed floor.

"Girls, girls . . ." They turned to see Captain Roxburgh enter the dugout. "We just got our marching orders," he said.

HE DIDN'T SEE THE PROFESSOR FOR TWO DAYS. Conrad's unit was one of those chosen to spearhead the drive out of the beachhead, and they left at dawn the next morning. It was a warm May day, a day of slaughter and confusion. You couldn't challenge the brass, but the decision to advance across open ground devoid of any cover in broad daylight displayed all the tactical wisdom of a general on the first day of the Battle of the Somme.

When they weren't being devastated by German machine-gun fire and artillery airbursts, they fell prey to friendly fire from the rear. The promised tank support evaporated, with many of the Shermans throwing their tracks when they ran over antipersonnel mines, the ones that didn't proving no match for the German Tigers with their superior firepower. It was a miracle that any of them managed to reach Highway 6 and the railway tracks by nightfall.

Fierce fighting on day two depleted their numbers further, but they continued their thrust towards the Alban hills, advancing well beyond the flanking units, arriving at the ancient village of Cori, perched high above the plain, as the afternoon heat was easing off. In stark contrast to the stiff German resistance, they were welcomed by hordes of cheering Italians. Many of the men were mistrustful of a people who had switched allegiance halfway through a war, but Conrad couldn't really care. He remembered something the Professor had once said: "The thing about the Italians is, they've seen civilizations rise and fall and they know it's all a lot of crap."

They rested up in the shade of the Roman temple beside the church, and Conrad wondered how many other soldiers had done exactly the same over the centuries.

Towards dusk, he was refilling his canteen from a nearby well when he heard a voice from behind him.

"Make mine a double."

It wasn't that the Professor looked tired—they'd been functioning at a level of terminal exhaustion for so long now that you no longer noticed it in others or yourself—but he looked depleted, as if some incubus had drained him of vital fluids. The ever-present chuckle behind his green eyes was gone, and his bloodied fatigues seemed to hang off him.

"Here," said Conrad, handing him the canteen.

The Professor emptied it then caught his breath.

"I'm sorry," said Conrad.

"Me too."

That night they went out together again, just like old times, searching for the dead. A section from 3rd Regiment had been worked over by a mortar crew earlier in the day to the west of Cori, taking numerous casualties, abandoned in the field. It was assumed the Germans had retreated to the hills, but you couldn't be too sure. They were dogged fighters, to be respected, and both sides knew there was too much at stake. If the Allies were allowed to reach Highway 7, the tide of battle would turn. The Appian Way would lead them straight into the heart of Rome, the coveted prize.

The moon was near full, the limestone path bright beneath his feet as Conrad scouted the lower slopes of the hills. He sniffed the air for cigarette smoke and freshly turned earth, but there was nothing. If they were up there and dug in, they were well beyond range. He padded back to the Professor, who was lurking in an olive grove, and they struck out through the adjacent pasture, the tall grass swishing against their legs.

The first body was intact, or near enough. While Conrad stood guard, the Professor gathered up something and placed it beside the corpse. This was how he liked to work, circumstances permitting— assessing the overall damage, reconstructing, before beginning the process of removal. Ten minutes later, he was ready. He unfolded a tarpaulin, laying it on the ground, and rolled the first body onto it.

The blast from the explosion knocked Conrad sideways, sending him sprawling into the grass. The screams began before the last of the debris had fallen to earth.

"Oh Christ! Oh Christ . . ."

Conrad stayed low as he scrabbled towards the Professor, the next mortar due any moment. Due now. Where was it?

"Oh Christ!"

The blast had taken the Professor's left leg off below the knee. His right foot was also missing, and he was staring at the void where his left hand had been, holding the ragged stump up to the moon for a better view.

"Shit," he said. "Shit . . ."

Conrad pushed him back down onto the ground and pumped two shots of morphine into him.

"Conrad."

"It's me, I'm here." He used his knife to cut a length of the parachute cord he always carried with him.

"They rigged it, they rigged the body, the sonsofbitches rigged the body."

Conrad fashioned a hasty tourniquet and secured it above the left knee.

"You sonsofbitches!" screamed the Professor. "YOU SONSOF-BITCHES!"

Conrad wanted to say "Keep quiet, don't give them the satisfaction," and he prayed the Germans were long gone.

The Professor struggled, resisting, as Conrad tried to apply a tourniquet to his other leg.

"Lie still, goddamnit."

"Don't do it, don't do it."

The Professor twisted, rolling away. Conrad went after him, straddling his chest, pinning him to the ground.

"I don't want to live. Not like this."

He was sobbing now, slapping at Conrad with his only hand, snatching at the loop of rope.

"Okay," said Conrad, holding up his hands in surrender.

The Professor stopped resisting. "Thanks, thanks . . ." he gasped.

Conrad slugged him on the jaw, fitted the tourniquets and applied sulfa to the stumps.

He was doing double time along a dirt track about a mile from Cori when the Professor came to, slung over his shoulder like a sack of fish meal. Conrad closed his ears to the curses. The pummeling of the fist on his back was too weak to have any effect. They said there were no atheists in trenches, but not once did the Professor call out to God, remaining an unbeliever till the end, which came a few minutes later, half a mile shy of the aid station. Not that they could have done anything for him. Way too much of his blood had already soaked into Conrad's fatigues.

He laid the Professor in the grass beside the track and sat with him awhile. Then he carried him the rest of the way in his arms.

The two medics on duty at the aid station were enjoying a well-earned rest, but they insisted on checking Conrad over for injuries. He could have told them that beneath all the gore he would be completely unmarked. When they were done, they set him up with a shot of brandy and stretchered the body away.

He was gone before they returned, pounding off down the track, back towards the hills.

It was reckless soldiering, but stealth wasn't the answer. He could have crept through the wooded slopes for the rest of the night and never found them. The answer lay in covering as much terrain as possible, crashing his way through the undergrowth, drawing attention to himself.

He was making his way up the side of a valley when a burst of fire raked the branches above his head. He hit the ground, scrabbling for cover behind a tree. Someone shouted in German—a challenge.

"*Schwarze Teufel!*" he called back: Black Devils. He heard the soldier relay the information to his comrades, a satisfying note of panic in his voice. Then the lead started flying again, tracers this time, which meant only one thing.

He was gone before the first mortar tore into the trees. If they were using the mortar they must be occupying an area of open ground beyond the tree line up near the ridge. He dismissed the idea of a direct assault, not because the terrain would play in their favor, but because he figured they'd soon be thinking about retreating. They knew who they were up against, they'd heard the stories, and the silence of the night would soon transmute into fear.

He was waiting for them near the foot of the neighboring valley—two mortar crews, six men, pounding down a woodland path, equipment clattering. Whether they were the ones responsible, he neither knew nor cared, his head thick with thoughts of vengeance.

He had already pulled the pins from the grenades, but he waited for the point man to pass before tossing them, opening fire before they exploded, ducking behind a tree as they did so.

The two who didn't die immediately, he finished off with the knife. One was very young, wispy hairs masquerading as a mustache, wheezing his last terrified breath as Conrad slowly slid the blade between his ribs, talking to him, cursing him, the same words the Professor had hurled at him, handing them on: take these with you.

When he was done, he smoked a cigarette then placed the barrel of the M-1 in his mouth, but he was unable to pull the trigger.

He returned to Cori via the pasture, recovering the Professor's shattered glasses from the long grass.

IT WAS A MIRACLE that the glasses had somehow stayed in his possession for the remainder of the war. He took it as a sign that they had, and he'd kept them on the writing desk in his bedroom ever since.

One evening, as Lillian was undressing, she had asked him, "What are these?"

She stood naked beside the bed—completely unabashed, as she had been from the very first—turning the glasses in her hands. "Nothing," said Conrad.

"Are they yours?"

"I don't want to talk about it."

She replaced the glasses on the desk, turned the light off, and joined him in the bed, snuggling up close.

"If I were you," she said softly, "and I didn't want to talk about it, I wouldn't have left them out."

He lay there in silence, hating her for seeing through him, loving her for exactly the same reason. She made no attempt to press him further, and that was probably why he began to speak.

He didn't start at the beginning and he didn't start at the end, he started in the middle and he leapt around, doubling back on himself. She asked very few questions. There was no need; the words tumbled out of him.

He told her about the Professor and his beaky nose and their games of chess and the gut-rot hooch they used to buy from the officer's mess—alcoholic footwash destined for the brass, but distilled through bread and flogged off to the rank and file by the batmen. He told her about the low, menacing profile of a Tiger tank, the silence of an 88 shell as the sound struggled to keep up with it, the spine-chilling shriek of the Nebelwerfer rockets, and he tried to describe the helpless terror of a sustained artillery barrage, bent double in a slit trench, the ground quaking, shaking your fillings loose.

He told her about the friends who had died, the ones who had cracked up and been shipped out, the ones who had been maimed. He described the horrors of the "far ward" at the field hospital, nurses holding cigarettes to the mouths of men who had lost their arms, others with whole parts of their faces missing, being fed ground liver squeezed through a tube.

He told her what he had done to the men who might or might not have been responsible for the Professor's death, and he described their triumphal entry into Rome a few days later. He detailed the baroque splendor of Castel Gandolfo, the pope's summer residence perched high above the shores of Lake Albano where they were sent to recuperate for a few weeks. Unreal afternoons spent lazing on the volcanic sand beaches of the lake, swimming in the aquamarine water, sipping crisp dry Frascati wine from the nearby hills and flirting with the local girls. Dreamlike memories they desperately clung to when their orders finally came through and they found themselves back in the thick of the action—in France this time, clearing Germans from a scattering of islands off the south coast, then fighting their way eastwards along the Riviera, securing the border with Italy, where the mountains collided with the sea and where Conrad's war came to an abrupt end.

He told her how it happened, though not why, because he wasn't sure of the answer himself, even then. All he knew was that war left you clinging to the raft of your own sanity, not because of the horror—that you grew used to—but because it tore at the heart of every man's being, his sense of who he was.

You could be brave one minute, a coward the next, selfless then cruel, compassionate and heartless within moments of each other. You spent a lifetime forging a view of what made you tick, what marked you out from other men, massaging yourself into being. Then war came along and ripped that construct limb from limb. It seized you by the neck, pressed your face to the mirror and showed you that you weren't one thing or another, but all things at the same time. The only question was: which bit of you would show itself next? That's what fucked you up. The not knowing.

He told Lillian all this. It was far more than he had ever told anyone, though that wasn't saying much. The only other person he had spoken to was the doctor at the hospital in England, and that had been under duress.

When he was finished, Lillian held him tight and kissed him on the neck, her cheek wet with tears, cold against his skin.

"It's okay now," she said.

And he had laughed, not in derision, not in amusement, but because she was absolutely right.

It was.

25

Wakeley waited till she was cleaning the bedrooms on the south side of the house before making his way outside to her car.

Returning to the study, he left the door ajar, and when she came downstairs he called to her.

"Rosa."

She deposited her mop, pail, and other cleaning items at the door and entered. "Mr. Wakeley."

"Would you make some coffee, please?"

"Of course, sir."

He didn't want coffee, but he hadn't quite finished reading the file, and he needed all the facts at his fingertips before springing it on her.

Rosa returned ten minutes later with a tray. He took a bite of a cookie while she poured the coffee from the pot. Unprompted, she stirred in half a teaspoon of sugar. She noted and remembered that sort of thing. It was the kind of attention to detail he demanded of himself and appreciated in others.

"Rosa."

"Yes, sir?"

"Why don't you tell me about Miss Lillian and the fisherman, Conrad Labarde."

"Excuse me?"

She was almost convincing.

"No doubt she swore you to secrecy, and I respect your loyalty, I do, but I need to know, Rosa."

"I'm sorry, sir, I don't know what you're saying."

He got to his feet, crossed to the door and closed it. "I don't have much time," he said, turning back, "so let me put it another way. If you don't tell me what I want to know, I'll have you arrested for stealing."

"What? I have never—"

He interrupted her, raising his hand. "Please, spare me the indignation, I know you haven't. But the police might see things differently when they find certain articles of Miss Lillian's hidden in your car."

She glared at him.

"You can deny it, of course, but who do you think will believe you, who do you think will hire you after such a scandal?" He paused. "Am I making myself clear?"

She nodded, making no attempt to mask the hatred in her face.

"Now, why don't you tell me everything you know about Miss Lillian and this Conrad Labarde."

MANFRED AND JUSTIN returned from the Maidstone Club around six o'clock. They were flush with victory, Justin having chipped in at the eighteenth to take the match for them, and they insisted on a bottle of Champagne by way of celebration.

"We'll have it by the pool, please," said Wakeley to Rosa.

The poor thing was in turmoil, but he'd made it clear to her that it wouldn't be in her best interests to do anything foolish, like resign her position. There was no reason for the Wallaces to suffer because of the bad feelings she now harbored towards him.

He was pleased to see she'd come around to his way of thinking over the course of the afternoon—in between the bouts of tears—her only protest being the brusque and silent manner in which she poured the drinks before leaving them.

"Is something the matter with Rosa?" asked Manfred.

"She's had better days," said Wakeley, and he told them what he'd learned from Rosa about Lillian.

"She was screwing a fisherman?!"

"And had been for a few months."

"Jesus Christ," mumbled Justin.

"How did they meet?" asked Manfred.

"By chance, I don't know, Rosa's not sure, and it's not important. This, on the other hand, is." Wakeley slid the file across the table. "It's his military record. I had it flown up from Washington. You were right about the tattoo—the red arrowhead."

Manfred turned to the first page. "First Special Service Force? I've never heard of them."

"Sounds like some kind of support unit," said Justin.

"That was the idea. Unfortunately, they were anything but that. It was a joint U.S.–Canadian commando outfit. They recruited outdoorsmen—hunters, trappers, loggers, quarrymen—men already accustomed to harsh weather, a hard life. Read it."

Manfred placed the file on the table and they perused it, side by side. After a couple of pages, Justin muttered, "Jesus Christ, how many silver stars does a man need?"

"There's also a Distinguished Service Cross in there."

"I think we get the picture," said Manfred.

"Only part of it. That was the bad news." Wakeley handed over the other file.

"And this is good?"

"It helps us, yes, quite a bit."

"Skip the dramatics, Richard," said Justin irritably. "Just tell us."

"He cracked up in southern France. Badly. He spent the last year of the war in a psychiatric hospital in England."

"That's the good news?" asked Justin. "We're not just dealing with a war hero, we're dealing with a deranged war hero?!"

"He's unreliable," said Manfred, catching on. "It discredits anything he says."

"Exactly," said Wakeley. "The question then becomes: what does he know? I think we can safely say he didn't witness the accident, so we have to assume he heard about it from Lillian."

"It's hearsay."

"Right. The word of a dead woman, relayed via her mentally unstable lover, against ours, the three of us. It would never stand up."

"But it might create a scandal," offered Manfred. "The sort of talk we'd never recover from."

"We'd gag him as soon as he went to the police with it. Which begs the question: why hasn't he, gone to the police, I mean?"

"Because he knows he doesn't have enough."

"And he'll never get it, as long as we all keep our heads."

Justin unwound his long legs from beneath the chair and leaned forward, pensive.

"Justin . . . ?" said Wakeley.

"Huh?"

"Is something bothering you?"

"It's probably nothing."

"Tell us anyway."

"The day of Lilly's funeral, just after she was buried, this policeman approached me. He asked a bunch of questions about her."

"What did he look like?"

"Small . . . nondescript," shrugged Justin.

"Deputy Chief Hollis."

"Yes, that was his name."

"What kind of questions?" asked Wakeley.

"I don't know . . . my relationship with her. He seemed to know we'd been engaged. I really can't remember, I was pretty upset at the time."

"Try and remember."

Wakeley could feel Manfred tensing beside him and he wished he was alone with Justin right now.

"He wanted to know how she was, the last time I saw her."

"What did you tell him?"

"Well not the truth," snorted Justin, "if that's what you're worried about."

He had told *them* the truth, by phone, within a few hours of that walk on the beach with her. He had described Lillian's worrying appeal to his conscience, the extent of her own crushing guilt, which seemed to have grown since her move out to East Hampton. He had told them, and they had told him not to worry, they would talk to her, make her see sense. But she hadn't, she had stood her ground.

"Why the hell didn't you say something about this before?!" snapped Manfred.

Justin was clearly taken aback by the vehemence of the question. "What . . . ?"

"Manfred . . ." said Wakeley, trying to silence him with a look.

"You should have told us before," insisted Manfred.

"He was just a policeman doing his job, asking questions," said Justin defensively. "Anyway, her death's got nothing to do with this."

And then the unthinkable dawned across his face.

"It doesn't, does it?"

"Of course not," said Wakeley, stepping in.

"Don't be ridiculous."

It was an admirable recovery on Manfred's part, just the right note of dismissive indignation.

"But we can't afford to take any chances. Everything has to go through Richard, we agreed that—everything."

DINNER WAS A MUTED AFFAIR. Justin declined the offer of a nightcap, and they accompanied him to his car. As he pulled away into the night Manfred turned to Wakeley.

"I'm sorry, Richard, I messed up."

"You're inclined to speak before you think. It's your one fault."

"He knows, doesn't he?"

"He can't afford to."

"That's not the same thing."

"Yes it is."

Manfred offered him a cigarette and lit it for him.

"The policeman, Hollis, he's no fool. He has shrewd eyes."

"Christ, it's unraveling, isn't it?"

"No it's not. These things are rarely perfect, it's all about evidence, a game of percentages. If Hollis had anything concrete we'd know it by now." He paused. "It's Labarde who concerns me. We haven't heard the last of him."

"You think?"

"They were close, Manfred."

"You said they only knew each other a few months."

"She was in love with him."

Manfred snorted.

"You don't want to believe it, I understand. But why would she lie to Rosa about something like that?"

"Rosa said that?"

Wakeley nodded.

Manfred shook his head in disbelief. "What did she think, that we'd welcome him into the fold?" He flicked his cigarette away in anger. "A fucking fisherman?!"

"Our opponent. And you never underestimate an opponent. We have to assume he's not going away."

"That's very comforting, Richard."

"It's no time for sarcasm."

"You know what bothers me? What bothers me is that we didn't know about him in the first place. Why is that, Richard? Why wasn't that in the fucking plan?"

"It was an oversight. It wasn't dealt with then, we're dealing with it now. We just have to stay calm."

Manfred laughed, amused by the notion. "Calm? You have any idea what's at stake here?"

"You know I do."

"Everything. I mean *everything*. And you're telling me to stay calm?"

"Don't forget," said Wakeley, "I wasn't the one driving the car that night."

Manfred's eyes locked onto him, but the anger went out of them. "I'm sorry," he said.

"This is what he wants, to rattle us. Try to think of it as a test. For the future. You'll learn from it, be stronger for it." He rested a comforting hand on Manfred's shoulder. "We'll get through this, you have my word."

"It's the waiting, I don't think I can stand the waiting."

"Who said anything about waiting? There are times when it's right to throw the first punch."

THEY WENT INDOORS and Wakeley spelled out his stratagem.

"It's a high-stakes game you're proposing," said Manfred.

"But the right one."

Manfred thought on it. "Okay," he said. "But I want your friend brought back in, just in case."

"He's not my friend," said Wakeley. "I don't even know who he is."

"But you know where to find him, right?"

Wakeley nodded.

26

HOLLIS HAD ALWAYS LOVED THE NIGHT SHIFT. EVEN AS A PATROLMAN HE'D never complained, often trading his days for others' nights. He preferred the stillness of the sleeping city, the company of the midnight folk—the tramps picking over the detritus of the day, hurrying to beat the street-sweepers and the garbagemen, heaping their treasures high upon creaky handcarts; the park bench philosophers and the outright crazies with their uncommon wisdoms; the cabbies gathered at the taxi ranks, smoking and joking, blue banter swathed in blue smoke.

Then there were the sounds, not smothered by the deafening white noise of the daylight hours—the distant peal of an ambulance, the snatches of music as customers rolled out of basement jazz clubs, the rumble of the early milk wagons. The night made you aware, it allowed you to pick up the trails of other people's lives.

A Monday night in East Hampton was a very different affair. It was as if word of an approaching plague had reached the community and everyone had left in haste, a few forgetting to extinguish their porch lights before fleeing.

Hollis set himself the challenge of finding any form of life. He was rewarded a few minutes later by the twin beacons of a cat casting a derisory glance in his direction as it loped across Dunemere Lane in front of the patrol car.

At the junction with Egypt Lane, the radio squawked into life. It was young Stringer—always so earnest—holding the fort back at headquarters.

"Calling Deputy Chief Hollis, calling Deputy Chief Hollis. Over."

"Calm down, Stringer, what is it?"

"An intruder, sir, I just got a call. They heard noises. Over."

"You want to tell me where?"

"Oh, yes . . . sixty-two Three Mile Harbor Road. Over."

"I'm on it."

"Do you want assistance? Over."

"I can handle it."

HE PARKED THE CAR some distance down from the house, approaching on foot. There were no lights burning, and he made his way around to the back door. It wasn't locked. He entered. A tap dripped in the kitchen sink. It was the only sound.

He stepped lightly across the wooden floor, creeping along the corridor, glancing into the living room. It was deserted. A loose board creaked beneath his feet as he climbed the stairs.

The door at the far end of the landing was ajar. He poked his head into the room before stealing inside.

Taking hold of the cotton sheet, he drew it slowly off the bed, inch by inch. She was lying facedown, one leg cocked.

His fingertips traced a lazy course from her ankle, up her calf, the back of her leg, gently delving into the warm fork of her thighs.

She stirred, moving her leg slightly to allow his fingers better access. He began unbuttoning his jacket with his free hand.

"No, don't take your uniform off," she said quietly.

———

HE WOKE LATE, his nose searching for the smell of brewing coffee. There was none. He was at home, and had been since four o'clock that morning. He glanced at his uniform discarded on the chair, smiled at the memory of the fleeting encounter with Mary, then swung his legs out of bed, moving with purpose.

He began by tossing the clothes Lydia had left behind into a pile in the middle of the room, hangers and all. Objects followed, the endless knickknacks she'd accumulated over the years—a family of clay mice with leather tails, a wire figure of a clown, a stuffed redheaded woodpecker clinging to a piece of bark—and worse, far worse. Out of guilt, she'd left him the lion's share of these, unaware that he'd only ever cooed over them out of politeness. They all ended up on the pile. He moved on, working his way through the other rooms, heaping up the litter of their marriage. He was ruthless in his selection. Anything that wasn't essential to his survival or comfort was tossed. He felt no bitterness, rather a lightness of head.

When he was done, he bundled the piles into his car and drove to the town dump. It occurred to him that much of what he was throwing out might be of interest to the ladies in charge of the rummage booth at the LVIS summer fair, but he dismissed the idea. He didn't relish the prospect of Mary hearing about the ceremonial purging; she might take it the wrong way.

What *was* the wrong way? Or the right way, for that matter? He wasn't sure. All he knew was that, for reasons he'd yet to fathom, she seemed very keen on him. It was all a little overwhelming, to say nothing of exhausting.

Was it normal to want to make love so frequently? He had assumed that the women who populated the pulp novels that used to make the rounds of the detective division were creatures of fiction, with their steamy glances and insatiable appetites.

The last few days had forced him to reconsider that position. Twice she had spurred him on in the scallop shack behind Joe's house, the mosquitoes feasting merrily on his back. Then, in the depths of the night, she had stirred him awake with her mouth, insisting that he just lie there this time, inert on his back, while she straddled him. She wasn't wholly to blame. In the morning, he'd been the instigator as they were dressing for breakfast.

Joe had prepared a small feast to set them up for the return journey, and when he shuffled off to church in his Sunday best, they too went on their way, following the boggy, twisting shoreline of Accabonac Harbor, emerging onto the shimmering sweep of Gardiner's Bay.

They headed south along the beach, beneath the bluffs, chatting idly as they strolled barefoot across the sand. It was a windless day, and they screwed up their eyes against the sun glancing off the mirrored surface of the bay. At first he resisted the sensation, wary and mistrustful, but he soon gave in to it, recognizing it for what it was: contentment, the simple yet complete pleasure of just being with Mary.

They cut inland, working their way up onto Stony Hill, just north of Amagansett. The narrow trail rose and fell, snaking through the dense woods. It was a rare glimpse of the ancient Appalachian forest that had once blanketed much of the East End, Mary explained. He knew he was meant to appreciate this virgin patch of untamed nature, but he didn't; it unsettled him, with its gloomy aspects, its rustlings of unseen creatures, and its chorus of amplified birdsong echoing off the canopy of leaves. He was relieved when they finally emerged once more into the sunlight, stepping out through the open pastures that lay to the west, and that led them eventually to the post-and-rail fence of Mary's home pasture.

They shared a bath then ate a late lunch, which left Hollis plenty of time to return home and get ready for his first of two night shifts. The next day, he had dropped by the LVIS offices on some false pretext to do with the summer fair. With five days to go till the big event, the place was in the grip of a barely contained panic, but Mary still found time to whisper what she intended to do to him the following evening.

She hadn't waited, summoning him to her house that same night with the call to police headquarters, and he had gone, unquestioningly. And now he was standing at the town dump, hurling away the last tangible remnants of his marriage, wondering what in the hell he was getting himself into: a divorced woman with a difficult son, a violent goose, and an unnatural attachment to a place he'd had every intention of leaving before the summer was out.

His confusion hadn't faded by the time he showed up for work at midday, but it was quickly replaced by another.

Tuesday was Milligan's day off, the day he set aside for fishing with his cronies, when they wouldn't have to do battle with the crush of weekend anglers for the best casting spots out at the Point. Yet there the chief was, sitting at his desk, going over some files. The squad room was deserted.

"You got a moment?" called Milligan, far too reasonably. Hollis entered the office.

"Take a seat."

"Not fishing today, Chief?"

"Doesn't look that way, does it?" He nodded at the chair, and Hollis sat himself down. "You've been asking questions about Lillian Wallace."

It was bad, worse than he thought.

"I spoke to the maid, yes." Did Milligan also know about his conversation with Justin Penrose?

"Rosa Cossedu," said Milligan, reading off a name from the notes in front of him.

"Yes. Routine stuff."

"Anyone else?"

Shit, thought Hollis, he knows.

"Her ex-fiancé. Julian . . . something."

"Penrose. And it's Justin."

"Right."

Milligan had bought it. If Hollis couldn't even recall the name, then that conversation must also have been routine.

"And the purpose of these discussions?"

"I was just trying to establish Miss Wallace's state of mind, eliminate the possibility of suicide."

"Maybe I'm wrong," said Milligan, "but hasn't the coroner's inquest already returned its verdict?"

"Yes."

"Accidental drowning."

"Like I say, sir, it was just routine."

"By the book."

"Right."

"Well sometimes you got to put that book of yours aside." Milligan was quite calm, his self-importance leaving no place for anger. "You missed something, Hollis. Labarde was seeing Lillian Wallace."

"Seeing . . . ?"

"Seeing. Screwing. The maid knew all along."

"I don't understand."

But he did, he just needed time to assimilate the news. It explained Rosa's nervousness when he'd pushed her on the matter of her mistress's bed, which hadn't been slept in. He had read her right, she'd been holding out on him, but this realization gave him little satisfaction, for he'd utterly failed to grasp the true nature of the Basque's involvement.

"What's there to understand?" asked Milligan.

What had he thought, that the big fisherman was playing at the

amateur sleuth, doing his bit for local law enforcement? Christ, had he
grown so blind in the last year?

"Hollis?"

"Is it relevant? I mean . . . to the question of her death?"

"It's relevant, Hollis, to the fact that Labarde has been harassing the
Wallaces. The girl's brother, Manfred, he was 'round here earlier raising a stink."

"Harassing?"

"Hartwell's bringing him in."

"Bringing him in?"

"What is it with the goddamn echo in here?" said Milligan. "Yes,
bringing him in. The Wallaces are worried. So would you be if you'd
read these."

He tossed a couple of files across the desk.

"They're Labarde's military records. The guy's a fucking fruitcake."

HOLLIS READ THE FILES IN THE PRIVACY OF HIS OFFICE. He felt bad, soiled.
No one had the right to peer into the depths of a man's soul uninvited.

The Basque clearly felt the same way. The reports by the English
psychiatrist were peppered with references to the patient's stubborn
resistance to discussion. The doctor's building frustration leapt off the
page. At least he seemed to care. There were several mentions in the
handwritten notes of the brother, Antton, and his death some years
before the war; but again, it was a line of discussion Labarde had refused to cooperate with.

Statements by fellow soldiers pointed to a marked deterioration in
his state of mind following the First Special Service Force's assignment
to southern France. There was a detailed account of an assault by the
2nd Regiment on a German position on the Île du Levant, wherever
that was. Ironically, in the light of what happened next, Labarde's

growing recklessness and disregard for his own life had only won him more accolades.

Labarde claimed to recall nothing of the incident near the Italian border that had ended his war and almost his life, but there were enough other testimonials to piece together the sequence of events. Labarde had been out scouting German positions in the mountains just back from the coast when some kind of firefight had erupted and he'd called in an artillery barrage. When the rest of his squad arrived on the scene, they found him badly wounded by shrapnel, barely alive. The Germans were all dead—from gunshot wounds. It was possible that other Germans had retreated before the barrage hit, but there was a chilling statement from a lieutenant that suggested otherwise. He had been watching from across the valley through his field glasses, and he described how he'd seen Labarde climb to the top of a large rock on the spur and just stand there in the open, facing the incoming shells. Everything pointed to Labarde killing the Germans then calling in the barrage right on top of himself.

Hollis closed the files and lit a cigarette. He had heard of men losing it in combat—shell shock, battle fatigue—catchphrases known to all. But this seemed different, more like a gradual heaping up of war, pressing down on a man, buckling him slowly. He reached for parallels in his own life, but there were none. What had he ever really seen that came close, what had he ever really done?

It was a sobering realization. He tamped out his cigarette and stared at the wall clock, the second hand ticking interminably by, hammering out the inescapable truth: he had lost the initiative, events had outrun him in the last few days while he'd been dallying around with Mary, at the mercy of his own lust like some overheated schoolboy.

Voices in the squad room brought him around. He entered as Chief Milligan was ushering the Basque into his office. Hollis caught the Basque's eye, but there was no sign of recognition.

"What's going on, Tom?" asked Bob Hartwell.

"I'll tell you later," he said, entering Milligan's office.

His earlier display of ignorance, stupidity even, had earned him the right to watch the great man at work.

MILLIGAN WENT IN HARD, way too hard. There was no teasing, no coaxing, no insinuation designed to unsettle; he just slapped it on the table like a side of meat.

"I'm not sure I know what you're saying," was the Basque's response.

"I'm not saying anything, I'm asking."

"You mean, why did I keep quiet about my involvement with Lillian Wallace?"

"What else do you think I mean?"

"Probably the same reason she didn't mention it to anyone."

"But she did—to the maid."

"They were very close," said the Basque.

Hollis was beginning to understand how the English psychiatrist must have felt.

"I'm waiting for your answer," said Milligan.

"I guess I think what happened between us wasn't anybody else's business but ours. I still don't. That's my answer. Will it do?"

"Don't you get smart with me, son. You're the subject of a formal complaint."

"By who?"

"Manfred Wallace."

"Oh," said the Basque indifferently. "You mind?" He pulled his tobacco pouch from the pocket of his pants. Milligan gestured impatiently that it was okay, then he launched into an account of a fishing trip the previous weekend. It was the first Hollis had heard of it.

"There was some tension, yes," said the Basque.

"He's accusing you of intimidation."

"He screwed up. He could have killed someone with a keg."

"A keg?"

"We were swordfishing," said the Basque, as if that explained everything, knowing full well that it didn't.

Milligan was floundering now, but he had a trump left to play. Holding it back was the only thing he'd done right.

"That's all fine, Mr. Labarde, except for the small matter of your war record."

The Basque visibly stiffened. Milligan allowed the silence to linger.

"If you've got a problem with Manfred Wallace I'd say he has cause for concern. Wouldn't you, if you were me?"

The Basque lit his cigarette with the Zippo. "I can't imagine," he said, "what it's like to be you."

Milligan's eyes narrowed. "You watch yourself."

"It was a long time ago," said the Basque.

"Two years?" Milligan glanced at Hollis. "You think that's a long time?"

The last thing Hollis wanted was to be drawn into the exchange, but both men were waiting on his reply.

"It's more like three years," he said.

Words for which he would be made to suffer later.

"Two, three . . . ten," said Milligan, leaning forward in his chair. "You leave the Wallaces well alone. I don't want you anywhere near them, you hear me?"

"I hear you."

Milligan looked at Hollis and nodded towards the door: get him out of here.

Hollis followed the Basque down the stairs and out of the building. The sunlight was spilling into Newtown Lane.

"I had nothing to do with that," said Hollis.

"I figured as much."

"I'll run you back."

"I'll walk."

He walked at a pace most men ran at, with a long, easy stride. Hollis felt foolish hurrying along beside him, dodging the pedestrians.

"It's him, isn't it—Manfred Wallace?"

"Is it?"

"He knows you're on to him. He's trying to head you off."

"Is he?"

"Talk to me."

"Why?"

"'Cos you did before."

"I was wrong to."

"You need me. What are you going to do, put a bullet in his head?"

The Basque drew to a halt, his cold, gray eyes fastening on Hollis. "Now why would I want to do that?" he asked. "Killing's easy."

From anyone else it would have sounded like an empty boast, but Hollis had read the files and the words chilled him. He was being closed out, and it was a moment before he figured a way to penetrate the Basque's guard.

"Just tell me one thing. Were you in her room the day she died?"

He could see the Basque battling with his curiosity.

"Why?"

"Because someone was. A man."

"How do you know?"

"The toilet seat in her bathroom . . . it was raised."

"It wasn't me."

"Then that's where they were waiting for her."

Hollis had run through the last moments of Lillian Wallace's life many times in his head, armed with information only he possessed. Now he was proposing to share those insights—an opportunity he figured the Basque was unlikely to pass up.

And he didn't.

"That offer of a ride still stand?"

———

THEY DROVE IN SILENCE until they reached the village limits, then Hollis began to speak. He explained that there'd been no visible signs of a struggle on Lillian's body, which suggested she'd been incapacitated in some way. Chloroform was a possibility. Some small residue of the drug would show up in an autopsy, but only if you were searching for it, which the medical examiner hadn't been. One possible scenario, the most credible one, was that Lillian had been drugged in her room, dressed in her swimsuit, carried to the swimming pool, and drowned. He explained that the autopsy was inconclusive regarding the sand in her lungs. The proper test hadn't been conducted. Only an exhumation and another autopsy would prove the theory, and that was out of the question right now.

The Basque stared out of the window while Hollis spoke, the muscles in his jaw clenching as he listened.

"They drowned her in the pool and dumped her body in the ocean later that night, didn't they?" said Hollis.

"They?"

Something in the Basque's voice hinted at a greater knowledge.

"They . . . he . . . you tell me."

"There was just the one."

"How do you know?"

"It doesn't matter."

"Manfred Wallace?"

"What do *you* think?"

"A professional," said Hollis. His mind turned to the bullnecked thug on duty in front of the church the day of the funeral, but he dismissed the idea. It was unlikely they'd thrust the killer into the limelight like that.

They had reached Amagansett by now and were heading east on Main Street.

"You can drop me here."

Hollis slowed, but didn't pull over. To stop would mean ending the conversation.

"I've got things to do," said the Basque firmly.

Hollis pulled to a halt beside the Presbyterian church and turned the engine off.

"Why?" asked Hollis.

"Why what?"

"Why kill her?" The question hanging over the investigation from the very first—the motive.

"I don't know."

"Sure you do," said Hollis. He offered the Basque a cigarette—a delaying tactic—but he declined. "Tell me what you're thinking. I can help."

"You're wrong."

"I'm helping already. If I shared what I knew with Milligan, you'd be a suspect. Maybe that's what they were hoping."

"That's ridiculous."

"Is it? You keep quiet about your relationship with Lillian, that's already pretty suspicious. She's rich, you're not, different worlds, she wanted to end the affair, you fought . . . 'Isn't that how it happened, Mr. Labarde? In fact, where were you on the night in question, Mr. Labarde?'" He paused. "Any lawyer worth his salt would have a field day with it. It was a neat move of his, going to Milligan. Unless you have evidence. He figures you haven't, or he wouldn't have done it. Do you?"

The Basque sat for a moment, his hand on the door lever. "Like I said, there's nothing you can do." He unfolded himself from the patrol car.

"I'm sorry," said Hollis, "about Lillian."

The Basque eyed him, judging the sincerity of the words, then he said, "She was a good person. She deserved a longer life." He shut the car door, but hesitated, stooping and peering through the open window. "Lizzie Jencks," he said.

Lizzie Jencks. The rag doll in the hedgerow.

"What about her?" asked Hollis.

But the Basque was gone.

27

THE MAN WAS UNREMARKABLE IN ALMOST EVERY REGARD. HE WAS OF medium height and build, he was neither handsome nor plain, and his hair was a neutral brown color. His clothes, the cheaper end of smart, looked as though they'd been ordered from a Sears catalog. He wore dark gabardine pants and a lightweight houndstooth sports jacket. The geometric design of his hand-painted silk necktie was discreet and not too colorful.

In fact, there was nothing whatsoever memorable about the man. Which was just the way he liked it.

As he climbed down from the train at East Hampton station, a casual observer might have taken him for a furniture-polish salesman, and assumed that the brown leather case he was carrying held a selection of his wares.

It did indeed contain the tools of his trade, but these consisted of a leather cosh, a three-foot wire garrotte, a Colt 1911, a nonregistered .357 Magnum with a variation 8⅜-inch barrel for extra punch and accuracy, and a hunting knife. He carried his other blade—an ebony-handled stiletto—in an ankle scabbard.

He examined the small station building, flashing white in the afternoon sun. He hadn't noticed on his last visit, but it was perfectly symmetrical, its pitched roof extending at both sides to provide identical covered seating areas open to the elements. It was, it occurred to him, exactly the sort of station building any kid would be proud to have sitting beside the rails of his toy train track.

People were already queuing for taxis in front of the station. The man strolled past, heading west on Railroad Avenue, then south on Race Lane. The car was parked in front of a laundry. It was a black prewar sedan, a different one from the last time. He slid his case across onto the passenger seat, climbed in, started the engine, and pulled away.

A room had been reserved for him at a guest house on Buells Lane. He drove to it, but only out of curiosity. He disliked anyone knowing where he was, and that included his employers. He knew for a fact that this caution had saved his life on at least one occasion.

He stopped at a grocery store on Main Street, bought a few provisions, and, after quizzing the clerk, found himself at the Sea Spray Inn, right on the ocean. It was a large, sprawling establishment with wide sun porches, set just back from the beach. Better still, one of the inn's small cottages strung out along the dune beyond the main building had come free due to a cancellation. He took it. It offered the privacy to come and go freely at all hours.

He unpacked his clothes and slid the empty suitcase beneath the bed. It would take an expert eye to detect the false bottom with its small cache of weaponry. He poured himself a glass of milk, checked that all the doors and windows were locked, then he tore open the brown envelope he'd pulled from beneath the sedan's passenger seat.

He smoked two cigarettes while he read the contents, committing the information to memory. There was no fireplace in the cottage, or he would have burned the papers there and then. As it was, he shredded them and flushed the mulch down the toilet.

He changed into some shorts and a sleeveless shirt and strolled onto the beach, pleased to note that there were others as white and pasty as himself spread out along the shore. He headed east, the sun at his back, sticking to the packed sand at the water's edge where children frolicked, leaping the waves and bodysurfing.

By his calculation, it wasn't even a mile to the spot where he had put the girl's body in the sea, and he was curious to see what the place looked like in daylight.

28

HOLLIS HAD LITTLE CHOICE BUT TO WAIT FOR THE CHANGE OF SHIFT AT
eight o'clock. Past case files were located in a cabinet right beside Bob
Hartwell's desk in the squad room, and there was no way he could
justify rifling through them, certainly not for records of an incident
predating his arrival in East Hampton. He was skating on thin ice—
Milligan had almost caught him out twice—and while he trusted
Hartwell, now was not the time to be taking risks.

At a quarter of eight, he suggested that Hartwell head home a
bit early.

"You sure, Tom?"

"Say hi to Lisa and the kids."

As soon as Hartwell was gone, Hollis moved fast. Stringer had a
tendency to show up early for work. Locating the files was easy, figuring how to get them to his car unnoticed was another matter. It would
require two runs. The first went without a hitch. Hollis had dumped
the second batch of files on Hartwell's desk, and was arranging the
cabinet to conceal the gaps when he heard footsteps on the stairs.

He intercepted Stringer at the door of the squad room.

"Do me a favor, will you, and get me a pack of cigarettes?"

"Luckys, right?"

"You don't miss much, do you?"

Stringer beamed.

"That's good," said Hollis. But not so good that Stringer didn't ask himself why in the hell Hollis couldn't pick up his own cigarettes seeing as he was going off work.

HE OPTED FOR THE KITCHEN TABLE, sweeping the clutter onto the floor. He spread out the files around a notepad, set up an ashtray to his right, along with a bowl of ice, a glass, and a bottle of Gordon's. Then he launched in.

He had arrived in East Hampton almost a month after the incident, just as Milligan's investigation was petering out. Eager to contribute, Hollis had suggested that he call in a favor from an acquaintance who worked in the Motor Vehicle Homicide Squad back in the city, maybe get the guy to come up for a week.

It was his first mistake. The first of many.

Milligan shot the proposal down. Clearly, the last thing he wanted was some jumped-up city fellow telling him how things should be done—or, more to the point, exposing the gross procedural errors he'd already committed. When Hollis then gingerly brought up the possibility of sending a sample of the black paint chips recovered at the scene to the Broome Street crime lab for analysis by their spectroscope, Milligan actually laughed. He dismissed the new technology— which he'd evidently never heard of—as a passing fad. Hollis had quietly sent the sample anyway, not that there'd ever been a suspect vehicle to check against the lab's spectrogram.

The case, dead for over a year, was now very much alive again, and this time Hollis was in charge, no Milligan to keep him at bay. He quickly reacquainted himself with the sequence of events, scanning the reports, the chief's clipped and unfeeling prose. The body was first sighted a little after seven in the morning by a potato farmer from Wainscott heading east on Town Lane for a spot of Sunday fishing off Barnes Landing.

She lay in the hedgerow on the north side of the road, fifty yards west of the junction with Indian Wells Highway. Hollis had never actually visited the spot, but he could picture it. Almost three miles in length, Town Lane ran parallel to Montauk Highway, about half a mile to the north of it, cutting through open countryside, farming land studded with pastures. It was a straight road, a fast road; he had often found himself unwittingly pushing the throttle to the floor when driving it.

By the time Chief Milligan had arrived on the scene, Lizzie Jencks's parents, whose homestead lay a little to the west on Town Lane, were already present among the gathered. The scene was photographed, the body then removed by the medical examiner.

Examination of the road surface suggested that the vehicle had been traveling west on Town Lane at considerable speed, the autopsy subsequently setting the time of death at somewhere between midnight and three o'clock in the morning. The parents were unable to explain why their daughter had been out walking in the dead of night, and no one else had come forward with an explanation for her nocturnal ramble. It was this that had stuck in Hollis's craw at the time, and it was still there.

He poured some more gin into the glass, then began to peruse the statements, looking for a name: Manfred Wallace.

He quickly ascertained that Manfred Wallace had never been questioned over the hit-and-run. Justin Penrose, on the other hand, had been, though not as a possible suspect. It was in his statement that Manfred Wallace's name was buried away, along with that of his sister Lillian. The document was Bob Hartwell's follow-up report on the movements of all those who'd attended a dinner dance at the Devon

Yacht Club on the night in question. According to the club's secretary, Manfred and Lillian had left the event early in the evening to join Mr. Penrose at his house. The departure of two members well before the time of the incident would have marked the end of that particular investigative trail for most police officers; but Hartwell had made the effort to visit Penrose at his house and ask him when exactly the Wallaces had moved on from his place. Hollis silently praised him for his thoroughness, while struggling with the questions thrown up by the report.

The Devon Yacht Club connection with the hit-and-run was tenuous at best. Town Lane was far from being the most direct route back to the summer colony in East Hampton from the club. More important, if Manfred and Lillian Wallace were already back in East Hampton just after nine o'clock, what the hell were they doing heading west on Town Lane some three or four hours later?

The answer was staring him in the face, it just took him a while, and a couple of slugs of gin, to see it for what it was.

Penrose's given address was Water's Edge—a house name displaying as little imagination as that of the Wallaces' place: Oceanview. Or so he'd assumed. Maybe it wasn't a house after all.

He went to the hallway and picked up the phone.

"Operator."

"Olive, it's Tom Hollis."

Olive Hibbel worked the board most evenings over at the telephone exchange on Main Street.

"I'm looking for a local number," said Hollis. "Penrose, maybe Justin, maybe not."

"We've only one Penrose in East Hampton—Everett."

Probably the father; must be a family home.

"Any way I could get the address?"

"Hold on," she said. "Number Two Water's Edge."

Not a house, but a road. And not a road he'd ever heard of in the summer colony, though private tracks were constantly being opened up for new residences.

"Where is that, do you know?"

"It's near Springs, just off Old Stone Highway."

He felt his heart leap, the pieces falling into place, his eyes already searching the framed map on the wall across the corridor.

"Thanks, Olive," he said absently, then hung up.

The map laid bare the events of the evening in connecting lines, some straight as an arrow, others twisting and coiling, but all leading to and emanating from that dusty stretch of Town Lane west of the junction with Indian Wells Highway.

Manfred and Lillian Wallace hadn't headed back into East Hampton on leaving the Devon Yacht Club, because the Penroses' house lay directly to the north, on the western shore of Gardiner's Bay. And if driving from Water's Edge to East Hampton, then Town Lane was a likely route to take, especially if you felt like picking up a head of steam.

Hartwell had abandoned the trail after Justin Penrose's assertion that Manfred and Lillian Wallace had visited him for no more than an hour, leaving well before the time of the accident. And that had been that, just another of the many blind alleys Hartwell would have wandered down at the time.

Or maybe Hartwell hadn't bought the story. His keen observation of Hollis and Penrose at the funeral suggested that he recalled his meeting with Penrose the year before. Maybe he'd had his suspicions at the time. But what could he do? Challenge the word of a respectable member of the community, of larger society?

The wealthy had closed ranks. Penrose had been called on to serve up an alibi. But just how far had his sense of duty, loyalty, and friendship carried him? Was he also privy to the conspiracy to silence Lillian Wallace? For that would explain away the remaining anomalies in the story: Lillian's split from Penrose, her uncharacteristic move to East Hampton for the winter months.

Her guilt had gotten the better of her, destroying her relationship with Penrose, driving her back to the scene of the crime, jeopardizing the fragile edifice of the shared lie.

Hollis checked himself; he was speculating now. And all based on one name uttered by a fisherman whose motives remained far from clear.

The phone rang, shrill and loud in the confined space of the hallway, startling him.

"Hello."

"Tom?"

Oh Christ, thought Hollis.

"Mary."

"That's right," she said. "Your hostess for this evening."

Supper with Mary. How could he have forgotten?

"I'm sorry, I'm working."

"At home?"

"It's true," he said pathetically, and was rightly rewarded with a silence on the other end of the line. "I should have called."

"Why didn't you?"

What could he tell her? Not the truth—that the invitation had completely slipped his mind.

"I was about to. I was literally just walking to the phone when you called."

"Having literally just walked away from it a minute ago, I suppose."

"Huh?"

"I called. Your line was engaged."

The phone call to Olive at the telephone exchange.

"Look Mary—"

"It's okay, I think I understand."

"No you don't."

"Just tell me, are you going to come over or not?"

"I can't."

"Okay," she said, then hung up.

Hollis made to call her back then realized he didn't know her number. The directory wasn't in the drawer of the table in the hallway. When he finally located it on the floor of the larder and dialed her number, there was no reply.

He fought the urge to jump in the car and head on over. There was a lot more to be done on the case files before he could satisfy himself he hadn't missed anything.

Five minutes later, the doorbell rang.

He leapt into action. The first thing he concealed was the bottle of gin. He was gathering together the files for removal to the larder when Mary's face appeared at the back door.

He froze, caught in the act. Dumping the files back on the table, he went to the door and threw the latch.

"I didn't mean to surprise you," she said, "but I thought we should talk. Face to face."

He stepped aside, allowing her to enter, resigning himself to her reaction. It wasn't just the mess, it was the grime—the thin film of grease thrown up by his inexpert cracks at cooking, and to which the dust had then adhered.

"I've let things go a bit."

"I'll say you have."

She picked her way around the clutter on the floor. He cursed himself as she reached for the glass on the table and took a sip.

"Neat?" she asked.

"It helps me think."

"My husband used to say it helped him sleep."

His shame gave way to indignation. She had no right to come snooping on him.

Mary glanced at the files on the table. "I'm relieved," she said. "I thought maybe you were lying."

"I wouldn't do that."

"What then? You were so absorbed you forgot all about our date?"

Hollis hesitated. "That's pretty much the size of it, I'm afraid."

Mary glanced back at the files. "First Lillian Wallace, now Lizzie Jencks?"

He could see what was coming and he wished it wasn't.

"I said there might come a time when I'd ask what you're up to. Now's that time, Tom."

He hesitated. "I can't."

"Why not?"

"Because I don't know for sure, not yet."

"Enough to sneak a bunch of papers home."

"I didn't sneak them home."

"Come on," said Mary. "Why are you doing this?"

"Doing what?"

"This cloak-and-dagger stuff. I thought the whole idea was to leave this kind of thing behind you. Isn't that what you said? A quieter life?"

"It's probably nothing."

"A drowning and a hit-and-run?" She paused. "Are they connected?"

"Mary," sighed Hollis.

Now she was hurt, stung by his refusal to trust her. And he realized then that he'd seen that look before, in Lydia's eyes, the first time he'd shut her out, laying the foundations of the wall.

"Okay," said Mary.

She headed for the door.

"Mary . . ."

"No, Tom," she said as the door swung shut behind her.

For a moment he thought he might run after her and tell her all, but a sterner voice in his head questioned the wisdom of doing so. With the investigation so precariously poised, what good could possibly come from confiding in a person he cared for, but who, when it came to it, he hardly knew?

Besides, there was a lot to be done, much to be thought through, not least of all: how best to obtain samples of paintwork from all the vehicles at the Wallace residence.

29

Conrad checked his watch. Ten o'clock. Time to make himself scarce.

He allowed his eyes to adjust to the darkness outside, then headed for the beach. He walked west along the shore, the sky dirty with stars. He searched for distraction, but it was hard to find. The night, after all, had been theirs, the only time when they could roam freely, without fear of being seen together.

They had never discussed the need for discretion, it was a given from the first, the way things had to be. The world wasn't ready for them yet. The secrecy wasn't without its satisfactions, though. It added a spice to their encounters, an edge of illicitness.

At Lillian's suggestion they had sometimes met openly in public, as customers in a general store or as moviegoers obliged to sit next to each other. On these occasions they rarely spoke, except to apologize as they brushed past each other, or to exchange pleasantries about the weather under the unsuspecting gaze of a counter clerk. One time, Lillian had "dropped" her purse while paying for some goods, obliging Conrad to crouch at her feet and gather up the scattered coins. And she had made no attempt to deny him the lingering view up her linen skirt of her nakedness beneath.

The anticipation that went with these encounters was maddening, too maddening on one occasion, and they'd been unable to wait till later, Conrad's hand delving beneath Lillian's jacket, strategically folded on her lap, during a night sequence in *The Imperfect Lady,* the auditorium of Edwards Theater cast into welcome gloom. And with the giant faces of Ray Milland and Teresa Wright looking down on them from the screen, he had brought her to a rippling climax—bearing out her claim that she could reach her peak in total silence, a skill acquired in the dormitories of New England boarding schools, she maintained, where the slightest gasp in the drowsy darkness would attract howls of ridicule.

There was another side to the clandestine nature of their affair that they both welcomed. There was never a wasted moment, no time-consuming introductions to each other's friends, no social gatherings where both were present yet not together. It seemed that they had somehow managed to distill a year, more, into a few brief months. They were never lost for things to talk about, arguing for argument's sake about books and ideas, trading stories about their lives. She told him about her dream of becoming a theater actress, and how it had slipped away from her with the onset of war and the death of her mother, her ally. She said she had moved up to East Hampton for the winter to recover from the split with her fiancé—one part of the truth, he now suspected; her claim that Penrose had left her for another woman probably a lie.

They felt no compulsion to remain indoors once darkness had descended. Sometimes they would swim in her pool, then make their way across the sandhills to the beach, where they'd cook up whatever fish he'd brought with him that evening over a driftwood fire. Other times, when she visited him, they would strike out on foot, heading north over Montauk Highway, crossing the railroad, disturbing the snakes warming themselves on the tracks in the cool night air. Napeague was his world, and he shared it with her as they wandered. He pointed out the spot where he and Billy used to gather coal from beside the tracks during the early years of the Depression, big bituminous lumps tossed from the tender by sympathetic railroad men. He drew her attention to the cranberry bogs and the osprey nests, platforms of sticks and bone and rope and other debris, perched precariously atop the telegraph poles. They strolled the skirts of the salt meadows, and they pulled blue-claw crabs from the channels with scoop nets.

By flashlight, they foraged for Indian artifacts in the soft sand just back from the beach on Gardiner's Bay, unearthing shards of broken pottery and arrowheads discarded many centuries before. And though he never took her there, not wishing to tempt the fates, he told her about the whale skeleton buried beneath the straggle of bearberry bushes.

On windless nights they would take the catboat out and go fire-lighting for fluke. Sometimes they made love in the cockpit, rocking on the gentle swell. One time, the sounds of some event at the Devon Yacht Club had drifted across the water towards them—a Cole Porter number carried on the night breeze—and it struck Conrad that Lillian had chosen to be with him, lying in his arms, rather than consorting with her own kind. And though this puzzled him, he never questioned her motives, he never doubted her desires.

But that had all changed since her death.

He now saw himself as a figure in a bigger picture, the full and proper dimensions of which she'd chosen to keep from him. She had been party to a crime, a killing; and just as her move to East Hampton for the dead winter months could now be seen as part of an instinctual penance, some need to atone, so too could her relationship with him.

He was her link to the place, to Lizzie Jencks—a tool, perhaps, in the purging of her own guilt. Could he safely assume she would have struck up a relationship with him under normal circumstances? It was unlikely.

Worst of all, though—and it was this that had robbed him of all but

the most fitful sleep for the past week—was the creeping realization
that he might actually have been responsible for her death. She had
changed, he had witnessed the change, just as she had watched him recover his footing in the world. But had he unwittingly given her the
strength to act, to make a stand, to jeopardize the conspiracy of silence
surrounding Lizzie Jencks's death?

It was a question he would never know the answer to, never shrug
off, and that realization gnawed at him, the corrosive acid of doubt.

His one satisfaction was that those responsible for her murder were
now experiencing a torment of their own, inflicted by him. And
though they might suspect they hadn't seen the back of him, they had
no idea just how far he was willing to go.

A few unforeseen developments aside, his plan was on course,
moving ahead, narrowing down to the fine point. The policeman,
Hollis, had taken the bait, and seemed intent on keeping it to himself.
That was good, essential even. Whether he had judged Manfred Wallace correctly remained to be seen. He'd know soon enough.

He glanced at his watch, calculating the hours left to kill. He wasn't
tired; the prospect of the looming conflict sharpening his mind, blowing away the clouds of light-headed exhaustion.

He veered away from the water's edge, up over the frontal dune
into Beachampton, the grid of cheap new summer homes that lay beyond. The development was spreading at an alarming rate. Skeletal
structures loomed around him, the building stock destined to flesh out
their timber frames heaped up in piles. A bulldozer stood abandoned
at the end of the narrow swathe it had punched through the dunes to
the east—a new road yet to be named—reshaping in a few hours a
landscape sculpted over centuries by the wind and the ocean.

Had the bulldozer completed its task, or were its instructions to
keep right on going? If so, it should be showing up at his place somewhere towards the end of the week, huffing and puffing and cough-

ing black smoke, its current course destined to take it right through the middle of the barn, ever onwards across Napeague, little shingle-clad homes mushrooming in its wake, all the way to Montauk Point.

If it was a vision of the future, then, thankfully, it was a future he wouldn't live long enough to witness.

He kicked the Beachampton sand from his heels, heading west on Bluff Road past the big houses with their commanding views over the Glades towards the ocean. Nearing the Kemps' house, he glanced up at the roof, fearful that Rollo might be watching from the widow's walk—the little scuttlehole beside the chimney from which the women of the house once scanned the ocean for their husbands' safe return. It could only be accessed via Rollo's attic bedroom, and Rollo had always spent an inordinate amount of time peering down on the world from his crow's nest, as he liked to think of it. Fortunately, he wasn't there, and Conrad turned in to the leafy, tenebrous cool of Miankoma Lane.

The doctor from Manhattan and his family were in residence. The landing light was on, and there was a car parked in back of the house near the barn. He noticed that they'd removed the old hitching post that had always stood out front. The wooden go-cart lying abandoned near the front porch had been Conrad's, hammered together from fish crates around the time of his tenth birthday; and while he felt a slight pang of possessiveness on seeing it there, he was pleased it was being used.

He trod lightly up the driveway, round to the back of the house. The barn was as good a place as any to hole up for the night. Maybe he was being too cautious, but he somehow doubted it. They would have to take action against him. And soon.

He noted, a little sadly, that the garden had changed almost beyond recognition. There was a carpet of lawn where the fruit and vegetable patches had once stood—their stepmother's pride and joy, where she'd spent so many of her waking hours, growing pole beans and peas, car-

rots and cabbages, cucumbers, marrows, and beets. She planted pump-
kins around the small stand of corn so that the sticky vines would deter
the raccoons, she built strawberry frames sheathed in condemned
Promised Land bunker net, and her back grew strong from hauling up
buckets of water from the well.

As young boys they'd never understood her obsession with cultiva-
tion. Only later, when they realized she was unable to bear children,
did her endless planting and tending and reaping make any sense.

If she was upset by the barrenness she carried inside her, she never
allowed it to interfere with her devotions to them. They, on the other
hand, were less than fair in their dealings with her, certainly at the beginning, their young minds unable to grasp the idea—sprung on them
one evening by their father—that their teacher was to become their
mother. Miss Elliott, with her long wavy hair and her sticks of chalk
and her constant talk of Regents exams and passing grades and the
Palmer method of handwriting? It just didn't make any sense.

Miss Elliott was a "peach," an upstater, who boarded with a local
family during school terms. She wasn't around a whole lot, and their
father, it seemed to them, did nothing but fish from dawn till dark.
How had they even met? The critical encounter, it soon emerged, had
taken place at a dance held at Miankoma Hall by the Ladies' Society
of Busy Workers. They knew their father was good on his feet, they'd
seen him dance in the barroom at Valentin Aguirre's in New York,
surprisingly nimble for such a big man, proudly presenting the steps of
their region to the other Basques—the *kaskarotak,* the *volontak,* and
the *maskerada.* And now, it seemed, he had won Miss Elliott's heart
with his glides and his shuffles, his spins and his leaps.

Their housekeeper, Miss Smarden, promptly resigned in disgust—
the first and only sign that she'd been carrying a torch of her own for
their father. They'd become so accustomed to the strict regime at
home that they thought Miss Elliott must be joking when she insisted
they invite their friends around to the house whenever they wanted.

She rigged a rope from the tulip tree out back, and the grass beneath was soon worn away to dirt by small feet. She accompanied them on the great spring and fall cattle drives along the ocean beach to and from the sweeping pastures of Montauk. On winter weekends, she drove them to watch the gaff-rigged iceboats rattling across Mecox Bay at improbable speeds, and she took them by ferry across Long Island Sound to the amusement park in New London. It was all too good to be true, and they suspected that it was just a ploy to win their hearts and impress their father, that it wouldn't last.

She proved them wrong over and over again. With time they learned to return her hugs and other displays of affection, and they marveled at her ability to treat them no differently from the other kids once they'd crossed the threshold of the little white schoolhouse each morning. She drove them hard, Antton less than some because of his difficulties, Conrad far harder than most, slipping him extra books to read after school. She did this, she said, because she believed he had a gift.

To Conrad's mind, it was a thankless gift if it kept him from the new fishing shanty their father had built at the bottom end of Atlantic Avenue. Raised a few feet above the shifting sands on locust posts, it was little more than a long wooden box with a shingle roof and a pot-bellied stove. But to Conrad and Antton it was a palace, a place of wonderment, a symbol of their father's advancement in the world.

Together with Billy, they would hurry there as soon as they'd wolfed down their supper, Maude shouting after them that exertion on a full stomach was a sure way to an early grave. If they were lucky, they'd arrive breathless before the dory had come ashore, and they'd watch it negotiate the thundering surf, their father and Sam bent at the oars, moving in unison. In summer, their father and Sam hauled seine and set bluefish nets way out beyond the bar, two or three miles offshore, and they would help lug the fish from the boat to the shanty, threading beach grass through the gills, their fingers too tender still for the sharp plates. They learned to dress and pack the catch, their clothes crusted with scales, the boards of the shanty slick with gurry beneath their feet. The big treat was to be taken a little way out beyond the surf—squeezed in together in the bow, white knuckles on the gunwales—and go drop-lining for fluke.

Held back in school, Antton was fifteen years old when Conrad joined him in the eighth grade. At the end of the school year, Antton failed his Regents for the second time, but with his sixteenth birthday falling in August, he had seen through his obligations to the law. The same week that Conrad started at East Hampton High School, Antton joined their father on the beach, set-netting for the last of the blue-fish. Times were tough—the fish had been down all season—and they worked long hours, longer still when the cod appeared around Thanksgiving.

On those gray winter mornings, Conrad would wake to the sound of an icy nor'wester rattling the windows, and he would know that his father and Antton were already on the ocean, setting trawls way out beyond the bar: well over a thousand fathoms of line carefully coiled down in the tubs the evening before, hundreds upon hundreds of hooks baited with steamer clams. And while they fought their way back to the beach, bucking the offshore blow, the cod in the bilges already stiffened out solid from the cold, he would breakfast with Maude in the warm glow of the stove. This was where she wished him to be— he could sense it—far from the sea's toss and the wind's kick, talking of other matters, of his studies, of his new friends and of books.

He helped out down at the shanty whenever he could, but he felt foolish and alone. Elevated to the rank of surfman, Antton was eager to drive home his superior knowledge and expertise. Their father, sensing Conrad's frustration, told him to be patient; in a couple of years he too would be part of the crew.

This was not a consolation he relayed to Maude.

The showdown, when it came, was explosive, and all the more

shocking for the fact that he'd never known their father and Maude to argue before. The thump of the exchange carried clear through the woodwork to his attic bedroom. He only made out one word, and only then because it was repeated several times—*aintzinekoak*—"those who have gone before us." Or, in this case: what was good enough for me and my father is good enough for him.

Maude urged Conrad to fight his corner, to insist on seeing through his studies, to eighteen and beyond, on to college. What could he say? He couldn't betray the vision that had come to his father all those years before on the Amagansett sands, made concrete with the money from Eusebio—a man and his two boys fishing side by side, following the sea. Besides, he was threatened enough already by his father's special relationship with Antton. It had always been there, but it had deepened considerably of late. Foolish though it now seemed, he could remember thinking at the time that even his name was proof of his father's favoritism—Conrad, his mother's father, the only non-Basque anyone could recall on either side of the family.

Maude withdrew in order to fight another day, but she hadn't counted on her husband's stubborn Basque temperament, and her cause wasn't helped by the onset of the Depression. Along with a number of his Amagansett friends, Conrad exchanged the classroom for the fish shanty.

His time on the ocean beach was sweet and very brief. A third set of hands was not always required. It became an indulgence, as the Depression deepened, and Conrad was dispatched to join the pack of other local men roaming the South Fork in search of work at a few dollars a day. He helped pour the first concrete sidewalks in Amagansett, he filled holes in the cinder roads, and he cut ice from the ponds during the winter freeze. He teamed up with Hendrik on laboring jobs, he crewed with Billy on the draggers out of Fort Pond Bay from time to time, and almost everything he earned went into the family purse. He fished with his father and Antton whenever they needed him, but it was his friendships with others that sustained him. And this is how it stayed, right up until Antton was taken from them by the sea.

It was a January morning, not so different from any other, raw and gray. The wind had come around northwest, stiffening overnight, and everyone knew the cod bit best in a nor'wester. When the wind was off the land, it usually flattened out the surf, but that day there was a strong groundswell running, driven by some force far out in the ocean, and the seas rose up in defiance, breaking over the outer bar, their crests whipped into white mares' tails of freezing spray. By the time they'd loaded the tubs and dragged the dory down to the water's edge, both the wind and the swell had eased a little, and some of the other crews were going off through the clean, sharp breakers curling towards the beach.

There was no question of not following suit.

They gritted their teeth against the jolt of that first dowsing and wrestled the dory through the white water, their woollen mittens already beginning to harden with ice. Hauling themselves aboard, Antton took the bow oars, Conrad amidships, both setting their stroke, their father still in the water, gripping the bucking transom to keep the dory headed seaward, his eyes reading the surf.

"Pull, boys, pull!" he yelled, shoving off and hooking a leg over the port gunwale. The oars bit in unison; the dory surged forward, gaining headway, rising up the face of the capping sea. The bow split the wave as it broke around them, green water tumbling and crashing past on both sides, a fair quantity of it finding its way over the boat's high sides and down the back of their necks, washing into the bilges; but nothing unusual, nothing that couldn't be bailed out easily once they were clear of the break.

The bow dipped into the trough, nosing into the next sea as they bent their backs into the stroke. The dory rose and fell, clearing the wave as it crested, shipping less water this time. None the next. The surf line receding behind them.

He saw it first in his father's eyes, a cloud of confusion that also furrowed his brow. A moment later, he felt it beneath the boat, a building swell that should have dropped away. But it didn't, it just kept on coming, surging up from below. His father gripped the gunwales, the confusion in his eyes now replaced by the unmistakable glare of fear. And Conrad turned.

A wall of water already making up about eight feet reared up behind Antton, a glassy ridge, deep green in color, shutting out the ocean beyond. And he could recall his sense of indignation. It had no place being here, no right.

"Eyes in the boat!" screamed his father.

Conrad yanked on the oars as he turned back, fear running through his arms now, and his starboard oar popped clear of its oarlock.

Later, he would spend endless hours reliving the next few moments, clinging to the fractured memories, replaying them in his mind, refiguring them: both his oars in the water this time, that instant of hesitation written out, along with the moment he committed the cardinal error known to all surfmen, the moment he turned to look at the ocean.

He would try to factor in the words of consolation from those who actually saw that freak sea, that rogue wave which had started life hundreds, thousands of miles away, and which only found some meaning to its existence in its dying moments off the ocean beach. They said they'd never seen the like before, they said no crew on the beach would have cleared that wave, they said popping an oar had made no difference to the outcome.

The dory was near vertical when Antton leapt clear, passing by Conrad's right shoulder. Conrad released the oars and made to follow him, but he was too late. The dory, snatched up in the curl, pitchpoled backwards, stem over stern, upended with such force and speed that Conrad had no time to set himself for the impact with the water. He hit it face-on while still drawing breath.

He spun and twisted in the darkness beneath the upturned boat, lunging for a hold. He seized what must have been the thwart, but it was wrenched from his grasp as the wave powered on inexorably towards the beach. Something struck Conrad a blow in the side of the head: a limb, an arm or a leg belonging to his father. He pawed help-lessly, trying to latch on, but it was past him now, leaving him tumbling in its wake, all sense of orientation gone.

He felt a line whip past him, and he clutched at it. It was the cod trawl, unraveling from one of the tubs. It offered no purchase, though; it simply began to wrap itself around him, the barbed and baited hooks at the end of the little snood lines catching in his oilskins, binding him up tight.

That's when he felt the downward drag—the weight of the water filling his waders—and he knew then that he was done for. Even if he hadn't been ensnared by the trawl, it was too late to kick them off. And as he sank away, his lungs gave up the fight, allowing the ocean to flood in.

There was no tunnel, no shining light to guide his path. Nor was there any pain. Only blackness, sudden and absolute.

The Kemp crew was fishing just to the east, and it was Rollo—relegated to the beach as always—who was first to arrive on the scene. He pulled Conrad's father, unconscious but alive, from beneath the dory and dragged him up beyond the wash. Seeing that the other rescuers were still some distance off, stumbling along the shore, Rollo stripped off his oilskins and his waders and struck out through the breakers. It was a foolhardy thing to do, suicidal even—he must have known that just as well as the next man—yet he managed to snatch at some lines of cod trawl before being driven back by the cold and the surf.

So it was that Rollo hauled Conrad's lifeless body from the ocean, reeling him in, hand over hand, oblivious to the hooks tearing at his bare hands, his flesh. He later claimed that he'd only done as his grandfather, Cap'n Josh, had once instructed him: forcing the drowned man's knees to his chest and bearing down hard on his midriff.

Conrad came to, the last of the water convulsing from his lungs, to find Rollo's blurred face filling his field of vision.

"Hello," said Rollo through chattering teeth, while rubbing Conrad furiously with his hands.

It soon became clear that Antton was lost. They searched for his body, handlining with grappling hooks, setting gill nets straight offshore and hauling seine. At midday, the swell picked up again, dangerously so, and even Conrad's father was obliged to concede defeat.

Conrad was warming himself at Doc Meadows's hearth, nursing a mug of steaming broth, Maude at his side, when his father showed up. That's when Conrad saw the look, the one that said more than any words: "You were to blame."

It was a fleeting moment, and the question of Conrad's responsibility for the tragedy was never once voiced by his father. Indeed, he laid the blame squarely at the feet of that freak sea. But Conrad always knew what he believed in his heart, and it stood between them like a mountain range shrouded in mist.

Two services were held for Antton—one a memorial, the other a burial some three weeks later, when a few scraps washed ashore near Gurney's Inn. During this period, there was not one day when Conrad's father didn't walk the beach, searching for the remains of his firstborn son.

Close-knit as they were, the fishing families were hit hard by Antton's death. But things picked up again, as they had to. Come May, when the first of the striped bass appeared and struck in at the beach, Conrad found himself hauling seine again, with Sam and Billy Ockham making up the rest of their crew.

Conrad's father shrugged off his mantle of gloom. Conrad did his best to mimic the charade, but it was over a year before he was able to visit Antton's grave, by which time the arguments for and against America's entry into the war were on everyone's lips. Pearl Harbor settled the matter. Conrad was drafted and ordered to report to Camp Upton at Yaphank. The day his parents saw him off at East Hampton railroad station he sensed it was the last time he'd ever see his father.

The letter from Maude arrived during his recuperation at Barton Hall in England. Conrad had recovered sufficiently in the eyes of his doctors to be allowed out from time to time, along with a couple of the other patients. He carried the letter with him on the bus to Norwich, opening it in the shady cool of the cathedral cloister while his two companions prayed inside.

He felt curiously removed from the words on the page—the stomach pain, the diagnosis of cancer, his father's sudden decline. Maude said she was putting the house on the market, but that she would deposit the greater part of the proceeds with the Osborne Trust Company for his use. Her brother had suggested she join him in California. He was wealthy, quite capable of supporting her, and she intended to take up teaching again. She urged him to reconsider a college education on his return, to which end she would be leaving him her library of books.

He could tell from the deterioration of her normally neat italic hand that she was devastated and fighting hard to hold herself together.

When his companions joined him in the cloister, Conrad made some excuse and went in search of a pub. He drank several pints of strong Norfolk ale then picked a fight with a loud American bombardier on twenty-four-hour stand-down from one of the local airbases.

It was a few weeks before he realized that the greatest fear of his childhood had finally come to pass, that as he waited in line at Ellis Island, fresh off the boat from France, the doctor had indeed marked him with that stick of blue chalk, leading him away, never to see his father and Antton again.

It came to him then that he was alone in the world.

CONRAD WOKE WITH A START, orienting himself. He brushed the straw from his clothes and climbed down the ladder from the hayloft. He had planned on slipping away a little before daybreak, but the morning sun was already casting long shadows in the garden as he crept from the barn.

He could make out the sounds of the doctor and his family stirring in the house, obliging him to duck below the level of the windowsills as he left.

He felt sharp, alert, which was good. The sleep had helped, sweet and unexpected.

HE ASKED EARL GRIFFIN to drop him off at the head of the track, and he settled the fare.

He saw the tire marks in the sand immediately. Closer examination revealed that there were two sets—the same vehicle coming and going, suggesting that the visitor had left. But his hand still closed around the gun in his hip pocket as he set off through the pitch pines towards his house.

The vehicle had pulled to a halt just before the trees gave way to the dunes. The track was too narrow at this point to turn a motorcar around, and the visitor had been obliged to reverse it back to the highway, but not before abandoning it first and continuing on foot.

The footprints stood out clearly in the sand, the area around them smoothed unnaturally flat by Conrad the evening before. It hadn't taken him long to perform the task: simply a matter of dragging some heavy, tarred pound trap netting behind the Model A.

The footprints veered off to the right, into the dunes, but Conrad made no attempt to follow them. Neither did he glance in their direction in case he was being observed. It wasn't important; he knew where they were headed.

He picked them up again in the broad sweeps of leveled sand in and around the buildings. The visitor had entered the compound from the west, skirting the shack, making for the whaleboat house. He had then crossed to the barn, entering it. From here he'd returned to the shack, circling, keeping his distance, approaching only twice—once to examine the small lean-to at the back which housed the generator; the second time, to inspect the corner of the roof where the telephone cable entered the building.

Conrad knew then that if they had to, they were willing to go all the way in order to silence him.

He should have felt fear, some modicum of anxiety at the very least, but he didn't. It was with a pleasing sense of anticipation that he reached for the phone and asked the operator to put him through to a number in Sag Harbor.

30

"Tom? Are you there?"

The voice entering his head through the earpiece of the receiver had grown distant, hollow, strangely remote.

"Tom?"

"Are you sure?" asked Hollis.

"I checked each sample twice against the master. None of them match."

"One of them has to."

"They're not even close. Believe me."

"Okay," conceded Hollis.

"Are you on to something?"

"I was. Thanks anyway, Ed."

"Any time, you know that."

"Sure."

He hung up, pleased to silence the unmistakable note of pity creeping into Ed's voice.

How much more saddened would his old colleague from the crime lab have been if he'd seen the whole pathetic picture behind the favor he'd just performed: Hollis creeping through the grounds of the Wallaces' house in the dead of night, heart pounding, ears straining for the sounds of detection as he scraped away with the chisel, dropping the flakes of paint into the envelopes. Four motorcars, four envelopes dispatched express to the Broome Street crime lab for comparison with the sample taken at the time of the hit-and-run.

Ed had fired up his spectroscope, the two electrodes blazing white over the sample dish, the prisms seizing the light, breaking it up and firing it down the ten-foot tunnel onto the photographic negative.

The machine had spoken. It had all been a waste of time.

A match would have offered the breakthrough piece of evidence— the *only* piece of hard evidence so far—and a firm base on which to build a case.

He should have seen it coming. Only a fool wouldn't have got rid of the incriminating vehicle by now. Odds were it was long gone, scrapped and melted down, a small price to pay for a man of wealth.

He had wanted it too much. Even Ed had detected the desperation in him. He could see him now, sitting back in his chair and thinking: poor old Tom Hollis, put out to pasture but still trying to make amends.

He felt a sudden urge to call Mary, but he resisted it. Thoughts of her had been clogging his head for the past two days, rushing in unbidden, demanding to be heard—the curve of her spine as she bent over the bathtub to test the temperature of the water; the way she dropped her lower lip when she sulked; her throaty little chuckle . . . and the unmistakable look of hurt in her eyes when he'd reneged on his promise to her, refusing to let her in on his findings.

It had seemed like a reasonable thing to do at the time, gripped by the thrill of the chase, but he had broken the trust between them and done irreparable damage. He knew that, because he'd heard it in her voice when he'd called that morning.

She was polite, gracious—he had even made her laugh—but the delicate flutter of intimacy was gone from her voice. She had withdrawn that particular favor. With the summer fair only two days off, she ended the conversation on the pretext that there was some emergency to be dealt with. It had been an unconvincing excuse.

And now even the little scenario of reconciliation he'd constructed in his mind had evaporated: a positive match on the motorcar, the news breaking through the community as the case unfolded, Mary understanding his need for discretion at such a critical stage of the investigation . . .

Christ, he was pathetic.

As if she gave a damn about any of that.

Besides, there *was* no match, there was no nothing, nothing concrete.

He picked up the phone and called the Basque.

No reply.

Things were slipping away fast. He could afford to start taking some risks.

THE LITTLE HOMESTEAD LEAKED POVERTY from every cracked plank of the barn's cladding, every dried and curling shingle, every fissure in the parched earth of the pasture beyond the low saltbox house, where two skeletal ponies lurked mistrustfully in the shade of a tree.

Beside the barn, a truck had lost its battle with rust and had been cannibalized for parts. Nearby, the blades of an artesian well groaned in the light breeze.

And yet there were signs of a proud hand at work. The yard was almost devoid of clutter, and what there was was well ordered, heaped up neatly against the buildings—reclaimed timber and bricks waiting for some future purpose, and a small mound of old iron barrel hoops, whose prospects of reincarnation seemed considerably slimmer.

The narrow border that fronted the house was a blaze of color, and there were more flowers planted out in pots around the steps leading to the front door.

A woman appeared from the house. Her hands were dusty with flour, only a shade paler than her skin. Her long, copper-colored hair was tied back off her face, a few wavy strands curling free.

She waited for Hollis to approach, wiping her hands on her apron.

"Mrs. Jencks?"

"Yes?"

"Deputy Chief Hollis."

"Yes?"

"Pansies," he said.

She glanced down at the pots. "Violets. The leaf of a pansy widens to the tip." She looked up with her wide brown eyes. "An easy slip to make," she added graciously.

Hollis abandoned all further plans of ingratiating himself with her.

"You're the new policeman."

"Not so new anymore. It's been a year now."

"A year don't count for a whole load 'round these parts."

"No, I guess not."

She pushed a stray strand of hair out of her eyes with the back of her hand. "What's he gone done now?"

"Excuse me?"

"Eli."

She meant her husband, he knew that from the file.

"Nothing."

"Nothing?"

"Well, not that I know of."

Her narrow lips curled into a soft smile, and he saw that she must once have been a beautiful woman.

"Could I have a glass of water?" asked Hollis.

If he could only work his way indoors, she'd find it harder to rid herself of him.

"There's elder water," she said, heading inside. "That's the tree with the little white flowers." There was no mistaking the dose of irony in her voice.

She poured him a glass, then returned to kneading her dough at the kitchen table. The drink was cool, refreshing.

"Where *is* your husband, as a matter of interest?"

"Digging a hole." She allowed the ambiguity to linger a moment. "Swimming pool for some city folk over on Egypt Lane. All this water and still they want more. Eli used to fish some, but the fear got him since Lizzie . . ." The words died on her lips.

"Did he ever fish with Conrad Labarde?"

She looked up. "You know Conrad?"

"A little. I see him from time to time."

"He's a good one, always was, even as a boy, running all over being fresh with the older folk, him and his friends, always laughing."

It was hard to picture, and she could see he was struggling.

"You known him late," she said. "He's changed some since them days. Couldn't see the Devil lying in hide for him back then."

"You mean, his brother?"

"Near broke him when Antton drowned. That and the war, then losing his pa . . . I don't know, you got to wonder what a man done to deserve it. Takes a heap off me just thinking about it sometimes. I don't like to say it, but it's the truth."

"He seems to be holding up okay."

"The moment he leaves that house of his you'll know."

"How's that?"

"His brother drowned off the beach there. He went and built that place right at the spot."

Hollis hardly had time to ponder her words before she laid the dough aside and said, "But you're not come here to talk about Conrad."

"No."

"Then it's Lizzie."

He'd worked out his line of approach on the drive over, though having got to know Sarah Jencks a little, he wasn't so sure she'd buy it.

"It's routine to revisit unsolved cases after a year or so," he said. "You'd be surprised how often it throws up something. I just wanted to talk through some stuff."

"What . . . stuff?" she said with that look of hers.

Okay, so she'd smelled a rat, but she hadn't shut him out.

"You said at the time, you and your husband—I'm going off the files here—you said then that you had no idea what Lizzie was doing out at that time of night."

He watched her reaction closely. It revealed nothing.

"That's right."

"You weren't aware of it happening before, her going out like that?"

"She was a poor sleeper, even as a wee one. Nothing to be done about it."

He noted that she hadn't answered the question.

"So it's quite possible it wasn't the first time."

"I suppose."

He took a sip from the glass. "And your son—Adam, right?—did he share a room with Lizzie?"

She stiffened slightly. "Not by then."

"So I guess he didn't know either, about her wanderings."

"Isn't that in those files of yours?" she said tersely.

"As it happens, Adam wasn't asked to give a statement at the time." It had been one of Milligan's many oversights.

"Then I guess he had nothing to add."

Hollis took another sip from the glass. "Can I speak to him anyway? Like I say, you never know."

This time she shifted uncomfortably.

"He's not here."

"I can come back later."

"Won't do much good," she said. "He's in Carolina. 'Least he was, last we heard . . . working the croaker boats."

He didn't know what a croaker was, but he got the general impression.

"How long's he been gone?"

"Put it this way, the croaker's a winter fish down them parts."

There was much more he wanted to ask, like why had Adam gone south so soon after his sister's death? And why hadn't he been in touch? There seemed to be bad feeling between son and parents, bad enough to silence Sarah Jencks and set her kneading her dough again for want of anything better to do with her hands.

He decided to back off, see if she followed.

"That was great," he said, placing the glass on the table. "And thanks for your time."

Her eyes came up suddenly, as if she were about to say something. Maybe she wanted to, but she didn't, not until she'd seen him outside into the sunlight.

"You'll not catch the one who done it."

"Don't be so sure."

"I'm not. I want to believe you will."

"There's a good chance, Mrs. Jencks."

He tried to reach out to her with his eyes, to let her know he knew she was holding back, that she could trust him.

"If I think of anything," she said, "I'll be sure to give Chief Milligan a call."

It was a moment before he realized he'd been had. She'd seen him tense up.

"Or maybe I won't bother the chief," she added, holding him in her dark eyes.

"He's got a lot going on right now," said Hollis, nodding.

31

PASSING THROUGH EAST HAMPTON, CONRAD STOPPED BRIEFLY TO WITH-draw some money from the bank. For a moment he thought he had spotted the tail, but the man in question climbed into a car and drove west on Main Street.

It wasn't until he was a couple of miles north of town that he picked up the black sedan in the rearview mirror, hanging well back. He didn't slow or accelerate in order to confirm his suspicions. To have done so would have meant jeopardizing everything.

He entered the outskirts of Sag Harbor, turning into Union Street. He noted that the Whaler's Church was still in need of a coat of paint. As long as he'd known it, there had always been a pleasing air of shabbiness about Sag Harbor. Unable to sustain the glories of its whaling heyday, the town wore its past proudly, though a little uneasily. The streets were peppered with grand residences built in any number of styles—Federalist, Georgian, Italianate, and Greek Revival. Some verged on the ostentatious, and most had fallen into a state of disrepair. Their sills were rotting, their roofs patched, their paintwork flaking, their gardens neglected.

The merchants, whaling captains, and shipbuilders who had first thrown up these temples to their own prosperity were long gone, their families forced to sell to the manufacturers who had washed in on the back of the tide before it finally turned for good. The factories, foundries, and potteries had closed, and Sag Harbor had slipped into gracious decline.

Like some dowager princess fallen on hard times, the evening gown may have been a little frayed around the edges, but the jewels were real. No other South Fork town could boast a Main Street to match, with its imposing brick edifices, its mansions, and its stores with their generous plate-glass windows.

It was here, on Main Street, that Conrad parked the car, just up from the Municipal Building. A group of young men was gathered on the sidewalk, loafing—a favorite Sag Harbor pastime, and one which lent the town its unique whiff of torpor.

The black sedan had not followed Conrad into Union Street, but it now appeared at the foot of Main Street, down near the waterfront, where the masts of the ships had once bristled.

It turned, crawling slowly towards him.

Conrad crossed the street in front of it, fighting not to turn and stare.

There was no need.

He caught the profile of the driver reflected in the window of the haberdashers beside the narrow office building he was heading for.

UNDER USUAL CIRCUMSTANCES, it took Walter J. Scarlett exactly six and a half minutes to walk from his office to his house, a little less the other way, what with the gradient. Today, he made the journey in well under six minutes; but then he had known it was going to be an unusual day from the moment he first showed up for work.

His secretary of a year standing, Elsie, was sitting at her desk devoid of lipstick for the first time ever. He hadn't commented on this detail at the time, fearing that he might be flattering himself. By noon, it was clear that he wasn't. He was too much of a gentleman to make the first move, but not so much of one that he hadn't reciprocated when her lips, untainted by any incriminating color, had sought out his while he was helping her with some filing.

By two o'clock, he had squeezed both her breasts, though not at the same time, and attempted to slide his hand up her skirt.

A run of afternoon appointments put paid to any more shenanigans, and, as Elsie prepared to leave for the day, he feared she was already suffering from terminal regret.

She hadn't been. And now he was running ten minutes late, or a little under, he noted, as he pushed open the front door of his house.

They were seated at the table, waiting patiently, a supper of cold cuts spread out before them.

"Daddy, you're sweating," piped up his son.

"I didn't want to be late."

"But you *are* late," said his wife.

"I meant *any later*," he replied sweetly, pecking her on the cheek, ruffling the children's hair, then taking his place at the head of the table.

He had barely finished saying grace when there was a knock at the door. His wife went to answer it. From where he was seated, he had no view of the entrance hall, but he could hear the exchange with the gentleman.

"Is Mr. Scarlett in?"

"What's it regarding?"

"It's a private matter."

"We're having supper, I'm afraid—"

That was as far as she got. He heard a scuffle, a little yelp, and then the man appeared in the dining room, steering Walter's wife by the elbow. Walter pushed back his chair and got to his feet.

"Sit the hell down," snapped the man. "You too," he added, forcing his wife towards her chair.

"Who do you think you are, barging in here?" said Walter, reaching for the phone on the sideboard.

The man dropped to one knee at the skirting board, pulled a knife
from somewhere around his ankle and cut the telephone cable. Rising
to his feet, he said, "I'm the man who's going to mess you and your
family up unless you put your ass in that chair this second."

He pointed with the knife, its slender blade flashing in the sunlight
slanting through the window.

Walter's daughter began to sob. He glanced at his wife, her eyes
wide with fear, and they both sat down.

"That's better."

The man circled the table, examining the food.

"Looks good." He leaned over and speared a shard of ham just
sliced from the bone. "You want some, son?"

The ham hovered in front of Walter Jr.'s face, the tip of the blade
inches from his eyes.

"Go on, I insist."

Walter Jr.'s bottom lip began to tremble. The man shrugged, then
ate the ham off the tip of the knife.

"What do you want?" asked Walter, wishing there was more authority in his voice.

"Conrad Labarde."

Labarde—his four o'clock appointment—the tall man who'd come
to see him with the interesting legal conundrum.

"What about him?"

"He came to see you. I want to know why."

Walter was about to plead the sanctity of an individual's relationship with his lawyer, when the man said, "And don't give me any crap
about client-attorney confidentiality."

It was a principle Walter prided himself on upholding. And he abandoned it without hesitation. The man listened closely to his account of the discussion with Labarde, interrupting every so often to ask a question. Finally, he seemed satisfied.

"Enjoy your meal," he said, making for the entrance hall. "Oh." He stopped and turned. "If you tell anyone about this conversation I'll cut out your daughter's lips and feed them to your wife."

Later that evening, while discussing with his wife which real estate agent should handle the sale of their house, it occurred to Walter J. Scarlett that even if he had ignored the threat and gone straight to the police, he would have struggled to give them an accurate physical description of the man.

32

MANFRED LAY ON HIS BACK IN THE DARKNESS, TORN BETWEEN LEAVING AND sliding into alcoholic slumber. He glanced to his right, and the matter settled itself.

It was as though the moonlight washing through the window had melted her face. Her mouth sagged open, the flesh was slack and loose around her jaw, gathered in folds. She had lied about her age, he'd guessed that at the time, mentally topping up the tally by four or five years. Looking at her lying there, laid bare by sleep, he revised that estimate by another five years.

Where was she from? Savannah? Charleston? Somewhere down south. They had hardly spoken over dinner at the Maidstone Club, just enough to establish that she was staying with the Van Allens; not in their ghastly new house—the one that looked like the bridge of an ocean liner—but in the old guest cottage at the end of the garden. Manfred had taken the information as an invitation, and he'd been right to do so. But now it was time to leave.

He eased himself out of the bed, his head throbbing as he stooped to recover his clothes. He carried them into the lounge, dressing there so as not to wake her, already working through the consequences of his actions.

He could rely on his friends' discretion, he knew that. Not that it really mattered. It wasn't as if his relationship with Helen was set in stone. Not yet, anyway. What would Senator Dale really do if he got wind of a one-night tryst?

Nothing. Nothing whatsoever. That was the truth.

Beneath the puff and the posturing, the senator was a pragmatist. He knew better than anyone that his daughter's union with Manfred was little short of a business deal: the senator's considerable political muscle in exchange for his daughter's elevated status, one which would see the Dale name etched into the history books.

IT WAS ALMOST TWO IN THE MORNING when he returned to the house on Further Lane, and he was surprised to see the ground-floor lights burning bright through the trees as he wended his way down the drive. His father and Gayle weren't due out till the following evening, and Richard was inclined to turn in well before midnight.

He parked near the front door and entered.

"Hello."

Silence. No. The dim sound of music—Beethoven—coming from the drawing room.

The room was empty, but the doors to the terrace were open.

"Richard?"

"Out here."

He was seated in a rattan chair, staring out across the lawn. Manfred could tell immediately that something was wrong. The ashtray on the low table beside him was almost full, the wine bottle near empty.

"Who was she?" asked Wakeley without turning.

"No one. You don't need to worry."

"Oh, but I do. And so do you."

There was a manic edge to his voice, uncharacteristic and worrying.

"Richard . . . ?"

Richard pointed to a chair. Only when Manfred had pulled it up and sat down did Richard turn and look at him.

"It's Labarde. He went to see a lawyer."

Manfred felt breathless all of a sudden. "A lawyer?"

"It looks like he might have some kind of document."

"What document? What are you talking about?"

"Calm down."

"I am calm. What document, damn it?!"

"I don't know exactly. Our man . . . he managed to speak to the lawyer. It seems Labarde wanted to know what weight a document written by a dead person would carry in a court of law." He paused. "A document which had come to light since that person's death, implicating the author and others in a crime."

"A diary? A letter? What?"

"Labarde said it came to him via a lawyer. He didn't have it with him, he didn't say what exactly."

"A confession . . ."

"That's what it sounds like. Written to Labarde and to be delivered to him in the event of her death."

"Jesus Christ." He reached for one of Richard's cigarettes and lit it. "He's bluffing."

"Except he didn't come to us, Manfred, he sought legal advice, not knowing he was being followed."

He was right. It didn't hang together.

"No," continued Richard, "she saw what was coming."

How? He had been so persuasive with Lillian, so masterful in his manipulation. When Justin first came to him with the news that she was wavering badly, he hadn't gone in hard—going in hard with Lilly had always been counterproductive, ever since she'd been old enough to defend herself with fist or tongue.

No, he had approached her in a spirit of sympathy, laying his own torment on thick, even managing to squeeze out some tears. He had said he needed time to think about it, to figure how best to approach the issue of coming clean about the accident.

Christ, he had almost persuaded himself of his own sincerity. And she had seen right through it. Through him. As she always had done. She was the only person in the world who could make him feel naked, stripped bare. When she was present in the room, he would find himself questioning and doubting every word he uttered, every opinion he held. She was like a mirror always lurking at the periphery of his vision. Every now and then he'd glance over and catch sight of his own reflection, and he'd falter and stumble.

She had always praised his talents, more than any other member of the family. What she disliked, as she'd told him many times, was his application of those gifts to the wrong ends. He sometimes wondered if she hadn't struck up a relationship with Justin purely in order to stay close to him, to monitor him, setting herself up as his moral compass. He hadn't resented this; he'd embraced the challenge, the debate, their continual sparring. He was happy to have her play at being his conscience, if only because it helped him believe he might actually have one. Besides, in the end her words were just that—words—they counted for nothing.

The accident had changed all that. It had empowered her, it had allowed her to hold sway over him, it had given her control—not theoretical and intellectual, but real and immediate. His choices were now her choices, and hers his. They were bound together in perpetuity, his fate now in her hands.

And when it came to it, she had opted to take from him everything she knew he held dear. On a point of principle, she had chosen to destroy him. Now here she was again, still working from beyond the grave to bring him down, entrusting her wishes to a goddamn fisherman.

"What does it mean, Richard?"

"What does what mean?"

"The document, for Christ's sake."

"It means a lot of things, none of them good. Legally, we can maybe beat it, but the scandal . . ."

Manfred got to his feet and wandered onto the lawn. "There has to be another way," he said eventually.

"You know there is."

Manfred turned. "It has to end here. Can it be made to look convincing?"

"With Labarde's record?" said Richard. "I can't see that being a problem."

33

Women swarmed like worker ants across the Village Green. Those who weren't chivvying along the men erecting the stalls were chatting like magpies. Very few appeared to be actually achieving anything, just the small handful unpacking boxes of cotton drapes and colorful bunting near the pond.

"Hello."

She swept past Hollis like a galleon in full sail, snapped an order then came about, bearing off on another tack. Only then did Hollis recognize her, from Mary's party.

He moved to intercept her.

"Barbara."

"What now?! Oh, it's you."

"How's the Apron Booth coming along?" he asked, and promptly wished he hadn't.

"Don't *talk* to me about the Apron Booth," she said, rolling her eyes. "Wednesday, he said. But was it ready? Is it here now? Do you see it?"

He glanced around. "I'm not sure I'd know it if I did."

"What's that?"

"See it . . . the apron booth."

"That's because it's not here."

"I'm sure it'll show up before tomorrow."

"Lunch," she snapped. "Lunch today. At the latest. It takes time to dress a booth properly, you know."

"Is Mary around?" he asked.

"Never when you need her."

Definitely a pretender to the throne, as Mary had told him.

"She's picking up Edward from the station," she continued.

"Edward?"

"Her son. He gets back at . . . well, any minute," she said, glancing at the watch strangling her fleshy wrist. "Is it anything I can help with?"

"It's about the parking. I'm on traffic duty."

"Well, that *is* Mary's department," she conceded. "What did you do last year?"

"I think we banned parking along the curb there, and on James Lane—"

"Sounds good to me. I'd go for that if I were you. I'll tell her you stopped by." She raised her hand abruptly. "Gordon!" she bellowed, brushing past him and picking up headway. "Gordon, the latch on the door of the tombola's broken. See what you can do, will you?"

There was no question of intruding on Mary's reunion with her son, much as he needed to see her. He had hardly slept, the sense of loss deepening with each passing hour, until the cocktail of exhaustion and alcohol had finally prevailed. The dawn had brought a new clarity with it, but the hole was still there. He'd swung by the Village Green on his way to work in the hope of filling it a little.

It would just have to wait. He'd have another chance to drop by later.

HE WAS WRONG.

He arrived at police headquarters to find that Milligan had scheduled a string of fool's errands for him. First up was a trip to Montauk.

Two surfcasters had come to blows out at the Point that morning. A nose had been bloodied, a rod broken. Hollis was forced to sit with the wounded party in a room at Gurney's Inn, suffering a lengthy discourse on surfcasting etiquette. There had been a flagrant breach of protocol, it seemed, with the result that a large striped bass had got away. It was bad enough—two grown men fighting over a fish—but when it emerged that they were good friends, he lost all remaining interest.

His next assignment of the day was chauffeuring the chief's wife out to Southampton for some urgent shopping. Dawn Milligan was a short, shy woman, long since bullied into submission, if not servility, by her husband. Hollis liked her. There had always been an unspoken bond between them—the silent complicity of the abused—and he didn't begrudge her his time, even as she strolled around the shops, chatting idly to friends.

Returning to East Hampton, Hollis slowed the patrol car almost to a crawl as they passed the Village Green. He failed to spot Mary among the throng of women, and hopes of returning later that afternoon were shattered when the chief demanded to see his report on the fishermen's brawl.

By the time he was finished writing it up, Milligan had already left for the weekend, and the Village Green was deserted. Hollis strolled around it, reading off the names of the empty booths awaiting tomorrow's cargoes of hot dogs and ice cream, flowers and cakes, candy, cigarettes, and scarves.

He wasn't altogether surprised to see that the Apron Booth held center stage.

He smoked a cigarette, judging his options. Then he returned to the patrol car and set off for Springs.

JOE WAS SEATED at a table in the creeping shade, fiddling with a bunch of engine parts laid out before him. He looked up briefly as the patrol car entered the boatyard, but there was no recognition in his eyes. Even when Hollis wandered over and removed his cap, he wasn't sure if Joe knew who in the hell he was.

"A word of advice, bub—never get yourself a Marine Spark outboard."

"Having problems?"

"Near on thirty years now. Shoulda' named this thing *The Bastard*."

He grunted in defeat, his arthritic fingers discarding the two bits of metal refusing to mesh. "I'll have you yet," he said.

He wiped his hands on a rag and looked up at Hollis. "You come by to thank me for last weekend?"

Hollis didn't reply.

"Didn't think so." Joe levered himself to his feet. "You want a beer?"

"I'm on duty."

"What do you know," said Joe. "Me too."

HOLLIS STOOD ON THE VERANDA looking out over Accabonac Harbor while Joe busied himself inside. The wind came in light gusts, rippling the surface of the water, the reeds and rushes bending in obeisance.

"Garden of Eden, bub," said Joe, joining him at the rail and handing him a beer. "Everything a man needs lies right out there. Ain't nowhere like it. And that's from folk what's traveled some, men of good word."

"It's very peaceful."

"It's changing fast. There's artists and all sorts moving in now." He pointed straight across the water. "City fellow bought just in back there, hard-drinker, calls hisself a painter, but can't hit the canvas for shit. I put a stove in for him. You should see the floor in that studio. And the walls. Just tosses that paint all over. What lands in the square, he sells. Now that's a way to earn a life," he chortled, "not fiddlin' with the guts of a bastard old outboard."

He scanned the harbor, a rueful look in his eyes.

"I guess it don't matter who's got it. The Montauketts took it off the Accabonacs with spears—butchered the whole lot of 'em one evening—we took it off the Montauketts with a pen, the city folk takes it off us with their checkbooks. Men does as men is. It don't matter, just so long as who's got it looks after it. How's Mary?"

"Er . . . she's fine," said Hollis, caught off guard by the swift change of subject.

Joe's eyes searched his face. "You know," he said, "last week we buried old Underwood from over Molly's Hill there. He were well along in years, that crazy old he-goat. Worked the big clippers most of his life, seen and done more'n enough for ten men." He took a swig of beer and smiled. "The priest, he's a young'un from up island, he asks around, and he's got all these stories to tell of Underwood this and Underwood that, how Underwood done pretty near everything save beat Columbus to the Indies. And we're sitting at the back of the church, me and some others what knew him going back a ways, and Ted Durrant says in that voice of his, 'Underwood, Underwood . . . well he is now.' "

Joe erupted in laughter. "It got out, you know, around the church, got handed along till the whole place is just heavin'. You shoulda' seen the face of that priestling, bub. If he sees out the month . . ."

Hollis was beginning to fear for the old man's sanity, when Joe finally composed himself.

"I guess I mean we've all got us a box waiting for us. I know Underwood went to his with no regrets, and that's a life well lived in my book." He paused. "They don't come better than Mary. I were fifty years younger I'd want her for my bride, fight you or any man for her, I would. Don't screw it up."

"It's good advice," said Hollis, "it just comes a little late."

"Don't bet dollars to doughnuts on it. Nothing you done to her comes close to what that other one done."

Joe eased himself into the old spring-rocker.

"I'll stop my preaching now, and you tell me why you come all the way out here."

Hollis hesitated. "Lizzie Jencks."

"Young Lizzie . . ." said Joe wistfully.

"You knew her?"

"Her folks is from Springs. They was married right here, bought a little patch down Amagansett, been skinnin' fleas for their fat ever since. Sure, I knew her. Damn shame what happened."

"I think I know who killed her."

Joe stopped rocking. "You think?"

"I can't prove it," said Hollis. "There's more. Another killing. I can't prove that either."

"Sounds like one heap of killin' and not much proof."

"It is. That's why I need your help."

"*My* help?"

"I need to know what Lizzie was doing out at that time of night. It doesn't make sense, it never has."

"You talk like you think I know."

"Her mother knows; she's not saying."

Joe scrutinized him. "Even if I did, you think I'd go against a mother's wishes?"

Hollis cursed himself silently; he'd come at it all wrong.

"I need this, Joe."

"Why?"

"Because it's all I've got."

Aside from extracting a confession under duress, this was his last play—Lizzie's midnight stroll.

"She was going to meet someone, wasn't she?" said Hollis.

"Was she?" Joe's face was set like iron.

"I think it could have been the man who ran her down."

He had gone back over his chain of assumptions, challenging each of them, forcing them to earn their place in his thinking. One had failed the test: the idea that mere chance lay behind the accident, that the impact of two alien worlds on a dirt-grade road in the dead of night—young flesh and hurtling metal, poverty and wealth—owed itself to nothing more than an unhappy coincidence.

But what did he really know about Manfred Wallace's movements that night? Only that he'd gone with Lillian from the Devon Yacht Club to Penrose's place. The rest was alibi, it had to be, concocted after the event. Maybe Lillian had stayed with her boyfriend that night—it was quite natural that she should—maybe Manfred Wallace had left Penrose's house not in order to return home but to keep a meeting, a rendezvous with a local girl.

It was thin, he knew that, but his talk with Sarah Jencks had reinforced his suspicions. She knew a lot more than she was letting on, and he wondered if her silence had been bought, or even secured with threats.

"What if you're wrong?" asked Joe. "What if Lizzie was just out walkin'?"

"She wasn't."

"What if you're wrong?" insisted Joe.

Hollis couldn't bring himself to say the words at first.

"Then it's over. I've got nothing else."

Joe heaved himself up out of the rocker and wandered to the rail. He ran his hand over his crest of stiff white hair and glanced up at the sky. "Weather's set fair for Mary's bash."

It was a good minute before he spoke again.

"What I'm fixin' to tell you goes no further." He turned to face Hollis. "I need your word on it."

"I can't promise that, Joe, not if it leads to something."

"It don't. It *is* over."

"If you're right, you have my word."

"Why don't you give me the name you got and we'll go from there."

Hollis hesitated before speaking. "Manfred Wallace."

"It's the wrong name, bub."

34

THE MAN GLANCED AT HIS WATCH BUT WAS UNABLE TO READ THE TIME IN THE darkness. Almost ten o'clock, he guessed. With any luck he'd be back in his cottage and asleep by two a.m., maybe three. The call to New York could wait till the next morning. Nobody would want to be dragged from their bed at that time of the night.

He tried to picture the face that went with the voice at the other end of the telephone line, but failed. He wasn't well spoken, just well connected with those who were, that was clear from the kind of jobs he handed out. Who else had there been? The lawyer, the Chicago banker, the square-jawed young polo player who'd pissed himself at the last moment. Establishment types. He never knew why they'd been singled out for his attentions, never even thought to ask. Best to just do the job and clear out.

This one was different, though, intriguing—first the rich girl, now the big fisherman with the crappy truck. What was the connection between them? Something to do with the document, but he couldn't see what exactly. He might have to break with tradition on this one and ask the guy before doing the deed.

He got to his feet and wandered over to the window. He could still see lightning scything the night sky way out at sea. The storm had stayed offshore, heading east. That was good. Rain was problematic. It meant mud on the shoes, it meant tire tracks, it meant a big pain in the ass.

He froze. His first thought was that the wind buffeting the fisherman's house must have drowned out the noise of the truck. His second thought was that he'd been spotted. He hadn't been. The darkened figure moving across the deck outside didn't alter its course.

The man skipped lightly across the boards and took up his position.

The fisherman entered warily, but didn't think to look behind the door.

The cosh was already raised, and he brought it down on the back of his skull.

Not too hard, not too soft—just right, he thought—as the fisherman crumpled to the floor.

CONRAD CAME AT THE HOUSE FROM THE BEACH, the gun in his hand brushing against his thigh as he walked. The breakers were building, booming as they collapsed—snatches of thunder stolen from the storm that had given them life.

He peered over the crest of the frontal dune and thought at first he was seeing things. There appeared to be light coming from the barn. He wasn't mistaken. He could just make out the sound of the generator above the noise of the warm wind whistling through the beach grass.

He made straight for the house, skirting it, only approaching to examine the corner where the telephone cable entered the building. It hadn't been cut. He waited in the darkness a while, listening for noises from inside the house, then he headed for the whaleboat house. It was deserted. He tucked a gutting knife into his boot before leaving.

He approached the barn with caution, glancing around him as he went. Ideally he would have checked the interior from one of the high windows, but the ladder he required was inside the barn.

He made two tours, drawing progressively closer. There was no way of entering unnoticed, no loose cladding to be gently pried aside, he knew that, he'd nailed the boards in place himself not even a year before.

This only left the main doors, slightly ajar, the tall crack of inviting light. He made his way over, alert, strongly suspecting he was treading a path expected of him.

Nothing, though, prepared him for what he saw through the gap in the doors.

Rollo was lashed to a chair near the base of one of the main supports. He was gagged, and his chin rested on his chest. For a terrible moment, Conrad thought he was dead, but Rollo raised his head and glanced around, wild-eyed, struggling with his bonds, only to slump again in defeat.

Whoever was present must be somewhere behind Rollo, lurking in the shadows. This didn't help Conrad much. He would have to enter regardless.

He tucked the handgun into the back of his waistband, pulling his shirt down over it, then eased the doors open a fraction.

"Come in, Mr. Labarde."

Rollo's head snapped up, his desperate eyes fixing on Conrad. Conrad fought to stay calm: mustn't let his anger cloud his actions.

"I haven't got all night," said the voice from the shadows.

Conrad pulled open the doors and stepped inside.

"Move to the other end of the barn."

Conrad did as instructed, skirting the long workbench that ran down the center of the building beneath the whaleboat suspended in the rafters.

"Put your gun on the table."

"I'm not armed."

"Then you won't mind stripping down."

"What?"

"You heard me."

Conrad began unbuttoning his shirt.

"You should know I have a gun aimed at the back of your friend's head."

As he eased the shirt off his shoulders and down his arms, Conrad pulled the gun from his waistband, letting it fall to the ground in the shirt.

"Turn around," said the voice. "Now the pants."

Conrad loosened his belt and dropped his pants.

"And the underwear."

Conrad did as instructed. "Like I said, I'm not armed."

"Take off your shoes."

Conrad undid the laces and pulled off his boots, concealing the gutting knife in his pants as he stepped out of them.

"Now toss everything over there by the door."

Conrad bundled the clothes and boots up tightly so the weapons wouldn't spill out. Not that it would have mattered. At that distance, they'd play no further part in what was about to happen.

"Turn around."

Conrad stood naked, facing Rollo down the other end of the workbench. "It'll be all right," he said to his friend, only starting to believe his words as his eyes settled on a hand axe lying within reach on the workbench.

There was movement in the shadows behind Rollo, and a man stepped into the light. It was the same man who had followed him to Sag Harbor, though somehow he had looked taller behind the wheel of the black sedan. The long-barreled handgun was leveled at the center of Conrad's chest.

"I'll get straight to the point," said the man. "You've got something I want, and I've got something you want." He rested a hand on Rollo's shoulder.

"Who are you?"

"It doesn't matter. What matters is the document, the one you went to the lawyer about."

"What lawyer?"

The man placed the end of the barrel in Rollo's ear.

"Don't mess with me."

Conrad stared into Rollo's terrified eyes. Then it came to him—one slender chance.

"Well, I guess this is what you call a Nantucket sleigh ride," he said.

"A what?"

"Rollo knows what I mean, don't you Rollo?" said Conrad, willing him to understand. There was a flicker of confusion in Rollo's eyes, then he raised them to the whaleboat overhead.

The man cocked the hammer of the gun. "Say good-bye to the half-wit."

"Don't. You don't understand. I know you followed me to Sag Harbor."

"That's clear now, isn't it?"

"I know you carried on down to the waterfront when I turned into Union Street. I know you then drove up Main Street. And I know I crossed right in front of your car."

It was enough to unsettle the man. "It's a good try," he said.

"I knew you were coming here."

"Bullshit."

"Tell that to the two cops waiting outside."

The man's eyes narrowed almost to a squint.

"I'm here to offer you a deal," said Conrad.

"No." The man shook his head. "You're bluffing."

"Deputy Chief Hollis," shouted Conrad, "I think it's time you showed yourself."

The man's eyes flicked involuntarily to the barn doors.

Conrad made his move, lunging at the axe on the workbench,

spinning back and burying the head in the wood of the support behind him, cutting the rope and rolling aside in the same movement.

He had expected the man to fire; he hadn't expected him to miss.
As the severed rope whipped through the block and tackle supporting
the whaleboat, Rollo toppled his chair to the left.

The whaleboat crashed onto the workbench, its bow poleaxing the
man. Conrad didn't wait to assess the damage. He came out of the roll,
seized a lance from among the clutter of whaling gear stacked against
the wall and spun back.

Remarkably, the man was getting to his feet. His right arm hung
limp and useless from its shoulder joint, but his left hand was already
bringing the gun to bear on Conrad.

Conrad let fly with the lance—his stance, the action, those of their
boyhood games, the endless whale rallies enacted with Rollo and
Billy. He didn't have to think, the past came willingly to his aid.

The lance caught the man in the midriff, low down and to the side,
the steel point passing straight through him. Both his hands instinctively went to the wooden shaft protruding from his belly, and the gun
fell to the floor. He recognized his mistake almost immediately, lunging for the gun.

Conrad kicked him in the side of the head as his fingers closed
around the butt.

Recovering the gun, he backed away towards Rollo, who was
struggling on the ground, twisting his head vainly to see what was
happening.

"It's me," said Conrad. He pulled the gag down over Rollo's chin.
"You okay?"

Rollo nodded. Conrad bounded over to his clothes, recovered the
gutting knife, and cut the ropes binding Rollo's arms and ankles to the
chair.

"Conrad . . ."

"Shhhh, it's okay, it's over." Rollo was shaking as Conrad helped him to his feet, and Conrad held him tight in case his legs buckled beneath him. They stared at the man lying skewered on the floor.

"Here." He led Rollo to the workbench and leaned him against it for support. "I have to do this now."

He checked the man's heartbeat, the entry wound, the exit wound. There was bleeding, but no pulse of imminent death. The lance would have to stay put, though. He dragged the man over to the upright and sat him against it. Then he ran a length of rope beneath his arms and lashed him in place.

"I'm sorry," said Rollo. "I'm sorry, I'm sorry—"

"Hey," said Conrad.

"He promised, he said he wouldn't say nothin'. But he did, he lied to me."

It took Conrad a moment to figure that Rollo was talking about his father. Ned had extracted the information about Lillian from Rollo, then used it when he said he wouldn't, banning Rollo from seeing Conrad.

"He did it for you, Rollo, to protect you. And he was right. Look." He turned to the man.

"He still lied to me."

That Rollo placed his father's betrayal above his own brush with death came as little surprise to Conrad. It was the way Rollo's mind worked. It also offered an opportunity. Conrad tried not to think too hard about what he was about to do.

"It's true," he said, "he lied to you."

"He did."

"And now I need you to do the same for me, Rollo. I need you to lie for me—to your father."

Rollo frowned.

"It's not forever, just till I can work this all out."

"Lie?"

A cardinal sin in Rollo's book, one for which he'd have to account to God himself.

"It's not even a lie," said Conrad. "I just need you to keep quiet about this for a couple of days. Can you do that for me?"

"I . . ."

"They killed my friend, Rollo. I think that man there killed her. But I need to know a bit more, I need a bit more time. Only you can give that to me."

Rollo nodded gravely. "I won't tell no one," he said. "No one."

"Let's get you cleaned up."

Conrad led Rollo towards the doors, stopping to gather up his clothes and his boots as he went.

THE MAN CAME AROUND SLOWLY to find the fisherman seated on the floor in front of him, dressed now and smoking a cigarette. A gun rested in his lap.

It felt like someone had cleaved away the right side of his body. Then he remembered and he looked down.

"Christ," he said. "Christ."

"You'll live," said the fisherman.

"There's a fucking pole in me!"

"It's a killing lance—for whales."

"Whales?!"

"Shut up."

"I need a doctor."

"Shut up and listen. I'm going to say this once. I've got some questions. If you lie to me, I'll kill you. There are no second chances. Do you understand?"

"Yes."

"Look at me. I said look at me."

He looked up into the two pockets of shadow cast by the overhead light.

"I want you to know that I hope you lie to me."

"I won't."

"When did you first meet Manfred Wallace?"

"Never heard of him. It's the truth, I swear it."

"Who are you working for?"

"I don't know his name. He calls me with jobs, I don't know who he is."

"What were you going to do, kill me after you'd got the document?"

"Yes."

"How?"

"Make it look like a suicide."

"Then what?"

"Then nothing. You're dead, I get my money."

"How?"

"How what?"

"How do you get your money?"

"He leaves it. In places. Hotels usually."

"How much did he pay you to kill Lillian Wallace?"

He was too slow. He'd hesitated just that little bit too long for it to be convincing.

"I want to know," insisted the fisherman. "How much was her life worth to you?"

He realized then that he had the answer to his riddle, written in the fisherman's face, buried in his voice. It was suddenly clear to him that he was sitting across from the dead girl's lover. And for one of the few times in his life he felt the cold touch of fear on his heart.

"Eight hundred dollars," he said.

It took a while for the fisherman to absorb the news. "The price of a secondhand car?"

"That's what I got. I don't know what the guy who did it got."

He congratulated himself. He'd slipped it in nicely, naturally.

"There were two of you?"

"I was only there to help move the body. I didn't do it. He did. I swear to God, it's the truth."

"He drowned her in the swimming pool."

"Yes."

"Then you both put her in the ocean."

"Yes."

How the hell did he know so much?

"Where?" asked the fisherman.

"Wiborg's Beach. It's—"

"I know where it is."

The fisherman tossed his cigarette aside, then used the workbench to help himself to his feet, his left knee stiff and straightened out.

"Where's your car, the black sedan?"

"Why?"

"Where's the car?"

"Down the highway. There's a track."

"Where are you staying?"

"The Sea Spray Inn."

"Room number?"

"It's a cottage—number four. Why?"

"Is this the key?"

He recognized the signs; the fisherman was making plans for his disappearance.

"Look, I've been straight with you, I can help you, I can finger the guy who did it."

"Is this the key?"

"Yes it's the key."

The fisherman took a couple of steps towards him. "I was at Wiborg's Beach," he said. "You carried her through the bushes on the right and up the dune. You stopped for a rest then you dragged her backwards down onto the beach."

How in the hell did he know so much? Flattery suddenly seemed like a good idea.

"I'm impressed."

"I'm not," said the fisherman. "There was only one set of footprints in the sand."

It took the man a moment to realize that he'd been led by the hand to his own doom, that there was never going to be any other outcome.

"Fuck you and fuck your half-wit friend," he said.

The fisherman stepped on the end of the pole. The dull pain in the man's side exploded into life, and he screamed.

"Go on, do it," he spat. "You're no better than me, you just don't know it."

"You're wrong," said the fisherman as the gun came up. "I do know it."

35

GAYLE WALLACE ROSE LATE. SHE PULLED ON HER SWIMSUIT AND A PAIR OF sandals, slipped a loose cotton gown around her shoulders, and headed downstairs.

She could hear voices in the study, her father discussing the business of the past week with Manfred and Richard, bringing them up to speed. He was excited about a new idea, something to do with water; she hadn't been paying too much attention during the drive up the previous evening.

Rosa had cleared the breakfast things away, but had left the coffee percolator primed beside the stove.

Gayle made her way across the lawn to the pool. Cup of coffee, cigarettes, lighter, and a towel—the same trappings, the same routine every Saturday of the summer.

She was thinking about Justin, and about what dress to wear to dinner at the Maidstone Club that evening, when she reached the poolside.

She didn't scream. But she did drop the cup. And she did run.

MANFRED HAD TO CONCEDE IT; it was a damned good idea of his father's. Two years of low rainfall had placed the city's water supply under enormous strain. An obvious way to combat the shortage was by introducing water meters, which meant only one thing—someone had to manufacture them.

They were discussing the relative merits of taking a stake in the Buffalo Meter Company or the Pittsburgh Equitable Meter Company when Gayle burst in on them, dressed for a swim.

"There's a man in the pool," she gasped.

"We can't have that," said his father. "Go and deal with it, will you, Richard."

"He's dead!"

Gayle pointed towards the garden, clamping a hand over her mouth, and for a moment Manfred thought she was going to empty her stomach all over the Aubusson rug. But she didn't.

Richard led her over to a chair and sat her down. "Wait here," he said.

THE MAN WAS WEARING A DARK SUIT and brown shoes. He lay facedown in the deep end of the pool, and he appeared to be hovering just a few inches off the bottom.

Any doubts as to who he might be vanished when Manfred spotted something dangling from a length of string attached to a sun shade. It was the silver-and-jadeite hair clip he had given Lillian on her twenty-first birthday.

They all stared at the body in silence.

"Richard, go call the police."

Richard didn't move. "I'm not sure I should do that, George."

"What?"

"It could be a bad idea."

Richard glanced in Manfred's direction. His father picked up on the look and his eyes flicked between them.

"What? What's going on?"

"Before we do anything," said Richard, "we have to move the body."

"Move the body?! You tell me just what in the hell is going on here."

"Rosa's out shopping, but she'll be back soon. She must not see this, George. We have to do this now."

THE FOLLOWING FEW HOURS WERE, by some considerable margin, the very worst of Manfred's life to date. He was dispatched into the water to bring the body to the surface. There was a neat entry wound in the man's forehead, a not so neat exit wound in the back of his skull. They used the wheelbarrow to deliver him to the garage, and threw a tarpaulin over the grim bundle.

Rosa was intercepted when she returned with the groceries and was told to take the rest of the day off. Gayle, still in a state of shock, was accompanied upstairs to her bedroom, where Richard spun some yarn about the dead man being a representative of theirs in Cuba, and that going to the police would only mean opening a far greater can of worms. She took his words in good faith, then took to her bed.

Manfred still had no idea how Richard intended to play it; there had been no opportunity to confer in private. But as they all entered the drawing room, he muttered under his breath, "Just follow my lead."

Manfred felt like an observer wandering among actors on a stage, present in the drama, yet not a part of it, a sensation reinforced by the fact that his father didn't look at him once while Richard spoke.

He did a good job, casting Manfred as an unwitting victim of circumstance, playing up the details of the girl's bid to kill herself. He added a fine touch, maintaining that Lillian had been at the wheel of the Chrysler when the accident occurred. He sketched the bare bones of the subsequent cover-up before tackling the matter of Labarde's affair with Lillian, which had recently come to light along with the existence of the incriminating document. The dead man in the pool was a hireling they had brought in to steal the document from Labarde, nothing more. But their plan had evidently backfired.

George Wallace seemed to visibly shrink before Manfred's eyes as he listened, the chair swallowing him. When Richard was finished, he eased himself to his feet and walked uncertainly towards the door, leaving the room without uttering a word.

"He's going to call the police."

"No, he isn't," said Richard. "He'd have done it right here, in front of us."

"It doesn't mean he won't though."

"No, it doesn't mean he won't."

They watched him from the drawing room. He walked, he sat on a bench beneath a tree, then he walked some more, disappearing from view to the far end of the garden.

Manfred found himself staring into the void, facing oblivion yet again. He felt the hatred and rage build in his gut, spreading through the pathways of his body, tightening the sinews, constricting his chest.

"I'll kill him myself."

"Don't be ridiculous."

"I'm trained, aren't I?"

It sounded pathetic, even to his own ears, which only annoyed him more.

There might have been some truth in the words, but his training wasn't a patch on Labarde's. And as for his combat experience, the whole purpose of Fighter Direction was to guide others into warfare from the safety of the Combat Information Center. There had been hairy moments in the Solomon Islands, relentless night-bombing raids by the Japanese, the odd barrage from an enemy battleship. He had even seen live rounds fired when the Marines flushed out a handful of enemy troops left behind on the island of Rendova. That "invasion" had lasted no more than half an hour, and they'd quickly set up their big SCR-270 radars, feeding vectors to their own air crews to help them zero in on the Japanese planes.

This is how he'd spent a large part of the war, sitting in front of a cathode-ray tube, helping the navy leapfrog its way towards the Philippines. As things went, it was about as good as it got. He was a lieutenant attached to the 1st Marine Air Wing; the radar technology over which he lorded was new, exciting, even glamorous; and there was the added cachet of always being on or about the front line. Okay, so it was the pilots of the old P-30s and P-40s who actually laid their lives on the line every day, but you were there with them, at their side, assisting, always in the thick of it, always safe back at base.

Maximum credibility, minimum risk. His father had judged it well, though they'd never discussed the details of the strings he had pulled.

It was a war record beyond reproach, an essential stepping-stone towards the prize, playing the long game. The question was just how deep the dream ran in his father. After all his work—all the planning, the foresight—was he really going to throw it away now?

In his heart, Manfred knew there was only one answer, though for a moment he doubted the assumption—the moment his father strode back into the drawing room from the garden. He walked straight up to Manfred, his eyes blazing, and slapped him hard across the face.

"You stupid boy," he spat.

Manfred could only think how much worse his reaction would have been if he'd been told the whole truth.

His father walked to the sideboard, helped himself to a cigarette, and lit it with a trembling hand.

"This fisherman, Labarde, does he have a telephone?"

"I don't know."

"Yes," said Richard.

His father made for the door.

Richard intercepted him. "What are you going to do, George?"

"What you should have done in the first place—pay him off."

"I don't know about this one."

"Name me one man who can't be bought."

"Then let me handle it," said Richard. "For your own sake, you should stay out of it."

It was a good point, though not the real reason Richard didn't want him speaking to Labarde.

"You should have come to me," snapped his father as soon as Richard had left the room.

"Come to you?"

"Yes."

"Since when have I ever been able to come to you?"

His father glared at him.

"It's true," Manfred went on. "You know it is."

He lit a cigarette. His father wandered to the French windows and looked out over the garden. They both smoked in silence.

His father turned. "He's with you forever now—Richard, I mean—you know that, don't you? This is his ticket."

It hadn't occurred to Manfred before that Richard might have an agenda all his own. And he drew comfort from it. If he'd done wrong, it was because his hand had been guided by a man thinking only of himself.

At that moment, Richard returned to the drawing room.

"He wants two hundred thousand dollars for the document. To-night."

"Two hundred thousand?!"

"It's cheap at that price," said George Wallace. "Though I daresay it's doubled since you tried to steal it from him."

"Where are we going to find that kind of money on a Saturday?" said Richard.

"After everything else you've arranged," snarled Manfred's father. "I can't imagine it poses too much of a problem."

36

Hollis had come prepared with two handkerchiefs. By midday, when the first cars started to arrive, one was already sodden from mopping his brow, and he'd laid it on a nearby hedge to dry in the sun; the second was well on its way to reaching its saturation point.

Another car tried to park on the side of the road and he moved it on.

Christ, it was hot, the windless heat roasting him in his uniform.

"Ambulance! Ambulance!"

The urgent call came from behind him, and he span around.

Abel triggered the shutter of the Speed Graphic. "That's great," he said, appearing from behind the camera. "I can just see it on the front page of the *Star:* 'Deputy Chief Hollis Moments Before His Sad Demise.'"

"Very funny."

"Jesus, Tom, you look like you just went twelve rounds with Rita Hayworth."

Easy for him to say, in his sleeveless open-necked shirt and his cotton slacks.

"So, how's it going?" asked Abel.

"How's what going?"

"The fair, Tom, the ladies' fair."

"Great. Attendance is up this year."

Abel looked at him askance. "Tell me you're kidding."

"I'm kidding."

"Christ, for a moment there I thought they had you in their clutches."

"No danger of that," said Hollis. "Where's Lucy?"

"Sulking. We had an argument. She thinks I'm seeing someone on the side."

"Are you?"

"I sure as hell wouldn't tell you if I was. But no, as it happens, I'm not." He lit a cigarette. "How's the president?"

"The president?"

"Mrs. Calder, you remember, the one who invited you to a party, the one you were spotted with in Springs the next day."

"We went walking," said Hollis. "She likes to walk."

"You've got to start somewhere, I guess."

"I guess."

"Why the hangdog expression? No, don't tell me—you fucked it up."

"I might have."

"You idiot, Tom."

"Coming from you?"

"Well, go and sort it out. Tell her she's invited to dinner over at my place later. You can come too . . . assuming you survive."

"What about Lucy?"

"Don't worry about her," said Abel, "she'll be okay by then."

HOLLIS WAITED TILL THREE O'CLOCK before making his move. The fair was in full swing, the Village Green thronging with people clustered around the booths, the gypsy caravans, the wishing well and the wheel of chance, or waiting in line for boat rides on Town Pond. Mary's little entourage had thinned out, and she was sipping a drink in the shade of a tree, the glass beaded with sweat.

"Hi."

"Here," said Mary, handing him the glass.

He took a gulp of the cold lemonade.

"Finish it," she said.

"Are you sure?"

"Believe me, I'm sure."

He drained the glass, dabbed at his face with his handkerchief, and looked around. There were some children playing nearby, romping and running about.

"Edward . . . ?"

"The big one with the stick chasing the small one without a stick."

"Seems like a nice kid."

Mary laughed, and he felt his heart soar.

"How have you been, Tom?"

"Oh, you know . . . terrible."

"Really? Why?"

"Take a guess."

"Don't blame me," she said, hardening.

"I'm not. I let you down, I know that. And I'm sorry."

"So am I."

Her words sounded so final, but he wasn't going to give up, not now. "There's a lot I need to tell you."

"You mean your investigation."

"That came to nothing."

"I'm sorry to hear that."

"Other things," he said.

"I'm not sure this is the time."

She didn't want to hear it, thought Hollis, not now, not ever. She just couldn't bring herself to tell him straight.

"Maybe later," she said.

Two simple words kicking down the door.

"How about this evening?" he suggested. "You're invited to dinner at Abel's place."

"This evening's difficult. There's all the clearing up."

"Delegate it. You're the president."

"And there's Edward."

"Get someone to look after him. I think it's going to be a special occasion."

"A special occasion?"

"It's just a feeling."

She thought on it. "Okay, I'll ask my sister if she can have him for the night." She paused. "Don't read too much into that; it's easier if he sleeps over."

"I wasn't reading anything into it," he lied.

THE SISTER SAID YES. He even met her briefly, with her brood and her lanky husband who made no bones about eyeing him mistrustfully.

He stayed for Mary's speech and clapped politely with everyone else when some prizes were handed out. As he headed home he stopped by Dakers Wine and Liquor Store and asked for two bottles of Champagne to be put on ice.

37

MANFRED CHECKED HIMSELF IN THE MIRROR, ADJUSTED HIS BOW TIE, AND removed a fleck of lint from the shoulder of his tuxedo.

He was surprised that nothing in his appearance, his face, betrayed the turmoil inside.

He told himself it would be over soon, but the thought brought little satisfaction. He had been outmaneuvered by a fisherman. Labarde would still be at large and in possession of a considerable amount of money, destined to see out his days in comfort, at their expense. No, there was not a whole lot to be happy about.

The cash had arrived a few hours earlier, Manfred and Richard watching from the house as the black van pulled up by the garage. A dark little man pulled open the doors, the van disappeared inside, and the doors were closed again. A few minutes later, the van was gone, taking the body with it. A leather case containing the money had been left beside the wheelbarrow.

With the exchange now sure to go ahead, they needed Gayle out of the way, and Manfred had spent more than an hour persuading her to brave the dinner with him at the Maidstone Club. At the appointed hour, he would slip away, join Richard back at the house, and they

would go on together from there. Justin was under instructions to ensure Gayle stayed at the club.

That, at least, was the plan. Richard had assured him it would all be
over by midnight. Only, it wouldn't be. There would be no conclusion, simply an accommodation with a man who might haunt him for
the rest of his life.

Manfred checked himself once more in the mirror, then crossed to
the Wellington chest. He opened the top drawer and stared at the
handgun buried among his socks.

38

Hollis arrived at Mary's house to find that she was running a little late. She called to him from upstairs saying she'd be down in a minute. A few seconds later, Edward appeared at the top of the stairs. He slid down the banisters and landed beside Hollis.

"Where's your gun?"

"My gun?"

"Mom says you're a cop."

"That's right, but I don't always carry my gun. I'm Tom, by the way."

"I've got a catapult."

"That's great . . . Edward, right?"

"My dad made it for me."

The emphasis on the word "dad" was clearly intentional.

Their relationship deteriorated rapidly from there. Hollis proved to be an embarrassingly bad shot with a catapult, a source of considerable amusement to Edward, whom he then made the mistake of calling "Eddy." To cap it all, Hollis had to admit he'd never killed anyone, although he was beginning to believe he might have it in him.

He was rescued by Mary, beautiful and fragrant and carrying Edward's overnight bag and a stuffed bear.

"Hey, cute teddy," said Hollis, eliciting a satisfying scowl from Edward.

———

ABEL AND LUCY WERE WAITING FOR THEM on the front porch. Lucy was beaming. Even from a distance, Hollis could see why.

"Lou's got some news," said Abel.

"*We've* got some news," said Lucy, shooting him a look then holding up her hand.

It was an emerald, fringed with diamonds.

"Oh, Lucy . . ." said Hollis, taking her in his arms.

"Congratulations," said Mary.

The women drew each other close, the men shook hands before abandoning the formality for a hug.

"Well done," said Hollis to Abel.

"It's all your fault."

"I'm pleased to hear it."

Abel took the bag off him and peered inside. "Champagne?"

"Call it a hunch."

HOLLIS MADE A POINT OF NOT DRINKING TOO MUCH over dinner. They sat at the table out back and fought their way through the feast Abel had prepared for them. Lucy told the story of how a friend of hers had spotted Abel in Southampton earlier in the week. Puzzled by this, Lucy had casually asked Abel about his movements that day. When he failed to mention the trip to Southampton, she immediately assumed he was having an affair, and said as much to him. Abel had let her stew in her suspicions, only to propose to her that very afternoon, presenting her with a ring—the one he'd been picking up from the jeweler in Southampton earlier in the week.

They all cleared the table, and Hollis found himself alone with Abel in the kitchen, making coffee.

"So," he said, "you're finally going to take her up the aisle."

"What we get up to in the privacy of our bedroom is none of your damn business," retorted Abel.

They were still laughing when the phone rang.

"I guess the word's out," said Abel, heading for the hallway. He returned a few moments later.

"Tom, it's for you."

"For me?"

"Conrad Labarde."

Abel was at his shoulder when he picked up the receiver.

"Hello."

"I'm sorry to interrupt your evening," said the Basque.

"How the hell did you know I was here?"

"I followed you. Do you have a pen?"

"No," said Hollis, laying the indignation on thick.

"Then listen carefully."

He listened. At a certain point, he interrupted the Basque. "Let me go get a pen," he said.

Abel provided the pen and the paper, and Hollis scribbled furiously for more than a minute. Only when he hung up did he realize Lucy and Mary had joined them in the hallway.

"What is it, Tom?" asked Lucy.

"I have to go."

"Why? What's up?" asked Abel.

Hollis looked at Mary helplessly. "I have to."

"Go," she said. "Really. Go."

"I need a flashlight."

"I've got one in the car," said Abel.

Nearing the car, Abel said, "I lied." He opened the door and took his camera from the backseat. "I don't have a flashlight, but I am coming with you."

"It's too dangerous."

"Hey, nineteen forty-three. Where was my ass while yours was pol-ishing a chair?"

It was Bob Hartwell's weekend off. What if he was away? It wasn't a risk Hollis could afford to take. He might need assistance.

"You drive," said Hollis.

"Where to?"

"My place. I need my gun."

HOLLIS SPELLED IT OUT FOR ABEL as best he could in the few minutes it took them to get to his house: Lizzie Jencks, Lillian Wallace, the Basque, the lack of hard evidence, and the meeting set to take place in just over an hour's time.

"Jesus, Tom, no wonder you've been acting so weird."

"Have I?"

The gun was in the bedroom. He checked the chamber, shoved a fistful of shells into his hip pocket, then he phoned Bob Hartwell.

"Thank God," he said when Hartwell picked up.

Hollis told him to change into something dark and to have his gun and a flashlight ready; he'd pick him up in five minutes. He didn't tell him why, and Hartwell didn't ask.

"Sure thing," he said in that low, impassive voice of his.

39

CONRAD CAPPED THE FOUNTAIN PEN AND REPLACED IT IN THE CHIPPED MUG on the desk. Wandering through to the bedroom, he tugged at the bedspread, straightening it.

Everything in order. Just one last act to perform.

He took the deer trails through the pitch pines north of the highway. He hadn't walked on Napeague since her death, fearful that the memories would hunt him down. She was everywhere, it was true, but now he drew comfort from her presence: her narrow footprints pressed into the firm sand around him, the fallen branch she had once tripped over, the clearing with the lone tree in the middle, the one she felt so sorry for, shunned by its companions.

Maybe she had seen herself in that tree, standing apart from those around her. Strange that it hadn't occurred to him before. And as he stared at the twisted little pine, it struck him just how alone she must have felt at the end, during those final moments of her life—the long walk back along the beach to her house, striding in anger beside the water's edge, angry with him.

She had overreacted; if she had lived to see the new day she would have realized that, she would have understood his hesitancy at her proposal.

It had caught him unawares as they lay intertwined on the damp sheet.

"Come away with me, Conrad."

He had grunted, suspended in the sweet limbo between reality and dreams.

"I mean it. Come away with me."

"Where?"

"I don't know. You decide. It doesn't matter to me."

"You mean a vacation."

"I mean life."

"I have a life."

"A new life."

He swiveled to face her. "Why?"

She didn't reply at first. "Because I'm asking."

"Is this a test?"

If it was, the look in her eyes suggested he had failed it.

"I can't just move away like that."

Ten minutes later she was gone, still sulking at his challenge to her flight of fancy. At least that's how he'd read it then.

He saw it differently now.

They had killed her for a reason, they had killed her because they knew what he hadn't known at the time: that she was about to blow the lid on Lizzie Jencks.

No, there'd been nothing infantile about her anger that day, she was just fraught and scared, poised as she was to risk everything on a matter of principle—family, friends, even him.

How close had she been to sharing the truth with him that last time he saw her alive? Very close, he suspected. And he wondered how things might have turned out if he'd only been more enthusiastic about her talk of a new life, if he'd only offered her the assurance she was looking for, that he would be there for her, come what may.

One thing was for sure—she would have stayed with him that night as they'd planned, and the killer lying in wait for her would have been denied his victim.

CONRAD CUT OFF THE TRAIL. It was a short walk over the low dunes to the tangle of bearberry bushes.

He dropped to all fours and clawed at the sand with his fingers. He came upon something hard and rounded and shifted his attentions a little to the left, scooping out a deep hole.

Taking up the whale vertebra he had carried with him from the house, he turned it once in his hands, caressing its familiar contours, then he returned it to its original resting place.

He filled in the hole and patted down the sand.

40

HOLLIS LED THE WAY, HARTWELL BEHIND HIM, ABEL BRINGING UP THE REAR. Stony Hill Wood was less forbidding at night than it had been during daylight hours, when he'd cut through it with Mary. This was partly because he couldn't see anything—barely the overgrown trail at his feet, even with the aid of Hartwell's flashlight—but mainly because Abel was clearly far more frightened than himself.

"Maybe he's just a guy with a sick sense of humor."

"Who?" asked Hollis.

"Labarde," said Abel. "He's probably sitting at home with his feet up having a good old laugh."

Hartwell snorted, amused by the notion.

"Hey, slow down," said Abel. "Wait for me."

"Are you scared?" asked Hartwell.

"Damn right I am. I've been in enough woods at night to know there's better places for a man to be."

Now Hollis felt bad. He had seen Abel's photos of Hürtgen Forest and it hadn't even occurred to him.

"We're almost there."

"You said that half a mile back."

Hollis stopped. Ahead of him, the ground dipped steeply away. He trained the flashlight on the paper, his scrawled instructions from Labarde.

"Correction," he said. "We *are* there."

THEY SKIRTED THE RIM OF THE DEPRESSION. It looked like some kind of quarry scooped out of the hillside, long since abandoned and reclaimed by nature. The sides were thick with vegetation, impossible to descend through to the area of clear ground at its heart. The only way to enter was via a dirt track that approached through the trees from the south.

On spotting the track, Abel wondered aloud why they'd just spent twenty minutes pushing their way through the undergrowth from the north. He got his answer a few moments later with the sound of a vehicle. It was moving along in a low gear, the sweep of its headlights plucking the forest out of the night.

"Over here," said Hollis, leading them to a thick screen of bushes. "Stay low."

"What are we going to do?" hissed Abel.

"*You're* not going to do anything. That was the deal, remember?"

"Okay, what are *you* going to do?"

"He didn't say."

Labarde had been very specific in every other regard: about where exactly to park the car, where to walk and when to arrive. His timing was a little off, though. According to Hollis's watch, they still had fifteen minutes before anyone showed up.

Hollis recognized the car the moment it crept into the quarry. He'd taken a shaving of paintwork off its rear fender earlier in the week.

It wasn't possible to make out the faces of the two people inside, but he figured one to be Manfred Wallace. Wondering if he had brought a goon along with him, Hollis found himself unholstering his gun.

The car pulled to a halt, its engine idling, and Hollis shifted his position to get a better view through the undergrowth. Manfred Wallace was the first person to get out of the car. He was followed closely by Richard Wakeley.

The two men huddled together in discussion, then Wakeley got back behind the wheel and turned the car around so that it faced towards the mouth of the quarry.

Hollis, Abel, and Hartwell screwed their faces into the dirt, the light raking their hiding place, pinning them down. And that's how they remained, anticipating their discovery at any moment, until Labarde arrived.

Only one of the headlights on his truck was working, but it was enough to illuminate the two men waiting for him, to get them squinting.

Hollis crawled to his left, edging closer. He needed to hear what was said.

Labarde took a few steps into the no-man's-land between the vehicles. He had a large buff envelope in his hand.

"How do we know you're alone?" demanded Wakeley.

"I could ask you the same thing."

"Are you armed?"

"Are you?"

"No."

"And him?"

"No," said Manfred Wallace.

"Me neither," said Labarde as if that settled it. "Where's the money?"

It was some kind of exchange, but what exactly? What was in the envelope?

"We need to know you're not armed," said Wakeley.

"The man you sent to kill me made me strip, just to be sure. It didn't help him, so why don't we just drop it?"

"What man?" asked Wakeley.

Hollis asked himself the same question, his head reeling. Was he really so far behind the field?

"Think straight," said Labarde. "If I wanted you dead, you'd be dead by now. I just want my money. Where is it?"

Wakeley removed an attaché case from the rear seat of the car. He handed it to Manfred, who didn't look too pleased at the prospect of having to draw any closer to Labarde.

"Open it first."

Manfred opened the case. From where he was lying on his belly, Hollis couldn't make out the contents, but Labarde seemed satisfied.

The two men met each other halfway, eyes almost at a level, one dressed in torn twill trousers and a cotton shirt, the other in a tuxedo.

"Don't be bitter," said Labarde. "I earned it."

"Oh really? How do you figure that?"

"Manfred . . ." It was Wakeley again, a note of caution in his voice.

"You don't want to be here," said Labarde, "but you are. You don't want me to have it, but I'm going to walk away a rich man." He paused. "I must have done something right."

Manfred Wallace's face twisted into a rictus of pure hatred. "Here." He thrust the case at Labarde.

"You mind if I count it?"

"It's all there."

"You'll understand if I don't trust the word of a murderer."

He placed the case on the ground and began to count the bundles of bills.

Hollis turned to look at Hartwell beside him and only saw then that Abel was gone. He gesticulated. Hartwell shrugged. Shit, thought Hollis. Shit.

"This is ridiculous," said Manfred. "Give me the envelope."

"Just wait, Manfred."

"Tell me something," said Labarde. "What's it like to kill your own sister?"

"Don't answer that," said Wakeley.

"She loved you, you know that, don't you?"

"Just do what you have to do, and we can all go," said Wakeley.

"What the hell." Labarde snapped the case shut and got to his feet. "If it's short, I'll drop by some time for the rest."

He handed over the envelope. Manfred ripped it open, feeling inside, then peering inside.

"There's nothing in here." He turned to Wakeley. "It's empty."

Wakeley stepped forward and examined the envelope. "Where's the document?"

"What document?" said Labarde.

"The one you went to the lawyer about."

"The one we talked about on the phone," said Wakeley.

Labarde tossed the attaché case to Manfred. "There never was one," he said.

"What do you mean?"

"Just that—it never existed."

"I don't—" sputtered Manfred.

"It's simple. I just thought we should meet. Face to face. That way there'll be no misunderstanding."

He took a couple of steps towards Manfred.

"I want you to know that I'm not going away, not ever, that I'll dog you for the rest of your life. You better keep one eye over your shoulder, 'cos that's where I'll be. What I do and when I do it, who knows? But I'll tell you this—it won't be quick and it won't be painless."

"Come away," said Wakeley, taking Manfred by the arm.

Manfred pulled free.

"Who the hell do you think you are?" he spat.

"Get one thing straight, I don't care what you think of me. You're not in charge here."

That's when Manfred pulled out the handgun. And that's when Hollis began to understand.

"Manfred, put that away."

"You heard him, put it away."

Labarde was clearly provoking him; taunting a man just wasn't his style. Hollis was aware of Hartwell unholstering his gun, about to break cover, and he held him back.

"No," he whispered, his mind racing, the pieces falling into place.

Manfred Wallace had to pull the trigger. That was the point. If he didn't, nothing had been gained. They hadn't heard anything that a good defense attorney—and the Wallaces would hire the very best—couldn't tear apart in a court of law, twisting their testimony into any number of shapes.

Manfred Wallace had to pull the trigger, and Labarde had understood it from the very beginning. He had figured that no amount of circumstantial evidence would lead to the downfall of Manfred Wallace, but if he could only get him to commit another crime, another murder . . .

"Manfred." Wakeley took a step towards Manfred and found himself staring into the barrel of the gun.

"I can end this now. It's over. Gone."

"You don't have it in you," grinned Labarde.

Manfred spun back, on the point of firing.

"Tom," hissed Hartwell.

"No."

They had all been summoned here for a reason, steered and cajoled towards this stage, this amphitheater in the woods, each with his role to play: Labarde to lay down a life he no longer valued; Manfred Wallace to bring about his own ruin; Hollis to bear witness to the killing, no more.

"Manfred—" said Wakeley again. And that's when Manfred fired.

Labarde was jerked to the right by the impact of the bullet. Manfred fired a second time, and the moment he did so, the scene was lit
by a blinding white light, the tableau frozen for a split second: Wakeley recoiling, the muzzle flash from the handgun, Labarde seemingly
suspended in time and space, but in reality buckling towards the
ground.

Manfred Wallace was turning to the source of the flash of light
when Hollis and Hartwell burst from the bushes.

"Police," yelled Hollis. "Drop the gun. I said drop the gun!"

It was the shock more than anything that forced the gun from
Manfred Wallace's fingers.

"On the ground. Now. Both of you!"

As he recovered the weapon, Hollis glanced over at Labarde. He lay
facedown in the dirt, inert, an arm twisted behind his back.

In a fit of fury, Hollis found himself kicking Manfred Wallace in
the side of the chest.

"Spread your arms and legs."

"I—"

"Shut up!" snapped Hollis, kicking him again.

The moment was trapped for posterity by Abel as he emerged from
his hiding place.

41

THE FOLLOWING DAYS PASSED IN A BLUR OF LAWYERS AND SEEMINGLY END-
less debriefings by men from the DA's office as everyone shouldered in
looking for a slice of the cake. A pack of newshounds descended on
East Hampton. Most were obliged to sleep in their cars, the inns and
boardinghouses already at capacity, what with it being the height of
the season.

Justin Penrose was the first to crack. Those with the least to lose
always were. He cut himself a deal—accessory after the fact of
manslaughter— for his role in covering up the hit-and-run. It was the
turning point. Once Lizzie Jencks had entered the frame, there was a
motive for the murder of Lillian Wallace. The floodgates opened.
Now it was just a question of who would drown and who would be
saved. Wakeley and Manfred Wallace fought each other for the lone
life preserver.

Wakeley had done a good job of protecting his charge from any association with the murder—too good a job as it turned out; there was
almost nothing linking him to the crime. Manfred's lawyer drew a parallel with Henry II and Thomas à Becket, claiming that Wakeley had

taken it upon himself to rid Manfred of his meddlesome sister. This argument largely fell on deaf ears.

Hollis didn't witness it at first hand, the unsightly spectacle of the two former friends turning on each other. He had already removed himself from the scrum by then. So had George Wallace. The newspapers presented him as a broken man, destroyed by the revelations about the true circumstances of his daughter's death. The press was no better equipped than anyone to speculate in this way. Following his brief interrogation by the DA, George Wallace had simply disappeared.

Chief Milligan, on the other hand, had taken center stage, the winds of national interest fanning the flames of his ego into a firestorm. Strangely, Hollis found himself amused rather than angered by the sight of Milligan claiming credit for the arrests, the successful conclusion of his own monthlong investigation.

When it came to it, Hollis really didn't care, and that realization surprised him. Besides, his thoughts were elsewhere—with the man hanging between life and death in Southampton Hospital. The man who had been manipulating events from the moment he first dragged his lover's body from the ocean in a net.

Labarde had survived the initial surgery, only to be hit by a raging infection. He had not regained consciousness.

The fourth time Hollis visited him, there was a leather-cheeked old Indian seated at his bedside, clasping his hand. Hollis waited patiently in a chair for twenty minutes, unable to make out what the Indian was muttering in his soft voice.

When the old man finally left, he said, "Ain't nothin' to do if he don't want it. And he don't."

Who could blame him? There was a bunch of people poised to pounce all over him, eager for his version of events, should he survive. Hollis had made a point of charming the head nurse, a woman who

concealed a good heart behind a lofty demeanor. She had finally re-
lented, promising that he would be the first to know if there was any
news.

THE CALL CAME FOUR DAYS LATER, early in the morning, at Mary's place,
to which Hollis had decamped to avoid the overeager newspapermen
staking out his house. When the phone rang, his head was thick with
exhaustion, having hit the pillow only an hour or so before.

Abel and Lucy had come to dinner, and somehow they'd all found
themselves seeing in the dawn. There was a lot to catch up on. Abel
had been out of circulation all week, dealing with the commotion
over "the photo," as it was now referred to.

It had been bought many times over, syndicated around the world,
and he was still reeling from the shock of what he'd achieved: the big
picture, the photographer's dream. True to form, Abel dismissed the
image as a work of mediocrity, an instant of violence trapped on film,
with little else to recommend it apart from a certain ghoulish appeal.

He was wrong. It somehow captured more than the moment, pointing to a deeper, more universal injustice: two well-dressed types gathered at the execution of a working man. Wakeley was frozen in the act
of turning his head away and raising his arms protectively, an instinc-
tive gesture, but one which seemed to imply he was washing his hands
of the deed. Because of the angle, the gun wasn't visible, but the muzzle flash was, shards of lightning exploding from Manfred Wallace's
fingers, a faceless figure clad all in black, unleashing a thunderbolt.
There was something almost beatific about Labarde's expression as he
crumpled forward and to the right.

They said all this to Abel, but he stuck to his guns. He much preferred the shot of Hollis putting the boot into Manfred Wallace, a
print of which he had also brought along with him by way of a gift—

the only one in existence, framed in oak. Mary remarked that the look of hatred on Hollis's face scared her, and Abel told her that that was the point. It was the one time he'd seen the real Hollis, he said, the beast within; and he wanted her to know what she was letting herself in for.

Abel had a healthy mistrust of what was happening to him. Picture editors and agents, many of whom had never even bothered to return his portfolio, were now calling him at all hours of the day and night. He knew he had gotten lucky, stumbling on success in his own backyard. Later in the evening, he announced, a little drunkenly, that even if his career took off it wouldn't change him as a person.

"Oh go on, please," said Lucy, "just a bit."

Their laughter woke up Edward, who shouted down from his bedroom window for them to put a sock in it.

Finally the dawn light crept overhead, revealing a low, feathery mist on the paddock. Abel and Lucy made a halfhearted offer to help clear up, heading for their car almost in the same breath. Hollis and Mary left the table as it was and went inside to bed.

After they had made love, they lay on their backs side by side, their fingers intertwined, drifting off to sleep.

Unexpectedly, Mary turned to him and kissed him passionately.

"Mmmmm," he groaned.

"Tom, there's something you should know," said Mary ominously.

"What?"

"I want you to know this now, so there's no confusion. I don't think it's the right thing to say, in fact I'm sure it isn't, but seeing as it's the truth and it's not going to go away." She paused. "Besides, I figure we're too old to talk around this kind of thing."

"We'll be too old for anything if you don't come out with it soon."

"I want another child, Tom."

Hollis absorbed the news.

"I understand," he said, "I really do. But I'm not sure they're that easy to swap."

"I'm serious," she said, trying not to laugh.

"I know."

"That's why I kissed you."

"You thought you could swing it with a kiss?"

"I thought it might be the last time."

Hollis leaned towards her. "Well, let's put that idea to bed," he said.

Two hours later, and after one hour's sleep, the phone rang.

Mary offered to go with him, but he said it would be better if he went alone.

Labarde lay in the hospital bed, his pale, drawn features set in repose. Hollis pulled up a chair and just looked at him.

Labarde opened a tired eye. "You look terrible," he said.

Hollis smiled.

"They say I lost a kidney."

"Good thing they come in pairs."

It was Labarde's turn to smile.

"Was I right to let him fire?" asked Hollis.

"You were right."

"You used me, you played me right from the start."

"You'll get over it, Deputy."

"Tom."

"What, now we're friends?"

"No. I resigned."

Labarde opened both eyes this time. "Yeah?"

Hollis nodded.

"What'll you do?"

"I'll find something."

"You're staying around?"

"Yeah."

Hollis handed him two envelopes. "I took these from your place before they went through it."

He had found the envelopes propped up on the desk against a water glass. One was addressed to Rollo, the other to someone called Sam Ockham.

Labarde looked at them, but didn't take them. "You can throw them away."

"You sure you won't be needing them?"

Labarde didn't reply.

"I'll try and keep them off your back for a bit," said Hollis, "but there's a stack of people want to see you."

"I guess."

"There's been talk of a man, a man sent to kill you, seems he turned up dead in the Wallaces' pool with a bullet in his head."

"I wouldn't know anything about that."

"That's the story to go with," said Hollis, "just make sure you stick to it. The DA's blood is up right now, he's capable of anything."

"Thanks."

"There's another thing. Manfred Wallace is saying Lizzie Jencks stepped into the road in front of the car."

"How does he justify killing his sister?"

"I think he's telling the truth."

He'd been sworn to secrecy, but Labarde was the one man who had a right to know. Besides, Hollis needed his advice.

He told him what he'd learned from Joe the time he drove out to Springs: how a girl from a poor Bonacker family would have had little choice, how the Jenckses and their kind had been in the thrall of the wealthy Amagansett clans since the very earliest days, reliant on them for work, charity even, during tough years. It was a relationship open to abuse, and there'd been many over the years. Joe said he could list a whole lot of them, payment taken in kind from families with nothing else to offer besides their womenfolk. He said he could point out the sons and daughters of gentry fathers brought up in Bonacker homes. He said Hollis was sitting across from one, although he didn't go into details.

Hollis protested that that was then and this was now. Girls didn't go around giving themselves to men just because they demanded it.

"It's nineteen forty-seven, for Christ's sake."

"No need to bring him into it," said Joe sternly.

"You know what I mean."

"I know things move slow out here."

"Did her parents know?"

"Not till after. The brother did, he was the one pushed her to it. He liked the cards more'n they liked him. He needed work fast, the cash kind. His pa near killed him when he found out."

Well, that explained why Adam Jencks had gone south.

"It's one of them things is all," said Joe. "Ain't nothin' going to bring her back. It's all arranged now."

"How's that?"

"Put it this way, the Jenckses ain't making the payments on the house right now."

"Oh that's great, everyone's happy."

"I ain't saying that."

"Who was it, Joe?"

"I ain't saying that neither."

LABARDE HAD LISTENED IN SILENCE to Hollis's account of the conversation. "Well . . ." he now said.

"You know who it is, don't you?" said Hollis.

"No."

"But you've heard something."

"No."

"You're lying."

"You don't understand. There's those who've been here forever. Then there's the rest of us."

"None of this would have happened if Lizzie hadn't been out that night. It all springs from that. I believe Manfred Wallace. She stepped in front of his car."

"You caught him. Be happy with that. It's enough."

Labarde closed his eyes.

"I'm tired," he said.

"Sure."

Hollis got to his feet and placed the chair against the wall.

"Oh, Gayle Wallace came by a few days back."

"Gayle Wallace . . . ?"

"To see how you were doing. She's gone now. I just thought you should know."

Hollis walked to the door, then turned.

"It's good to meet you," he said. "Finally."

But Labarde had already drifted off.

42

THE WIND SWEPT DOWN ON THEM OUT OF THE NORTH, SPRAYING THE BEACH with stinging sand whipped from the frontal dune. Beyond the breakers, the ocean was hard, cold, granite-gray.

They eased the dory off the trailer into the wash, its gunwales filmed white with frost. While Rollo tended to it, Conrad pulled the Model A up the beach, the sand chattering against the windshield.

As he climbed down from the cab, a figure appeared on the crest of the dune. It was Ned Kemp, dressed in waders, oilskins, and a wool-knit cap.

"Cap," said Ned, approaching.

"Cap."

"Some blow."

"Sure is."

Ned looked at his boots, then up again, the stubble showing white against his chin, the awkwardness hanging heavy between them. They'd just exchanged more words than they'd managed in the past few months put together.

"You done good," said Ned. "You done what you had to, but you done it right. Even made us look good."

"It wasn't planned. That's just the way it turned out."

"That's what you say."

Ned looked past Conrad to Rollo struggling with the dory in the wash.

"Lost his voice around the home. Can't hardly look at me."

"What are you doing here, Ned?"

Ned turned back, squinting his tired eyes.

"I come to see my son," he said.

ROLLO SHIFTED UNEASILY AS THEY APPROACHED, looking every which way but theirs.

"There's a fellow here wants to know if he can lay trawl for us," said Conrad. "What do you reckon?"

Rollo shrugged, trying to look indifferent. "I don't know. What do *you* reckon?"

"Oh . . . I reckon every greenhorn's got to learn somewhere."

Rollo beamed nervously at his father's affronted scowl. "Sure," he said. "Why not?"

They clambered aboard the dory and took their places at the oars. Ned pushed them into deeper water, holding the stern steady, eyes on the breaking seas.

"I heard you was thinking of going to college."

"Figured I'd stick around instead," said Conrad.

Ned peered past them, reading the waves.

"Fishing don't teach you much," he said, "but it do teach you you don't need much."

A large wave broke under the dory.

"Go, boys, go!" yelled Ned, pushing off and dragging himself over the gunwale.

The oars bit, the dory sprang forward, rising steeply, its high, sharp bow splitting the face of the capping sea, carving a passage through.